# Tenderness

G·K Hall &C?

Also published in Large Print
from G.K. Hall by Dorothy Garlock:

*Homeplace*
*Ribbon in the Sky*

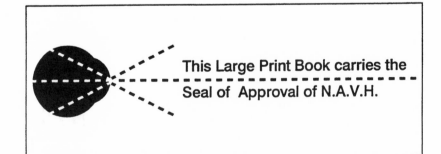

This Large Print Book carries the
Seal of Approval of N.A.V.H.

# *Tenderness*

# Dorothy Garlock

G.K. Hall & Co.
Thorndike, Maine

G.K. Hall Large Print Romance Collection.

Published in 1993 by arrangement with Warner Books, Inc.

The text of this Large Print edition is unabridged.
Other aspects of the book may vary from the original edition.

Set in 16 pt. News Plantin by Barbara Ingerson.

Printed in the United States on acid-free, high opacity paper.♾

---

**Library of Congress Cataloging in Publication Data**

Garlock, Dorothy.
    Tenderness / Dorothy Garlock.
      p.    cm.
    ISBN 0-8161-5851-7 (alk. paper : lg. print)
    1. Man-woman relationships — Fiction.  2. Large type books.
  I. Title.
  [PS3557.A71645T46     1993]
  813'.54—dc20                    93-26834

---

THIS BOOK IS DEDICATED

TO
GLENN HOSTETTER

and all my friends at
the BOOK NOOK
JACKSONVILLE, FLORIDA

WAY TO GO, Glenn!

# CHAPTER

## • 1 •

*H*e was . . . he was b-by the bed when I woke u-up . . . ohh . . . I was so scared."

"I can imagine!" Jesse hugged the young girl sitting on her father's examination table and wiped her tear-wet face with a damp cloth.

"Try not to cry, Bertha, and tell me exactly what happened."

"I . . . just saw his outline before he . . . before he covered m-my eyes with one hand and my m-mouth with the other."

"The . . . beast!"

"Then . . . he said he . . . was going to tie something over my eyes and if I made any noise he'd cut me with his . . . pocket knife."

"Did you recognize his voice?"

"He . . . he whispered."

"He made you take off your nightgown?"

"Yes, and . . . and made me put my arms up and my hands under my head."

"Lord have mercy! Then what did he do?"

"He lit the l-lamp. I heard him strike the match.

7

He sat down on the bed and put his hands all over me. I cried and he said not to cry, he just wanted to look at me and t-touch . . . me. He . . . rubbed my titties a long time and . . . and made me spread my legs."

With conscious effort, Jesse suppressed her indignation and encouraged the shy girl to say more. "Did he go inside you, Bertha?" she asked gently.

"No. Oh, it was so . . . awful. He felt of me with his hand and ah . . . spread me so . . . he could see — I guess. I just . . . wanted to die!" Wracking sobs shook her slight frame.

"You poor child." Jesse put her arms around Bertha and held her until she quieted. "How long did this go on?"

"A long t-time."

"Could you tell if he was young or old? Did he have whiskers or a beard?"

"His face was rough like he hadn't shaved, but he didn't have whiskers. He put his face on . . . on my belly."

"Try to remember everything you can so that we can tell Marshal Wright."

"No!" Bertha grabbed Jesse's arm. "If I tell, he'll come back and hurt me. He said he would. Please, Miss Jesse, don't tell anybody. You promised! Oh, I shouldn't have come —"

"Shh . . . you did the right thing to tell me. A girl can't keep something like this to herself. I'll keep my promise. I won't tell, Bertha, if you don't want me to. But I think your father should know."

"Not him! He'd . . . say it was my fault."

"How long will he be at the work camp?"

"Another month. The bridge isn't half finished yet."

Jesse thought for a long moment. The man who did this knew the children were alone! It made her blood boil.

"Bertha, didn't your little brother or little sister wake up?"

"No. They play hard and sleep like rocks."

"Is there anyone you can get to come stay with you?"

"I'd have to tell them . . . and I can't."

"From now on all of you sleep in the same room. And bring that old dog of yours into the house. Where was he last night?"

"I reckon he was off chasin' a coon. I got to be goin', Miss Jesse. The kids will be comin' home from school. I told 'em the reason I wasn't goin' to school was cause I was sick."

"If you remember anything else, come tell me. I'll not tell anyone but my father, and you can trust him not to say anything unless you want him to. But he should know this in case it happens to someone else."

"Bye, Miss Jesse."

"Bye, Bertha. Come by tomorrow. I'll be anxious to know how you're getting along."

Jesse watched the girl hurry out the side door, run past the lilac bushes and dart between the gap in the hedge of bridal wreath that divided their yard from that of their neighbor. She followed the girl's path across the yard to the sidewalk that paralleled the brick paved street.

In the town of Harpersville, Tennessee (population two thousand and forty, or two thousand and forty-one if Doctor Forbes had delivered the Burlesons' sixth child), what had happened to Bertha, and to one other woman of whom Jesse knew, was not supposed to happen, even in the wild and promiscuous year of 1902.

Jesse clenched her fists in outrage. Something should be done to find this sick, miserable excuse for a man. But what?

"It's a disgrace that something like this can happen here in Harpersville."

Jesse had just finished repeating Bertha's story to her father. She spoke over her shoulder while she put away gauze, swabs and iodine. The last patient, a boy who had gashed his bare foot on a piece of glass, had limped from the office and Jesse finally had the chance to speak to her father alone. Doctor Hollis Forbes had watched with pride while his daughter cleaned and stitched the cut on the boy's foot. She had spent two years at nursing school, but the two years she had been his nurse had increased her knowledge tenfold. She was as calm and efficient in an emergency as anyone he had ever known. He mused, as he often did, whether it was fair to his bright, elder daughter that she spend eight to ten hours a day here in the surgery and then manage the rest of the house and see to the upbringing of her sister and brother. So much responsibility piled on her shoulders didn't give her much time for herself.

"Papa, who could be doing this terrible thing?"

"A pervert," Doctor Forbes said tiredly. "The women are lucky that all he wants to do is look. I only hope that's all he does until he's caught."

"It could be someone passing through town," Jesse suggested.

"My guess is that it's someone from nearby who comes to Harpersville occasionally. Bertha makes two women that we know of who have been subjected to this. There may be more who aren't telling."

"Someone knew when Mrs. Johnson's husband was gone and when Bertha's papa was working on the bridge and staying in the work camp."

"That information could have been picked up at any store in town. You know how people like to talk."

"Surely no one who lives here would dare do such things to a woman. Mr. Harper would have him tarred and feathered for dirtying his lily-white town."

"Now, now. You sound bitter."

"Not bitter, Papa, just tired of the Harpers telling people what to do — and think. Did you know Mrs. Harper is still trying to match me up with Edsel? I saw her yesterday at the post office. 'Oh, there you are, dear,' she said. 'Just this morning Edsel was speaking of you. He thinks you're the prettiest girl in Harpersville.' " Jesse's mocking

11

of Mrs. Harper's voice brought a smile to her father's tired face.

"What did *you* say?"

The doctor's eyes twinkled as he watched Jesse poke at the knot of chestnut hair at the nape of her neck with her index finger. She tilted her head, held up her hand as if to put on nose-pinching spectacles and looked down her straight nose in a perfect imitation of the town's leading socialite, Roberta Harper.

"I told her I was too busy to think of affairs of the heart; we were expecting an epidemic of the black plague and had to get a place ready to lay out the dead."

"Shame on you." Doctor Forbes wore an expression of amused affection on his face.

Jesse's grin was mischievous. Large blue-gray eyes sparkled and her even white teeth flashed. Jesse had a beautiful smile, her father thought, and worried again that he was stealing her youth. She was graceful and . . . womanly, and it was too easy for him to take for granted that she was perfectly happy spending her days in the surgery, tending the house, or calling on their patients. She must sometimes want to go to parties, dances, picnics or ball games.

"There's a ball game Sunday afternoon. Why don't you and Susan go and take Todd? You know how Todd loves ball games."

"What brought that on?" Jesse asked, the smile fading from her face.

"It'll do you good to get away from the house.

Bushman's Dairy is playing Burleson Lumber. They're calling it the battle of the B's." The doctor's twinkling blue eyes watched her over the top of his spectacles.

"The battle of the B's? Oh, that's clever, very clever. They'll have to fight it out without me. On Sunday afternoon I catch up on things I can't get done through the week. You know that, Papa."

"Reverend Pennyfield says it's a sin to work on Sunday."

"Reverend Pennyfield doesn't have a ten-year-old brother with holes in the knees of his britches, or berries to pick, or a kitchen floor to scrub."

"Can't Susan do some of that?"

"She helps. She hangs the clothes on the line and does most of the ironing. But fourteen-year-old girls have more interesting things on their minds than picking berries, making jam and scrubbing floors." Jesse watched her father rub his tired eyes. "Go take a nap, Papa, while I clean in here. You've been up since two o'clock this morning," she said gently. "Supper will be ready when you wake up. I've got a chicken roasting in the oven."

"Chicken on a week night. Aren't you getting a mite extravagant?"

"I bought it from Mrs. Arnold. It was all cleaned and dressed and ready for the pot. She said she was culling out the hens that had stopped laying. But I suspect they need the money."

"And you couldn't resist?"

"Go on with you," Jesse retorted affectionately.

"You wouldn't have resisted either."

In the weeks that followed, two more women spoke about having been stripped and fondled by The Looker, as he was now being called since the word had spread through the town like wildfire. That brought the total of women and girls whom Jesse knew about to four. It was reasonable to believe that others had suffered the same treatment and were too ashamed to make it public. And some must have remained silent because, although they felt violated, they had not suffered any bodily injury nor been raped.

Boyd Harper was furious when the story appeared in the *Harpersville Observer*. Ralph Marsh, the owner and publisher, was the only man in town, other than Doctor Forbes, who dared to stand up to the Harpers. The headline read: LADIES BEWARE. In the article, the editor cautioned women to lock their doors and stay off the streets at night. Outraged at the unwritten suggestion that the offender was a town resident, Boyd Harper or his son, Edsel, appeared at every public gathering declaring that The Looker was someone from the colored town on the other side of the wooded hills that ringed Harpersville, or from nearby Frederick or Grover.

At supper one night, Doctor Forbes told his family the latest rumor was that The Looker was Wade Simmer, a man who lived in the hills and who came into town only when necessary.

"Wade Simmer? He's got a mean look. I saw

him real close up . . . once. Yup, I bet it's him."
Susan, at fourteen, had more than a mild interest in anything that had to do with sex.

"Why do they think he's the one?" Jesse passed the cabbage and pepper slaw to her father.

" 'Cause most folks don't like him."

"Why not?"

" 'Cause he doesn't give them the time of day, I reckon."

"What's that got to do with it? You don't accuse a man of such a terrible thing just because you don't like him."

"Some do."

"H-h-his p-p-pap-a w-w-was —" Todd's stuttering was much worse when he had what he considered valuable news to impart to the family.

"Talk slowly, son, and the words will come out," Doctor Forbes said.

"Papa h-hanged."

"His papa was hanged?" Susan's interest was piqued. "For what?"

"K-k-killin' Mr. H-H-Harper's brother."

"Lord!" Susan exclaimed. "That'd do it. That'd twist the tail on the donkey. How'd you find that out, you little twerp?"

"I-Ike S-Spangler."

"That greasy old man who's always foolin' with motor cars? What does he know 'bout anything?"

"H-h-he knows M-M-Mr. S-S-Simmer, that's w-why." Todd looked defiantly at his sister, glanced to see if his father was looking, then stuck out his tongue.

15

"Mr. Simmer is a man who tends to his own business and expects everyone else to do the same." Doctor Forbes helped himself to another helping of creamed potatoes and peas.

"You've met him?" Jesse asked.

"Yeah, I've met him. Remember the woodcutter who split his leg open with an axe last fall? It was Wade Simmer who carried him out of the woods to the road. Another time he stopped me and asked me to look at the colored boy who lives on his place."

"Well?" Jesse and Susan said at the same time.

"Well, what?" The doctor was being deliberately obtuse.

"You know," Susan said. "What was he like?"

"He had the belly ache from eating too many green apples. Simmer thought maybe it might be something serious."

"I mean Mr. Simmer. What was he like? Does he and that nigger boy live under a brush arbor? Does he have a woman up there? Is he mean as folks say he is?"

"Susan, for crying out loud," Jesse exclaimed. "Do you listen to every gossip? And I told you not to say 'nigger.'"

"How am I going to know anything unless I ask? I bet you don't plug up your ears when Papa tells us about Mr. Simmer."

No, she wouldn't, Jesse admitted silently. She had been as curious about him as everyone else. It was simple curiosity, a perfectly normal reaction to a man who was practically a recluse.

"He lives in a house. I didn't see any women,"

the doctor said. "Jesse, is there more cornbread?"

"Of course. I'll get it." Jesse left the table and went to the kitchen. "Oh, for goodness sake. Todd, you didn't empty the pan under the ice box. There's water all over the floor."

"I-I-I f-f-forgot."

"That's your chore, young man," Jesse said, returning to her seat at the table. "You can clean up the mess before Susan and I do the dishes. And don't forget to put the card in the window. The iceman comes tomorrow."

The next morning on her way out of town to visit families in the hill country, Jesse stopped at the modern two-storied brick schoolhouse, the pride of Harpersville. She had glimpsed the blond head of her friend, Pauline Anthony. The teacher was holding a child who had fallen from the giant stride, an iron pole that sat in the ground much like a maypole. Instead of ribbons and flowers, chains with hand grips hung from this pole. Holding onto the chains, the children ran around the pole until the momentum lifted them off the ground so that they made "giant strides" around the pole, hence the name. If one of the chains was not in use, it oftentimes swung free and struck one of the children. Jesse had always thought it a frightfully dangerous thing to have on the playground.

She pulled the horse to a stop, stepped quickly from the buggy and called to Pauline before she entered the school.

"Is she hurt?"

17

"No, I don't think so. She got a little bump on the head. You all right now, Fredda?" She set the small girl on her feet. "Go in and get a drink of water. You'll feel better."

"That plaything Mr. Harper insisted on having in the school yard is a menace," Jesse said.

"I agree. I try to keep the big kids off while the little ones are playing nearby." Pauline looped her arm into that of her friend. "Where are you off to, Nurse Forbes? Wherever it is, I wish I were going with you. I hate being cooped up in a schoolroom on such a lovely spring day."

"I'm going up to Mill Springs to check on Mrs. Bailey's ingrown toenail. Papa cut a hunk of it out last week. Granny Lester's goiter is getting bigger. Soon her neck will be the size of a waterbucket. Papa wants me to try once again to get her to come down and let him send her to Knoxville and have it taken out." Jesse grinned at her friend. "How is that for a romantic afternoon?"

"Oh, you!" Pauline's brown eyes sparkled. She was not as tall or as willowy as Jesse, but her skin was flawless and she had a ready smile. The two had been friends for two years — since Pauline had come from Knoxville to teach in the new school.

"How do you find them?"

"There's only one road, silly. I'll just keep going until I get there. It isn't as if I haven't been up there before."

"My foot! You shouldn't go alone. You could run into that idiot that's got the women in this

18

town scared out of their wits."

"The Looker? I'll be back before dark."

"Wade Simmer lives up there."

"You think he's The Looker?"

"Everybody else does."

"Papa wouldn't let me go up there if he thought it was dangerous."

"I saw Wade Simmer at the depot once. He looked mad enough to bite a nail in two. He was having a set-to with the agent about something he'd expected to come in on the train. He seemed wild and . . . kind of exciting. Now that I think about it, he didn't seem the type to *look* and not do anything else. He was pure-dee male from top to bottom. But then . . . you never know. Could be a horse kicked *it* or he got *it* caught in a fence and all he can do is look." She giggled at the look of exasperation on Jesse's face.

"Pauline! For goodness sake —"

"Yes, yes, I know. I've got a nasty mind. Tell you what. I'll come help you put up your raspberry jam if you'll go to the ball game Sunday."

"That's a bribe. You know how I hate making jam, but I also hate letting berries go to waste."

"It's a deal? I'll be over Saturday morning." The school bell rang, and, laughing over her shoulder, Pauline dashed for the school door.

"I've been hornswoggled," Jesse called.

"You sure have," Pauline retorted, and disappeared inside.

Jesse stood on the walk for a moment and watched the children file back into the school.

19

Some of them were in awe of her, she knew. Once a month she visited the school to talk about the importance of clean hands and teeth. While she was there, she swabbed throats, treated boils and ringworm and a dozen other minor ailments.

Today she wore her nurse's apron, white and starched, over her blue gingham dress. The square bib came up to the neckline. The long, wide straps that went over her shoulders crossed in back, fit into loops at the waist and tied. The little round, stiff white headpiece that was anchored to the crown of her head and the apron that covered her skirt identified her as a nurse. Jesse was proud of her uniform; she had spent two years away from home and family to earn it.

She walked back to the buggy, climbed in and slapped the reins against the animal's back. It was a wasted motion. Molly was a well-trained horse. She knew that when Jesse or the doctor got into the buggy, she was to go. She also knew that when they got out, she was to stay until they came back.

The buggy moved past the creamery, crossed the bridge that spanned the creek and turned onto the road that led up the mountain. It really wasn't a mountain. The Great Smokies were ten or fifteen miles to the east. What Jesse was driving through was more like a cluster of high wooded hills that rammed against each other, divided only by the rocky streams that cut a deep gash to the rich bottomlands. The ride was quiet and peaceful. Jesse let Molly travel at her own speed while her ears drank in the birdsong and her eyes feasted on the beauty of wildflowers.

Where the road rounded a curve, the trees opened up and Jesse could see the town below — Mr. Harper's town. The wide brick-paved streets were laid out in straight lines, fanning out from the main street that ran through town. Business places filled the four-block area around the park square. In the center of the park was a statue of the town's founder. To the intense irritation of Boyd Harper, the statue had become a favorite resting place for pigeons and starlings and needed periodic washing down to maintain its dignity.

Farther out on Main Street Jesse glimpsed the large, Victorian house where she had lived since she and her father had moved here from Knoxville when she was five years old. Here he had met and married Dora Gilbert. Jesse's own mother had died giving birth to her, and much of the time she had been shuffled among relatives until her papa remarried; Dora, his new wife, had been all Jesse's young heart had dreamed a mother could be. The family had had ten wonderful years together before Dora died when Todd was still a baby in diapers.

The windows of the white, gabled house gleamed in the morning sun. Set well back from the street with a narrow walk leading to the wide steps of the veranda that curved around two sides, the home was much like the others that lined the main street beyond the business section.

The Harper house, of course, was much bigger. The town's leading family lived in a square red brick building set in the middle of two acres of well-tended lawn. The white pillars rose up to support an upper porch. On the side were two sets of bay windows on both the ground floor and the upper floor that extended to smaller bays on the third-floor attic rooms. A fretwork railing circled the flat roof. Every eave was decorated with the elaborate scrollwork. And, fluttering in the breeze, the United States flag hung from a pole that jutted out from the porch, as if, Jesse thought, to identify it as an official residence.

Jesse's smile was one of indulgence as the horse followed the meanderings of the road. Unlike most people in Harpersville, she felt no animosity toward the Harpers because they were rich or because they thought they owned the town fifty-five years after their ancestors founded it. To her, their struggle to be important was almost childish.

At the crossroads Jesse took the trail through an unfenced pasture and passed a tobacco patch before entering the cool woods again. All was quiet except for the chirping of the birds and the chatter of a squirrel now and then as it scampered to the tops of the birches that stood white and clean. A mockingbird trilled high up in a treetop and a bluejay scolded him from the sumac below.

"You old fussbudget," Jesse teased as she passed by.

Molly pulled the buggy on up the hill. The sun was warm and bright. It was a sweet-smelling May day, a bright blue day and one that would stay in Jesse's memory for a long, long time.

# CHAPTER
## • 2 •

*M*ules, horses and teams were hitched to the rail in front of the mill when Jesse drove by. A man was unloading sacks of corn and a woman with a stiff-brimmed sunbonnet stood holding the hand of a small child. The woman waved. Everyone in a four-county area knew Doctor Forbes's buggy. They also knew that it was his daughter in the white uniform of a nurse.

Jesse promised herself that if she had time, she would stop at the store on the way back and visit for a moment with the miller's wife, Mrs. Frony. She usually found the tiny woman crocheting. She made everything from baby booties to doilies and tidies to bed and table covers. On her last trip Jesse had delivered a box of thread that had come in on the train, and Mrs. Frony had given her a lacy dresser scarf.

On down the road she found Mrs. Bailey barefoot in the garden with only a dirty stocking covering the toe that had been a bloody mess a few days earlier. Jesse persuaded the woman to soak her foot in a washpan of warm water, then liberally doused it with iodine and put a bandage on it. A half hour later she took her leave with a jar of dill pickles and a glass of chokecherry jelly that had been carefully sealed with beeswax. The poor but proud hill folk never sent the doctor or his nurse away empty-handed.

When Jesse reached the Lesters' neat little house set back in the woods, Granny was sitting in a bent-willow rocker on the front porch with the ever-present snuff stick in the corner of her mouth. Before she got out of the buggy, Jesse could see that the goiter in Granny's neck was larger than when she and the doctor had visited a month earlier.

The house Grandpa Lester had brought Granny to as a bride was four rooms now — the original two in front and the two across the back that had been added when the family increased. The porch was narrow and was sheltered by the sloping roof of the house. The two front doors stood open to allow the breeze to circulate.

"Now ain't ya just as pretty as a buttercup." Granny spat snuff juice in the small tin can beside her chair before she spoke.

"Hello, Granny," Jesse said, coming up the two steps to the porch. "Isn't this a lovely day?"

"It's as sightly a day as I ever did see. Come sit a spell."

"Thank you, I will. How are you feeling?"

"As good as can be expected with this devilish thin' growin' in my craw."

Jesse noticed that Granny's eyes had started to bulge and that she was short of breath.

"How's Grandpa?" Jesse asked while trying to think of a way to bring up the subject of the trip to Knoxville.

"Fair to middlin'. The boy come and helped him put his tobaccy in the shed."

"One of your boys came home? How nice! The one from Huntsville or the one from Atlanta?"

"Neither. Ain't one of 'em goin' to dirty his hands with tobaccy. They be too high-toned fer that."

"Oh, I didn't know you had but the two."

"We don't." Granny cocked her head to listen. "That's Mr. Lester comin' in." Although everyone called the couple Granny and Grandpa, they called each other Mr. and Mrs. Lester.

The bald-headed old man in the patched overalls came through the house and out onto the porch.

"Howdy," he said to Jesse, then held up two dead squirrels by their bushy tails.

"Looky here, Mrs. Lester. They was on the back step, shot through the head like they is, ain't no doubt 'out who left 'em."

"The boy." Grandpa nodded and Granny said, "Well, clean 'em, Mr. Lester, so the doctor can have squirrel for his supper."

"Oh, no," Jesse said quickly. "I'd dearly love to take them, but I'm afraid they'd not keep in this hot weather. I want to stop and visit with Mrs. Frony on the way home."

"Well, now, reckon there's somethin' to what ya say. Mr. Lester, didn't ya say them vines was

25

making taters? Go dig her a mess to take home."

"Grandpa," Jesse said as the old man started to leave, "Papa sent some ointment for your hemorr— for your piles." She bent over the gaping top of the leather bag she had brought from the buggy and took out a flat, white tin. "Did sitting in the warm, then cold water, help?"

"Some," Grandpa said without looking at her. He took the tin. "Thanky."

Because Jesse knew he was embarrassed, she said nothing more. When she was alone again with Granny Lester, she broached the subject of the operation.

"Granny, your goiter is going to keep growing. It's beginning to affect your eyes and your heart. Have you given any thought to going to Knoxville and having it removed? Papa says it's not a complicated operation, and seventy-five percent of the patients get along fine. Of course, it depends on a person's general health, and you seem to be fine otherwise."

"I thought 'bout it oncet." Granny spat snuff juice out of her mouth. "I ain't goin'. Ain't leavin' Mr. Lester here all by his own self. When it comes my time and the Lord calls me to the pearly gates, I'll go. There ain't no two ways about it."

"You may leave Mr. Lester alone for quite a few years if you don't have the goiter removed."

"Fiddle-faddle. He'd not get along a winter without me. When ya get old yore supposed to die and that's that. Hot, ain't it? Have a fan, it'll stir the breeze."

Granny handed Jesse a cardboard fan that advertised ROSADALIS BLOOD PURIFIER. Bold black print stated that the medicine would positively cure nervous debility, rheumatism, gout, goiter, bronchitis, consumption. The list went on, but Jesse didn't bother to read it. She did notice the claim that many "Physicians and Ministers of the Gospel" recommended the product.

Her cause was lost. Granny Lester would never have the operation. Jesse handed the fan back to Granny, closed her satchel and rose to go.

Grandpa led Molly around the house to the watering tank. When he returned, a gunnysack half-filled with potatoes was on the floor of the buggy. Jesse thanked him and exclaimed on the size and the quality of the gift. She waved good-bye and turned the horse on up the trail.

Granny was taking the quack medicine recommended by ministers of the gospel and had faith it would dissolve the goiter. Ministers of the gospel, indeed, Jesse fumed. She bet the man who had written the label had invented them — and the "physicians" too. If the growth wasn't removed, Granny would be dead by Christmas, if not sooner.

Wade Simmer came out of the woods and squatted on his heels beside the trail. When the doctor's buggy left the Lesters' and turned north, he had cut through the woods in order to reach this place. This was not the first time he had waited for the buggy carrying Jesse Forbes. Usually he faded into the woods and watched her pass. Today he intended to stop the buggy and talk to her. What he had to tell her could delay her so long that it would be dark by the time she came back down out of the hills. That meant he'd have to follow her home to see that nothing happened to her.

Wade cursed himself for not approaching her while she sat on the porch with Granny, but he'd waited too long to meet her face-to-face to do it in front of Granny Lester's sharp eyes. Old Granny had been telling him for years to get himself a good woman — as if *good* women were like apples hanging on a tree just waiting to be plucked.

He had been back at the family homestead for about a year when he had seen Jesse for the first time. What he saw only made him want to see more. He began to carry a small pair of field glasses with him when it was time for her to visit Granny or the Fronys'. Just curiosity, he told himself when a little part of his mind told him he was a damn fool. That was about a year and a half ago. Now he knew her face as well as he knew his own.

Wade had also caught glimpses of the doctor's daughter in town when he occasionally went down to the post office or to get freight at the depot. He wondered how she would react to him. Did she think he was the one who was stripping women naked and looking at them?

Not much that went on in Harpersville escaped Wade's notice. A couple times a week he went to Ike Spangler's garage to tinker with a motor. Ike had told him he was suspected of being The

28

Looker. He'd got a chuckle over that.

Hell, there hadn't been this much excitement in Harpersville since he was a kid and he and some of his friends had come down from the hills and hoisted Boyd Harper's privy to the top of the bank building.

The jingle of harness brought Wade to his feet. Suddenly he was as breathless as if he had run five miles, and it irritated him. Godamighty. She was only a woman, for Christ's sake. Then it occurred to him that in his mind he had built an image of her; not her physical appearance, but what kind of person she was on the inside. And he didn't want to be disappointed.

Jesse was so deep in thought that at first she didn't see the man standing in the center of the trail holding a rifle in his arms. When she did, the first thing she noticed was the scowl on a face that was dark with whiskers, a face that she suspected would be dark even if he had just shaved. He stood, booted feet spread, as if he were facing an enemy. His brimmed hat was pulled low over his forehead so that she was unable to see the color of his eyes, but she could tell that they were looking at her.

She pulled up on the reins, aware that her heart was beating awfully fast. Somehow she knew that this was the notorious Wade Simmer. If he were The Looker, as everyone in town believed, he'd not harm her here in broad daylight, would he? Her father wouldn't have sent her up here if he had thought she would be in danger. She had not known him to make a mistake in judging a man's character.

"Hello, Mr. Simmer," Jesse said calmly, although a mad, frightened dance was going on inside her.

He came slowly to the side of the buggy. From the road, she'd been able to tell that he was a wide-shouldered, slim-hipped man with long arms and legs. Up close, she could see that his eyes were green with amber flecks and his hair black as midnight. His jaw was solid and hard and looked as if it had withstood many a barroom brawl.

"You know who I am," he said, his eyes holding hers.

"Am I wrong?"

"No. Aren't you afraid to be out here alone with the one they call The Looker?"

"You've heard that? Naturally, they want to believe you're The Looker because they don't like you. If Papa thought I'd run into that revolting excuse for a man, I'd not be here."

"Your papa is too trusting," he said drily.

"Is he wrong?"

Time seemed to stop as they looked at each other. Without embarrassment, Jesse looked directly until she was sure that his features would be imprinted in her memory forever. Wade was a tall man. His face was almost on a level with hers, though she sat above the wagon wheel. A sudden smile formed on his lips and spread to his eyes.

"Well?" Jesse asked crossly, thinking he was laughing at her.

Instead of answering her question, he said, "I'm not the least bit disappointed."

"I don't know what you're talking about, but I'm glad to hear it," she snapped. "Now, I must be going."

He seemed to sigh and his shoulders relaxed.

"I stopped you to ask you to look in on some sick kids — the Merfelds and the Gordons."

"Of course. Where do they live?"

"Back up in the woods on Downy Creek. It's about three miles to the Merfelds and two more to the Gordons."

"All right. How do I get there?"

"I'll take you."

"Thank you very much, Mr. Simmer. It's kind of you to offer."

"You're willing to go off into the woods with me?"

"Do I have reason for fearing you?"

"Maybe." He turned his head so she couldn't see his face.

"Well, I'm not afraid of you. You go to Ike Spangler's garage. He's a friend of my little brother, Todd. I'm sure Ike wouldn't have you around if you were dangerous."

Wade continued to stare at her. "Your pa may be a fine doctor, but he hasn't taught you anything about men."

"I've got to be going, Mr. Simmer, if I'm going to get home before dark."

"You won't make it," he said, placing his rifle on the buggy floor and climbing onto the seat.

31

"But I'll see you to your door."

"Thank you, but no. I'm perfectly capable —"

He took the reins from her hands and gave them a shake. "Get goin', boy —"

"— Girl," Jesse said sternly. "Molly doesn't like being called a boy. She's very feminine and . . . sensitive."

Wade saw the defiant look in her eyes, and he suddenly felt light as a cloud. *Sweetheart, you're sure as hell no disappointment.*

Jesse didn't understand herself at all. Here she was, miles from anywhere with a man most folk considered dangerous. Why hadn't she refused to let him get into the buggy? Come to think of it, she had no choice. When he had first walked up to the buggy, there had been a question mark lurking in the back of his eyes. She wondered what he had been thinking. Had he expected her to scream or faint? The thought brought the question to her lips. She was unable to hold it back and turned her head to look at him.

"You thought I'd swoon when you popped out of the woods," she said accusingly. "I've never swooned in my life and I've seen some grisly things."

"More grisly than I am?"

"Much more." She lifted her head proudly. She was determined not to let him think she was afraid of him.

Their heads turned simultaneously toward the trail ahead. For several minutes they were silent, both busy with their own thoughts and each too intensely aware of the other to note how wonderfully cool it was here in the woods. The air smelled sweet and fresh as they followed the trail cut between sloping, timbered hills.

"Tell me about the Gordon children," Jesse said, breaking the silence.

"All I know is their pa came down to the mill yesterday and said a couple of them were real sick. He said the Merfeld and the Foster kids had come down with something too, and if we saw the Doc, to ask him to come over. He'd pay with a sack of corn."

"Hmmm. Where does this other family live?"

"About a mile from the Gordons."

"Where do these children go to school?"

"Coon Rapids."

"Is that a town?"

"It's an area."

"I've never heard of it."

"No reason to. Not much there."

Wade could hardly believe he was sitting here talking to her about sick kids and schools. He wanted to look at her. The white thing that covered her dress brushed against the legs of his duck britches. She was as crisp and clean as a spring morning. He glanced at her hands in her lap. They were smooth and white, her fingers long, her nails clipped. He wondered how her hands would feel on his face. Disgusted with himself, he turned his face toward the side of the trail. In all his twenty-eight years he'd not ever been this interested in a woman. Why in hell did it have to be one that was so . . . unobtainable?

"This is the Merfelds'?" Jesse said, when they came in sight of a homestead that was so run down that it was a wonder the house was still standing. The yard around the house was littered with debris of every kind. The vegetable garden was almost overgrown with weeds, and a big sow rooted among the few scattered logs that served as a woodpile.

Molly stopped at the broken rail fence. Jesse straightened her cap and stepped down from the buggy before Wade came around to help her. She reached for the leather satchel and looked up to see him beside her.

"If Merfeld gives you any trouble, sing out."

"Why would he . . . give me trouble?"

"He's got a whiskey still up here and drinks most of what he makes."

"Oh."

By the time Jesse passed through the broken fence, a woman had come out onto the porch where the roof sagged so low it almost touched the top of her head. She was thin and weary-looking, and well along in her pregnancy. As Jesse approached, she combed strands of hair back from her face with her fingers.

"Mrs. Merfeld, I'm Nurse Forbes. Doctor Forbes is my father. I hear you have sick children."

"Yeah, I got sick kids. Would you come look at 'em?"

"Of course. How long have they been sick?"

"My oldest boy got sick a week or two ago.

He's better, but now the younger ones come down with it and they're sicker than Dude was."

Jesse followed the woman into the house that smelled strongly of vomit and excrement. Three children lay on pallets on the floor. They were all naked except for what would pass as underwear on the two boys and a thin shift on a girl who was about eight or nine years old. Jesse knelt down beside her.

"Turn over, honey, so I can take a look at you." The child was feverish and red as a strawberry. "Open your mouth, so I can look at your throat. Hmmm. . . . Mrs. Merfeld, did they vomit and run off at the bowels?"

"Yes'm, they did."

Jesse looked at the other two children. "Did their brother break out like this?"

"Yes'm, but not so much."

"Did all of them complain of their heads hurting?"

"Yes'm."

"They've got scarlet fever, and I suspect they caught it from their brother."

"Do you have medicine for it? We'll pay . . . somehow."

"I don't have any with me, but I'll get some. Doctor Forbes has medicine that will drive the rash to the surface. When that happens, they'll begin to feel better. Meanwhile give them milk and soup and as much water as they can drink. Put some soda in water and sponge them off from head to foot. Do you have anyone to help you, Mrs. Merfeld?"

"I got Dude. He's hangin' round out back. And Flora, she went to the Gordons 'cause we heard their kids was sick. We hoped Mrs. Gordon would know what to do."

Jesse looked down at the woman's worried face and her heart went out to her.

"When Flora gets back, keep her here at home and don't let anyone outside the family in the house. Scarlet fever is catching and can be spread very easily. Pour boiling water over the children's dishes and eating utensils. When they drink from the dipper don't let them put it back in the water bucket until you scald it."

"Will Flora get sick?"

"I'm not sure, but don't worry. They'll be all right if you can get the fever down. If you have sage, make a weak tea and force them, if necessary, to drink as much as they can. Don't forget, sponge them down with the soda water — no soap. Make them drink the tea or plain water. And get them to eat. I saw a chicken out back. Boil her and give the broth to the children. I'll be back as soon as I can with some medicine."

"Thank you, miss. Oh, thank you. I was worried sick."

"We can't have that. When is your baby due?"

"I don't know. I kind of lost track. Should be pretty soon."

"We'll talk about it when I come back."

"When, miss?" Mrs. Merfeld asked anxiously.

"Bright and early in the morning."

Jesse hurried out to where Wade Simmer was rubbing Molly with a gunnysack to wipe the sweat away.

"Mr. Simmer, the children have scarlet fever. I need to get back to town and get medicine — but first, I'd better see about the other families. If they have scarlet fever, I must warn them of how contagious it is."

"Then let's go. The horse has been watered."

"First, I must disinfect my hands." She took a bottle from the satchel. "Pour some of this onto them. It's alcohol."

"The drinking kind?" he asked, as he watched her rub the liquid over her hands and wrists.

"If you want to go out like a light. It's one hundred proof. Papa gets it from a distillery that makes medical supplies."

Wade helped her into the buggy and set the satchel on the floor. He climbed in beside her just as Molly began to pull at the traces.

"Your father will be worried. You'd better write a note and tell him you'll be late."

"How'll I get it to him?"

"Jody will take it. He'd rather run than eat."

"Jody? Is he your son?"

"Some think so, but he isn't. He's a darkie who lives with me. You got any problem with that?"

She scowled and snapped. "Why should I? He isn't living with me."

"Don't get your dander up. I only asked. Write the message. Jody'll take it down to the doctor."

"And bring the medicine back?"

"Just explain to the doctor what you want."

"Another thing. Do you think Granny Lester would put me up for the night? If the boy brought back the medicine, I could be at the Merfelds' by daybreak."

"I'm sure Granny would be happy to oblige."

Wade stopped the buggy, put two fingers in his mouth and whistled two short blasts then a long one.

"What in the world are you doing?" Jesse asked, as she fumbled in the bag for paper and pencil.

"Calling Jody. He's around here somewhere. He'll be wanting to know what's going on — why I'm in your buggy. He's just naturally curious about everything." Wade whistled again.

Jesse shook her head and began to write.

"Jody," Wade called. "Can you hear me?"

" 'Course, I hears ya. I'd have to be daid not to hear ya, the way ya beller."

A tall thin boy in his early teens came out of the woods and leaned casually against a tree beside the trail. His skin was the color of coffee with a dab of cream added, and his hair was cut close to a well-shaped head.

"The lady has a message for the doctor. I don't suppose you could take it down and bring back some medicine before dark. Naw," Wade said with a shrug. "It's too far. I guess I'll have to do it."

"What ya mean, white man? I can be in and outta that town 'fore sundown. I knows the sun don't set on no nigga in that town."

"Oh, gracious me," Jesse exclaimed. "I'd forgotten about that stupid law."

"Ain't no worry, lady." Jody swaggered up beside the buggy.

"Do you know where the doctor lives?"

"Yes'm, I knows. I ain't no dumb nigga."

Jesse looked at him sharply and handed him the folded paper.

"I didn't imply that you were, so don't be lippy. It's very important that I get the medicine as soon as possible. Tell Doctor Forbes not to worry about me. Oh, never mind. I told him in the message."

Jody looked at the paper in his hand, then pushed it deeply into his pocket.

"Well, what'a ya say, slue-foot?" Wade dug into his pocket and pulled out a coin.

"What do *ya* think, bucket-bottom?"

"Betcha a nickel."

"I ain't runnin' *that* cheap."

"Dime, then."

"— And the nickel."

"You're on, but you'll not make it. You've already lost a half-mile standing here jawing. Lose and you'll finish that woodpile by yourself."

Jesse looked from one to the other, disbelieving what she was hearing. The relationship between this colored boy and the white man was amazing. *Slue-foot? Bucket-bottom?*

"Jist you watch my smoke, white *boy*."

Jody crouched down, one foot out, the other behind him, his hands touching the ground. Jesse wasn't prepared for Wade's shrill whistle and was startled. Jody took off down the track, head up, shoulders back, his arms and legs pumping like pistons. Wade chuckled.

Jesse turned to look at him. *Laughing, he was handsome as sin and dangerous as a coiled rattler!*

"He's showing off for you now. As soon as he's out of sight he'll slow down and set a pace."

"He's going to *run* to town and back? It's ten miles and you goaded him into doing it."

"Not as the crow flies. He'll take shortcuts. I told you he'd rather run than eat, and he likes nothing better than to make me eat my words."

"I hope he does," she retorted with a toss of her head. "Bucket-bottom. I never heard the like."

Wade heard a little giggle. He couldn't take his eyes off her, and something funny happened to his heart.

# CHAPTER
## • 3 •

*T*he trail Wade followed could be called that only because there were faint wheel tracks on the thick sod and because it cut a narrow path through the woods. At times the trail became a mere thread clinging to the hillside, and the top of the buggy brushed overhanging bushes as it moved along. High above, a pair of hawks circled in amorous pursuit of each other, and from the underbrush beside the trail ahead, a fox, drawn by his irresistible curiosity to inspect the unfamiliar sound, scurried away as the buggy approached.

It seemed to Jesse that she and this man she had met just a few hours before were the only two people in the world. Yet she was surprised to discover that she was not afraid. Wade Simmer was at once strange and yet familiar.

"It's so pretty here," she said in an awed tone.

"You think so?" He turned slightly to face her more directly. A shaft of sunlight sifting through the trees shone on his deeply tanned face, so that his eyes seemed especially light. They reminded

41

her of clear green glass. She realized this suddenly as if it were of great importance.

"Don't you?"

"I wouldn't live anywhere else."

As he gazed at her, Jesse sensed something disturbing in the way he looked at her and felt uneasy in the region of her heart.

"Are you hungry?" She was grateful for the thought that gave her something to do, and she reached for the cloth-wrapped package on the buggy floor. "My sister Susan packed my lunch. No telling what's in it." Jesse, who rarely was made ill at ease by a man's gaze, felt her cheeks grow warm under his bold scrutiny. "She eats like a field hand so there'll be plenty."

Jesse unfolded the cloth to find two slices of bread spread with butter, two hard-boiled eggs, four of the cookies she had baked the night before and a fried apple pie.

"See? She must have thought I was going to be gone a week."

"I've seen your sister. She doesn't look anything like you. Her hair is light."

"Susan and Todd are my half-sister and half-brother. Oh, my. I haven't thought of them in that way for a long time." Jesse held out a thick slice of bread spread with butter and one of the eggs. "My mother died shortly after I was born. I lived with various relatives while Papa was in medical school. He married again when I was five, and oh, it was wonderful to have a mother. I loved her so —" Her voice trailed.

42

*Shut up the nervous chatter, Jesse Forbes. You're babbling like a brook.*

"Good light bread," Wade said, after he had eaten the bread and the egg.

"Thank you. I make about six loaves a week. We all have hearty appetites. Ready for more?"

"I didn't expect you to feed me."

"You're not getting a fancy meal. You eat the pie, I'll eat the cookies. They're my favorite. We call them cry babies."

"I suppose because babies cry for more."

"How did you guess?"

"I'm no dummy. I've been out of the woods a time or two."

"Or three, or four," she said drily.

He was fascinated. His eyes smiled into hers. He took the plump pie from her hand, being careful not to touch her fingers. She was everything he had imagined her to be and more. Much, much more. His adamant wish was for the day never to end because beyond this there could be nothing more between them.

He was what was commonly referred to as a hillbilly, and the son of a man hanged for murdering a Harper. She was the daughter of the town doctor. Well, hell, he had known that from the start. His curiosity had goaded him into stopping her buggy when the Lesters could have given her the message about the Merfelds and the Gordons and saved him the grief that was sure to come. Wade silently cursed himself for being a stupid son of a bitch. He feared that what he had done

43

today was going to make him miserable for the rest of his life.

"Tell me about Jody," Jesse said, uneasy in the silence between them. Now that she was no longer uncomfortable with this strange man, she wanted to know more about him.

"What do you want to know?"

"Where did he come from? How did he come to be staying with you?"

"He came from Violet, the colored town over near the mountains. I don't know where he was before that. I found him in a cave in the woods, hungry and sick." Wade chuckled. "He spit and hissed like a cornered cat. I thought I'd have to throw a net over him to get him out of the cave. I got him home, fed him, and doctored him up. He's been with me since."

"I've never been around a Negro who talks to a white man the way he talks to you."

"No?" There was a coolness in Wade's voice. "What's wrong with the way he talks to me?"

"Well, you know. Colored folk don't usually —"

"Speak to white folk as if they were equals?"

"Something like that. I didn't mean —"

"— Yes, you did. You mean he's a *nigger* so he should bow and scrape and be grateful for a kind word from the high-and-mighty *white* man. You, me, Jody, the Lesters and even the lofty Harpers are all equal in the eyes of our creator. We're all human. We eat, breath, live and die. Jody's got more intelligence in his little finger than that pea-brained Edsel Harper has in his whole mol-

44

lycoddled, gutless body. If Jody had the opportunities Edsel's had, he would amount to a hell of a lot more than being old Boyd's flunky." Quiet anger was in Wade's voice and his stare was as cold as a wall of ice.

"I'm sorry if I made you angry. You must admit your opinion is not a common or a popular one."

"Who the hell cares about popular opinions? I damn sure don't. That's a sore spot with me, lady. What I see is a lot of good potential brain power going to waste because the boy's skin is dark."

Silence settled heavily between them, a silence Wade regretted. He knew their time together was short and didn't want to waste a minute of it.

"Why do you dislike Edsel Harper?" Jesse asked the first thing that came to her mind.

Wade snorted with disgust. "I don't dislike him. He isn't important enough to me to bother to dislike."

"I've always felt kind of sorry for him because he's so dominated by his parents."

"Are you going to marry him?"

"Good heav . . . ens!" Jesse's eyes registered shock and indignation. "Where did you get an idea like that?"

"It's common talk in town that the Harpers want you in the family."

"That doesn't mean that I'd even consider —"

"— Think of all that money."

"You're . . . you're being vulgar!"

"Money isn't vulgar. Some folk think it's what makes the world go round."

45

"I didn't say *money* was vulgar," Jesse almost shouted. "I said *you* were."

"Then you're not going to marry him?" His eyes had a teasing glint in them and the corners of his mouth twitched.

"Absolutely, positively not! I'd not marry that namby-pamby mamma's boy if he were the last man alive. You certainly don't credit me with much intelligence, do you? I know what Roberta Harper is up to. Let me tell you another thing, Mr. Know-It-All Simmer, I *may* be just about as smart up here" — she tapped her temple with her forefinger — "as your Jody."

He looked at her from beneath furrowed brows, and for a moment their eyes locked and clashed.

"Why are you so all-fired mad all of a sudden?"

Her face sobered. She tilted her head to one side and placed a finger at the corner of her mouth.

"I . . . don't know."

The expression on her face changed with lightning speed. Laughter rumbled up and out of her sweetly curved mouth. Wade could only stare. Jesse Forbes was like no one he'd ever met before. She had a quick mind and a ready wit, and was as pretty as a covey of quail. He had heard more happy laughter during the past few hours than he had during the past few years. The attraction he felt for her was something he would never dare bring out in the open. Nevertheless, it was there, a power he was going to have to reckon with sooner or later.

The Gordon homestead was tidy compared to the Merfelds'. The house was small, scarcely more than two or three rooms and set up from the ground on stumps so that beneath it the breeze could circulate and the chickens could move about freely. A wild rose vine planted beside the door followed thin wires to the roof. The vegetable garden was weeded and fenced. Two hogs were penned back from the house, but their stench still reached Jesse where Wade had stopped the buggy beneath a huge ash tree.

A thin, gaunt-faced man in overalls hurried out to meet them.

"Hello, Mr. Gordon," Wade said. "I heard at the store that your children are sick. I've brought the nurse."

"Thank God you did. Come in, ma'am. Come in. Our littlest one is bad off. Took bad about noontime. Fever's high. The others ain't quite so bad."

Jesse's mind cleared of everything except the work at hand. She grabbed her satchel and hurried into the house after Mr. Gordon. In one of the two front rooms two children lay quietly in a double bed, and on a bunk attached to the wall beneath the window, a small girl, judging by the short curly hair, lay thrashing about beneath a heavy quilt. A pale, haggard-looking woman sat on the edge of the bunk fanning the child's face with a piece of cardboard. She stood when Jesse came into the room.

"Hello. I'm Nurse Forbes —"

"Thank the good Lord. She's bad, awful bad."

Jesse set her satchel on the floor and bent over the child on the bunk. Her little face was covered with a red rash. Jesse threw back the cover and saw that the same rash covered the child's body, and her skin was fiery. Scarlet fever.

"Get a bucket of fresh cool water, please, and hurry." Jesse issued the order briskly. "I need a cloth to bathe her and an oilcloth if you have one to put on the bed beneath her. I'll have to give her a cold enema and try to bring down the fever before she goes into convulsions."

Jesse worked over the child for an hour before she had the first hint that the fever had gone down and the child was breathing more easily. She examined the other two children and instructed Mrs. Gordon about sponging them down with soda water and forcing them to drink as much water as they could hold.

"Fever takes moisture from their bodies," Jesse explained. "It must be replaced. Sage tea is good for fever."

"I ain't got one bit a sage on the place."

"I'll bring some when I return."

"When will that be, miss?" Mrs. Gordon asked anxiously while Jesse carefully cleaned the pipe on the end of the syringe with alcohol.

"I sent a note to Doctor Forbes. Medicine should be here shortly after sundown. If Mr. Simmer will show me the way" — she glanced at Wade leaning against the porch post and saw

48

him nod — "I'll be back tonight."

"Thank you. God bless you."

"Keep bathing Madaline with warm soda water. Don't let her scratch herself. The medicine Doctor Forbes is sending will bring out more rash. That must all come out before she can get better. Cover her with a light cover until evening.

"Scarlet fever is catching, but it's unlikely you or Mr. Gordon will get it. Don't let anyone else in the house. Scald all their eating utensils and when you empty the chamber pots, bury the waste or cover it with lime." Jesse put her hand on the woman's shoulder. "Don't worry. I'll be back as soon as I can."

Jesse walked briskly to the buggy. Wade had been busy too. A fresh bucket of water sat at Molly's head, and she was munching on a pile of cut grass. Jesse took out the bottle of alcohol and he poured some over Jesse's hands without her having to ask him. While she was rubbing her hands, he recapped the bottle and put it back in the satchel.

On the way to the Fosters', Jesse asked, "How will Jody find us?"

"He'll go to my place. We'll go there after we leave the Fosters'."

"I'd rather go directly to Granny Lester's."

"You're afraid I'll get you to my place and have my way with you?" he asked almost angrily.

"Of course not! But it's not proper for me to go there when you are . . . are a single man."

"Maybe I'm married and have six kids."

She looked at him sharply and saw the teasing light in his eyes.

"If you're married, word hasn't reached town yet."

"So you *have* heard of me."

"Who in Harpersville hasn't?" she answered sharply.

"Then you know my pa was hanged in the town square."

"I heard he was."

"— And I'm a chip off the old block."

"I haven't gotten around to analyzing you yet, Mr. Simmer."

"But you will."

"If I've nothing better to do."

She heard him chuckle and it made her angry. If she didn't need his help she would order him out of the buggy.

They rode without talking until they reached the Foster homestead. The children were in the first stages of the fever and were not as sick as the Gordons. Jesse gave Mrs. Foster the same instructions that she had given the others.

One of the Foster children had pinworms, which meant that the other two children who slept in the same bed would probably have them too. Jesse told Mrs. Foster about the pinworms and asked her if she had a syringe. The woman shook her head.

"I'll leave mine for you to use until I return later with medicine to bring out the rash. Give each of the children an enema using a big spoonful of salt. Put them over the chamber pot, then take the pot to the woods to dump it. Let an hour go by and do the same thing again. By the way, be sure to grease the pipe on the end of the syringe with butter or lard and wash it well before you use it on the next child."

"Ma'am, Mrs. Preston was over this mornin'. She said her two was comin' down with sore throat and couldn't hold nothin' on their stomachs. She was worried sick they was comin' down with what my kids got."

Jesse's eyes met Wade's and he nodded.

"We'll stop by."

The Preston children were indeed coming down with scarlet fever. After leaving instructions on how to care for the children and promising to return, Jesse and Wade departed.

It was the twilight time of day.

"Jody should be at my place by the time we get there. We've made a half-circle. About three miles through the woods" — Wade pointed to his right — "is Grandpa Lester's place."

"And where do you live?"

"Three, four miles from here."

"It'll be dark soon. I promised I'd be back with the medicine."

"Don't worry, I know this country like the back of my hand."

"I appreciate your taking the time —"

"Forget it. We can make that trip faster tonight on horseback. A horse can go places a buggy can't."

51

"I don't ride and even if I did I'm not dressed for it. Brrrr . . . it gets cold up here in the hills when the sun goes down."

Jesse was pleasantly surprised when they reached Wade's home. Although it was almost dark, she could see that he was neat about the place. His barn and sheds were mended, his fences clean. The house that sat amid pines looked as permanent and peaceful as the timbered hills surrounding it. Made of heavy logs that fit snugly together, it not only seemed to belong there, but as if it could be depended on to be there forever. Light shone from one of the windows.

"Jody's here," Wade said quietly after he stopped the horse. He had not looked at her, had not wanted to see her reaction to his home. "I'll take you inside, then I'll unharness Molly. She deserves a rest after what she's been through today."

Jesse allowed him to help her down. With his hand firmly supporting her elbow, he guided her up onto a narrow porch and into a well-lighted kitchen. The instant she stepped through the door, the familiarity of home closed around her. The room was oblong with the great fireplace at one end and at the other a big cooking range, flanked by a kitchen cabinet, a wash bench, and a sink with a red iron handpump. A lamp hung over a huge round oak table, its top scrubbed down to the bare wood.

This room, Jesse decided, is the heart of the house.

Jody sat at the table hunched over a plate of

food. He stared but made no move to stand.

"Get to your feet when a lady comes into a room." Wade spoke softly but firmly.

Jody rose and stood scowling.

"Hello, Jody. Did Papa send —" Jesse paused when she saw the carpetbag on the table. "Oh, my, what all did he send for goodness sake?"

She opened the bag and found not only the medicine she had requested, but some sage, a dress, two nurse's aprons, a nightgown, toilet articles and underwear that she quickly covered with the dress. There was also a letter. She scanned it quickly, then read it aloud.

"Nurse Forbes, you have what appears to be an epidemic on your hands. Treat your patients sparingly with the extract of smartweed. I have more coming in on the train day after tomorrow. Have Wade Simmer take you to the schoolhouse. Tell the teacher to close school for at least three weeks. I will not be able to come help you. There are two cases of diphtheria in town, and I must administer vaccine to a child over near Allison who was bitten by a rabid skunk. Thank God for Louis Pasteur! Take heart, daughter. This is what you were trained to do. The people up there are good God-fearing people and they will listen to you. Wade Simmer will take care of you and find a family to give you a bed. Susan packed what she thought you would need. Don't worry about her and Todd. Things are well in hand here. Your loving father. P.S. That boy of Wade's runs like a deer. Susan said he thumbed his nose at Dusty

Wright as he sped down Main. I had the best laugh I've had in a week. I'd give a nickel to have seen the look on Dusty's face."

Jesse finished reading the letter.

"He expects me to stay a while. Tomorrow is Saturday. I can't see the teacher until Monday."

"I'll take care of it for you."

"Have you met Papa when he's come up here?"

"A time or two." He shrugged and turned to Jody. "Why did you thumb your nose at the marshal?"

"Jist hankered to, that's why."

"Dusty been ridin' you about something?"

"Not yet. He ain't had no chance."

"Better put a rein on those hankerings. We have enough trouble without going out and looking for more." Wade looked at him with an unmistakable but silent threat. "Heat up the ham and beans for the lady. And make her a cup of tea. I'll tend to Molly." He paused beside the open door.

Jesse could feel his gaze upon her, studying her. She was unable to meet his eyes, afraid that he would see the uncertainty in hers. The responsibility of being in this man's house and handling the epidemic alone was weighing on her.

"I'll light the lantern and set it out by the convenience to guide you."

"Thank you."

As soon as the door closed behind Wade, Jesse removed the starched cap and set it on the table. She would have loved to unpin her hair and scrape her scalp with her hairbrush. Since that was impossible now, she combed into her hair with her fingers.

"Why you wearin' that silly thin' on your head, lady? Don't keep off no sun." Jody stood beside the cookstove shoving kindling into the firebox.

"It's part of a nurse's uniform. The uniform serves as a means of identification."

"Can't ya jist tell people you doctor-folks?"

"Yes, I could, but when I'm wearing a uniform they can tell at a glance that I'm a nurse. A uniform says a man is a soldier or a train conductor even if people don't know them. Can you read, Jody?"

" 'Course, I can read," he said belligerently. "I ain't no dumb nigga. I done read all the books Wade's got." After giving her a scornful glance, he carried the teakettle to the pump and filled it.

Jesse went quietly out the door and stood for a moment on the step. She had relieved her bladder only one time since noon and she badly needed to use the "convenience." A glow of light led her to the small building. She picked up the lantern and went inside. The privy was spacious and clean. Half of a Sears Roebuck catalog lay on the seat, ready for her to use its pages. Liberal use of lime had kept the stench to a minimum. Again, Jesse was pleasantly surprised.

Wade was waiting beside the stoop when she returned to the house. He took the lantern, raised the globe and blew out the flame. In the kitchen he hung his hat on the peg beside the door, filled the washpan with water from the teakettle and set it in the sink.

"Wash up and we'll eat," he said. "It's been a long day and it's going to be longer." He took a towel from the drawer of a chiffonier and hung it on the pump handle.

"Thank you." Jesse soaped and rinsed her hands, then splashed water on her face. The cloth she dried with was edged with tatted lace — a company towel. "Beautiful lace," she said, folding the towel. "It's almost too pretty to use."

"They need to be used once in a while," he said while pumping water into the pan to wash.

"Did your mother make the lace?"

"Humpt!" he snorted, his hands splashing water on his face. It was a noncommittal sound. Finally, as he was drying his face, he said, "My granny."

Jesse stood behind the ladder-backed cane-bottomed chair. Wade was acutely aware that she was watching him. It was a diabolical combination of pleasure and agony having her here in his home. All the beauty that he had ever suspected life held was summed up in her. She was indeed a paradox: strong, resourceful, quick-witted, with a sparkling sense of humor, not beautiful, but still alluringly feminine. He had known women more beautiful, but none had stirred him like this one.

Usually he went to women for the gratification of very elemental needs. That he would want more from a woman had not often occurred to him. Jesse had impressed him the moment he had seen her face in his field glasses. She had won his esteem by her actions today. Now, he was eager that she regard him in a favorable light.

He couldn't imagine what she was thinking. Her face was calm, but the fingers gripping the back of the chair told him that she was nervous. Surely she wasn't worried for her safety. *It could be that she feared she would have to sit at the table with Jody.* Wade knew a moment of panic. *Was she all he had thought her to be or a bigot like the rest of the folk in Harpersville?*

Wade dragged his eyes away from her, cursing himself and this sudden attack of self-consciousness. He felt like a gawky kid instead of a man who had been around the world and seen everything he considered worth seeing.

Jody moved between them carrying a black iron kettle to the table.

"Put the beans in a bowl, Jody. We have company."

"Don't regard me as company, please." Jesse moved away from the chair. "I feel I've been thrust upon your hospitality. I'll set the table." She opened the glass doors of the china cabinet and lifted three plates from the shelf, and from a drawer beneath the doors, she chose three sets of utensils. She laid out the place settings knowing that Wade was watching her, testing her to see how she would react to eating at the table with a Negro.

At an early age Doctor Forbes had emphasized to his children that Negro people were no less human than white people. He looked beneath the color of a man's skin and saw what lay in his heart and judged him by his character.

"I done et," Jody said and placed an ironstone bowl of steaming beans and ham on the table.

"You didn't finish your meal," Jesse said lightly. "Sit down, Jody. A growing boy can surely eat more than one plateful. Isn't that right, Mr. Simmer?"

Wade waited to speak until her blue eyes were looking directly into his.

"Right as rain, Nurse Forbes." His voice was deep, husky, his expression remote. Holding her eyes with his, Wade moved around the table and pulled out her chair.

Jesse sat down. She was emotionally shaken. She would never have dreamed when she left home this morning that she would be completely at the mercy of this notorious man — not that he had made an ungentlemanly move, she assured herself. Still, her logical mind told her, he was so . . . big and dark and unpredictable. One moment he smiled and the next moment he looked as if he would bite the head off a snake. He did have a beautiful smile, she finally admitted, and wondered why he was so stingy with it.

# CHAPTER
# • 4 •

**D**ick Efthim closed and locked the double glass doors of his emporium and put the key in his pocket. He stood for a moment looking up and down the street. This was the quiet time of day — suppertime. Most of the businesses were closed, but a light blinked here and there. Two men came toward him on the raised boardwalk that fronted the stores in the block.

"Evenin', Mr. Harper. Evenin', Marshal."

"Evenin'." Boyd Harper's voice boomed so loudly in the quiet that Dick wondered if the man was going deaf. The short, notably plump banker was puffing on the stub of a cigar he would toss away before he reached home. Roberta Harper, his wife, frowned on tobacco and spirits. They were allowed in the house only on special occasions when it was socially necessary.

"Howdy, Dick." Dusty Wright was big, sandy-haired, freckle-faced, and so easy-going that he had managed to get along with Boyd Harper for the past fifteen years. Named Dunstan at birth, a fact he generally concealed, the marshal had been called Dusty for as long as he could remember.

"I was just tellin' the marshal that half the town saw Wade Simmer's uppity nigger runnin' slap-dab down the middle of Main Street. It was a sorry sight to see, but when trash like that thumbs his nose at our town marshal, it's more'n a body should have to put up with. Disgraceful, I say. Disgraceful!" Harper continued in his loud voice as he lifted his watch from his vest pocket and flipped open the case. "Them niggers are just gettin' uppitier and uppitier. But they know better than to be in my town after sundown. Isn't that right, Marshal?"

Dusty nodded and glanced at Dick. He listened to the banker's advice, then did what he thought was right according to the law. Now he could scarcely keep the grin off his face. The handlebar mustache that covered his upper lip jerked, the only sign of his amusement. Both men remained silent and let Boyd talk.

"Keep that trash in the hills, Marshal. We can't let them sully our town. My granddaddy built this town with his sweat and blood. He didn't build it for lazy hill trash."

When Boyd got on this subject, it always made the storekeeper uncomfortable. A number of hill families did business in his store. He had extended credit to a few of them and they had always paid when they promised, unlike Boyd, who let his bill run a year or more and then pretended to have forgotten it. Dick also knew of hillfolk who did business with Boyd's bank. The man seemed to forget about that when he launched into one of his tirades.

"You should've gone right out and arrested that darkie for indecent behavior."

"Indecent behavior?" Dusty scratched the back of his head, tilting his hat over his face to hide his amusement. "I don't even know what it means when a person 'thumbs his nose.' Do you, Boyd?"

"Why, 'course, I know," the banker blustered. "It means . . . it means somethin' . . . nasty."

"If I arrested everyone who called me somethin' nasty, Boyd, I'd have that new jailhouse full and overflowin'. Think of the expense havin' to feed that bunch. I'd be havin' tramps and rotters and good-for-nothin's thumbin' their nose just to get a good warm bed and three squares a day."

"Well, now." Boyd chewed vigorously on the end of the cigar. "We'll write up a new ordinance. Any nigger that acts disrespectful while in Harpersville —"

"It wouldn't stand up in court, Boyd. Tennessee law says we can't have one set of rules for whites and another for coloreds."

"What do those high-binders over there in Nashville know about what goes on over here in this part of the state?" Boyd puffed rapidly on his cigar, then took it from his mouth. "I never thought I'd see the day Harpersville would have to put up with uppity niggers and womenfolk not bein' safe in their own homes. My granddaddy would turn over in his grave if he knew what's been goin' on in his town."

"Has another woman been attacked?" Dick asked.

"Not that I know of," Dusty said. "But women are shamed about talkin' about such things. I suspect there's been more'n what we know about."

"Do you have any idea who it could be?"

Before Dusty could answer, Boyd's voice boomed.

" 'Course, we got a idea. Wade Simmer. He's got to be brought to justice. There's been nothing but trouble since he come back here. Bad blood!" Boyd shook his head so vigorously his jowls quivered. "I got proof written in my granddaddy's hand, God rest his soul, that Simmer's old granddaddy was a smuggler, a thief, a womanizer, and a Yankee to boot. Bad blood was passed on down to Alvin, then to Wade. Everybody knows Alvin Simmer killed my brother, Buford, and got hung for it."

*What everybody doesn't know,* Dusty thought to himself, *is the truth about that killing.*

"I can't arrest Wade Simmer without some evidence he's guilty," Dusty said.

"Arrest his nigger then."

"I have no evidence it's him either. He's no more'n fourteen or fifteen. I figger he's not smart enough to get in and do what's been done to these women without being seen."

"Hell, man! You got to arrest somebody."

"I will when I catch the guilty man. This bird is bound to slip up sooner or later, and one of the women will be able to identify him."

"It better be soon. I never thought I'd see the day a white woman wasn't safe in my granddaddy's town." Harper looked so indignant that Dusty wanted to laugh. "Why, I'm havin' to send Edsel home early to stay with Mrs. Harper. She's near scared out of her wits."

Dusty had a difficult time holding back a smile at the thought of The Looker getting the corsets off Mrs. Harper's barrel-shaped body. So far, the man had picked sightly young women and girls. Unless he got the urge to look at a belly shaped like a watermelon and breasts like two good-sized cantaloupes, Roberta Harper was as safe as if she were locked in the bank vault.

When the banker said goodnight and walked on down the street leaving the marshal and the storekeeper standing on the boardwalk, they looked at each other, careful to wait until Boyd Harper was out of hearing, and they both laughed.

"A man would have to be really sick to want to see Mrs. Harper naked," Dick said, then added, "I don't mean to make light of what's happened. It's not a jokin' matter. I keep wonderin' who's doin' it and if it's somebody I know."

"It's a bet it's someone who knows what's going on in town. So far he's picked women whose men-folk were out of the house. I don't think it's one of the hill people. I don't have any idea who it is. It's not one of the bridge crew. I'm almost sure of that. They don't bathe from one month to the next and stink like a slop bucket. A woman would notice such as that. It's hard for me to believe it's Wade Simmer. I'm thinkin' that if he took a notion for a woman, he'd not be sneaky about it. Besides, he can go up to Knoxville or over to Frederick or Grover or Finny and get a woman who'll give him a fine time for four bits. Why risk gettin' caught just lookin'?"

"Maybe it's a game with him. Maybe he feels he's getting back at the town for what it did to his pa."

"Preyin' on women?" Dusty snorted. "Ain't Wade's style."

"But you don't know for sure."

"No. I don't know for sure. Could be you, Dick."

"Or you, Dusty." Dick laughed and clapped his friend on the shoulder. "I heard they got a run of scarlet fever in the hills," he said after a pause. "Susan Forbes was in the store and bought sage to send back by that darkie. He was down to get medicine from the doctor. Miss Jesse will have her hands full. It don't seem right her bein' up there all by herself."

"She's probably as safe there as she'd be in town right now. If she's tending the younguns, the hill people'll look after her."

"You a friend of Simmer's, Dusty?"

"I know him. I was raised in the hills myself. My pa knew his pa. Wade's a ornery son of a bitch when he's riled, but he tends to his own business if folks leave him be."

"He comes to the store four or five times a year.

Seems to have money to buy what he wants. Gives me a bill to fill, pays and leaves. Don't say three words all the while."

"He ain't a talker, that's certain. Well, I got to be makin' my rounds. Night, Dick."

"Night, Dusty."

"This piccalilli is delicious." Jesse spooned a second helping of the relish onto her plate. "Which one of you made it?" She tried to smile into Wade's eyes, but he refused to look at her.

"Mrs. Bailey gave us a half dozen quarts last fall," Wade finally said reluctantly.

"After we sawed up a bunch of —" A quelling glance from Wade stopped Jody's words.

"I'll have to ask for the recipe," Jesse said. "Mine never tastes this good."

She glanced at Jody and found him looking at her. He scooped a piece of ham out of his plate with his fingers and filled his mouth, letting the juice run down his chin. *He was being deliberately ill-mannered.* Why? She slanted a quick look at Wade. His face had tightened with a scowl, but he said nothing.

Jesse finished her meal in silence after that. Jody was doing his best to live up to what he thought she expected of him, and she was tired of trying to make conversation with Wade. Since she had stepped inside his home, he had been different — as if he didn't want her here. Sitting at the table with a colored was not something she did every day. Not that it bothered her. It was just strange, and she had tried to make everyone feel at ease with her ceaseless chatter. She could see now that it had been a mistake.

Wade finished eating, moved his chair back from the table, and carried his plate to the dishpan in the sink. Jesse quickly followed.

"I'll wash these before we go."

"No. We'd better not take the time." Wade stacked the dishes in the pan and covered them with water from the teakettle. "Jody, take Nurse Forbes's bundle over to Granny Lester and tell her the nurse will be spending the night there. Tomorrow night she'll go to the Baileys. We can't be playing favorites."

"Favorites? What do you mean?"

"To these folk it's an honor to have the nurse in their homes. It's only fair to pass you around."

"My . . . goodness."

*And you, Wade?* Jesse wanted to say, *are you glad I'm here? You act as if you can't get me out of here fast enough.*

"I'll go saddle up Samson."

"Oh, Mr. Simmer . . . I've had very little experience riding horseback."

"You won't ride alone. You'll ride in front of me. We can make the rounds in half the time." Wade plucked a wool shirt jacket from a peg and slipped into it. "Jody, I didn't see Delilah when I came in."

"She was layin' by the chicken house. Think she's gone off to have her pups?"

"It's about time." At the door, Wade spoke to

Jody again. "Get Nurse Forbes a shawl out of Granny's chest."

"Please . . . don't bother. I'll be all right."

"You'll be cold. It's chilly up here at night, even in the summertime." With that, he was out the door.

Granny Simmer had been the only person in the world ever to be close to Wade. Since her death he had constantly guarded against letting anyone, even Jody, get too close. He had controlled every aspect of his adult life, closing his mind to what had happened in the past. After years of drifting first into one job and then another, he had returned to the place of his birth. The decision had been made suddenly after fate had stepped in and placed him at the right place at the right time.

He had been standing on the wharf looking at the Statue of Liberty in the Upper Bay of New York Harbor, marveling at the colossal figure that had been a gift of the people of France. It was dusk and the wharf was deserted, or so he thought. But suddenly he heard a muffled cry and turned to seek out its source. With a shout he ran toward two men who, with clubs raised, were ready to strike again the couple they had knocked to the rough boards of the wharf.

Wade had brawled in the coal mines, aboard merchant ships, and in the roughest dives that lined the seaports of the world. The two toughs didn't stand a chance against him, even though they were armed with heavy clubs. He kicked one in the groin, broke the arm of the other, and tossed the two of them into the cold water of the bay.

The couple he rescued were elderly. As he helped them to their feet, making sure they had come to no serious harm, a big man in the uniform of a servant ran up to them.

"Oh, Lord! I shouldn't've left ya."

"We're all right," the man said shakily, reaching to straighten his wife's hat. "This young man saved our lives."

After thanking Wade profusely, the feeble old man escorted his wife to the waiting carriage.

The incident and the surprising event that occurred the following morning were turning points in Wade's life. For the first time he accepted himself as he really was. The realization made him feel oddly secure and able to face all the hideous details of his birth and childhood. A few days later he began the journey back to the hills of Tennessee, back home to the place where he was born.

Wade had been fairly content — until now.

He groaned inwardly as he saddled the horse. He had once thought of himself as invulnerable. Now he wasn't sure he could get Jesse Forbes or the empty, lonely years that stretched ahead out of his mind. He was certain that waiting for Jesse beside the road, getting to know her, bringing her to his home, was a mistake.

When she came out of his house, Wade was glad to see she was not wearing the nurse's cap and that she had one of his granny's shawls wrapped around her shoulders. He moved the horse up close

68

to the porch where it would be easier for her to mount.

"Do you have chores to do before we go?" she asked.

"None that won't keep until I get back." Wade hung her nurse's bag over the saddlehorn and stepped into the saddle. "Put your foot on mine and I'll boost you up."

She hesitated and gestured to where lightning flickered in the sky. "It looks like it's going to rain."

"I have a slicker." He held out his hand.

"I . . . don't know about this —"

"Don't tell me a woman who will go alone into the woods with a strange man — even come to his home — is afraid of riding a horse."

"It isn't that. It's just that I'm not dressed —"

Wade leaned from the saddle and placed his hands on her waist, and before she could even think of what he was doing, she was sitting on his lap.

"Swing your leg over. You'll be more comfortable without the saddlehorn poking you in the side."

"But . . . my skirt —"

"— Will come up and show your legs. Who'll see them out here, but me? I've already seen every color, shape and size of female legs. Yours won't excite me one bit," he added in a bored tone.

"In that case — what the heck!" she snapped and swung her leg over the horse's neck.

The skirt of her dress was full enough to cover

her knees. As she tugged on it, she was aware that her bottom was nestled snugly against the V made by his spread thighs. She could feel the warmth of him through her clothing and his. He adjusted the shawl around her shoulders, then his arms were around her, pulling her back against him. The horse tossed his head. Wade spoke sternly and the animal stood motionless again.

"Relax. I'll not let you fall." His voice was a low rumble close to her ear.

The nearness of Wade's hard body was something Jesse hadn't anticipated. His arms pressed her close to his chest, her thighs lay alongside his. Lord help her! The intimacy was wildly exciting, and she prayed he couldn't hear the pounding of her heart.

"Ready?" Warm breath fanned her ear.

Jesse nodded uncertainly, for she was trying desperately to cope not only with the unaccustomed experience of being on horseback, but also his physical nearness, the way in which he held her and the fact that every nerve in her body was aware of the lean hardness of his.

Wade put his heels to the flanks of their mount. The animal responded and they moved out away from the house. Jesse looked straight ahead, not daring to look down and see how far she was from the ground.

"Relax," Wade said again. "You're stiff as a board. You'll be worn out by the time we get to the Prestons'."

"We're going there first?" She felt the need to say something.

"We'll reverse the trip we made today."

"The Gordon girl was the sickest."

"We'll be there in an hour unless you have to spend extra time at Prestons' and Fosters'."

"Why were you walking when I met you today?"

"I was strolling around — seeing the sights."

"In the woods?"

"Lots of interesting things to see in the woods." When she had nothing more to say, he said, "I'll draw you a map tomorrow so you can see where each family lives."

*He'd draw her a map so he wouldn't have to bother with her again. That was fine with her!*

Jesse shook herself mentally. She was here to do a job and should be grateful for his help, but she wasn't. She wished the help would have come from anyone but him.

The horse's movements brought her into rhythmic contact with his body from his chest to his knees. There was no way she could escape his closeness. It would never do to let him know that being in his encircling arms made her heartbeat accelerate and her silly brain stop functioning. No wonder, she told herself. Being alone in the dark woods with this strange wild man was enough to give a person heart failure. The horse moved carefully down an incline, crossed a dry creekbed and scrambled up the steep bank on the other side.

Jesse's hand grasped Wade's wrist in sudden fright.

71

"Don't be afraid," he murmured. "Samson has good night vision. He can see better than we can."

"Thank heavens! I can hardly see my hand in front of me." She laughed. "Are you sure you know where we're going?"

"Sure as shootin'." A chuckle escaped him. His voice was low and soft, and she had felt the vibration in his chest when he laughed.

Conscious of a loud and determined thumping between them, she wondered whether it was his heart or hers. She did not have time to consider the question. Something swished in front of them. The horse shied and danced in place.

"Whoa!" Wade commanded. "It was only an owl."

"My goodness!" Jesse exclaimed. "It's scary in the woods at night."

"Not as scary as in a big city or even in a town the size of Harpersville. Two-legged animals can be far more dangerous than four-legged ones."

"You've been to a lot of big cities?"

"A few."

"I've never been to a *big* city."

"You haven't missed anything."

They came into a clearing. A backlash of lightning showed momentarily against the overhead blackness, followed by a low rumble of thunder.

Jesse's mouth curved at the thought of what her friend, Pauline, would say if she could see her now — in the dark woods, astraddle a horse, with the man the whole town believed was The Looker.

# CHAPTER
## • 5 •

*O*tis Merfeld sat sprawled in a chair watching every move Jesse made. Aware of the gaze of the thin, wiry man with a head of straw-colored hair, thick, loose lips and watery eyes, Jesse was glad that Wade was just a call away. She realized Otis was drunk when he grabbed his eldest daughter, Flora, and tried to pull her down on his lap. When she hit him with her fist and darted to the other side of the room, he laughed as if being struck by his daughter were the funniest thing in the world.

Jesse was giving Mrs. Merfeld instructions on how to administer the medicine her father had sent when a stunning crash of thunder shook the house. It was still echoing when another roared in its wake. Otis staggered to his feet.

"Hit's gettin' ready to rain pitchforks and nigger babies. Ya'll jist have ta stay the night, missy. Flora," he shouted to be heard over the now constant rumble of thunder, "Fix up a pallet for the nurse."

"Never mind, Flora. I'm expected at the

Lesters'. Be sure to keep the children covered, Mrs. Merfeld —"

"Ain't no need a'tall fer ya to go to old Granny's. She ain't —"

"I'm going, Mr. Merfeld," Jesse said firmly. "But I thank you for your concern."

"Ain't decent ya goin' off in the dead a night with that nigger-lover," Otis mumbled and shouldered his way past his wife to reach Jesse and grasp her arm. "Yore pa'd think me lax —"

"Let go of my arm," Jesse said quietly.

"Otis!" Mrs. Merfeld whispered fearfully.

"Go sit, Pa," Flora demanded. "Yo're bein' a jackass."

"Watch yore mouth, girl," Otis snarled and raised the hand he removed from Jesse's arm in a threatening gesture.

"Ready, Nurse Forbes?" Wade's voice came from the door leading to the porch.

"Just about. Mrs. Merfeld, I'll caution you again about not allowing the children to get chilled. Don't allow anyone in the house who could carry the germs to another household. If you were in town you would be under quarantine."

"Under what?" Otis pushed his face so close to Jesse's that she backed away.

"Quarantine. A red sign would be put on your door and no one would be allowed in or out until the doctor declared the patient no longer contagious."

"Ain't no son of a bitch puttin' no sign on my door, by Gawd."

"No one is planning to do that. I said — if you lived in town —"

"They'd not do it in town either."

Knowing she was about to lose her temper, Jesse focused her mind on a motto that hung in her father's surgery: *"Patience is a Virtue."*

"I'll be back tomorrow, Mrs. Merfeld." Jesse picked up her bag. "You've done a good job keeping the fever down. I don't think there's much danger of you or Flora getting the disease, but you could carry it to other children. So stay close to home."

"Yo're just bound to go traipsin' off in the night with Wade Simmer. Ain't ya carin' what folks'll think? Yo're shamin' yore pa is what yo're doin'. Ya been offered a decent bed —"

"Otis . . . please —" Mrs. Merfeld followed Jesse to the porch. "Don't pay him no mind, miss. He ain't hisself when he's drinkin'."

"Don't worry about it. Try to rest. Let Flora take a turn sitting with the children. I'll be back tomorrow."

Wade appeared out of the darkness and settled the shawl over her head and around her shoulders. She cupped her hands and he poured a small amount of the disinfectant in them before capping the bottle and putting it in her bag.

The routine had been the same at each place they had stopped. He lifted her into the saddle, mounted behind her, then unfurled the poncho slicker and settled it over their heads.

"Your feet will get wet, but there's nothing

we can do about that."

Wade turned the horse away from the house and down the road. The first spattering of raindrops began to fall onto the poncho that covered them like a tent. With her back pressed snugly against Wade's big hard and curiously gentle body, his arms around her, Jesse felt cozy and safe. There was no doubt in her mind now that he would see her safely to Granny Lester's.

"Poor Mrs. Merfeld. I don't see how she stands that . . . that lout of a husband!"

"She has no choice," Wade said.

"He'd have to sleep sometime, and when he did I'd work him over with a stick of stove wood." Jesse's voice rose heatedly.

"I bet you would at that." Wade chuckled. "I thought for a minute I'd have to barge in and rescue you. But you were holding your own pretty good."

"Only because I knew you were just outside the door."

Wade felt a surge of pleasure. She overwhelmed him, driving all logical thought from his mind. She melted back into him as if it were the most natural thing in the world. He struggled against the passion she aroused in him. Her body moving softly against his was seductively dangerous to his self-control. He breathed in the scent of her, a faint antiseptic and woman scent, mingling with the clean night air. His chest rose and fell with his breathing. He hoped desperately to control the part of him that would embarrass both of them if she became aware of it.

"Here it comes," Wade said almost welcoming the sheet of wind-driven rain that hit them. "Are you scared of storms?"

"Sometimes."

She turned her face to his shoulder. His back and bowed head were to the wind and the slicker shed the rain that pounded them. He held her tightly against his chest in a protective, sheltering way. She could feel the beat of his heart. She couldn't remember ever being held this close to anyone except her brother and sister. Like all young girls she had had her dreams. One of them had been to wonder what it would be like to be held by a lover. Of course, she admonished herself, Wade Simmer was not her lover, but just a man taking care of her because he admired her father.

The thunder and flash lightning rolled and crackled over them, and with it came the heavy downpour that lasted for what seemed a long time. When the deluge finally let up, a gentle constant rain continued. Jesse rested against Wade in sweet comfort while the rain curtained them and bestowed upon her a sense of belonging, enriching her faith in this man she had known for less than twelve hours. The rain gradually receded until it became a light drizzle, then stopped.

Jesse moved her face back to look into his. Water from his hat brim spilled down on the slicker when he tipped his head. Moisture clung to his lashes and ran down his cheeks. They were a breath apart, so close she could see the shine of his eyes as they moved intently over her face. Seconds slipped by and he said nothing. As the quiet between them stretched, and the horse carried them onward, Jesse blinked at him in confusion.

When they came, his whispered words were a shock that caused her heart to make a frantic leap.

"Jesse." He said her name softly. "I'm afraid I'm going to have to kiss you."

"No!"

"I . . . won't bite you." He knew the words were stupid, but it was too late to take them back.

They looked at each other for a long while before he lowered his head slowly, giving her time to turn her face away. Jesse was mesmerized. She knew what was about to happen but was unable to stop it. He brought his mouth down on hers; his lips were wet with rain but warm and gentle. He brushed her lips with his, lightly, like the wings of a butterfly. It wasn't enough.

"God help me!" It was a groan that ended as his lips, hard and intense, found hers again, covering, taking control, feasting on her mouth as if it were a warm ripe peach.

Never before had she felt quite like this. Never had she known this melting, letting-go sensation that now invaded her innermost being. The sudden joy was startling, and yet so lovely it was breathtaking.

*Why couldn't she think?* Now his lips were playing with the corners of her mouth, tracing a path to her eyes and then back to close over hers. Their lips met with an eagerness and familiarity that was unique for two who had not been lovers. Her senses commanded her to move back out of his embrace, but her body ignored the order, remained pliable, and molded itself against him. She could feel the steady thumping of his heart and feel the hard muscles and bones of his chest and arms.

A warning crept into the back of her mind. She knew she should have found his kiss distasteful, but it was wildly exciting, deliciously sweet. Her sanity argued, this is madness! For once she refused to listen to that inner voice and delighted in the wondrous warmth, the sensation of his lips on hers, to the feel of arms encircling her, to his strength, to the masculine smell of his skin, to the roughness of his cheeks.

"Damn! Damn! Damn!" Wade groaned in frustrated agony and pressed his cheek tightly to hers. "I'm sorry. I didn't mean to do that." His voice was husky with regret.

"I don't know what possessed me to let you —" Her lower lip trembled. She was glad he couldn't see her face. "I'm not . . . I don't . . . go around kissing strange men."

"I know that," he said quickly. "It was my fault. I should have resisted. But you're enough to tempt a saint and I'm sure as hell no saint."

She was aware of the heavy beat of her heart and his. His mouth had had the bittersweet taste of tobacco. Her nose, when pressed to the roughness of his cheek, had caught the whiff of smoke. These scattered thoughts floated through her mind as her eyes focused on the space between the horse's ears and her mind fought for something casual to say.

"Why don't you have a mustache?"

"Too much work."

"I don't like them anyway," she said lamely, turning her head and moving it slightly away from him.

Jesse sat still, dazed, aware that Wade no longer held her tightly against him. Coldness was seeping in where she had been so glowingly warm before. With shaking fingers she adjusted the wet shawl on her head.

"Looks like the rain is over." Wade spoke as if nothing out of the ordinary had happened. "That's the Lesters' ahead. Grandpa put a lantern on the porch."

Too late, too late. The refrain echoed in Wade's brain as he rode home through the rain-soaked woods after he left Jesse at the Lesters'. His insides churned and twisted painfully. He couldn't even excuse himself on the grounds that he hadn't known what was happening, would happen if he kissed her. From the beginning he had known. The first time he had looked at Jesse Forbes through the field glasses he had known that he would have to be very careful. And knowing that, he had gone full tilt ahead, paying no deed to the warning signals.

Jesse was so far above him they didn't even breathe the same air, he reminded himself sternly.

80

His brain knew that, but his body and his emotions lacked that understanding. What he needed was to go to Knoxville and visit a woman he knew who was skilled in giving him relief. After visiting her, he didn't give her another thought until time for the next session, and she didn't expect him to.

The frenzy of his obsession with Jesse frightened him. He had tried all day to analyze his feelings. It was not that he was desperate to get her into bed — although he had to admit that he had thought about how it would be to bury himself in the soft warmth of her body. It was more than that. Never before had he wanted someone to belong exclusively to *him,* care for *him.*

Even now he could smell the clean, sweet scent of her, see her eyes as calm and serene as a mountain pool one moment and sparkling with laughter the next.

*She could destroy you, you idiot!*

Wade was disgusted with himself and vowed to stop thinking about her. He had done foolish things in his life but never any quite as foolish as kissing the doctor's daughter.

Still, the warmth that had settled inside him and the odd feeling of belonging when she returned his kiss were the most pleasurable moments of his life. He allowed himself the luxury of imagining how it would be if she were in his kitchen, standing at the stove, waiting for him. She would have a sweet smile on her pretty mouth and her dark hair would be loose and hanging down her back.

Damn, damn. In one short day she had turned his life upside down.

The smell of coffee roused Jesse. She identified it and became aware that she was snuggled down in Granny Lester's featherbed. She turned on her back and found herself looking out on a clear morning. She stretched luxuriously. Then a clatter of iron brought her full awake. She sprang out of bed and scrambled into her clothes, brushed and pinned up her hair, and hastily made the bed. She glanced around the small room where the neat iron bedstead was now spread with a patchwork quilt, then walked barefoot into the kitchen. Granny stood at the cookstove stirring a pan of raw-fried potatoes.

"Morning."

"Hit's goin' to be a fair day. Mr. Lester says there ain't a cloud in the sky. Sleep good? Bed not too lumpy?"

"The bed was wonderful." Jesse had not slept well. Her mind would not release thoughts of Wade Simmer and the devastating effect of his kiss. As she washed her face and hands and dried them on the towel that hung on a nail above the wash bench, she strove without much success to put him out of her mind. "What can I do?"

"Ya can sit. Mr. Lester is comin'. I heard the gate swing shut." Jesse stood behind the high-backed kitchen chair feeling awkward at being waited on by this elderly woman with the goiter that was choking the life out of her. But knowing the pride of the hill people, she waited quietly.

The screen door banged behind Grandpa Lester. He set a dishpan on the wash bench and poured water from the bucket over a small skinned animal in the pan.

"Caught us a possum, Mrs. Lester."

"We ain't had a possum in a coon's age." Grandma Lester wiped her hands on her apron and went to peer into the pan. "It'll be plumb larrupin' fer Sunday dinner. Got to let it stand a day and night in salt and sody water," she explained to Jesse. "Ain't nothin' better 'n possum and sweet 'taters." Granny went back to dishing up fried potatoes, white milk gravy and buttermilk biscuits.

Jesse's stomach did a slow roll at the thought of eating the possum and she gave thanks silently that she'd be spending the next night with the Baileys.

After they were seated at the table and Grandpa Lester had said the blessing, he announced that the "boy" had come early this morning with Jesse's buggy.

"Jody brought it over?" Jesse asked.

"Wade brung it."

"When you said boy, I thought you meant Jody."

"Wade brung it," Granny repeated. "Said tell ya Hod Gordon'd meet you at Merfelds'. Boy ain't got but one flaw. He's dead-set on treatin' that darkie like he was white. Ain't natural." Granny's mouth twisted in lines of disapproval.

"Now, Mrs. Lester, don't get yoreself all flustered," Grandpa said soothingly, then to Jesse, "Wade's goin' to Coon Rapids and tell the teacher to close the school."

"Oh," Jesse said and busied herself with pouring sorghum onto a buttered biscuit.

"Mine is the first face the boy saw when he come into this world o' woe." Granny pushed the gravy bowl toward her husband when he reached for it. "Scrawny, skinny little beggar. Looked like a skinned rat, he did. Humpt! No wonder. The woman that birthed him bein' what she was. But he let out a whoop when I whapped his behind and I knew sure he was a Simmer."

"Were you a midwife, Granny?"

"Only one fer miles in them days. Brung more'n a hundred younguns in the world. Didn't lose more'n a dozen."

"You must know everyone around here."

"— And their folks and their folks' folks. Some come from good sturdy stock. Pure hickory, they is. Some's offshoots of a rotten vine and ain't never goin' to be nothin' else but rotten like their folks. Ya ain't goin' to have to kill a chicken for Sunday, Mr. Lester, now we got the possum."

Hod Gordon was waiting at Merfelds'. He escorted Jesse on her rounds and to four additional families who had sent word that they had sick children. Her supplies were running dangerously low by mid-afternoon, and she knew that she would have to send another message to her father

84

or make the trip to Harpersville herself.

No sign had been seen of her escort of the previous day. And no word about him other than an insulting remark made by Otis Merfeld.

"Fed up with the nigger-lover already?" He whispered the words slyly when he caught Jesse alone. "Told ya not to go off in the dark with 'im. Feel ya up, did he?"

Never in her life had she detested anyone as much as she detested Otis Merfeld, and she longed to tell him what a pitiful excuse for a man he was. But she ignored him because his wife and his children needed her.

The hill people welcomed Jesse into their homes but seemed in awe of her; she had to work hard to make them comfortable with her presence. By the time she reached the Baileys', where she would spend the night, she was bone-tired, and her back ached from bending over the beds and pallets of her patients. Mrs. Bailey's son, Homer, a forty-year-old with the intelligence of a ten-year-old child, was waiting to take Molly to the shed behind the house.

Jesse hadn't counted on Mrs. Bailey's delight in having her as an overnight guest. The supper table was covered with a rose-patterned oilcloth and set with heavy stoneware, some pieces of which were cracked and chipped, but obviously the best she had. The delicious aroma of roasted chicken and gooseberry cobbler filled the house. A platter of pickled pigs' feet and a bowl of pickled beets sat on the table alongside several dishes of relishes and jams.

"This is a regular feast, Mrs. Bailey. You shouldn't have gone to all this trouble."

"Fiddle!" Mrs. Bailey's plain face beamed with pleasure. "Go on in the room there and wash up. Wade brung ya a satchel from your pa."

"Mr. Simmer went into town? Oh, I wish I had known he was going. I need more medical supplies."

"Brought it just afore ya got here. Said you'd be needin' what's in it."

The suitcase was on the bed. She opened it anxiously. On top were two dresses, two aprons, and a note from her father. Beneath the clothes, wrapped in newspaper, were the precious medical supplies. Relief mingled with puzzlement. Wade Simmer not only had made the trip to the schoolhouse, but had been to Harpersville. He had covered a lot of territory today unless he had sent Jody into town again.

Jesse unfolded the note and scanned it quickly. Her father was confident she could handle the epidemic and told her that if there was anything she needed to tell Wade Simmer. He or Jody would come for it. Simmer had assured him, he said, that she would have an escort as she made her rounds. *So he had gone to Harpersville.* Doctor Forbes closed his letter by saying she had a nice surprise waiting for her when she got home.

Jesse smiled, folded the note and tucked it into her pocket. Had Susan attempted to make the berries into jam by herself? Then she remembered

86

that this was Saturday. Oh, foot! Pauline was going to come today and help put up raspberry jam. The surprise would be no surprise at all — Pauline and Susan had picked the berries and made the jam.

Later Jesse felt guilty lying in Mrs. Bailey's bed while that good woman occupied her son's cot in the kitchen. Homer had taken his blankets to the shed. After supper Mrs. Bailey had urged her son to show Jesse the handles he made for hoes, rakes and shovels. Carved from white ash, they were hard and strong and as smooth as silk. Jesse was suitably impressed with the fine workmanship and told him so. Before they retired, he had proudly given her a beautifully crafted rolling pin. The look on his homely features was adoring when she told him that she would treasure his gift forever.

Snuggled in the soft featherbed, Jesse's thoughts turned to Wade Simmer. In truth, the man had invaded her thoughts all day. She felt a stirring of self-disgust when she recalled his kiss, and her fingertips went automatically to her lips. She had sat there like a dumb ox while he kissed her!

Heaven help her! She hadn't felt the least bit put-out or afraid of him. She had felt no awkwardness about the arms she had wrapped about his hard body, no guilt about the warmth she had received from leaning on his strength. It had been so sweet and . . . natural.

What kind of an idiot are you? Jesse questioned herself. *The man took advantage of you! He probably*

87

*thinks you're just a love-starved old maid.* He had hardly been able to get away from her fast enough after he took her to Granny Lester.

But damn him for being so gentle, so attractive . . . so thought-provoking.

# CHAPTER
## • 6 •

*P*auline Anthony came out of the store where she had purchased embroidery floss and walked past the rooming house, being careful to keep her eyes from the male boarders who sat in the bentwood chairs on the porch. She wore a dark skirt and white middy blouse with an elbow-length cape flung over her shoulders; yet she felt exposed, vulnerable and uncomfortable. She hastened her steps.

She had had her share of suitors since she had been in Harpersville, none of whom was serious. Teachers, reasonably attractive teachers, were usually married within two years. Some didn't even last out the school year. Pauline loved to teach and was determined not to lose her job by marrying unless she were madly in love.

It was evening. Lights were beginning to shine from the windows of the houses she passed. She turned the corner and walked slowly toward the house at the end of the block where she had roomed since coming to Harpersville. The house looked empty and desolate without her cheerful landlady sitting on the porch. Mrs. Poole had taken the train to Grover to visit her daughter and to see her new grandchild.

Pauline went straight to her room at the back of the house and lit a lamp. This was the first time she had stayed alone since the stories had begun circulating about The Looker. Until now doors in Harpersville had seldom been locked. Pauline looked for keys to the front and back doors. Unable to find them, she wedged a kitchen chair under each doorknob and went back to her room feeling reasonably safe.

At the library table she worked on papers she had brought from the school, but her thoughts were troubled. How would Jesse react to the changes that had taken place in her home since she had gone to the hills to care for the sick? Four days had passed since Pauline and Susan had picked the raspberries and made the jam, or rather tried to make the jam. It seemed they could do nothing *right*. Susan had certainly been in a surly mood at school the last few days. And was it her imagination, or had Todd's stuttering worsened?

While Pauline's thoughts were occupied with what she considered would be a serious problem for her friend, another's thoughts were occupied with her.

One of the men who sprawled in the chairs on the porch of the rooming house had left the porch after Pauline passed and walked leisurely in the opposite direction from the one that she had taken. Once out of sight of the others, he had cut through the alley behind the stores and come out on the street where he could watch her until she entered the house at the end of the block.

The tall slender man with the quiet blue eyes stood for a moment, pretending to light the cigar he held clamped between his teeth. His mind methodically sorted out what he had found out about the teacher. She had been in Harpersville two years and had spent the better part of Saturday afternoon at the doctor's house. Of course, he had heard about the scarlet fever epidemic in the hills and had heard that her friend, the doctor's daughter, was up there. The doctor's other daughter was just an adolescent girl. Why would the teacher visit her student for hours? One would think she saw enough of her at school.

The tall man pulled his watch from his vest pocket, flipped open the lid, peered at the time, and decided to take a leisurely walk down Main Street past the doctor's house. It was essential that he find out more about Pauline Anthony and her connection to the Forbes family. She could be the missing piece of the puzzle that would bring everything together.

Later that night Pauline awakened in utter terror. A hand was clamped over her eyes, and fingers squeezed her nostrils together. She opened her mouth to scream and it was filled with a soft cloth. Just as she was about to black out, the fingers on her nose eased their pressure and she filled her lungs with air.

"Shhh . . . Shhh . . . I won't hurt you if you behave." The whisper was husky and had a nasal twang. Pauline felt the point of a knife beneath her chin and fear kept hysteria at bay. "Good girl," her attacker muttered soothingly when she stopped struggling.

A long soft cloth was quickly wrapped tightly around her head, covering her eyes. Sounds of newly awakened terror came from Pauline's throat, and she tried to force the gag from her mouth.

"Shhh . . . I don't want to hurt you. Put your arms over your head and grab hold of the bedstead. Do it now," he commanded sharply. When she obeyed, he quickly bound her wrists to the bed-post.

Realizing how helpless she was, how vulnerable, Pauline panicked. She raised her legs and tried to kick him. Immediately the knife point beneath her chin made itself known.

"Now cut that out! I'm only going to look at you."

Whimpers came from her throat as she heard the scrape of a match when he lit the lamp. The knife left her chin and quickly cut down through the thin lawn of her nightgown. She felt the cool air on her skin as the gown was folded back exposing her naked body.

"Ahhh . . . you're blond down here too." Fingers combed through her pubic hair. Humiliated almost beyond endurance, Pauline stiffened. "Ahh . . . don't be scared." The guttural whisper came again.

"Pretty." The tip of the knife moved around to her cheek as his hand caressed her belly on its way to her breasts. He rubbed them almost roughly and rolled her nipples between his thumb and forefinger. "I like titties," he murmured. "Yours are so pretty." Suddenly his mouth was there sucking vigorously.

Shocked, Pauline bucked, but the hand moved down to her mound and held her down. "Be still," he growled menacingly. Pauline froze, paralyzed. He sucked first one breast and then the other, pulling on her nipples with firm lips.

*God help me! I can't endure this!*

"Spread your legs."

*Oh, please —*

"Now!" The knife tip pressed against her cheek. The hand on her mound moved and a finger wiggled its way inside her.

*Oh, Lord help me —*

"Bend your knees and spread so I can see."

*I can't! Help me . . . someone help me —*

He put his hand beneath her knees, lifted them until her feet were flat on the bed, and roughly shoved them apart. He bent his head over her exposed femininity. She could feel the warmth of his breath on her quivering flesh. Dazed and terrified anew, she lay there helplessly, trapped, exhausted, gasping and trembling.

The man was breathing heavily now. His fingers spread and probed and rubbed her tender flesh. In desperation Pauline tried to close her legs.

"No!" He struck her a sharp blow on her inner

thigh. "I only want to look."

*I'll kill you! Someday, I'll kill you!*

His fingers left her, but his palm continued to hold her to the bed. He kissed her breasts, her belly, his hand going over every inch of her body.

"I didn't hurt you. You're the prettiest one yet. You didn't mind me looking at you, did you?"

*Yes! Yes! I minded. You . . . pervert —*

"I've got to go now. I'm taking the cloth out of your mouth and untying your hands. You be good now." He began to roll her in the quilt that was on the bed. "Lie still and count to two hundred before you try to get out. I don't want to come back and cut those pretty titties. That's a sweet girl. Thank you, darlin', for leaving the window open. Thank you for a lovely time."

Paralyzed with fear, Pauline, rolled tightly in the quilt, strained her ears for sounds of him leaving. There were none. She began to sob, forgetting to count. After a while she could bear the confinement of the quilt no longer and began to roll across the bed. When her head and her arms were free, she was afraid to open her eyes for fear he would still be there.

Pauline lay there for a long time, filled with misery and shame, her mind going in a thousand directions. So this is what the other victims of The Looker had endured. Only now could she appreciate the humiliation, the indignities they had suffered at the hands of this pervert.

Finally, convincing herself that he was gone, she stood up, then, legs atremble, sat down hard on the side of the bed. After a while she lit the lamp with shaking hands. There was no sign, no sign at all, that anyone had been in her room. The papers she had been grading had not been disturbed. Her hairpins were on the table, her skirt over the back of the rocker. Everything was just as it had been before . . . only *she* was different.

Pauline wrapped the quilt around herself and sat down in the rocking chair wondering if she would ever be able to sleep in the dark again. She began to catalog in her mind everything she could remember about the man who had made the night visit. He had smelled of cigar smoke. Most of the men in town smoked cigars. He didn't have a mustache. Half the men in town were clean shaven. He was light on his feet — she had not heard a sound when he crossed the floor to the window. His hands had been big, or had they just felt big on her body? They were slightly rough, not a plowman's hands, but not the hands of a man who did no work at all. He had whispered and hissed, so she would never recognize his voice. One thing was sure; he had known who she was and that she would be alone in the house tonight.

It could have been Wade Simmer. People suspected he was The Looker. Or it could just as easily have been one of the men on the porch of the rooming house.

Shame set the blood pounding in her ears. She vowed that she would never, never tell anyone what had happened here tonight. If anyone knew, she would be so mortified she'd not be able to stay in town. She had to complete the school year in order to get a recommendation so that she could get another job. It was only one month until school was out for the summer. One more night until Mrs. Poole returned. She would stick it out, then she would leave this town forever.

"I'm going home today, Granny." Jesse had come back to the Lesters' to spend her sixth night in the hills. "Papa will be up to see you just as soon as he has time."

"Now don't ya be startin' *that* over again, girl. I ain't wantin' ya to be pesterin' your pa about me. Hear? I be spendin' my last days right here with Mr. Lester." Granny had filled her lower lip with powdered snuff, which was now trickling down the corner of her mouth.

"But, Granny, you might have quite a few more days to spend with him if you would do something about the goiter."

"Ain't God's will to go cuttin' stuff outta folk's craw and that's that."

Jesse kissed the old woman's wrinkled cheek. "If you change your mind —"

"I won't," she said emphatically and spit snuff juice in the can beside her chair. "Ya done good here, girl. Your pa ort to be proud. Folks won't forget ya."

"There haven't been any new cases of scarlet fever the last couple of days. I'm sure the worst is over. I'll leave medicine at the mill store just in case. Everyone has been generous. I'm loaded

96

down with gifts to take home." She laughed. "Molly will be worn to a nubbin by the time she gets us home."

Granny's eyes twinkled merrily. "It's downhill all the way to town."

Jesse climbed into the buggy, picked up the reins and waved at the old couple on the porch. She was glad to be going home, although she had enjoyed her stay in the hills and had come to know and appreciate the people. They were, for the most part, good people, hard-working. Of course, there were loathsome creatures like Otis Merfeld, but there were some like him in Harpersville too.

She had not seen Wade Simmer since that first day, but his presence had been felt. He had smoothed the way for her, providing an escort for her rounds and a designated place for her to spend the night. He had made two trips to Harpersville for medicine and instructions from her father. At first she had been puzzled that he kept his distance. Then it occurred to her that he was avoiding her. Did he think that she expected him to court her because of the kiss they had shared? When she thought of it, the blood rushed to her face. She was glad to be leaving. She didn't want to face him. She never wanted to face him again. Even as she had the thought, she knew it wasn't true.

Jesse paused to say good-bye to Mrs. Bailey and Homer and to thank them for their hospitality. She stopped again to say good-bye to Mrs. Frony. It was almost noon when she left the mill store after declining the invitation to stay for dinner.

The sun sprinkled the ground with gold dust. The birches that lined the road stood whitely clean. A mockingbird trilled high up in the trees and a jay scolded him from the bushes below. Jesse smelled the clean May air and felt the warm sun of the bright blue day.

Suddenly a horseman appeared out of the trees at the side of the road. Jesse drew a deep steadying breath and pulled up on the reins. Her eyes were wide and confused, her face flushed with surprise. Her mouth formed a silent O. She and Wade looked at each other for what seemed to be a long while before he spoke.

"You're leaving." His voice was strained.

With an effort she pulled her gaze away from him, determined that he not know how upsetting it was to see him. A thought came unbidden to her brain, undeniable in its truth. He knew that I was going home today. He wanted to see me again.

"Why are you surprised? You've known every move I've made since I've been up here." Something dark and angry welled up inside her.

He nodded in agreement.

"Well, good-bye and . . . thanks for your help."

"I've brought a picnic."

"Picnic? What on earth for?"

"To pay back for eating the lunch your sister packed."

"Oh, that — I was invited to eat with the Fronys."

"But you didn't."

"How do you know?"

"You weren't in there long enough."

Jesse stared at him as he edged the horse up closer to the buggy. All she could think of to say was, "It was presumptuous of you to think I'd picnic with you."

He smiled at that. "I guess it was. Down ahead is a stream where Molly can get a drink of water."

"She had one at Fronys'."

"She'll need another one. Come on, Nurse Forbes. Don't be difficult." His laughing eyes held hers. The devilish grin on his face made him so incredibly handsome that, if asked, Jesse would have been unable to recall her own name.

He led Molly off the road and into a clearing beside a slow-moving stream. Stones along the bank were white in the sun, and tiny silver minnows darted frantically from shallow to shallow. The roots of a large sycamore tree sprawled out toward the water. It was a beautiful, peaceful place.

Wade tied his horse and, carrying a cloth bag, came to the buggy. Jesse was standing beside it.

"It's pretty here. Listen to the lark."

"You like birds?"

"Love them. Who doesn't?"

"You'd be surprised at how many people don't even hear them, can't even identify one from the other."

She looked up at him and later realized that she had said something absolutely stupid.

"Were you this tall the other day?"

He laughed, spreading charm all over his usually

99

serious face. His lips widened, making deep creases in his cheeks. His green eyes shone like a mountain pool in the sunshine. Again, she was aware that when he smiled he was breathtakingly good looking in a wild sort of way.

"I'm walking on stilts. Didn't you notice?"

Her eyes went quickly to his booted feet and back to his eyes before she turned her head away. He cupped her elbow in his hand and led her toward a grassy spot near the stream.

"I forgot the blanket." He placed the bag on the ground and loped back to his horse to take a roll from behind the saddle.

"You've thought of everything. I'd not be surprised if you produced a freezer of ice cream," Jesse said irritably, and took a corner of the blanket to help him spread it on the ground. "I really don't have time for this."

"You have time for a piece of chicken. I fried it this morning."

"You fried it?"

"You'd better hope so. Jody's cooking isn't fit for the hogs."

"I've not seen Jody since that first day."

"He keeps busy."

"Doing what?"

"Studying."

"Studying? Who teaches him?"

"I do — with the help of the teacher at Coon Rapids. There's a school of sorts at Violet, but he refuses to go. He wants to go to a school where he can run on their track team, but he has a lot of studying to do first."

"Oh."

"Oh? You think it's a waste of time teaching a . . . nigger." His tone more than his words made her angry.

"Climb down off your high horse, Mr. Simmer, and stop being so defensive where Jody is concerned. I don't think anything of the kind."

He grinned at her sheepishly. "I guess I do get defensive, but it's an uphill battle to see that Jody gets his chance. Who knows, Jody could be the next Booker T. Washington."

"I've heard of him. President Roosevelt invited him to the White House. Caused quite a stir."

"I took Jody to the Chautauqua down in Chattanooga to hear him speak. It got him all fired up to go to a colored college. Folks up here don't understand how important it is to send their own kids to school, much less a colored boy. Hill people are more closed-minded about some things than town people."

"Papa says that some folk have so little self-worth that they need to feel that they are better than someone. Jody is handy."

"I never thought about it like that."

He opened the bag and laid out fried chicken, bread-and-butter pickles, slices of light bread spread with butter and two pieces of applesauce cake.

"Cake? You have all sorts of hidden talents."

Wade grinned. "I was a little short on time so

101

I got the cake from Mrs. Frony."

"What would you have done if I had accepted her invitation to dinner?"

"I was holding my breath that you wouldn't." Wade produced a tin cup, went to the stream and brought it back brimming with clear, cool water. He set the cup between them. "Go ahead and eat. I promise I didn't fry the chicken in croton oil."

Color tinged Jesse's cheeks. "You say the darndest things."

"That's the first time I've heard you swear."

"I know a couple more swear words, all of which describe Otis Merfeld."

"Did he give you any trouble?" The smile had left Wade's eyes.

"None to speak of."

They ate in silence, Wade leaning on his elbow, Jesse sitting with her legs drawn up under her, each stealing sly glances at the other.

Wade waited to drink from the cup until after she had drunk. He told himself that he was ten times a fool. He had vowed to stay away from this woman, and here he was with her in this secluded place. He had convinced himself that he only wanted to see her, talk to her one last time. The idea of the picnic came to mind and he, idiot that he was, gave in to the impulse.

Talk to her? Hell! He wanted to lay her down on the blanket and kiss her all over. He wanted to hold her, feel her bare breasts against his chest, feel her arms curl around his neck in sweet surrender. He wanted to take her in his arms, carry her back to his home and lock the doors against the world. He had never been so enamored, so completely captivated by a woman before. It was scary as hell.

Say something, you numskull, Jesse told herself. She searched her mind for something casual to say. The weather! That was a safe topic.

"It's warm for May. I suppose we'll have a hot summer."

She looked at Wade, trying to smile, but her smile faded as the seconds ticked by and Wade said absolutely nothing. The silence stretched. Jesse felt a knot of discomfort forming in her stomach.

"Goodness, it's getting late," she said in a tight, jerking voice. "I should be getting on toward home."

"When will you be back?"

"Oh, I don't know." She got to her feet and shook the cake crumbs from her skirt. "Thank you for the lunch."

"My pleasure." Wade stood and folded the blanket. "I'll ride with you to the flatland."

"Oh, you needn't bother —" Jesse followed along behind him and climbed into the buggy.

"It's no bother." His voice was curt. He mounted his horse and rode up beside the buggy. "When will you be back?" he asked for the second time.

"I don't know," she said again. "Thank you for helping me. I couldn't have reached all those families without you."

"Doc shouldn't have let you come up here by yourself."

"I suppose you told him that."

"Bet your life I did."

"What did he say?"

"He said you were not a weakling and that you could take care of yourself."

"Well, forevermore! People in Harpersville think you're The Looker. Why would he think I was safe with you up here?"

"Do *you* think I'm The Looker?"

"I haven't given it any thought."

"Liar!" He turned to look at her. She forced herself to meet his eyes. All this fluttery stuff in her stomach was distracting.

"I'd not have picnicked with you if I thought you were that . . . pervert."

"Good answer. I'll have to stop making my night trips to Ike's garage and maybe, just maybe, folks will stop talking."

"Why do you go to Ike's garage?"

"We're building a gasoline engine. As a matter of fact I was there last night."

"My little brother loves to go to Ike's garage."

"Yeah, I know. I've met him."

They came out of the woods and onto the flatland road.

"Were you put out with me for kissing you the other night?"

"Nooo . . ." She lifted her shoulders in a careless shrug as if it were nothing.

Their eyes met and held for a timeless moment.

Jesse was mesmerized, and what she saw in the green depth of his gaze barely registered in her mind. Later she was to decide that it was loneliness, fear of rejection.

"You're perfectly safe with me. You know that, don't you?"

"I know that. I just don't go around kissing every man I meet —" Her voice trailed and she became lost in the tender concern she saw in his eyes.

"Thank God for that. Jesse," he whispered, her name a caress. The eyes that looked into hers were dark with emotion.

Jesse was almost moved to tears. She knew with certainty that this man would never hurt her, never force his attentions on her. The decisions would be hers.

"You'll be all right. I'll watch until you reach town." His voice was tight, strained.

"You don't have to —"

"I'll watch. Bye, Miss Jesse."

"B-bye, Mr. Simmer."

# CHAPTER
## • 7 •

*J*esse held the reins as Molly trotted down the road toward Harpersville. She refused to dwell on whether or not she had acted properly when she had allowed Wade Simmer to kiss her. It had come about naturally. The sweetness of it is what surprised her and even more than that, how comfortable she had felt being held close in his arms. The few quick kisses she had shared with suitors from time to time had not stirred her at all. Wade's kiss was different. It had opened up a whole new world of feeling for her.

Jesse decided that she was attracted to Wade because he was considered dangerous, wild and unsuitable for a doctor's daughter. She had heard tales about Wade Simmer and the reasons he had left the hills after his granny died. Some said he had been in prison; others said he had been involved in some illegal activity and had made a pocketful of money. They speculated that he would leave again when his money ran out. The tales had not seemed so outlandish at the time she heard them, but now that she had met him she had reason to question their validity. If he were as bad as people said he was, would he be concerned about sick children and about the education of a homeless colored boy?

The buggy rolled smoothly down the road. Jesse, lost in her thoughts, was oblivious to her surroundings. Few in Harpersville had taken the trouble to know Wade Simmer. It was unfair to condemn him for what his father had done.

Molly's hooves were loud on the plank floor of the bridge that spanned the creek just outside of town, and Jesse was abruptly jolted back to the present. She passed the creamery where milk wagons lined the dock. The flag still fluttered from the pole when she passed the school. It told her that school was still in session. She would be home before Todd and Susan. She was eager to see her sister and brother. She had not been away from them for so long since she'd been at nursing school.

Wishing she didn't need to pass the bank and the mercantile but knowing there was no help for it, she drove down Main Street, nodding to those who waved, grateful that no one stopped her to ask about the epidemic. In the alley behind the house she guided Molly to the barn, where the mare nickered a greeting to the doctor's riding horse. Old Mr. Adams, who cared for the animals, came leisurely down the alley from his little house at the end of the block.

" 'Lo, Mr. Adams."

"Howdy, miss. You been gone a long time."

"Yes, and I'm glad to be home."

Carrying her medical bag and suitcase, Jesse walked up the drive to the house and let herself into the surgery. A note on the desk said her father had gone on a house call. She surveyed the office, grimaced at the disorder, and wondered why her father thought it unimportant to return things to their proper place. Tired, but knowing that sooner or later she would have to tackle the job of restoring order, she set about putting away bottles of tonic, gauze and swabs, and boxes of pills in the medicine cabinet.

A voice from behind Jesse startled her so that she almost dropped the bag she was emptying.

"What are you doing in here?"

She whirled to stare at the woman who stood in the doorway leading to the private part of the house. Her hands were on her hips and a look of indignation darkened her face.

"Close that cabinet at once."

Jesse was jarred from her stupor when the woman brushed past her, closed the door to the cabinet firmly, twisted the key in the lock and put it in her apron pocket.

"Who in blazes are you?" Jesse blurted when she finally found her tongue.

"I'm the doctor's housekeeper. I'm in charge when he's away."

"Are you now!" Anger made Jesse's voice sharp. "I'm the doctor's daughter and I was not aware that *we* had a housekeeper."

The woman's face registered shock, then

108

changed in an instant. The frown was replaced with a cheerful smile.

"You're Jesse Louise," she exclaimed. "My dear, I thought you would be older, plainer. I wasn't expecting someone so young . . . so pretty. It didn't occur to me —" Her voice trailed. "Oh, dear, I've put my foot in it, haven't I? I'm Louella Lindstrom." She held out her hand.

Good manners forced Jesse to take it. "How do you do?" Her voice was quiet and flat. "How long have you been here?"

"I came in on the train last Friday. Hollis, ah . . . Doctor Forbes said you had left that day to go up into the hills to care for the sick. You're tired, aren't you? Would you like help in putting away your things?" There was an absence of real inquiry in the woman's voice, and Jesse suspected she was merely being polite.

"No, thank you. The key, please." She held out her hand and the woman promptly returned the key.

She's pretty in a pink and white way, Jesse thought as she emptied her medical bag — almost too pretty. Not one blond hair was out of place. It was folded and pinned at the nape of her slender neck. Her face was very white and wrinkle-free although Jesse guessed her age to be near that of her father. Her lips and cheeks were pink, her eyes large and cornflower blue. The dress and apron she wore looked as if they had just come from the ironing board.

"Jes-se-eee!" As Todd's voice reached Jesse, she

heard his running steps coming down the hall. "You — 're h-h-home!"

Jesse crowded past Mrs. Lindstrom, who remained in the doorway, and hurried to meet her brother. They met in the hall. He threw his arms about her waist and she hugged him to her.

"Yes, I'm home. How are you?"

"F-f-fine, I g-guess."

Jesse ran her fingers through his dark hair. "You look fine. I've missed you."

"I-I-I m-m-miss-ed you."

"How did you know I was home?"

"I-I saw you p-p-pass the s-school."

"You sly fox. You were looking out the window when you should have been looking at the blackboard." Jesse kissed the top of her brother's head.

"Change your clothes, Todd. You have chores to do." Mrs. Lindstrom spoke gently and placed her hand on the boy's shoulder.

Jesse felt her brother stiffen and turned to look at the woman. She was smiling sweetly.

"What chores?" Jesse asked.

"His father insists that he keep the woodbox filled and that he do at least one other chore each evening. I've hung the hall runners on the line. The rug beater is on the back porch. When you finish, I want you to go to the creamery for a pail of buttermilk. Hurry along, dear. Dinner is served at six o'clock sharp."

There was something so quiet and implacable about Mrs. Lindstrom's manner that it chilled Jesse's heart like the touch of cold fingers. The woman's words echoed in her mind. *Dinner at six o'clock sharp.* They had always had *supper* in the evening and it was never at six o'clock sharp.

Todd was looking at her, his eyes pleading.

"The woodbox has always been one of your chores, honey. Fill it and go get the milk. I'll beat the rugs —"

"Oh, I don't think the doctor —"

"I'll speak to Papa, Mrs. Lindstrom. Todd needs a little time for himself before *supper.*"

"Very well. I was merely passing along his father's instructions."

Todd was looking at his toes, his cap in his hands. Jesse gave him a gentle push toward the stairs. He didn't move until the new housekeeper had disappeared into the dining room.

"I-I-I don't l-l-like h-her."

Jesse put her lips to his ear. "I don't think I do either, but let's go along with it until I can talk to Papa."

A grin split Todd's face and he raced up the stairs.

Jesse looked around the house as if seeing it for the first time. It fairly shone. Chairs had been arranged in groups for conversation. The windows sparkled and freshly washed and stretched lace panels hung to the floor. Starched doilies covered tables that gleamed. Lace tidies lay on the backs and arms of the chairs and sofa. Bridal wreath filled vases she had forgotten they owned. She walked slowly down the hallway that divided the house. In the dining room her stepmother's crocheted tablecloth covered the table, and in the middle a single pink peony floated in a bowl of water.

The swinging door to the kitchen was closed. It had stood open for so long that Jesse had almost forgotten it could be closed. She pushed it open. The room in no way resembled the kitchen she had left six days ago. The breakfast table had been moved to the space next to the pantry. The rocking chair from her father's room and a small table with a book and reading glasses now sat beside the windows. The kitchen cabinet had been moved over beside the enameled sink. Neatly folded towels hung from a rack that had been attached above the high back. The new housekeeper had lost no time in making the house her own.

Feeling like a stranger in her own home, Jesse backed out of the room and went down the hall to the front door. Through the side glass she could see Susan coming up the walk.

Her sister was going to be a beauty, Jesse thought, as she waited for her to reach the door. Her light brown hair was tied at the nape of her neck with a black ribbon. She wore a dark, two-piece sailor suit with a wide collar trimmed in red braid. The skirt was the new mid-calf length, her stockings black. But Jesse was disturbed to see the usually high-spirited Susan trudging along with such a dejected slump to her shoulders.

Jesse threw open the door. "Hurry up, slow-poke, and give me a hug."

"Jesse! When did you get home?"

"A while ago. Todd saw me pass the school."

112

Jesse hugged her sister. "You look so pretty. That sailor suit finally came from Sears Roebuck. Oh, I've missed you."

"I'm glad you're back. Have you met . . . her?" It was like Susan to get right to the point.

"I've met her. What do you think of the new housekeeper?"

"Not much! She's got Papa wrapped around her finger."

"Where did she come from?"

"She came to the door with her suitcases and told Papa she was mamma's girlhood friend and had come to visit. She acted as if she didn't know mamma was gone and cried big crocodile tears. She and Papa went into the surgery, and before I knew it, I was moving out of my room and into yours so she could have my room." Susan's jaw jutted a little.

"Hmmm . . ."

"She's all sweetness around Papa, but when he isn't here she's as mean as a snake."

"What do you mean?"

"It's do this, do that. Proper young ladies don't do this, don't do that. Do you want to shame your papa?" Susan mimicked Mrs. Lindstrom's voice.

"I suppose you have chores —"

"Do I have chores? She hasn't washed a supper dish since she's been here. Do you know what she's done? She talked Papa into letting Mrs. Klein go. She said that Todd and I could get up an hour early on Monday and work the lever on the washing machine before we go to school and that soon school would be out and there was no reason to pay Mrs. Klein when we could do it."

"Mrs. Klein has been coming for years. She depends on the money she makes."

"Old Ghost-face said washing was part of a housekeeper's duties and she would be most *happy* to do it. What she meant was she would be most happy for me and Todd to do it."

"Ghost-face?"

"It's milk-white, isn't it? I've caught her putting buttermilk on her face three times since she's been here. She says I'll be sorry for going without a hat when I have freckles all over my face. Well, poot on her!"

"What does Papa say to all of this?"

"He says it's what he's always wanted — someone to take the household duties off your shoulders so you can have more of a social life."

"Hmmm . . ." Jesse said again.

"Talk to Papa, Jesse. Maybe he'll listen to you. He's doing this because he doesn't think it's fair that you work in the surgery and have to run the house. I'll help more. I promise."

"I'll talk to him. In the meanwhile change clothes and help me unload the buggy. The boot is full of payment for my services — full of everything but money."

As soon as they left the house Susan began to ask questions.

"What was it like up there all by yourself? Where did you stay? Did you see where Wade Simmer lives? It is true he lives with that darkie?"

"In the first place I wasn't by myself. There are families scattered all through the hills, and, believe it or not, they are a tight-knit group who, in a way, look after each other. I stayed with a different family each night. Wade Simmer does not live in a dugout or a lean-to. He lives in a very comfortable house made of log and stone. His great-grandfather built the original cabin and his grandfather added to it. Jody lives with him. Does that answer your questions?"

"Wade Simmer came twice to see Papa. It's the first time I've got a good look at him. He's handsome in a rough sort of way. The first time they were in the surgery a couple of hours with the door shut."

"He was very . . . helpful."

Susan was too engrossed in her tale to notice the hesitancy in her sister's voice.

"You would have laughed your head off when that darkie came to the door with your letter. Old Ghost-face tried to run him off with the broom; but he wouldn't go, and he wouldn't tell her what he wanted. She was madder than a wet hen. He just squatted out by the lilac bushes and waited until Papa came home. When he left he ran right down the middle of Main Street and thumbed his nose at Marshal Wright. I laughed till I nearly peed my pants."

"You'd better not let ah . . . Old Ghost-face hear you say that." The sisters giggled and hugged each other.

When they entered the kitchen with the first

load from the buggy, Mrs. Lindstrom was bringing a custard pie from the oven. Jesse ignored her and headed for the pantry, where she found the shelves definitely tidier than when she had last seen them. She and Susan placed the jars of pickled peaches, beets, relishes and jams on the shelves and without a word went back to the buggy for a second load. They returned with sacks of new potatoes, winter onions, dried pumpkin and squash. Susan carried a tin of rendered lard.

"Where in the world did all this come from?" Mrs. Lindstrom asked.

"From my patients."

"Forevermore." It was all she said but it was enough for Jesse to detect the disapproval in her voice. "Set the table, please, Susan. It's twenty minutes till six."

"But . . . Papa isn't here yet."

"He will be." Mrs. Lindstrom turned back to the stove and Susan poked out her tongue.

"I'd help you, but I've got to beat the rugs." Jesse caught her sister's eye and winked.

A few minutes before six o'clock Doctor Forbes came into the house, dropped his bag beside the surgery door, tossed his hat on the hatrack and hurried down the hall to the lavatory. A few minutes later he came out, hair combed, tie straightened, and entered the dining room.

"Hello, Papa." Jesse came from the kitchen.

"At least ten people told me they saw you come through town. You all right?"

"Fine. No new cases in two days."

116

"Good. Good. What do you think of my surprise? You didn't even have to cook supper."

"Dinner is ready, Doctor. Please sit down." Mrs. Lindstrom, coming in from the kitchen, saved Jesse from having to answer. "Children," she called.

Lacking the exuberance they usually had at suppertime, Susan and Todd came to the table. "Hello, Papa," they both said at the same time.

Jesse moved to her regular place opposite her father and near the kitchen. Before she could sit down, Mrs. Lindstrom slid gracefully into the chair.

"Oh, dear! Is this where you usually sit, Jesse? I've been sitting here so I could serve Todd. If you'd rather —"

"It isn't important." Jesse slipped into the chair beside her brother. "But I think Todd can serve himself. He's been doing it for years."

"I'm sure. He's such a little gentleman at the table."

Doctor Forbes didn't seem to notice the bite in Jesse's voice or the housekeeper's smooth reply. He was helping himself to the pot roast. Susan rolled her eyes to the ceiling; Todd nudged Jesse with his foot.

The meal Mrs. Lindstrom had prepared could not be faulted. Doctor Forbes ate his roast, mashed potatoes and gravy with obvious enjoyment. He attempted to talk with Jesse about the epidemic; but after she said that they could discuss it later, he too fell silent.

Mrs. Lindstrom moved smoothly in to fill the void.

"How was your patient, Doctor?"

"He'll make it. Damn fool waited long enough to call me."

"He's lucky you went at all, considering —"

"Some people have more pride than brains."

"And some have none at all. How fortunate they are to have such an unselfish doctor."

"Delicious meal, Mrs. Lindstrom."

"Thank you, Doctor. Save room for the custard pie."

Jesse's eyes went from the housekeeper to her father. A tight knot began to form in her throat; and although the meal was very good and she was hungry, it was difficult to swallow.

"I-I'm g-glad Je-Jes-se's ho-ho-ho—" Todd glanced at Mrs. Lindstrom before looking down at his plate. His face reddened because he couldn't get out the word.

"I'm sure your sister knows that you're glad she's home, dear," Mrs. Lindstrom said kindly and then spoke to the doctor, effectively shutting off further conversation from the boy. "I met a very nice lady today. She invited me to join the Harpersville Historical Society."

"I can guess who that was." Jesse placed her knife and fork on the edge of her plate.

"Old Barrel-belly," Susan said, under her breath but loud enough for Mrs. Lindstrom's sharp ears.

"Whom did you say, dear?" The voice had lost some of the sweetness.

"It could be none other than Roberta Harper." Jesse grinned at her sister before looking directly into Mrs. Lindstrom's eyes. "She's terribly proud of the fact that her husband's grandfather founded the town."

"Yes, she told me. Well, if we've finished, I'll serve the pie. Susan, dear, will you remove the plates?"

"Sit still, Susan. I'll do it." Jesse picked up her plate and Todd's and followed the housekeeper to the kitchen. After placing the dishes on the kitchen cabinet, she returned to the dining room for her father's and Susan's. She met the eyes of the housekeeper after she butted open the swinging door with her backside. The woman's eyes had a strange, cold faraway look that made Jesse uncomfortable.

"You're spoiling her, you know."

"Susan?" Jesse set the plates down none too gently. "You've not been here long enough to make that judgment, Mrs. Lindstrom. And if I were, it would be a family matter."

"The doctor has expressed his concern to me." There was a note of self-assurance in her voice.

A qualm of uneasiness went with Jesse back to the table, but she wore a bright cheerful smile and spoke to her brother.

"Did you go to the ball game on Sunday?"

Todd looked toward the kitchen door and nodded his head.

"Well . . . who won?"

"B-B-Bush-man D-da-dai-ry."

"Did Pauline go with you?" Jesse looked across the table to where Susan sat slumped in her chair.

"She went. She came to make jam too. I don't think she'll come back."

"Why is that?"

"She just . . . she just couldn't do it right. Mrs. Lindstrom made it — after we picked the berries, of course." Susan glanced at her father. He was leaning back in his chair studying his eldest daughter.

Something had happened to her during her stay in the hills. Her eyes were bright, her cheeks tanned, her hair loose and tied at her nape with a ribbon. She had bloomed like a woman in love. Well, she was pretty and capable and deserved to find a man who would love her as he had loved his Dora.

Mrs. Lindstrom came through the swinging door carrying a tray she placed on the buffet after moving aside a large crystal bowl. The bowl had belonged to Susan's grandmother, and Jesse had carefully packed it away until Susan had a home of her own.

The housekeeper served the neat wedges of pie and took her seat at the table. Jesse looked at Susan and winked, remembering other meals when she had set the pie in the middle of the table, and they had helped themselves until every crumb was gone, arguing loudly about who was entitled to the last piece.

Tonight they ate in silence. When he finished, Doctor Forbes complimented Mrs. Lindstrom on the meal, moved his chair and stood.

"Do you want your coffee in the parlor, Doctor?"

"In the surgery."

"I'll be in, Papa, as soon as Susan and I do the dishes." Jesse began to pick up the plates.

Doctor Forbes smiled a trifle ruefully at his daughter. "We have a housekeeper now. Susan can help her —"

"I-I-I do-don't have to he-help?"

"I don't think it takes three people to do a few dishes." The doctor ruffled his son's hair. "Do your lessons. Soon you'll be having end-of-the-year tests."

"That's right," Mrs. Lindstrom said brightly. "Mrs. Harper says school will be out in another three weeks. Come along, Susan. We'll make quick work of this chore."

Susan wrinkled her nose at her sister, worked her mouth in silent protest and picked up the dessert plates.

# CHAPTER

# · 8 ·

*J*esse followed her father into the surgery and closed the door. He sat in his swivel chair, she in the chair beside his desk.

"It was a pleasant dinner we had, huh, Jess?"

"The food was good. Where did she come from, Papa?"

"Delaware, I think she said. She came in on the morning train the day you left."

"And came directly here seeking a job?"

"No. She came to see Dora. She didn't know Dora had passed away. She was going to say hello and go to the hotel. Seemed broken up about Dora's passing. They were girlhood friends in Knoxville years ago."

"It's strange they didn't keep in touch."

"Not so strange considering Mrs. Lindstrom lived in Sweden for a number of years. Her husband died there and she came back to her native country."

"She's hardly the type to be a housekeeper."

"For the last two years she was a mistress in

122

a girls' school. I know she's bossy and Susan resents her —" His voice trailed when he saw the impatient look on his daughter's face.

"Did she tell you why she left the school?"

"Said she got homesick for Tennessee."

There was a soft knock on the door before it opened. Mrs. Lindstrom came in balancing a tray with two steaming cups of coffee.

"If you want more, Jesse, I'll bring in the coffee server. Doctor usually drinks one cup after dinner."

"One is enough for me, thank you." Jesse knew immediately that Mrs. Lindstrom wanted her to know that she usually had coffee with her employer after supper.

After the housekeeper left, the doctor leaned back in his chair and grinned at his daughter.

"Nice to be waited on, isn't it?"

"Oh, I don't know about that. I'm used to doing things for myself."

"You've got to admit she's got things in tip-top shape."

"She does everything beautifully —"

"— And she'll be good for Susan. She knows how to handle girls."

"Susan doesn't need *handling*, Papa. She's growing up. All girls her age try to spread their wings."

"She spreads hers right out of the house when there is work to be done."

"Of course she does. She'll do as little as she can get away with, but that's normal."

"Mrs. Lindstrom will see that she does her share

of the chores. You have enough to do."

"And Todd? Is every minute of his time after school to be filled with chores? His stuttering is worse —"

"I've not noticed that. Mrs. Lindstrom will take the burden of the house off your shoulders and give you time to enjoy life. You're young —"

"You want me to go out and kick up my heels. Is that it?"

"You'll have time to go to ball games, dances, church socials. You'll have time for a beau."

"Glory be! Do you have someone in mind?"

His eyes twinkled. "I'll leave that up to you."

Something in his tone and the look on his face caused Jesse's cheeks to burn. "Todd and Susan don't like her," she said bluntly.

"Of course not. She has authority. Children resent authority. She explained that to me."

"I bet she did." Jesse's voice held resignation.

"Give her a chance, Jess. She's a very pleasant woman."

"Susan tells me that Mrs. Klein will not be coming to do the washing."

"Well, yes. Mrs. Lindstrom said that she would do it."

"Does she know about boiling the towels from the surgery?"

"I don't know. I never thought to mention it."

"Is it the money, Papa? I'll pay Mrs. Klein out of my wages. She depends on the pay she gets here."

"Mrs. Lindstrom said it was the housekeeper's

duty to take care of the wash, and I just left it up to her."

"Well?"

"Keep Mrs. Klein. And don't be lippy about paying her out of your wages. You don't get enough as it is."

"I get room and board as well."

"Jess, you're about to make me angry. Is that your intention?"

"No. It was a shock to come home and find everything . . . different. Has anything else happened since I've been gone? Has The Looker struck again?"

"If he has, it's not been reported to me." Doctor Forbes drained his cup and set it back on the saucer. "Simmer told me you did a fine job up in the hills. The people liked you."

Jesse felt the heat rush to her cheeks again and hoped her father wouldn't notice.

"I did the best I could. The people are proud. I brought home a boot full of pay; everything from jelly to rendered lard."

"How was Granny Lester?"

"Granny refuses to go to Knoxville for treatment. She's dead-set against it. Her eyes are beginning to bulge and she's short of breath. I'm almost sure she's taking a cure-all medicine recommended by some quack."

The doctor sighed and shook his head. "They're a different breed up there — pigheaded and proud. We can't force her to go."

"Mrs. Bailey's toe is healing, although I don't

125

know why. She was in the garden digging potatoes with just a dirty sock on her foot. Mrs. Merfeld is thin as a rail except for her stomach. I'll be surprised if she delivers a normal baby."

Jesse opened a notebook and read to her father the data she had recorded about each of the families she visited, including the ages of the children in the family and some personal information.

"Mr. Merfeld is trouble. I would not like to go there alone."

"One of us should go back up there in about a week and check on the young ones. And as soon as I get the government smallpox vaccine, we'll go up there and innoculate."

"When will that be?"

"Month or so." He studied his daughter for a long moment, rocking back and forth in his swivel chair. "I had a couple of good visits with Wade Simmer. He helped you out, did he?"

Jesse felt her face grow hot again and gulped down the last of her coffee before she spoke.

"He was very helpful. He arranged for me to have an escort each day and a place to spend the night. The hill people are very hospitable and went out of their way to make me comfortable. They gave me the best they had. I liked them, Papa."

"Plenty of good people up there. You treat them right and they'll treat you right. But I wouldn't want to get on their bad side." The doctor continued to rock and to observe his daughter. "Simmer is determined to send that darkie to a boarding school for colored."

"Boarding schools cost money." Jesse looked intently at the toe of her shoe.

"Money doesn't seem to be a problem. He was asking me if I knew a teacher who would tutor the boy during the summer. I suggested Pauline."

"Mr. Harper wouldn't let Jody darken the door of that schoolhouse and you know it."

"I know it and Wade knows it. She can't teach him at the school, and Mrs. Poole is going away for the summer. She couldn't teach him there anyway. That woman would have a fit. And, of course, she can't stay at Simmer's. I've thought of hiring the boy to do jobs around the place. He could sleep in the barn if it wasn't for that stupid law about darkies being in town after dark. He'd have to go back to Wade's at night. If Pauline came here to spend the summer on the pretext of giving Todd extra lessons, she could teach the boy. Simmer will pay her."

"Is this your idea or his?"

"Both, I reckon."

"Why are you doing this?"

"Because, as Wade says, the colored man is here to stay. White folk brought them here. They deserve a chance for an education the same as white folk. And the boy is hungry to learn."

"You two must have gotten pretty friendly. Do people still think he's The Looker?"

"Some do."

"You don't?"

"Use your head, Jess. Would I have sent you up there if I thought there was one chance in a thousand Simmer was that pervert?"

"How can you be so sure he isn't?"

"You think he is?"

"No! You know I don't," she said in a cool no-nonsense voice.

Her father chuckled. "Then how can *you* be so sure?" His low-voiced query hung in the air between them.

"Well . . ." He had backed her into a corner and was actually enjoying her discomfort. Her blue-gray eyes flashed him a look of irritation. "He hasn't spent his entire life in the hills of Tennessee, you know. Why would he be interested in looking at a naked woman?"

The doctor laughed. "He's a healthy male. I doubt he'd shut his eyes if the opportunity arose."

"I don't think he's the type to sneak around to do anything."

"That's all?"

"That's all."

The doctor noted his usually unflappable daughter's agitation and changed the subject. "Do you want to talk to Pauline or do you want me to?"

"The house is full, Papa. Where would she sleep?"

"Louella . . . Mrs. Lindstrom suggested we fix up the storage room for Todd so Susan could have his room. It would be plenty big enough after all that stuff is carried to the barn."

Resentment boiled in Jesse. "You've discussed this with *her*."

"She brought it up after she realized that you and Susan were sharing a room."

"I don't mind sharing with Susan."

"I didn't think you would. Don't get on your high horse about Mrs. Lindstrom. You'll see how pleasant it is to have a well-ordered house and dinner ready. You'll find you've gained a new freedom."

"I'm not on my high horse. Have you considered our home up to now to be *not* well ordered?"

"Now you're defensive."

"I can't help being defensive, Papa. It's strange having an outsider in the house. I . . . don't think we need her."

"I do. When you're not in the surgery, you're devoting your time to this house and to your brother and sister. I want you to leave the house entirely in Mrs. Lindstrom's hands and enjoy yourself for a change."

Jesse drew a deep, shaky breath. She was sure that if her spirits dropped any lower she would cry. Shielding the hurt in her eyes with her long thick lashes, she went to the door.

"I'll talk to Pauline," she said just before she went out.

Jesse lay on her back beside her sister, her arm under her head, and gazed out the window at the starlit sky. She longed for a way to turn off her thoughts so that she could sleep. She resented having Mrs. Lindstrom in the house. Mrs. Lindstrom planned to stay or she would not have already entrenched herself so firmly in the household. Jesse also admitted a worry over her father's satisfaction with the woman. Yet she couldn't believe it of herself that she was shallow enough to be jealous of someone her father admired. It was just *this* woman. There was something disturbing about Mrs. Lindstrom that she couldn't put her finger on.

Her thoughts also dwelled on her conversation with her father about Wade Simmer. The reality was that a couple of kisses would mean nothing to a man who had been all over the world, had seen all shapes and colors of women's legs, or so he had said. Now it was easy to believe he had used her as a means of getting a teacher for Jody. Sudden embarrassment made her want to cry. She had submitted to his kiss like a love-starved old maid. Deep inside she was bitterly ashamed. She also wondered why he hadn't mentioned his visits to her father or their plans to get a tutor for Jody.

An unwanted thought crept into her mind and she pondered what life with Wade Simmer would be like. Wade would never leave the hills, so his family would live in his house. There would be dogs and horses and . . . children . . . long summer days in the open air, long winter nights in a warm bed.

Her thoughts dwelled on the intimate side of married life. Wade would be a demanding lover. Oh, Lord! What did she know about a lover? What did she know about Wade Simmer?

Jesse battled the storm of confusion that

pounded inside her and came to realize that there was only one course of action. When she saw him again, and there was no doubt she would, she would treat him politely, but coolly. He must never know that she was even mildly attracted to him. She flopped over on her side. The very next invitation she received from a man she would accept. Hastily she qualified the promise to herself by adding unless it came from Edsel Harper.

As Jesse walked past the bank on her way to the school to catch Pauline before she left for home, Edsel Harper came out the door and called to her.

"Miss Jesse, do you have a minute?"

Jesse paused and watched Edsel come toward her. He was not an unattractive man when seen from a distance. He was tall, broad-shouldered and dressed in the latest fashion. Up close, however, one could see that his light hair was thinning, his eyes were close-set, his brows met over his nose and his full red lips were shaped like a woman's. Edsel's chin receded sharply, and Jesse wondered why he didn't wear a beard to cover it. Probably his mother wouldn't allow it.

"I was concerned when I heard you had gone to the hills, Miss Jesse. I'm glad you're back unharmed."

"There was no need for concern —"

"Oh, but there was. Beside all the other undesirables that live in the hills, this man, Wade Simmer, lives there. He's most likely the man who has been invading the bedrooms of our womenfolk. I tell you, Papa's in a regular snit over it."

"Why do you say it's Mr. Simmer? Has anyone seen him crawling into a bedroom window?"

"Not that, my dear." He patted her arm. "But he's been seen in town on the nights women have been molested."

"That doesn't make him the culprit. Papa thinks it's someone from Fredrick or Grover. Surely a man wouldn't be dumb enough to do something like that in his own town."

"Your papa is absolutely right, but we must include hill people. They are a dangerous lot."

Jesse felt her anger rising. "That's debatable, Edsel, but I don't have the time right now."

"Of course. Of course. By the way, Mama is having a musicale followed by a tea on Sunday afternoon. She asked me to extend an invitation. I would be honored to come and escort you and Mrs. Lindstrom. Mama is quite taken with her. She thinks it admirable the lady has come to take care of her dear friend's home and children."

"Edsel, I'm sure our *housekeeper* would be honored to have you escort her to your mother's little social. I've made plans to go to a ball game with my brother."

"Oh, but couldn't you — ?"

"No, I couldn't. Good-bye, Edsel. I hope you have a lovely time with . . . our housekeeper."

Seething at the way Mrs. Lindstrom had whitewashed her job with the family, Jesse proceeded down the boardwalk. She stopped and gazed unseeing at the hats in the window of the millinery shop. How dare that woman tie herself to the family because of a friendship of twenty years ago — a doubtful friendship at that.

The newspaper office was next to the millinery. Jesse opened the door and went in. Mr. Marsh, the publisher of the *Harpersville Gazette*, was sorting type. When the bell on the door jingled, he looked up, tilted the visor cap back, and picked up a rag to wipe his hands.

"Hello, Miss Jesse. How was your stay in the hill country?"

Jesse laughed. She liked Ralph Marsh, liked his wife, Geneva, and his two married daughters. He was one of only a few men in town who stood up to Boyd Harper.

"Very uneventful except for the scarlet fever epidemic, which will probably hit town in the next few weeks. I've written a news story telling parents to watch for early symptoms."

When she extended a folded paper, he motioned for her to place it on his desk.

"My hands are inky," he explained. "I need a printer's devil to sort this type. My helper got itchy feet and took off last week. I have to break down this week's edition by myself."

"Don't let me interrupt. We can visit while you work."

"And I'll be putting the A's in the W's and the S's in the L's. Now if I were rich like some people I know, I'd buy one of those linotype machines. I saw one in Knoxville. Works slicker than a whistle."

"What in the world is a linotype machine?"

"It's a machine that makes type out of hot lead. It has a keyboard somewhat like a typewriter. The characters are cast in metal in a complete line the exact width of a column. You can set a whole column in less time than it would take to set ten lines by picking out individual letters. After the type is used, it's melted down and reused."

"Forevermore! I had no idea such a machine existed."

"Well, I can forget about it. It costs a lot of money and I'll not make it here in Harpersville."

Jesse picked up a newspaper and read a headline on the front. LADIES! LOCK YOUR DOORS. She glanced at Mr. Marsh and grinned.

"Boyd Harper won't like that."

Marsh grinned back. "I'm sure."

"According to Marshal Wright," Jesse read, "no new attacks have been reported. However, that does not mean The Looker is no longer active. According to the Marshal, the ladies who have had this harrowing experience are reluctant to discuss it, and he has only a very few clues as to the man's identity."

"Sorry business, but you can't sweep it under the rug and pretend it isn't happening. The more womenfolk are aware of it the more precautions they will take."

"The Harpers think it's Wade Simmer." Jesse looked directly into Mr. Marsh's eyes to gauge his reaction to her statement. He laughed. "You don't agree?" she asked.

"No, I don't agree. It's convenient to lay the blame on Simmer. Harpers and Simmers have been at each other's throats since before the war. It's been passed down from generation to generation. Boyd's daddy had Wade's daddy hanged with only a mockery of a trial. 'Course, there was no doubt that Alvin Simmer shot Buford Harper. What was covered up was the fact Buford was in bed with Alvin's wife at the time."

Jesse drew in a deep breath. "How awful. I've never heard that side of it before."

"Few have. That girl was nothing but trouble. Alvin married her in Chattanooga and brought her down here. She was pretty as a picture and wild as a deer. She took off after the killing, leaving Wade with his granny. As far as I know, it's the last anyone has heard of her."

"Why do the Harpers hate Wade? He had nothing to do with that. Heavens, he was just a little boy."

"For one thing, Boyd discovered that Wade's got quite a bit of money in banks in Knoxville and Chattanooga and not a dime in his bank. He's eaten up with curiosity as to where Wade got the money."

"I suppose he thinks he stole it."

Ralph's eyes twinkled. "That's exactly what he thinks."

"My goodness. It's like Boyd to think the worst."

The bell jingled and they both looked toward the door. The man who entered removed his hat

135

quickly when he saw Jesse. He had an engaging grin and a jaunty air when he tipped his head in greeting.

"Afternoon, ma'am."

"Afternoon," she replied. "I'll be running along, Mr. Marsh. Give my regards to Geneva."

"I'll do that, Miss Jesse."

"Ma'am, don't let me interrupt," the young man said quickly. "I'm Ethan Bredlow, looking for a job. I can come back later." He stood awkwardly on first one foot and then the other, twirling his hat in his hand, a shy smile of embarrassment on his face as he looked from Ralph to Jesse.

It was hard for Jesse not to return his smile. He had a pleasant face, a headful of curly blond hair and sky-blue eyes that were plainly admiring as she passed him on her way to the door.

"No need. I was leaving anyway." He sprang to open the door for her. "Thank you," she said as she stepped out onto the boardwalk.

Ethan Bredlow closed the door behind Jesse and turned to Ralph. His expression was quiet and serious, far different from the one he had worn when he had entered the newspaper office.

"Ralph Marsh?"

Ralph nodded. "What did you say your name was?"

"Ethan Bredlow. I would like to speak to you in private."

"It's private here."

"Someone may walk in on us. Do you have an office?"

"What's this all about?"

Bredlow handed him a card. Ralph studied it and looked the man in the eye when he returned it. "This way."

Seated at his desk with the door ajar so that he could hear the bell if someone came in, Ralph motioned the stranger to a chair.

"How did you get my name?"

"I was told to contact you if I should need help."

"But it's been so long —"

"Your records are on file. Once an agent, always an agent."

"What do you want from me?"

"A job. I hear your printer's devil left you. I need a reason to stay around for a while."

"The only job I can give you is sorting type."

"I'll do it."

They were silent while each studied the other. Finally, Ralph said, "I can't imagine the Bureau being interested in a degenerate who likes to look at naked women."

"They're not."

"Then I don't suppose you'll tell me what you're working on."

"You suppose right. Who was the young lady who just left?"

"Jesse Forbes. She's a nurse. Her father is Doctor Forbes."

"That's what I thought. Nice-looking woman. How come she's not married?"

"How in the hell would I know?"

"I need to know as much about people as I can.

Any new arrivals in town beside me?"

"None that comes to mind. People come and go."

"I hear the doctor has a new housekeeper."

"Friend of the family. Knew his wife long ago."

"Hmmm . . . How about the teacher, Pauline Anthony? Know her?"

"Of course, I know her. It would be hard not to in a town this size."

"I take it she's friends with the nurse."

Ralph was suddenly irritated with the whole situation. "Pauline Anthony is a damn nice woman. So is Miss Jesse. She just spent a week in the hill country taking care of sick kids. She just might have been paid a sack of potatoes and a crock of lard for her trouble." He stood and tossed a greasy apron at the man who sat calmly in the chair. "I've got three pages of print to knock down. Are you working or just pretending to work?"

Ethan caught the apron. "I'm working."

# CHAPTER
## • 9 •

Stay here this summer? I've made plans to go home. As a matter of fact, Jess, I'm going to look for another teaching job."

Jesse's mouth fell open in shock. "Pauline! You don't mean it. You've always said you like it here."

Pauline continued to wash the blackboard as if she had only seconds to clean it. When she finished, she dropped the rag in the bucket beside the door, took the erasers to the open window and clapped them together to shake out the chalk dust.

"I did — at first. Now I need a change." She smiled a smile that did not reach her eyes, which Jesse suddenly realized were sad. "Maybe I'm homesick."

"You've not been homesick before. Didn't you tell me that since your mother remarried —"

"— Oh, yes, I told you that, but —" Her words trailed and the sadness in her eyes intensified.

Jesse watched intently, wondering at the tremor around her friend's mouth and why she was so nervous and kept glancing at the door as if she expected someone to come barging in.

"What's happened? You're not the Pauline I saw last week. Is Mr. Harper causing trouble here at the school again?"

"No." She shook her head.

"Can't you tell me what's wrong?"

"Oh, Jess —" Tears filled her eyes and began to roll down her cheeks. She came around the desk, crying like a child, her shoulders shaking. Jesse held her while she sobbed on her smoothly ironed white shirtwaist.

Pauline had been trying to keep out of her mind the man who had stripped her naked and invaded her body. But he was there all the time, buried in her subconscious like a wart she could not help rubbing. Thinking about him made her sick — sick and scared. In a twisted way, he knew more about her body than any person alive, had seen more than she had seen herself. The thought made her stomach tighten as though someone had hit her there with a clenched fist.

The awful part was that he might be someone she knew. She hadn't seen his face or heard him speak in a natural tone of voice. Perhaps he had seen her in the street. How could she ever recognize him when all she could remember was the feel of his hands on her body and his heavy breathing when he looked at her private parts? Why had he wanted to hurt, humiliate and degrade her?

"What in the world could put you in such a state?" Jesse dug a handkerchief out of her skirt pocket.

"I'm sorry." Pauline averted her head and wiped her eyes. "I'm sorry," she said again after she cleared her throat.

"Don't apologize. What are friends for if not to share their troubles? As a matter of fact, I was about to unburden myself on you. Please tell me what's upset you."

Pauline's eyes followed the crack in the blackboard made when the end had come loose from the wall and fallen to the floor. A sudden anger mingled with the pain and humiliation that stirred inside her, boiling up until she thought she would choke. Holding the handkerchief to her nose, she blew vigorously, then turned back to Jesse.

"It . . . was . . . it was . . . *him!*" she said, trying to hold back the sobs.

"Him?" Jesse's face reflected her bafflement.

"The . . . Looker."

"Good Heavens! Oh, my dear, no wonder you're so upset." Jesse put her arms around Pauline's shaking shoulders. "Did he hurt you?"

"He . . . killed my . . . pride. He looked at . . . the part of me I've not even seen m-myself."

"Did he go inside you?"

"With h-his . . . f-finger." Pauline's quivering voice was barely above a whisper. "Oh, Jesse, I've never been so helpless, so humiliated. It was . . . a nightmare."

"Of course it was. The beast!"

Once the words started to come, they poured out of Pauline like the water from a broken dam. She told of being awakened, blindfolded and tied,

141

of the man looking at and feeling her naked body. When she finished, a deep, hoarse sigh came from her and she seemed calmer.

"He's a wicked monster!"

"Thank God he didn't rape you."

"He did with his hands . . . and his eyes," she stated angrily.

"Have you told the marshal?"

"No! I've not told a soul. And don't tell anyone. Please!"

"The marshal should know. He won't spread your name around."

"How do I know? It could be him."

"Oh, Pauline, not Dusty. He was a friend of my stepmother before Papa and I came to Harpersville."

Pauline turned quickly when the door to her classroom opened.

"I didn't know you were still here, Miss Anthony. I thought to borrow your slide rule. Mine seems to have disappeared. Hello, Miss Forbes. It's nice seeing you again."

James Crane's Adam's apple slid up and down his long neck and his small mouth beneath his rather large bony nose smiled shyly. Jesse felt rather sorry for the young man her sister had nicknamed Ichabod Crane. The boys in the upper class had given him a rough time until he thrashed one with the razor strop. Jesse was sure his action had surprised him as much as it had the boys.

"Here's the rule." Pauline spoke abruptly.

"Thank you. Sorry I interrupted your visit." He

backed out the door as if he couldn't get away fast enough.

"Do you think he heard?" Pauline asked frantically.

"I'm sure he didn't. If he had, he wouldn't have come in. He would have waited to see what else he could hear."

"That's true. See, I'm afraid to look at every man I meet, even Mr. Crane, thinking it could be *him* and he's looking at me, laughing at me, knowing how I look under my clothes."

"I don't think you need to worry about . . . Ichabod." Jesse wanted to get a smile out of her friend, but it didn't work. After a moment she asked, "Was the man big, little, young or old? Were his hands soft or rough?"

"His hands were . . . kind of scratchy. He was clean-shaven and I could feel his hair on my . . . s-stomach, so he isn't bald," she added bitterly. "When he moved across the floor and out the window, I didn't hear a sound." She gave a muffled whine of anguish. "He held the tip of a knife to my cheek and . . . I was frightened almost out of my mind! It's a wonder I can remember anything."

"You must have been scared half to death. I only wish we had some idea of who he is so he could be watched and caught. Papa thinks it's someone from a nearby town."

"I think it's Wade Simmer!" Pauline blurted angrily.

The words went right through Jesse and sent

a jab of pain along its path. She was shaken by the hardness in Pauline's eyes, by the straight, contemptuous line of her mouth. Her mind told her that what had been done to her friend was brutal, terrifying and sick and that she was lashing out blindly.

"What makes you think it was Wade Simmer?" Jesse asked quietly.

"Everyone else thinks it's him. He's mean, isn't he? He doesn't socialize with anyone, acts like he's better than everyone here in Harpersville. And . . . he moves like a cat. When that . . . man went out that window, I never heard a sound. I've heard Wade Simmer can walk up on a deer in the woods, and . . . he's strange. Everyone says so."

"That's no reason to think he would be doing this despicable thing. Why would he try to socialize in town when people snub him? I'd bet my life it isn't Wade Simmer." Jesse spoke so passionately that her friend looked at her intently. "I got to know him while I was in the hills. He's a quiet man who tends to his own business like Papa said. He just isn't the type to sneak around looking at naked women. He'd be more likely to go to the city and visit a loose woman." The thought of Wade being with a woman like that sent a shiver of dread down her spine.

"He was seen in town that night."

"He goes to Ike's garage to work on an engine they are building. He's a caring person, Pauline. He cares that the boy Jody gets an education and a chance to run in competition. He cares about his neighbors and the sick children. He went with me on my rounds the first day and provided me with an escort the other days. He made the trip over to Coon Rapids to tell the teacher to close the school. Papa trusts him and thinks it's ridiculous people are saying these things about him. I think it's the Harpers that are spreading the rumors."

"Why would they do that if they didn't have some evidence?"

"They are a self-serving family. You know that. The Harpers and the Simmers have been at each other's throats for years. It started with their great-grandfathers. Another thing, and maybe the most important, I've heard that Wade has some money and he didn't put it in Harper's bank. It could be as simple as that."

"You sound as if you actually like him."

"I . . . don't dislike him," Jesse said hesitantly.

"You actually talked to him?"

"Of course. The next time I go up there, come with me. Meet him and see if you still think he's the type of man who would crawl into a woman's bedroom window."

"You seem so sure —"

"I am, Pauline. Papa wouldn't send me up there if he thought I'd be in any danger. The hill people treated me with utmost respect." Jesse crossed her fingers when she remembered Otis Merfeld. "I'd like for you to meet Mr. Simmer and Jody before you make up your mind about spending the summer with us to tutor Jody and Todd."

"Todd doesn't need tutoring."

"Exceptionally good grades will give Todd confidence and help him with his stuttering."

"Mrs. Poole is going to her daughter's for the summer, and I certainly don't intend to stay in that house alone."

"Then come stay with us."

"Let me think about it."

"You wouldn't have to be alone with Jody if you're afraid of him," Jesse said.

"It isn't that."

"Will you go with me the next time I make my rounds and meet him and Mr. Simmer? I'll arrange to go on a Saturday. Some of the hill families are very poor, some are just shiftless; but most are good people. I liked them, Pauline. They were so grateful for my help and gave me the best they had."

Pauline went to the cloakroom for her hat and cape. When she came out she seemed more like her old self and smiled mischievously.

"What do you think of your father's hiring a housekeeper?"

"It was a shock. Papa has asked me to give her a chance. Susan and Todd are unhappy with her, and, frankly, I don't care for the woman myself. I'm hoping to give her enough rope so that she'll hang herself — in Papa's eyes, that is."

"I suppose Susan told you about our jam-making session?"

"She told me the two of you could do nothing

right and were only allowed to pick the berries."

"Allowed? Ha! The biddy is like an army sergeant. She commanded; we obeyed. We picked berries and washed them outside at the pump. She made the jam and made sure Doctor Forbes knew about it. Oh, yes, she also *allowed* us to wash the jars."

Jesse was relieved. This was the Pauline she knew. She laughed aloud and squeezed her arm as they walked out of the school.

"I can tell you'll never be bosom pals with our housekeeper."

"I'll never be anything with your housekeeper if I can help it."

"I think she's got her sights set on Papa, Pauline. I don't know what to do about it. It's not that I wouldn't want Papa to remarry if he found a woman he could love and who would be a companion to him, but this woman is taking over too fast."

"Maybe I should stay with you this summer. I know a few tricks that would make her life miserable." Pauline laughed softly.

"For instance?"

"Well, we could put a garter snake in the flour barrel and rub itchweed on her bedsheets. Better yet, we can rub poison oak on her pillow. That would fix that milk-white face! She's as vain as a peacock. Did Susan tell you we call her Ghostface?"

"She told me. Was that your idea, teacher?"

"No. I'd take credit if I could. Susan thought

147

of it all on her own." Pauline giggled happily and then became quiet as they began to meet people on the street.

Jesse stopped to look into the window of the Efthim Mercantile.

"Oh, look, Pauline. Mr. Efthim must have a new shipment of dress goods. Do you want to look?"

"You go ahead, Jesse. I'd better get on home."

Jesse shrugged. "I'll walk you to the corner. I'm not in the sewing mood anyway."

Mrs. Harper came out of the store as they moved down the walk.

"Jesse, my dear, dear girl!" she exclaimed, flinging her arm around Jesse and pressing her to her barrel-shaped body. Jesse extracted herself as quickly as possible and stepped away. Ignoring Pauline, Mrs. Harper began to babble, "Oh, I've been so worried about you, child. When Edsel came home to tell me you were staying in the hills to treat that . . . worthless trash, I was beside myself with worry. Dear girl, I'm so relieved that you're home. How in the world did you endure that awful experience? Edsel threatened to scold your father for sending you up there."

"I'm glad he didn't, Mrs. Harper. My father wouldn't have taken kindly to being scolded by Edsel. It was a wonderful experience. I was able to help sick children and the hill people treated me with utmost respect —"

"But, dear, that awful man and his nigger live up there. You didn't run into them, did you?"

148

"As a matter of fact I did. Jody, the colored boy, was kind enough to bring a note down to my father telling him I needed medicine and to fetch it back to me."

"Oh, my!"

"Mr. Simmer," Jesse hurried to continue before Roberta Harper interrupted her, "was very helpful. He either escorted me himself or found someone to escort me to the various homesteads each day."

"Oh, my!" Mrs. Harper gasped again. "You poor, poor child!"

Jesse rolled her eyes toward Pauline. "We must be going, Mrs. Harper. Pauline and I are considering buying some of the new dress goods Mr. Efthim just got in."

"You should look across the street at the Emporium before you buy. They have a much better selection."

"We'll do that," Jesse said and tugged on Pauline's arm.

The two girls stood inside the mercantile and watched Roberta Harper move down the sidewalk until she encountered Mr. Crane, the teacher. She stopped him and began to talk, and as they watched she pointed her finger toward the city park. He stood with his chin almost resting on his chest and listened. Finally, with a toss of her head, Mrs. Harper moved on, and Mr. Crane, with his ungainly stride, continued on down the walk.

"Poor man," Jesse whispered as he passed. "She was giving him a lecture about something."

"She probably wanted him to go wash the pigeon do-do off granddaddy's statue."

They left the store, and as they were passing the newspaper office, the door opened and Ethan Bredlow stepped out in front of them. He quickly doffed his hat, a huge smile making creases in his cheeks.

"Hel . . . lo. We meet again. This must be my lucky day."

Jesse nodded. "Did you get the job?"

"By the skin of my teeth. I had to show how fast I can sort type. What I really want to do is write feature articles, but in this business you take what you can get." His interested eyes traveled back and forth between the two women as he spoke. Pauline had turned her face away and was gazing at some object across the street.

"This is Pauline Anthony. Pauline," Jesse placed her hand on her friend's arm to get her attention, "Meet Mr. Bredlow."

"Ethan Bredlow, ma'am. How do you do?"

"Hello." Pauline spoke curtly and turned away again.

"I can say one thing about Harpersville; they've got the prettiest girls in Tennessee."

Jesse laughed. "You're speaking from experience? You've been in every town in Tennessee?"

Ethan's expression was not the least bit sheepish. His grin widened. "You've caught me up there. Guess I have to add that Harpersville has the smartest girls too."

"I'm going, Jesse." Pauline said. "See you later.

Nice meeting you, Mr. Bredlow." Her tone of voice indicated complete disinterest.

Ethan chose to ignore her cool manner and said, "We're going the same way. I'll walk you to the corner."

Pauline turned on him, her face reflecting a fight for control of her emotions. "You'll do no such thing."

"Gol . . . ly! What'd I do?" he said to the retreating back held stiff as a board. With his hands on his hips he turned to Jesse with a concerned look on his face. "She acts as if I've got the plague."

"It isn't you," Jesse said quickly, seeing the bewildered look on his face. "My friend has a lot on her mind right now."

"I'm relieved to know that. I mean I'm sorry she's troubled but relieved to know that I wasn't the reason she was out of sorts." His engaging smile returned. "May I walk *you* to your corner, Miss Jesse?"

"I'll be glad for your company," Jesse replied, and she meant it when she saw Edsel waiting in front of the bank. "Where are you from, Mr. Bredlow?"

"Ethan, please. I was born in Arkansas, raised in Missouri, worked in Iowa, Illinois and Ohio. Guess I'm a roamer. Done a little of this, a little of that, but the ink in my veins just won't go away. I'd love to have a newspaper in a little town about this size."

"Do you plan to stay a while?"

"As long as I have a job." They walked in silence

151

for a few minutes, then he said, "Mr. Marsh tells me you're a nurse and your father is a doctor. I think I feel a fever coming on."

"It could be the scarlet fever," Jesse said laughingly. "We're expecting it to hit town in a few days."

"It'll have to be something else that brings me to your door. I've had scarlet fever."

"How about a loose, glib tongue? I'll save you the cost of an office call. I don't think the doctor can do anything about that." They both laughed.

Jesse decided she liked Ethan Bredlow. He was light-hearted and fun. She wished Pauline hadn't been so abrupt with him. Her friend had said she would like to meet a man who was fun and made her laugh. Ethan was a stranger in town and was trying to make friends. On the other hand, considering what Pauline had been through, Jesse could understand her attitude.

"Is your friend a nurse too?"

"Pauline is a teacher."

They approached the bank. Edsel stood on the steps with a disapproving frown on his face. Jesse glanced at him as they passed, nodded politely, and pretended to be very interested in what Ethan was saying.

"Is she married? Is that why she gave me the icy glare? I didn't see a ring."

"No, she's not married."

"Steady beau?"

"No." She gave him a sideways look and caught his laughing eyes.

152

"She's awfully pretty," he said.

"Yes, and she's a very nice person. Any more questions?"

"Oh, Lordy. I've shown my hand, haven't I? To tell the truth, I was sitting on the porch of the rooming house one evening and saw her walk by. I thought then that she was mighty pretty. I couldn't believe my luck when I stepped out on the walk today, and there she was. Not that I wasn't glad to see you again, Miss Jesse," he added quickly.

"That's nice of you to say, Ethan. Don't worry about it. I understand perfectly."

"It's lonesome being in a town and not knowing anyone."

"You'll get acquainted quickly enough when it's known you work in the newspaper office. There's nothing the ladies like more than seeing their name in print."

"Ladies like Mrs. Harper?"

"You've met the town's socialite?"

"She has a musician visiting from North Carolina. Actually he's from Asheville, but she said to say North Carolina because it sounded farther away. I think he plays the piccolo or something. Maybe I'll make a mistake and say he plays the Jew's harp or a harmonica."

Jesse laughed. "You wouldn't dare! You'd lose your job."

"Maybe not. Mr. Marsh was happy when she left." Ethan stopped. "We're here already. That just proves what fascinating company you are, Miss Jesse."

"Mr. Bredlow, you are a flatterer of the first degree."

"Ethan. And thank you. I have always wanted to be something of the first degree."

Jesse laughed. "Good-bye, Ethan."

"Good-bye, Miss Jesse."

Ethan watched Jesse proceed on down the brick walk. She was a woman a man could be proud of. He wished he were free to present his real self to her. Well, so much for daydreaming. He was here to do a job and he was satisfied with the day's progress.

Wade Simmer rode his horse down the main street of Harpersville. A few people nodded a greeting; others with solemn, disapproving faces stopped and stared. He passed close by two men unloading a wagon. One spit contemptuously.

"Somethin' ort to be done 'bout that bird," he said.

"What's he done?" The other man cut a chew from a plug of tobacco and shoved it into his mouth before he lifted a heavy grain sack to his shoulder. They both watched as Wade turned his horse into the alley beside the marshal's office.

"If you ain't knowing' that, yo're dumb as a stump."

"Guess I'm dumb then."

"I'd betcha my bottom dollar he's in town spottin' the next woman he'll strip 'n' scare the shit outta."

"Ya think it's *him* doin' that?"

" 'Course it's him. He ort to be hung . . . like his pa was."

Wade saw the men eyeing him and ignored them. In the alley next to the marshal's office he alighted and tied his horse to an iron ring set in the stone wall. He patted the animal's rump as he went around him and walked back down the alley to the Main Street entrance of the office rather than entering through the back door.

Marshal Wright was seated behind a desk, his booted feet on the cluttered top. A thick mug was clutched in his hand.

"Howdy, Dusty."

"Howdy, Wade. Help yourself to the coffee."

"Thanks." Wade wrapped the rag Dusty used as a potholder around the handle of a blackened coffee pot and filled a cracked mug. He took a sip and grimaced. "How long have you been boiling these coffee grounds, Dusty?"

Dusty grinned. The handlebar mustache on his upper lip lifted. "What day is this?"

"Friday."

"Four days."

"Tastes like it's been a month or more." Wade placed the mug on the desk and dropped down in a chair.

"We operate on a tight budget. How's things up around Mill Springs?"

"The same. How's things here in Harpersville?"

Dusty took his feet off the desk and leaned on it with his elbows. "Shitty."

"I hear that folks think I'm the man that's doing

the looking at naked women."

"Yeah, some think that."

"The Harpers?"

"Yeah."

"And you, Dusty?"

"Hell, Wade. I've got no evidence it's you or anyone else for that matter." The marshal picked up a pencil and jabbed at a paper on his desk. "Whoever it is, I've got to catch the bastard before he rapes some poor woman. I can't think he'll go on *looking* for much longer."

"No, I suppose not."

"Why'er you here, Wade?"

"Visiting an old friend," Wade said with a grin. "You don't come up to the high ground anymore, Dusty."

"I've not had enough reason to. 'Course, I could come up there and bust up Merfeld's still or go over to Jensons' and try to settle the feud between them and the Maxwells. Wouldn't do any good. They'd be right back at it as soon as I left."

"Yeah. You're right about that. They've been at it for a hundred years."

"At least the killing has stopped. All they do now is harass each other."

Dusty sat back in his chair, propped his feet on the desk and clasped his hands over his stomach. He had known Wade since he was a stripling, had followed behind him and his granny when they came to town for Alvin's body after he was hanged. He wasn't the marshal then, and he thanked God for it. Wade would tell him the purpose of the visit in his own good time. All he had to do was wait.

"I hear Jody thumbed his nose at you as he ran down the middle of the street." Wade tried hard to keep his lips from twitching.

"Yeah. The brassy little bugger. Boyd thought I should've arrested him."

"On what charge?"

"Being uppity." Dusty laughed and Wade laughed with him.

"Doc Forbes wants Jody to do some work around his place this summer."

"Yeah? Is he a good worker?"

"Like any other kid . . . when he's pushed. I want him to be around white folk and know how to live with their attitude toward Negroes. He needs to know that he's got a tough row to hoe and that he'll have to fight twice as hard as a white boy for everything he gets out of life."

"What do your neighbors think about you taking in a darkie?"

Wade snorted. "They're more narrow-minded than town folk. I made it plain it was none of their business, so they ignore him."

"What do you want me to do about it?"

"Keep an eye out. Jody won't cause trouble un-less someone jumps him; then he'll fight. I don't want him beating the hell out of some white kid and getting sent to a work camp."

"That law Boyd got the city council to pass for-bidding darkies in town after sundown wouldn't stick if taken to court, but Boyd would see to it that it caused a stink and stirred up folks against you and the boy."

"Jody'll come home at night. I wouldn't want him to sully the Harpers' lily-white town." Bitterness crept into Wade's voice. "Another thing, Dusty. For the past few months I've been coming to town on Wednesdays and Fridays to work with Ike Spangler on a motor."

"I know that. Not much goes on that I don't hear about."

"How do those dates coincide with what's been going on in town?"

"I've heard of one that was on a Wednesday. No telling how many women this low-life skunk has messed with in this town and other towns. The women are so embarrassed they won't come forward. One begged me not to tell her husband because he would think it was her fault, that she'd seen this bird on the street and encouraged him."

"If there's anything I can do, let me know."

"It's best you stay out of it, Wade."

"Well, thanks for the coffee if that's what you call it." Wade went to the door. Before he opened it, he turned back. "If you catch the bastard they're calling The Looker, I'd like a few minutes alone with him before you throw him in jail."

Dusty raised his brows. "You'll have to stand in line behind me."

Wade nodded and went out. He liked Dusty Wright. He was a fair man — always had been. He'd do the best he could for Jody, but he was in a tough spot if he wanted to keep his job. The

158

damn Harpers owned the town council.

He mounted his horse and rode down Main Street. Edsel Harper was standing in front of the bank. Wade followed the direction of his gaze and saw a tall, slim woman walking beside a man in a derby. He didn't have to see the chestnut hair beneath the straw hat to know the woman was Jesse.

A pang of jealousy hit him in the gut like a baseball bat. He turned his horse in the middle of the street lest he overtake them and with a lonely, vacant feeling in his chest, rode through the alley behind the stores and on down toward Ike's garage.

# CHAPTER
## · 10 ·

*T*he family was at breakfast on Monday morning when Mrs. Klein arrived to do the wash. Jesse knew immediately there was going to be trouble when Louella Lindstrom began giving orders about how the starch should be made and how Doctor Forbes' shirts should be washed.

"I been makin' this here starch for six years. Doctor ain't had no complaint."

"He's too nice a man to complain. He realizes how badly you need the job. However, from now on I will make the starch and I'll add the bluing to it. After washing the first two loads of clothes, I want you to change both the wash and rinse waters. And —"

"— Doctor don't like scratchy collars." Mrs. Klein's voice quivered.

"I'm well aware of that. Doctor also doesn't like his collars starched with lumpy starch. I suggest you get started with your work. The doctor is paying you wages to wash, not to stand around arguing. If this arrangement is not satisfactory, you know what you can do."

Mrs. Klein let the back door slam as she left the kitchen.

"How dare you talk to Mrs. Klein like that!" Jesse came into the room as Mrs. Klein left it. She rudely brushed the housekeeper aside and went out the door.

The washhouse was only a few steps from the back porch. Mrs. Klein was inside, her eyes wet with tears.

"I'm sorry, Mrs. Klein. I'm so sorry. I never dreamed that woman would have the gall to say such things to you."

"Ain't I been doin' good work, Miss Jess?"

"You certainly have. We couldn't have managed without you."

"I ain't never scorched but one of doctor's shirts."

"— And it wasn't so bad he couldn't wear it. Don't worry about Mrs. Lindstrom. I'll speak to her."

"I ain't wantin' to cause no trouble for doctor. He's been so good —"

"What's old Ghost-face done to Mrs. Klein?" Susan burst through the door, went straight to the crying woman and put her arms around her. "That gal-dammed old biddy!"

"Stop yore swearin', girl, or I'll spank yore behind," Mrs. Klein said between sniffs.

Susan turned to Jesse, her eyes blazing. "I hate that old poot! When's Papa going to get rid of her? Does he know what she said to Mrs. Klein?"

"Papa is out on a call."

"She just makes me so mad —"

"You better get moving," Jesse said. "I heard the first school bell."

"I'll see you at noon, Mrs. Klein." Susan kissed the woman's wet cheek. Jesse had never been prouder of her little sister.

That afternoon when Jesse complained to her father about the housekeeper's treatment of Mrs. Klein, she was concerned about how readily he jumped to the woman's defense.

"It was a misunderstanding. Louella said she didn't mean to hurt the woman's feelings, and she's sorry she upset you and Susan. You must realize, Jess, she's not used to the way we do things here in this small town."

"I'm beginning to feel as if I'm a guest in my own home, Papa. It's difficult for me to stand by and see our way of life changing right before my eyes."

The doctor looked at his daughter affectionately. "You've run the house very well. You've done your duty to the family, but it's time you turned loose and stopped finding fault with Louella. She's good at running things. She's quiet, capable, obviously self-possessed, and I find her a truly charming person, interested in people. I surprised myself by being chatty when I'm around her . . . and she's a pleasant-looking woman too."

Jesse felt an odd ache within her. She wanted to dismiss her reaction to her father's words as jealousy, but she felt sick — sick at heart and sick in her legs. They could hardly carry her out of the room.

She had thought her father too smart not to see through the woman.

While she was busy in the surgery, and her brother and sister were in school, it was easy for Jesse to ignore Mrs. Lindstrom. However, the evenings, which she had always enjoyed with her father, brother and sister were severely strained.

The evening Mrs. Lindstrom announced she would serve after-dinner coffee in the parlor, then seated herself behind the service and proceeded to pour three cups, Jesse realized the woman was going to horn in on the private time she spent with her father. She left the parlor and went to the dining room, where her brother and sister had started clearing the table.

"How about a game of hide and seek?" Her mouth was smiling, her eyes twinkling mischievously.

"Y-You m-mean it?"

"Now?" Susan asked.

"What better time?"

"Glory! Old Ghost-face will have a fit."

"Good," Jesse muttered as Susan ran through the kitchen and out the door.

"You're it, Todd. Hide your eyes and count to ten."

Louella almost choked on her anger when she went into the dining room and saw the dinner dishes still on the table. The doctor had retired to his study, and she could think of no tactful way to bring his children's neglect of their chores to his attention tonight.

Quietly and efficiently she carried the dinner dishes to the kitchen and began the cleanup. She was making progress here and was determined not to let anything or anyone keep her from her goal. She had not realized the golden opportunity before her when she had first arrived. It had fallen right in her lap. The only obstacle was Jesse, who should have been married and out of the house long ago.

Mrs. Harper had hinted, more than hinted, that she would like a match between the doctor's daughter and her son. Louella decided that she would have to give it some thought. Surely there was something she could do to help bring that about. A marriage between the two would remove Jesse and put her in solidly with the town's leading family.

She had her arms in dishwater up to her elbows when the laughing trio came in the back door.

"Wash up, Todd, and get ready for bed." Jesse gave her brother a gentle push toward the door. "We'll have time to put the hem in your new skirt if we hurry, Susan." Her eyes met those of the housekeeper and held them until her brother and sister were out of the room. "Good night, Mrs. Lindstrom." She waited. The housekeeper turned her back and Jesse left the room.

Later in the week when Louella learned that Pauline Anthony would be staying with them for the summer, she was not happy about it but was careful not to let Doctor Forbes know of her displeasure. Around him she was efficiency personified, with a double dose of sweetness and refinement thrown in.

Todd was delighted that the storage room would be made into a room for him.

"Us . . . m-men will be d-down here," he said in his halting speech.

"And us women will be up there." Jesse hugged his head to her breast. She loved this little brother of hers fiercely.

"I'll need help carrying all this to the barn," Louella declared.

"We'll help, won't we, Todd?" Jesse turned cool eyes on the housekeeper. "We'll do it tonight after school and tomorrow you can clean the room."

Pauline moved into Todd's room as soon as school was out for the summer. While Jesse worked in the surgery, Pauline spent time with Susan and Todd. Mrs. Lindstrom was barely civil to her when they were alone. This amused Pauline more than it angered her.

Jesse had delayed her trip to the hills until Pauline could go with her. She persuaded her father to allow Todd and Susan to go with them. Because her brother had not had scarlet fever, he would stay with Mrs. Frony at Mill Springs or with Granny Lester while Jesse called on her former patients.

With Molly hitched to the buggy, a huge picnic basket and Todd sitting on the platform in back, they crossed the bridge spanning the creek and headed up the hill road.

The June morning was warm and soft. The air was filled with the sweet aroma of thousands of blossoms. Long fingers of sunlight meshed through the tree branches and made lacy patterns on the road. Birds fluttered from tree to bush to waving grasses. When Jesse heard the song of a lark, it brought back vividly the memory of being beside the stream with Wade, his smiling green eyes, and the way they had lingered on her face.

She acknowledged the budding excitement in the pit of her stomach at the possibility of seeing him again. She had debated with herself about her hair and what to wear today. One part of her wanted Wade to see her in something other than the nurse's uniform; the other part didn't want to see him at all. She had chosen to wear a pale-green-and-white striped calico dress with a small neat ruffle edging the yoke. Her chestnut hair, freshly washed in rainwater, was so soft and shiny it could hardly hold the hairpins that held the knot at the nape of her neck. She was glad now that she had let Susan talk her into cutting a thin layer of hair around her face. In the slight breeze it caressed her forehead and cheeks.

Susan and Pauline were chatting like a couple of magpies.

"I don't know how Jess ever persuaded Papa to let us come." Susan was so excited that she could hardly contain herself. She had been to Mill Springs but not up into what was called the high country.

"I cried." Jesse looked past her sister to Pauline and winked. "It worked too."

"You did not! You never cry."

"I told him I needed you to help Pauline push this buggy up the hill in case Molly gives out."

"Old Ghost-face will be glad we're gone. She'll have Papa all to herself today."

"He's taking the morning train to Frederick and the evening train back home."

"Goody, goody, goody," Susan chortled. "That'll throw a kink in the rope she's using to reel Papa in."

"Papa won't be so easy to reel in," Jesse said firmly. "He still keeps Mama's picture beside the bed and her things in the dresser." She said the words to convince herself as much as to convince Susan. The fear was there in the back of her mind that her father would wake up too late to see Mrs. Lindstrom for the greedy, manipulating woman she was.

"I remember how sad he was when Mama died. I was just little bitty then, but I remember. It about killed him to lose her," Susan said.

Pauline grasped Susan's hand. "Just be patient. Doctor Forbes will see through her sooner or later."

"With our help it could be sooner." Susan giggled happily and imitated Louella's voice. "Oh, Miss Anthony, I'm so glad you'll be staying with us this summer." Then in true Susan fashion she turned to her sister with a complete change of subject. "Do you think we'll see Wade Simmer, Jess?"

"I think so." Jesse tried to keep the eagerness out of her voice. "I want Pauline to meet him and Jody."

Jesse looked at her friend and saw the tension on her face. She had lost weight during the past few weeks, but it only enhanced her beauty. Her pale hair was pulled back and tied with a lavender ribbon that matched the one at the neck of the white shirtwaist. Her blouse was tucked neatly into a tan skirt. A wide belt cinched her small waist. She was pretty — so pretty. Just looking at her made Jesse feel gauche and . . . plain.

Susan continued to chatter, jumping from one subject to the other.

"If Ichabod got wind that you were teaching a darkie he'd go straight to Mr. Harper and raise a stink."

"And if Mr. Crane got wind that you call him Ichabod, you'd have a rough time next term," Pauline retorted.

"He's got his nose buried so deep in his books, he'll be the last to know." Susan giggled. "Anyway he brought it on himself by reading *The Legend of Sleepy Hollow* aloud to his class. The description of the school teacher fit him perfectly."

Jesse was so occupied with her own thoughts that she hardly heard the conversation. They had passed the turnoff that led to the clearing beside the creek where she and Wade had picnicked. Her mind was busy trying to decide how she should act when she met him. Should she be cool and businesslike? She certainly didn't want to act as if the kisses they'd shared meant anything to her.

Her mind was suddenly cleared of all thought when Wade, on his big black horse, appeared in the middle of the road. It was just as it had been before. If her mind had been able to sustain a thought, it would have been to wonder how the man could move through these hills like a phantom. Molly stopped on her own accord because Jesse was too befuddled to pull back on the reins.

Wade sat quietly on his horse and looked at Jesse, his eyes beneath the pulled-down brim of his hat devouring her face. He was hungry for the sight of her. Just looking at her spread a feeling of peace over him. He slowly moved his horse up beside the buggy.

"Mornin'." His hand went to the brim of his hat. His eyes flicked over Susan and Pauline and came back to Jesse.

"Morning, Mr. Simmer. This is my sister, Susan, and Miss Anthony, the teacher Papa told you about." Jesse was proud of the way she was able to control her voice despite the heavy thumping of her heart.

"Ladies." Wade put his fingertips to the brim of his hat again.

"H-H-Hi, Mr. S-S-Simmer." Todd called from the back of the buggy.

"Hello, Todd. I wondered why poor old Molly was working so hard to get this buggy up the hill." A genuine smile of pleasure lit Wade's face when he spoke to the boy.

"W-We got a p-picnic."

"That's good news. I left Jody at the house to watch a turkey I put on to cook. If it's burnt up we'll have something to fall back on."

"Oh, but we can't impose —" Jesse said hurriedly. "I have rounds to make. I wanted Pauline to meet you and Jody so she can —" Her voice trailed.

"He was expecting us," Susan exclaimed.

"Todd left word with Ike last night." He winked at the boy and looked back at Jesse. "I promised him a ride on Samson. Now is a good time if it's all right with you."

"G-G-ee whill-liker!" Todd was already standing on the platform reaching for Wade.

Jesse watched while Wade lifted her grinning brother to the horse. Snug against Wade's back, both arms about his waist, he turned shining eyes to his sister.

"I-I-I won't f-fall, Jess. I sat on Samson before." The happiness on his face brought mist to Jesse's eyes when she smiled up at the man who was the cause of it.

"And when was that?"

"Only a time or two at Ike's." Wade commanded the fidgeting horse to stand still. "We'll turn off just before we get to the Mill Store and take the shortcut home." Wade moved the horse out ahead of the buggy as if previous arrangements had been made for them go to his place. Molly followed.

*Take the shortcut home.* The words echoed in Jesse's mind. She could hear her brother's chatter and the low tones of Wade's voice. He liked her brother . . . he liked children. He'd had a special look on his face when he looked and spoke to them. In her heart she knew that he was a special man regardless of what anyone else said or thought about him.

Jesse looked around Susan to Pauline. There was a slight frown on her face. In the excitement of seeing Wade again she had forgotten how disturbing the meeting must have been for her friend.

"Pauline? Do you mind going to his house?"

Pauline turned and smiled. A silent message passed between the two friends. *Pauline no longer suspected it was Wade who had subjected her to such appalling indignity.*

"No, Jess. I don't mind at all."

Jesse's shoulders slumped with relief. She felt as if a weight had been lifted, and she could fly as free as the butterflies that darted amid the wildflowers alongside the road. She was eager to get her friend alone and ask her what it was about Wade that had caused her to change her mind. Jesse had been sure that Pauline would come to that conclusion once she had met Wade, talked to him, but she hadn't expected it to be quite so soon.

"So that's *him*. This is the first I've seen him up close." Susan rolled her eyes toward her sister. "Imagine that little stinker leaving word at Mr. Spangler's that we would be up here today. Jess, do you think Mr. Simmer asked Todd to let him know when you would be coming up here again?"

"I don't know about that. He and Todd are better acquainted than I thought. I wonder why Todd never said anything before about riding his horse."

"Todd likes him a lot." Susan chattered on. "He's handsome as all get out, but kind of scary too, isn't he, Miss Anthony?"

"And too old for you," Pauline said.

"But not too old for Jess. He looked at her as if he could eat her."

"Susan, you say the most outlandish things!" Jesse could feel the heat rise to her face. "And don't talk so loud. He might hear you."

They turned off the main road and onto a trail cut through a thick stand of oak and ash trees. The well-worn trail began to slope gradually upward. It was quiet and cool in the woods, the only sound being the creak of the buggy and the soft thud of the horses' hooves. Even Susan had stopped chattering.

"I want to tell you something before we get to Wade's house." Jesse spoke in a low murmur. "I don't want you to be shocked." When she was sure she had Susan's and Pauline's complete attention, she continued. "Wade treats Jody as if he were his son. He'll eat at the table with us."

"Is Mr. Simmer a Yankee?" Pauline asked. "He didn't sound like a Yankee."

"No, he isn't a Yankee. He was born and raised right here in these hills, but he spent quite a few years as a stevedore and traveled all over the world."

"How exciting!" Susan exclaimed. "Well, if he

wants his nigger to eat at the table it's all right with me."

"Susan! You know how I hate that word. Don't you dare use it again."

"I'm sorry. I meant Negro."

"— And Wade doesn't consider Jody *his*. He treats him as his equal."

"It's strange," Pauline said, shaking her head. "I've heard of that being done up north, but not here in Tennessee. Hill people are clannish. I can't imagine them accepting a colored in their homes."

"I got the feeling, although Wade didn't say so, that the people here are less than kind to Jody. I think that those who are especially fond of Wade, like the Lesters and the Fronys, just ignore Jody's existence."

"Wouldn't it be a lark if he ran in the Olympics and won?" Susan chortled. "Wouldn't that put some folks's noses out of joint?"

"I don't know the rules," Pauline said. "But I doubt they would let him enter the races."

"That's not fair, is it, Jess?"

"Not it isn't, but many things in life are not fair."

Jesse was getting nervous. Her hands inside her gloves were damp. Wade and Todd had gone on ahead and were out of sight. The image of Wade's sun-bronzed face with its high cheekbones, well-formed nose, and sharp but kind green eyes floated before her. His kissing her did not mean he had any serious interest in her, she told herself sternly. He had been in town several times since they met

173

and had not called on her and she wasn't sure she wanted him to. She could easily get to liking him too much and she was too young to live with a broken heart.

Jesse had not seen the stone-and-log house in the daylight and was surprised that it was larger than she had remembered. Almost all the houses in the hills had tin roofs. Wade's house was roofed with cedar shingles. It was neat, the grounds surrounding it well tended. The barnyard was on a lower slope than the house. The runoff went downhill and away from the clear creek that at one time had been the occupants' only source of water. The house sat there among the trees, amid railed fences and wild rosebush hedges, as if it had always been there.

"This is nice. Not at all what I expected." Susan's eyes were bright. "I thought everyone up here lived in tumbled-down shacks."

Wade was waiting when they reached the yard behind the house. He patted Molly on the rump as he passed to help Jesse from the buggy. His hand clasped her gloved one tightly; his eyes looked directly into hers. She was so breathless that she just barely managed to speak.

"Where's Todd?"

"In the barn with the new pups."

Pauline got out on the other side, but Susan, flirt that she was, moved over so Wade would lift her down.

"I've heard all sorts of untrue things about you, Mr. Simmer. That you were ugly and mean —"

"From your sister?" Wade's smiling eyes lingered on Jesse's face, which was turning a light pink.

"Not that you were ugly or mean. She said that —"

"Susan. You're making me wish I hadn't brought you along."

Wade chuckled. "That would have been a shame. I can't have a pretty girl thinking I'm mean. I need all the friends I can get in Harpersville."

"You're not ugly either." Susan tossed her head and smiled up at him.

"It's kind of you to say so." Wade reached for the picnic basket. "Come in the house, ladies. Jody and Todd will tend to Molly." Then to Jesse, "I hope you intended for me and Jody to share what's in this basket."

"Why do you think she packed so much?" Susan, ahead, turned to walk backward so that she faced them and saw the "wait until I get you home" look on her sister's face. "Uh-oh," she murmured, and turned to walk ahead with her chin lowered and her hand over her mouth to stifle a giggle.

Jesse could tell that Pauline was pleasantly surprised when she stepped into Wade's house. She looked with interest at the scrubbed wooden floor, the table covered with an oilcloth, the neatly arranged cookpots that hung over the stove, and the rows of books in a glassed-in bookcase.

Susan, with unabashed curiosity, went to the bookcase to look at the book titles. She touched the heavy glass pitcher and goblets that sat on the oak buffet, looked closely at the picture of the Dutch windmill on the handsome wall pocket. After touching the high-backed rocking chair and putting it in motion, she went to the doorway to look into the other part of the house.

"I like your house," Susan said. "Old Ghost-face has got ours so gussied up we can't even sit in the parlor anymore."

"Thank you, but who is Old Ghost-face?" Wade had hung his hat on the peg beside the door and had set the basket on the counter between the kitchen cabinet and the sink.

"That's a story that will take some time to tell." Jesse moved to halt Susan's recounting of the family situation.

Wade didn't like the fluttery uneasy feeling in the pit of his stomach. He blamed it partially on the fact that he seldom had people in his home other than a neighbor who dropped by occasionally. Having three women in his kitchen was unnerving, especially if one of them was a woman who had been constantly in his thoughts and dreams for days, weeks, for a year or more.

He felt as if he were standing on the edge of a high cliff. One false move and all he yearned for would be lost to him forever. He would know before the end of the day if he had a chance with Jesse. His eyes constantly strayed to her even as he removed a large baking pan from the oven.

"This old fellow didn't burn up after all."

Susan came to stand beside him and peer in the pan when he lifted the lid.

"We have turkey only on special occasions like Thanksgiving and Christmas."

"*This* is a special occasion." Wade spoke quietly, and over Susan's head his eyes met Jesse's in silent yearning.

"Let's go see the puppies, Susan." Pauline had seen the look that passed between Wade and her friend.

"Now? I was goin' to —"

"Now." Pauline pushed Susan gently toward the door.

# CHAPTER
## • 11 •

*A* rosy flush flooded Jesse's face and her tongue stuck to the roof of her mouth. Her mind groped like a bat in bright daylight for something to say.

Wade saved her from trying to erase the sudden silence.

"I'm glad you brought the teacher."

"She's a good teacher and likes a challenge. Knowing that Mr. Harper would be furious if he knew she was teaching Jody makes it all the more exciting for Pauline."

Wade came close to her. All his senses were focused on the woman standing before him. He remembered the day he had stopped her in the road. She had smiled at him, the sun shining on her glorious hair. Before the day was over he had known that she would be his only love, his only joy, the all-consuming factor in his life. He was not half good enough for her, and God knew he had tried to get her out of his thoughts. She had stuck there like a burr; whether he was awake or asleep, she was there in the back of his mind.

"Right now the teacher is the farthest thing from my mind."

Jesse's heart began to surge wildly; she couldn't speak, but she smiled up at him. With his dark unruly hair and his dark skin, he was good-looking as all men are who have character stamped on their faces. His air of competence set him head and shoulders above other men. It was hard for Jesse to use these words even in her mind. She just knew that when Wade was around everyone was aware of him, even if he was standing still and not saying anything.

Her eyes found his, and they were soft with amber lights. When he smiled back at her, his face was younger and free of the somber expression it usually wore. She knew immediately that this was a turning point in her life. Nothing would ever again be the same.

"I'm glad you're here, Jesse." His hands gripped her shoulders. It wasn't what he had meant to say, and he held his breath as he waited for her to say something.

"I'm glad to be here. We'd better get dinner on so I can make my rounds," she whispered, her lips barely moving, her eyes lost in his. The hands on her shoulders tightened and he stared at her.

"You're really glad you're here?"

"Yes." Jesse felt her heart jump out of rhythm. When he lowered his face and pressed his lips reverently to her forehead it was so sweet that she wanted to cry. This big hill-country man was capable of incredible tenderness. Her eyes were moist when they met his.

He gripped her hand and led her to the door, then stopped. "I'll take you on your rounds. I take it you didn't intend for your brother and sister or the teacher to go with you."

"I'd planned to leave them with Mrs. Frony or Granny. Todd hasn't had scarlet fever."

"It would be a good time for Jody to get acquainted with them. This is his territory. He's more comfortable here."

"Do you want to send him north someday?"

"He can't stay here in these hills and amount to any more than what he does now. He's heard about track meets and he wants to compete. He also wants to learn. He's got to get in there and fight for what he wants. I need to find a place where he can get the education he needs."

"Jody is lucky to have you. You're a very special man, Wade Simmer."

Jesse walked beside him. They were at the barn door before she realized it. Inside the cool, dim barn, he gave her fingers a gentle squeeze and released them.

Todd came from one end of the barn holding a fat, wiggling pup in his arms

"Looky, Jesse. Jody s-says maybe I c-can have him when he don't need his mamma any m-more."

"I've been after Papa to let you have a dog." Jesse stroked the puppy's head.

"Susan s-said old Ghost-f-face won't l-l-let m-me h-h-ave him." Todd's stuttering always became worse when he was upset.

"Don't worry about that now. Enjoy the puppy. It will be a while before he can leave his mamma, and in the meantime I'll talk to Papa."

When Jesse and Wade reached the stall, Pauline was holding one of the pups and Jody was on his knees beside the mother, stroking her head and crooning to her.

"Hello, Jody." The boy's glance was brief, but Jesse saw his scowl.

"Howdy," he mumbled.

"How many pups did Delilah have?"

"Six."

Jesse saw the frown on Wade's face. No doubt he had instructed Jody on how to act toward her and Pauline and the boy was pouting. It suddenly occurred to her that Jody was jealous and frightened that she was a threat to his security here with Wade. She made a mental note to speak to Wade about it.

"Where's Susan?"

"I'm up here, Jess. Up here in the hayloft." Susan's head appeared over the edge of the loft floor. She had lost her hair ribbon and spikes of straw stuck to her hair. "I've wondered what a hayloft was like since Mary Sue told me it was where she and Jeff Stealy . . . uh-oh —" She paused when she saw the stern look come over her sister's face. "I'd better come down."

Jesse had stepped back to look up at her sister and had come up against Wade's chest. She could feel his silent laughter.

"Mercy me," Jesse murmured. "What will I ever

181

do with that girl?"

"She's a corker, isn't she?" His hand moved up and down her arm, and Jesse's thoughts scattered like dry leaves in a windstorm.

Not wanting to leave the touch of his hand, but knowing she must because she saw her sister watching from the loft, she moved away from him to speak to her brother.

"Take the puppy back to its mother, Todd. Maybe Jody will let you hold it again after we eat. I must get started on my rounds."

"Where do you plan to go?" Wade asked as they left the barn.

"I want to visit the little Gordon girl; she was very sick. Papa wants me to urge Mrs. Merfeld to come in when it's time for her baby. Then I'll see Granny and Mrs. Bailey. Papa also wants me to put a notice in the store. Two weeks from now we'll be there to vaccinate for smallpox."

"Would you like me to take a notice to Coon Rapids? The school is closed for the summer, but I could leave word at the church."

"It would help. I'll ask the Gordon and the Merfeld children to spread the word. We want to inoculate as many as we can that day. Papa thought two weeks would be enough time to get the word around. He's getting the vaccine from the Public Health Department."

Jesse and Pauline set the table and laid out the contents of the picnic basket: deviled eggs, bread, cheese, sliced ham and several dozen cry-baby cookies.

As Wade sliced the turkey, he watched Jesse out of the corner of his eye. He had never even touched her hand until three weeks ago. Now all the beauty he had ever dreamed of was summed up in her. He had to be careful or his rough ways would scare her away.

"I told Todd to wash, but he didn't do it very well. And . . . he threw water on me." Susan came storming into the kitchen, letting the screen door slam.

Jesse glanced at the few wet spots on Susan's dress. "You're not hurt. Come fill this pitcher and fill the water glasses."

Todd came in wiping his hands on his pants. The front of his shirt was wet. He looked at Susan and poked out his tongue.

"S-Susan threw w-water on me."

"You did it first, bird-brain."

"I-I-I didn't."

"Hush, both of you," Jesse said. "Where's Jody?"

"On t-the porch."

Jesse saw the worried look on Wade's face. *He was afraid of what the others would do when Jody came to the table.* She imagined that Jody was worried too. She went to the door.

"Hurry, Jody. We're ready to sit down." When she turned, Wade was holding out a chair for her. He indicated for the others to sit down and went to the head of the table. Pauline and Susan sat on one side, Todd and the empty place was on the other. "We'll wait for Jody."

183

The boy came in with a rebellious look on his face. Jesse recognized it as a defense against what he was afraid would happen when he sat at the table with Wade's white guests.

"Sit down there by Todd, Jody," Wade said.

"It's a good thing you're not eating at our house," Susan sat primly, her hands in her lap. "Papa makes us wait if we're late."

"T-This ain't our h-house, blabber-f-face."

"I'm just telling him . . . block-head."

Jody looked down at his plate and said nothing.

Jesse sent Wade a look of apology. He was gazing at her. On his face was a look of patient waiting, and in his eyes a shadow of longing. It was as if he was unaware of what was going on around him.

"My granny always said the blessing." He spoke quietly about the pleasant memory. His eyes held Jesse's.

"Would you like me to do it?"

When he nodded, she held her hand out to Pauline on one side and to Jody on the other. When Jody didn't respond, Todd reached down and clasped his hand and brought it up to rest on the table and held his other hand out to Wade. Hesitantly, Jody put his hand in Jesse's. She bowed her head.

"Dear Lord, we thank Thee for this food, and for allowing us to be here today with our friends, Wade and Jody. Bless this house and keep it safe. Amen."

Silently, Jesse thanked God for her little brother's compassion and understanding.

184

"I-I want turkey. I g-get those old deviled eggs at home. Wait'll y-you eat Jesse's cry-b-baby cookies, Jody. They're r-r-really good."

The dishes were passed. Susan chattered about the colt she had seen in the pasture behind the barn. Todd asked questions about the geese and the pups. Wade answered all questions patiently. Pauline watched and listened as if she could hardly believe she was here in the hills in a comfortable home.

Jody did not utter one word until they had almost finished the meal. "We got a pet deer," he said suddenly.

Both Susan and Todd looked at him with astonishment.

"Ah . . . you don't," Susan scoffed.

"We do too."

"If Jody s-says he's g-got a pet deer, he's g-got one. S-so shut-up, S-Susan."

"I won't believe it till I see it." Susan reached for a cookie. "I never heard of such a thing."

"It comes and licks salt." Jody glared across the table at Susan. "Ya don't know nothin' 'bout deer, *white girl.*"

Jesse glanced quickly at Wade. He didn't seem to be perturbed. His green eyes went from one to the other. Jesse could almost read his thoughts. *This exchange with the Forbes children was good for Jody.*

"At least I know enough not to run down the middle of Main Street and thumb my nose at the marshal . . . smart-mouth."

185

Jody lifted his chin proudly. "Yeah, I did that. I'll do it again."

Susan giggled. "Everyone in town laughed about it. Old Man Harper had a fit and fell in it. He wanted to have you arrested."

"How'd ya know that?"

"I get around. I hear things. Now about this pet deer —"

"It ain't a real pet like Delilah." Jody admitted. "Wade says if we tame it, it'll not be scared of folks 'n' they'll kill it. But we got a pet coon."

"That's more like it. When can I see it?"

"D-Don't s-show her, Jody. She's just a-a s-silly g-girl."

Wade burst out laughing. "I guess I'm out of touch with the younger generation. Miss Anthony, is this what goes on in your classroom?"

"Some of the time. The rest of the time I'm cracking the whip." She saw the startled look on Jody's face and said quickly, "What I mean is, I assign them so much work they don't have time for getting into mischief."

"Ya think ya can learn me?" Jody asked.

"No. But I can teach you if you want to learn."

"I gonna be like Wade. I gonna be smart 'n' read ever' book in dis world."

"Oh, Lord." Wade shook his head. "That's not a very high goal to set for yourself. You'll have to learn a lot more than I know in order to get into a good school."

"I'll write to the colored colleges and ask about the entry exams and what classes are offered,"

Pauline said. "We'll have to plan a course of study for Jody."

"I'll help you with your homework." Susan rolled her eyes upward. "Miss Anthony pours on the homework."

"I ain't needin' no help from you. I ain't no dumb nigga!"

"Maybe not, but right now you're actin' like one."

Jesse stood. "Pauline, if you want to change your mind about staying with us this summer, I'll not blame you."

Pauline laughed. "Not on your life. It would make Mrs. Lindstrom too happy." She took the teakettle from the stove and poured hot water into the dishpan.

"You can see what you're in for. Three smart-mouthed kids."

"I've handled twenty smart-mouthed kids. I can certainly handle these three."

"Lou . . . el . . . la —" Susan drew out the housekeeper's name dramatically — "won't let her dress tail touch her hind end until she tells Mrs. Harper the goin's on in the doctor's house."

"My word, Susan!" Jesse glanced at Wade. He was trying to keep the grin off his face. "Papa talked to Mrs. Lindstrom and he assured me that she understood the situation and would say nothing about it."

"She'd say anything to keep on Papa's good side. She's got her eye on him. If he marries that bossy, dried-up old prune, I'll run away from home."

"I swan to goodness, Susan —"

187

Hiding behind a casual attitude because she knew her sister would lecture her on the way home, Susan reached for another cookie. Her hand collided with her brother's.

"J-Jody hasn't h-had hardly any. You're a p-p-pig!"

"Go on, Jesse." Pauline carried dishes to the pan of hot water. "Susan and I will clean up."

"What about Todd and Jody?" Susan complained. "They ate too, and a heck of a lot more than I did."

"W-We got work o-outside, ain't we, J-Jody?"

"Ain't? You said, ain't?" Pauline exclaimed. "If you were in my class, Todd Forbes, you would write 'we don't say ain't' on the blackboard a hundred times."

"B-But we ain't . . . we're not in s-school." Todd giggled and grabbed the last of the cookies from the plate. "Come on, Jody. Let's g-get out of here. Can you s-spit through your t-teeth, Jody? Will you s-show me how?"

Jesse knew her friend well enough to know that she was comfortable here, that she had accepted Wade and Jody without the slightest qualm.

"It shouldn't take us more than three hours, Pauline. We'll be back so we can start home before sundown."

"Don't worry about us. Have a good time." She lifted her brows and laughed when Jesse's pink cheeks told her she had caught her meaning.

"Oh . . . you!" Jesse said as she went out the door.

Wade was hitching a lively young mare to the buggy. She was a beautiful golden color with a white mane and tail.

"She needs a good workout," he explained.

"What's her name?"

"You won't believe it. I let Jody name her."

"Tell me. I've got to call her something."

"Christmas. Jody couldn't decide so I suggested something he liked. I should have kept my mouth shut."

"Christmas. I must admit that it is an unusual name for a horse. She's pretty though."

"So are you," he said softly and helped her into the buggy.

The young mare was frisky and wanted to run. Wade held her to a fast trot and the buggy rolled smoothly down the road toward the trail that would take them to the Gordons'.

Now that she was alone with him, Jesse could think of nothing to say. Wade was silent also. He drove with one foot on the footboard, both hands on the reins.

"Papa has always encouraged my brother and sister to say what's on their minds," Jesse finally said. "They did a good job of it today. I hope you don't think they're brats. They're really good kids."

He turned to look at her. "They accepted Jody. That's what's important to me. He accepted them, but not quite so much. It will take time."

"Susan is a freethinker. That's what Papa calls her. If Jody is her friend, she'll look out for him."

Jesse laughed into his eyes and almost forgot what she was going to say. "Just the other day, our new housekeeper said some unkind things to the woman who comes to do the wash. Susan was furious. I held my breath for fear she would kick Mrs. Lindstrom's shins."

"She's Old Ghost-face?" Wade chuckled. "It fits. I saw her the couple times I went in to talk to the doc."

"Papa hired her while I was up here. Susan named her because she puts buttermilk on her face to bleach her skin." Jesse's laugh rang out. "It's a habit of Susan's to tack nicknames on people. She swears she caught her putting egg white on her face, and later she sneaked around to see what it was like when it dried."

"And?"

"The way Susan described it, her face looked as if it was all drawn up tight and if she smiled it would crack."

"She could have named her Old Egg-face."

They laughed together, then smiled into each other's eyes. Soon the smile left Wade's mouth and eyes, and a look of pure longing took its place. He turned his attention back to the mare and pulled her over into a stand of oak trees. He loosened the reins so the mare could lower her head and crop the grass, then wound them around the brake handle. It was cool and quiet in the woods except for an occasional birdsong.

When he turned sideways in the seat and opened his arms, Jesse went to him willingly. He gathered

190

her to him gently, carefully, as if she were the most fragile thing in the world. A warm protective feeling slowly filled him. He felt her hand on his face and his body became one silent groan of pleasure. He longed to crush her to him, plunder her mouth with his own. Instead when she turned her face for his kiss, it was, in a way, an innocent kiss — soft, generous, uninhibited and incredibly sweet.

Wade closed his eyes and whispered, "Jesse." His lips touched hers as he whispered again. "Sweet Jesse."

Whatever it was that had happened when he first saw her over a year ago had been growing steadily. Now it almost consumed him. She was so open, so giving, as unrestrained as a summer breeze when she responded to his kiss. Her mouth parted beneath his, yielding and vulnerable to the invasion of his lips and gentle tongue.

Wade had saved his love, stored it away, sharing it only with his granny and, to a certain extent, with Jody. Now all the love he had to give was hers; this wonderful, beautiful angel of a woman who had come into his life and turned it upside down. His heart was drumming so hard that he could hardly breathe; his love for her was choking him. He burrowed his face deep into the fragrance of her hair and felt his whole self harden and tremble.

Jesse abandoned herself to the heavenly feeling of being in his arms. Her fingers touched his hair and his nape and felt along the hard line of his jawbone. A low moan escaped from her lips when they were freed, and she clung to him as if she could merge with his body.

"Wade . . . I didn't know . . . kisses were like this."

Half-laughing, he locked his arms around her more tightly. He smoothed her rumpled hair and traced along the side of her face with his lips and gently kissed her trembling mouth. His whispered words came against her lips.

"Neither did I, love." His lips moved to her hair. "I've been crazy about you for a long time," he said with a touch of desperation. "The feel of you in my arms is like no other feeling in the world. I'm so damn scared that I'll lose you and we'll never get to know how wonderful our lives together could have been."

Jesse pulled back and cradled his face with her hands. "I understand what you mean. I was scared to come up here again, afraid I had read too much in the kiss we shared and would be disappointed. We have the power to hurt each other, Wade, simply because we care about each other." She felt the tremors rippling through his body. "We must wait and see if what we feel is just mutual attraction or something more."

As he looked into her blue-gray eyes, soft with caring, the fear went out of him, and strength flowed in to fill the hollows that fear of losing her had dug. Seeing her smile and the flash of a dimple in her cheek made Wade feel as if he could take on the whole world. A surge of love for her flowed through him like a river. How was it possible that this woman, and only this woman, with her soft smile and calm words could make him feel like this?

"Right now we'd better get on up to the Gordons'." Her mouth curved into a wanton little smile that grew into low, throated laughter.

He kissed her with lusty delight. "Yes, ma'am." His eyes, shining green between a hedge of thick lashes, danced over her face. "Your cheeks are pink," he teased. "Everyone will know it was my rough whiskers that scratched your soft skin."

"Oh, no!" She put her hand on his cheek. It was dark, but not rough. "You lied, Wade Simmer. You lied to scare me."

"I don't care if the whole world knows I kissed you." He turned the buggy out from under the trees and once again they were on the road.

For the first time in years Wade asked God for something. *Please, God, make me worthy of this woman.*

# CHAPTER
## • 12 •

*T*hey made two stops before they reached the
Gordons'. Wade turned off down a lane to the
Prestons', then to the Fosters' so Jesse could tell
them about the inoculations coming up in two
weeks.

"The vaccine is being furnished by the Public
Health Department," she explained. "By vaccinating everyone the world's health organizations
are hoping to eradicate the disease that kills mil-
lions of people each year. A sore will appear on
the arm where the serum has been rubbed into
the skin. My father will explain the treatment it
will require. Spread the word to your friends and
neighbors."

Before she left, Jesse passed out stick candy to
the children and promised another when they came
to get their smallpox vaccinations.

The Gordon home was as neat as Jesse remembered it. The children playing on a swing in the
yard stopped to stare at the buggy as it approached.
One ran to the house yelling, "Maw."

Wade helped Jesse from the buggy. She smiled into his eyes and squeezed his hand. Happiness sang in her heart like the lark they had heard the day of the picnic by the creek. He stood beside the buggy while she went to the house.

Mrs. Gordon was on the porch. A small shy girl hid behind her skirts.

"Howdy." Mrs. Gordon held out her hand. Jesse shook it, returned the greeting, and then placed her hand on the head of the little girl.

"Hello, Madaline. Remember me? I had on my nurse's uniform the day I was here. You're not sick anymore. You look fit as a fiddle now."

"Yes'm, she's doin' tolerable. Don't have no lustre yet, but perkin' up ever'day. We don't know how we kin ever thank ya —"

"No thanks are necessary, Mrs. Gordon. Just seeing Madaline well is thanks enough. Have you heard of any new cases of scarlet fever?"

"No, ma'am. Now school's out we don't get much news. Hello, Mr. Simmer," she called. "Won't you and the lady step in for a cool drink of water? I'll get one of the boys to draw a fresh bucket."

"Thank you. And I'll gladly fetch the water."

"Bucket's there on the shelf. Watch that pulley. It don't take to the rope like it ort to no more. Come in outta the sun, ma'am."

The half hour they spent with the Gordons was pleasant. Jesse explained about the smallpox inoculations. Mrs. Gordon asked sensible questions and promised to send the older children to homesteads farther back in the woods to spread the news. Jesse passed out the stick candy and spoke to each of the children. They responded politely while their mother smiled with unconcealed pride in her brood.

As soon as they were away from the house, Wade grabbed Jesse's hand and held it tightly.

"I'm proud of you, sweetheart. I'm so proud of you I could burst."

"Well, for heaven's sake." Jesse gave him a pleased smile. "What brought that on?"

"You're so patient. You act as if you actually like these people."

"I do like them, Wade. Why in the world wouldn't I like them? As far as I can tell, most of them are good, honest people trying to make a living. And they love their children and want what's best for them."

"You don't understand, do you? To them you're someone far above them. You live in town, you wear nice clothes, your father is a doctor. Yet you treat them as if you were their friend."

"— But I'm not *above* anyone!"

"You really believe that."

"I'm just doing my job. This is what I was trained to do."

"And you do it very well." He pulled the mare to a stop. "Enough talk. I've got to steal kisses while I can."

"We shouldn't."

"I remember you saying that to me once before. As a matter of fact, I think I can remember every word you've ever said to me."

"Well, if you're going to kiss me you'd better get at it. Christmas isn't fond of standing still. She'll think we're slow as . . . Christmas." She tipped back her head and laughed.

Small warm puffs of her breath fanned his face. He could feel the beat of her heart against his chest, smell the freshness of her skin and the fragrance of her hair. He watched with intense pleasure as she lowered her lashes. Her eyes were on his mouth. He could wait no longer to taste the sweetness of her lips. Dear God, what had he ever done to deserve this pleasure?

His lips touched hers, lightly at first, then with longer and more intense kisses, sending his blood thundering through his ears. He pulled back and looked into her face.

"Jesse, Jesse, Jesse," he said her name as if he loved saying it. "How I yearn to love you all night long." His hands framed her face, and he looked deeply, lovingly into her eyes.

Caught in a spinning whirlwind of desire, Jesse was aware that his heart was racing as fast as hers. She placed her hands over his.

"Right now we've got to get to the Merfelds'," she whispered.

At the Merfeld homestead Otis was sitting on a stump in the yard with a crock jug held between his bare feet. His face was covered with thin light whiskers; rope suspenders held up his britches. Mrs. Merfeld sat in a willow rocker on the porch.

"Oh, shoot," Jesse said in a low murmur. "I was hoping he wouldn't be here."

"Don't worry about him. If he gives you trouble, he'll lose a few more teeth."

"No, Wade. Don't let it come to that. He could keep his children from getting the vaccination. Let him say whatever he wants. If he lays a hand on me, I'll poke him with the hatpin I carry for just that purpose."

"You're a wonder," he whispered as he helped her out of the buggy.

"Afternoon, Mr. Merfeld," she said and kept walking toward the porch without giving him a chance to answer. "Hello, Mrs. Merfeld. Isn't this a lovely June day. I swear, I've never seen so many wildflowers. They thrive up here."

"Howdy, ma'am. Won't you sit?" Mrs. Merfeld made an effort to get up.

"Thank you. I'll sit here on the edge of the porch." Jesse watched the woman sink back down in the chair gratefully. "Did the children get over the fever all right?"

"Yes'm, they did. And Flora never came down with it. She was a mighty big help." The woman glanced nervously toward the yard where her husband had lifted the jug to his mouth.

"I'm sure she was. How is she? I'd like to say hello to her and the other children."

"Well . . . she's out back . . . some'ers with the kids. They're . . . they're playin'."

"I'll just say hello to her." Jesse got to her feet. "And I want to see how the little ones fared after their bout with the fever."

"But . . ."

Jesse ignored Mrs. Merfeld's protest, walked around the porch, and headed for the back of the house. Something was not right. The woman was scared to death. Otis jumped up and came across the yard to intercept her.

"Where ya think yo're goin'? Ya ain't had no invite to go prowlin' 'round. Yo're still hangin' out with that nigger-lover, ain't ya?" He reached for her arm, but halted when Wade spoke behind him.

"Touch her and I'll break your arm in four places."

"Ya, got no say-so here, Simmer. This here is my place."

"And what a sorry-looking place it is. Torn-down fences, hogs running loose, scattered woodpile. A good wind would blow that shack away. Look at that garden, Otis. Your wife planted it, and you're letting it go to ruin cause you're too damned lazy to pull a few weeds."

Jesse, leaving Wade to handle Otis, continued to walk toward the children who were bunched with their older sister in the shade of a birch tree. A boy, a head shorter than Flora, had a thread tied to the leg of a june bug and was amusing two small boys and a thin little girl by letting them hold the end of the thread while the bug flew above their heads.

"Hello," she called cheerfully. "Remember me? Nurse Forbes. Maybe you don't want to remember me. I made you drink that awful medicine."

When she was close enough to the children to see their faces, she could see that Flora's eyes were both blackened, and her lip was puffed and split. The boy with the june bug had a bruise on his swollen jaw and one eye was swollen shut. Jesse's mind groped wildly for a way to handle the situation and decided it would be best to ignore, for the time being, the obvious signs that these children had been beaten recently.

"Hello, Flora." The girl murmured and turned her face away.

Jesse spoke to the boy. "I used to love to play with june bugs when I was your age. Your name is Dude, isn't it?"

"Yes'm."

"You were a big help when I was here before. You brought in water and helped cool the little boys while I worked with your sister. They all have fully recovered, I see."

The children seemed to be awed into silence. They looked at her with the quiet patient eyes of their mother. Sad eyes, Jesse thought, and silently wished she had their father's neck under her foot.

"Thank ya fer what ya done," Flora murmured.

"You're very welcome. I was trained to help sick people and I love doing it. Not that I want people to be sick so I can help them." She laughed lightly and asked if she could hold the thread tied to the june bug. She held it for a moment and then passed it to the youngest boy.

"How'd ya get to learn all that?" Flora asked.

"I went to nursing school in Knoxville for two years."

"I wish I could."

"Maybe you can someday."

"I can't leave Maw."

"If you still want to be a nurse when you finish school, come down and talk to my father. He may be able to arrange something for you." Jesse reached down and took the hand of the thin little girl. "I'm going to talk to your mother about you children having a vaccination for smallpox. Come up to the house so you can listen and understand." Jesse desperately wanted Wade to see what that beastly man had done to his children.

"Pa seen ya comin' 'n' said fer us to stay here till yo're gone." The boy spoke, barely moving his lips. It made Jesse wonder if his jaw was broken or just badly bruised. She watched as he carefully untied the thread from the leg of the june bug and held it on the palm of his hand until it flew away.

"Mr. Simmer will explain to your father that it's important for you to hear what I've got to tell your mother. Besides," she added in a conspiratorial manner, "I've got stick candy to pass out."

Jesse prayed she wasn't going to cause these children more pain. She was counting on Wade to throw the fear of death into Otis should he do it again. Holding the little girl's hand she started walking toward the house. After a few steps, she glanced over her shoulder to see the three boys following and Flora slowly trailing along behind.

Otis was sitting on the end of the porch and Wade stood near by trying to make conversation with Mrs. Merfeld. When Jesse and the children came around the corner, Otis stood.

"I done tol' ya —"

Jesse cut him off. "I insisted they come and hear what I want to tell you and Mrs. Merfeld about the smallpox vaccination program."

Jesse saw Wade's scowl as he looked at Flora's and Dude's faces. The children sat down on the edge of the porch as far away from their father as possible. Flora stood behind her mother's chair.

Otis snorted disdainfully at various times as Jesse explained the necessity of the vaccinations, how the vaccine worked and its effect.

"Foolishness. I ain't heared of no pox in these parts. Injins and niggers have pox, not decent white folks."

"Mr. Merfeld, smallpox doesn't care about color or class. It hits the rich, the poor, and people of every color. The germs will live a year and a half in a cotton bale or on a blanket. Once an epidemic starts it spreads like wildfire. Hundreds could die in these hills before it could be stopped."

"My kids ain't goin' down to no store 'n' havin' no prissy-tail woman scratch 'em and put germs in 'em."

"To set your mind at rest, Mr. Merfeld, my father, a doctor of medicine, will be doing the vaccinating. I'll just assist him." She turned her back on him, her face red with anger. "Mrs. Merfeld, have you given any thought to coming down to Harpersville when your baby comes?"

"Law, no, ma'am. It's more'n ten miles. I'd never make it astraddle that mule."

"I see. I didn't realize you didn't have a wagon."

"Ya think we're poor trash, don't ya?" Otis stood again. "Didn't realize ya didn't have a wagon," he mimicked. "She ain't needed yore help to pop out a youngun. Popped out five slick as catgut."

Jesse ignored his outburst. "If you have time, get word to Mr. Simmer. He'll pass it along to my father. Papa will come if at all possible."

"Gettin' chummy, air ya? *Mister* Simmer, the nigger-lover, will pass the word —"

"Shut up, Papa!" Flora yelled.

"Why ya shitty little —" Wade's hand came down heavily on Otis's shoulder, pressing him down and cutting off his words.

"Before I go," Jesse said, opening the bag she had left on the porch, "I have something for the children to thank them for being so good at taking their medicine when I was here last." She brought out the stick candy, gave one to each child, and gave a handful to Flora for later.

"No, by Gawd. Ya ain't taking her handouts." Otis shouted so loud the little ones flinched. They looked longingly at the candy, but made no attempt to eat it.

"I think it's time you and I had a man-to-man talk, Otis," Wade said calmly. He reached down, hooked his hand in the rope suspenders and effortlessly hauled Otis to his feet.

"I ain't palaverin' with no nigger —"

"Don't say it again unless you want to walk spraddle-legged for the rest of your life." Wade hissed the words and yanked on the suspenders until the overalls rode high in the man's crotch. He walked him that way to the back of the house, slammed him up against the wall and fastened his hand to his neck, holding him there.

"What ya doin? Ya can't —"

"Shut your mouth, you filthy, half-assed son of a bitch, or I'll shut it for you. You used your fists on those kids, didn't you? You're a big man, tough man with kids that can't fight back. Hit me, Otis. Your hands are free. Hit me, so I can smear your nose all over your face."

"They sassed, talked back —"

"Sassed, talked back." Wade banged Otis's head against the house. "It would give me a great deal of pleasure to smash your jaw and shut your lying mouth. If I hear of you beatin' your kids again, I'll break every bone in your worthless body. Get the message, you puking fathead?"

"Ya don't . . . ya ain't —"

"I do . . . and I am. Lay a hard hand on them again and you'll get a hard hand laid on you. Another thing, I hear you're fond of young girls."

"Naw. Naw." Otis tried to shake his head in denial.

"You were seen trying to feel up the little Foster girl at the camp meeting over at Coon Rapids.

If her pa gets wind of it he'll kill you."

"Naw!"

"Lying bastard!"

"Naw . . . I swear —"

"Have you been tryin' to get in Flora's pants? Is that why you hit her? Ruin her, Otis, and I'll hunt you down and kill you. You know I'll do it, don't you?" Wade's hand tightened on the man's throat. "You know I'll do it because I'm a mean, nigger-loving son of a bitch. The day you die, you'll never know what hit you. I'll be shootin' at a squirrel and suddenly your ugly head will be in my sight when I pull the trigger. It'll pop like a ripe melon."

"Ya can't . . . I'll tell the marshal."

"Dead men don't tell anything. They just lie in the woods and stink."

"Yo're . . . crazy!"

"You're the one that's crazy if you think I won't do it." Otis tried to break away from the hand holding him. Wade put his knee in his groin. "I'm not through with you yet. See to it that your kids are down to get the vaccination, or I'll set the revenuers on you. They'll bust up that still and haul your rear off to jail faster than a chicken on a wooly worm."

"You don't know —"

"I know exactly where it is and who you sell to. You're paying off a debt with whiskey. You know what that man will do to you when the deliveries stop. He'll be up here like a shot and before he leaves you'll wish you were dead."

"How'er ya knowin' that?"

"You're stupid, Otis. Everyone in the hills knows it. Don't try to move that still or I'll bust it up myself. Do we have an understanding? If not, say so. I'd just as soon break your neck now as later. It would be a relief to your family to be rid of you."

"Aw . . . all right —"

"All right what?" Wade snarled.

"Kids'll be thar."

"What else?" Wade's booted foot came down hard on Otis's bare toes.

"Aw . . . shit, don't — I . . . won't . . . hit 'em."

"You go back on that and I'll find you. When I do you'll be walking on a stump if you're walking at all. Now you get out there and tell that nurse who is trying to help your family that you appreciate what she's done and what she's going to do."


Jesse looked back at the group on the porch as the buggy pulled out of the yard. The children were bunched together, and Flora stood protectively beside her mother. Otis had gone back to the stump in the yard.

"What will he do? Will he beat them as soon as we're out of sight?"

"He won't beat them." Wade saw the worried look on her face and wanted to erase it. "Don't worry. He won't beat them," he said again. "He's too big a coward."

"What makes you so sure he won't?"

"We had a little man-to-man talk. The only kind a man like Merfeld understands."

"Whatever you said to him had an effect. He was meek as a lamb. I hope it lasts, and he doesn't take it out on Mrs. Merfeld and the children. I could have cried when I saw Flora's face. And Dude. That bully could have broken his jaw. Dude was so kind to his little brothers and his sister. He even took the thread from a june bug's leg before he let it go. Most kids would have let the poor thing fly away with the thread hanging to get caught on something."

"Otis knows what will happen to him if he uses his fists on his kids again. He also knows what will happen if his kids fail to show up for the vaccinations." Wade grinned at Jesse wickedly and moved close to her so that they were touching from shoulder to thigh.

She answered his grin with one of her own. "Wade Simmer! You're a bully. You threatened poor Mr. Merfeld with bodily harm." She tucked her hand into the curve of his when he reached for it. Her eyes danced with delight. "I'd like to have been a bird so I could have heard and seen it. Oh, I wish you'd blackened both his eyes and . . . knocked out his teeth."

A rumbling laugh bubbled up out of Wade. "I didn't know that my girl was such a bloodthirsty little vixen." His eyes, full of teasing laughter, traveled lovingly over her face.

*My girl.* The two words held a world of meaning.

She belonged to someone — Wade — in a special way. Her face reflected her happiness when she lifted her chin and looked down her nose at him with a haughty expression on her face and a teasing glint in her eyes.

"My good man, I like a good fight as well as the next fellow."

They both burst out laughing.

The attraction between them was like a living flame, and yet there was something more — a comfortable sharing of thought and feeling. When Jesse looked into his dark face and green eyes, she felt that she could tell him anything, everything, share her innermost thoughts, fears, and dreams with him. At times that afternoon she was so happy that her heart shook with apprehension. To be so happy was dangerous, her inner voice cautioned. What had happened between her and this man was too good to be real.

Granny Lester had known immediately that there was something brewing between them.

"Ya courtin' her, boy?" she asked bluntly and switched her snuff stick to the other side of her mouth. "If you ain't, yo're a blame fool."

Not the least embarrassed, Wade watched the color come up to flood Jesse's cheeks, while she watched his eyes crinkle at the corners and his wide mouth stretch in a grin that enveloped his whole face.

"Well, I don't know, Granny. She's not asked me to court her yet."

"Law, boy. Yo're hard put if yo're waitin' to

be asked." Granny turned her eyes to her husband of more than fifty years. "I'd not ever set eyes on Mr. Lester till he walked right up to me at a camp meetin'. He were bold as brass. 'Yo're the one fer me,' he said. 'I'm comin' courtin' Saturday night.' He walked off 'n' didn't give me a chance to say aye or nay. But come Saturday ya can bet yore britches I was all duded up in my best bib and tucker 'n' ready to walk out with him. Ya ort to take a lesson from Mr. Lester, boy, 'n' go after what yo're wantin'."

"Maybe I should come over and have a little talk with Grandpa and get some pointers on how to court from someone who has done it before." Wade's bright teasing eyes watched Jesse fidget and throw him a threatening glance.

"Ain't ya ever courted a gal, boy?" Granny asked. "Pshaw! Guess ya never needed to. Ever loose thin' in these hills has been beatin' a path to yore door. Talk to Mr. Lester. I guarantee ya'll learn a thin' or two 'bout courtin' a *good* woman."

After they left the Lesters' and before they reached his place, Wade turned off the road and drove deep into the woods before he stopped the buggy.

"This is a favorite place of mine. I wanted you to see it. I come here sometimes, sit under a tree and marvel at the stillness."

It was a beautiful glen, cool, secretive, enchanting. Tall branches shadowed the sun, allowing only shimmering streaks of sunlight through and here and there a splash of blue sky. A light breeze rustled the leaves and from far away came the lonely call of a mourning dove.

"It's peaceful. Do you come here to get away from all those women who beat a path to your door?"

"I was afraid you'd pick up on that."

"I ain't no dumb . . . nurse," she said, mimicking Jody's voice.

"Thank you for the best day of my life."

"You're very welcome," she said because she didn't know what else to say.

"Will there be others?" His voice was husky, strained.

"I doubt there will ever be another day like this one." She spoke with rock-hard certainty and drew back so that she could look in his eyes.

"Ah, love." The soft, awed murmur echoed though Jesse's scattered senses. "Are you real?"

"What a silly question."

After a long, lingering kiss he released her lips to search her eyes. This thing between them was almost too wonderful to bear.

"Are you going to ask me to court you?" he whispered, his eyes teasingly soft.

"You'll have to take your turn. I've already asked two very fine gentleman to call on me." Jesse's laugh was more like the giggle of a young girl. She peered at him through half-closed eyes.

"Good Lord," he groaned. "How big are they? Bigger than I am? I'll have to have a man-to-man talk with them — the kind I just had with Otis Merfeld."

Jesse wound her arms around his neck. "I think I lost my mind this afternoon." Her voice was low and soft.

"Sweetheart, I lost my heart."

The kiss they shared was fresh and clean and sweet, nothing of passion and heat and clinging closeness, just tenderness.

# CHAPTER
## • 13 •

*W*hile Molly was being hitched to the buggy and the picnic basket loaded, Jesse had a few minutes alone with Wade on the back porch.

"I'll be down one evening soon. Will your father object if I call on you?"

"Papa considers me a grown woman, perfectly capable of making my own decisions."

"— And, I know, I'll have to stand in line behind those two other fellows." He laughed a deep chuckling laugh as his hand reached out to squeeze her shoulder.

Jesse smiled up at him and said softly, "If you come, I'll see that you go to the head of the line."

Wade's heart beat with pure joy. He caressed her with his eyes. His throat was so tight that he couldn't speak for a long moment. When he did, it was to say something he was determined to tell her before she left.

"About this fellow they call The Looker. I talked to Dusty Wright the other day. He hasn't a clue as to who he is. Promise me you won't go out after dark alone and that you women will stay together at night."

"He's not likely to come to our house even if Papa is gone. Susan and I sleep in one room. Pauline and Mrs. Lindstrom are across the hall."

"He might not know that until he's in the house."

"It's strange. Papa and I have talked about it. This man knows when the women are alone. Papa used to think it was someone from out of town. Now he thinks that he's someone we know, someone who lives in Harpersville and has a reputation beyond reproach."

"That lets me out. Dusty tells me that I'm the prime suspect."

"But . . . that's silly!"

"The Harpers will hang it on me until the man is caught. Does that bother you?"

"Yes, it bothers me because it's so unfair."

"Have you thought about your own reputation? It will suffer if you're seen with me."

"No, I've not thought about it and I don't intend to. I have a right to choose my friends. If people don't like it, the . . . devil can take the lot of them." Jesse's tone more than her words showed her frustration.

"I want to be more than a friend, Jesse."

What she read in his eyes brought a flush to her cheeks.

"I know." Her soft whisper came to him. Her eyes were misty. Here in the hills it seemed so natural to be with him, but down below people in the town would be horrified that Jesse Forbes would even consider being friends with the notorious Wade Simmer.

His body throbbed with the need to hold her, and it took a supreme act of will to let his hand slide down her arm to take hers. Only God knew how much he wanted her, how he dreaded the lonely days until he could see her again.

"You've got to go, honey. I want you home before dark."

*Honey.* Jesse's insides warmed with pleasure as she looked into his quiet dark face. She wanted once again the warmth of his arms, the scrape of his afternoon whiskers on her cheek. She wanted to feel the pounding of his heart against hers. But there was nothing to do but put her feet into motion and head for the buggy.

With their hands clasped tightly, they stepped off the porch and into the yard. Wade's horse was saddled and waiting. Jody had known that Wade would escort them out of the hills.

"B-Bye, Jody. I had a good time. See you M-Monday." Todd climbed up on the platform behind the buggy. C-C-Can I ride as far as you go, Mr. Simmer?"

"Sure." Wade helped Jesse into the buggy, then stepped into the saddle and lifted Todd up behind him. "Hold onto my belt, big fellow."

"Bye, Jody," Susan called. "Thanks for showing me the baby rabbits and for letting me play your fiddle. I'm still mad 'cause you threw that cow pie at me. I'll never get that green out of my dress and it's all your fault. Jess, did you know Jody made a fiddle out of a cigar box? You should see it; it has strings and everything."

Pauline and Jesse waved to Jody as Molly pulled the buggy out of the yard. Wade and Todd rode behind. Since Wade had volunteered to take the sign announcing the date of the vaccinations to the store, they could take the shortcut to the main road.

"This has been a great day. It's probably the most fun I'll have all summer. Wait'll I tell Mary Sue and Jeff I was in Wade Simmer's hayloft. She thinks he's a jailbird and has done terrible things. Maybe he did when he was young, but now that he's old, maybe he's had a change of heart. Mary Sue was sure that if we came up here, he'd *ravish* us."

"Ravish? Susan, for land sakes. Where do you get such notions?"

"It wasn't my notion, Jess. It was Mary Sue's. She knows a lot about ravishing and things like that." Susan slouched down in the seat and rested her head against the back. "I wish we didn't have to go home to old Lou . . . el . . . la."

"Are you disappointed that you're going home . . . unravished?"

"Oh, silly. Why don't you marry Mr. Simmer? I could come up here and live with you."

"That's not a bad idea, Jesse," Pauline said. "Susan could go to that school over at Coon Rapids. It has two rooms but only one teacher. Three grades are in one room and three in the other."

Susan sat up straight. "I'm not going to any dinky old school out in the woods somewhere. And Jess won't marry and leave me and Todd with old Ghost-face, will you, Jess?"

"You're getting the cart before the horse. I've not been asked. Get along, Molly." Jesse slapped the reins against the mare's back. "We've got to get this smart-mouthed girl home."

When the curving road began to dip deeply into the valley, Jesse stopped the buggy. Wade settled Todd on the platform in back and came around to the side.

"From the cliff yonder, I can see you until you reach the bridge."

"You don't have to wait. We'll be all right."

"I intend to make sure. Bye, ladies." He tipped his hat to Pauline and Susan.

"Bye, Mr. Simmer. I had a really good time."

"I'm glad, Susan. Come back again."

"I will if Jess will let me." With a little suggestive smile on her face she rolled her eyes to her sister.

"Thanks, Miss Anthony, for taking on the job of teaching Jody. If you get into difficulty with the school board, I'll certainly compensate you for the trouble."

"Don't worry about it. I'm not certain I want to stay in Harpersville anyway. Perhaps a school like the one at Coon Rapids would be more to my liking."

"Let me know if there are any books you need. I'll get them from Knoxville or Chattanooga."

As he spoke to Pauline, his eyes, dark and in-

216

tense, wandered to Jesse and clung like a caressing hand. They traveled over her face, her soft red mouth, blue-gray eyes, wind-tousled hair, and down the tight, slim body and firm round breasts as if to imprint her image forever in his mind.

This woman was his, the love of his life.

A silent prayer formed in his heart: *Dear God, keep her safe until I can be with her again.*

"Bye, Jesse. See you soon."

"Bye, Wade. Thank you for going the round with me."

"My pleasure."

Since there seemed to be nothing else to say, Jesse moved Molly on down the road.

"Such formality," Pauline said to Jesse as soon as they were out of hearing distance. "You'd think the two of you had just met."

"Do you like him, Jess?" Susan asked. "He's not as bad as I thought he'd be. Everyone said he was mean. I don't think he's mean at all. He sure takes a lot from that brat, Jody. I've never seen a nig . . . a colored that talks back like he does. He's a smart-mouth. I can tell you that."

"Yes, he's smart-mouthed," Pauline said. "But he's smart as a whip. He reads fast and absorbs what he reads. Mr. Simmer has worked with him. I'll have to get books from the school on the pretext that I'm helping you, Susan."

"Who would believe that? Everyone knows I get good marks in school."

"They may think that you're wanting to skip a grade."

"Yeah? Do you think I could?"

The voices of her sister and her friend drifted over Jesse's head. She had no thoughts except of the man she had left sitting on the big horse, the time they had spent together and the words that had passed between them.

Jesse was so occupied with her thoughts of Wade that the time flew by, and soon they were crossing the bridge and entering Harpersville.

It had been a very satisfying day for Louella Lindstrom.

Alone in the house for the entire day, she had decided it would be a good time to clean the doctor's bedroom. Until today she had only made the bed, run the carpet sweeper over the rug and the dust mop over the hardwood floor around the edges. Jesse had made it plain to her that that was all she needed to do.

The room was large and airy with beautiful walnut furniture and a bed with posters that reached within a foot of the ceiling. Papers and medical journals littered the room except for the table beside the doctor's bed. A gas lamp hung from the ceiling. An oil lamp with twining pink roses painted on the shade, a framed picture of Dora Forbes and the doctor's pipe sat on an embroidered scarf on the bedside table.

Louella picked up the picture and looked at it curiously. Dora had not been beautiful by any means, but she was pleasant-looking, just as she had been when she was a girl. Time had blurred

Dora's features in Louella's memory until she had seen Susan. The girl resembled her mother; there was no doubt about that, but she hadn't inherited her mother's ways. Dora had always been sweet, demure and easily manipulated. Susan was strong-willed and to Louella's way of thinking, a rude little snip.

Only through the chance meeting with an old acquaintance had Louella learned that Dora had married a doctor, had borne two children and had passed on several years ago. The information had come just in the nick of time when Louella desperately needed a place to go.

By mid-afternoon the furniture except for the bed (because she couldn't move it) had been re-arranged, and the room had been cleaned until not a particle of dust could be found. The polished surface of the walnut furniture gleamed. Its beautiful grain was caught by the sunlight that came through the freshly washed windows. Long-unused dresser scarfs with fancy crocheted edges, which she had found in a bottom drawer, covered the tops of the chiffonier, the dresser and the table beside the bed. Louella had thought of moving Dora's picture to a corner shelf, but decided to let it stay on the table for now as it was best not to make too many changes all at once.

The lady's writing desk with the French bevel plate mirror was the only piece of furniture in the room that was not walnut. It was solid oak with a high gloss finish. The writing lid let down to reveal a series of pigeonholes with one drawer in the middle. It was locked. In the pigeonholes were a collection of calling cards. Stationery was heaped helter-skelter just as Dora had left it.

After arranging the contents of the desk to her satisfaction, Louella, working with a shoe hook, opened the locked drawer, took out the handful of letters and went to the chair beside the window. After sorting the letters by handwriting and date, she began to read.

Thirty minutes later, smiling, Louella realized there was more to Dora Forbes than she'd ever dreamed. She put the letter from Dusty Wright, the marshal, in her apron pocket. It always paid, she told herself, to have an extra ace in the hole when the stakes were high. She returned the rest of the letters to the drawer and carefully relocked it.

It was dusk when Jesse walked into the house. The parlor was alight in the glow of the gas lamps. The rest of the house was in semi-darkness. She sniffed and realized that what she smelled was the furniture polish her stepmother had taught her to make by using a cup of vinegar, a cup of turpentine and a cup of boiled linseed oil. She followed the path of light that came from the open door of her father's room.

As she stood in the doorway and surveyed the room, Jesse felt anger boiling up inside her. The housekeeper sat in Dora's platform rocker reading by the light of an oil lamp on the onyx-top brass table from the parlor. The rearranged furniture stood in splendid polished silence. The bed was covered with the white fringed honeycomb bedspread that she had washed, folded carefully, and put away at her father's request.

"You're back. I was beginning to worry." Louella stood. "I've been sitting here reading the doctor's journals. My goodness, I never realized that medicine was so interesting."

"I distinctly remember telling you, Mrs. Lindstrom, to leave Papa's room alone. He didn't want it rearranged, or I would have done it myself."

"But, dear, isn't it lovely? The furniture is valuable, you know, and shouldn't be left to stand in dust —"

"It was not your decision to make."

"You must not allow sentiment to keep such a pleasant room in gloom. I know it will cause Hollis a pang at first, but afterwards he will be glad to put the past behind him."

Jesse, trying to ignore the housekeeper's use of her father's first name, walked over to Dora's desk and pulled down the slanted lid. Stationery was neatly tied with ribbon. Envelopes and cards were in the pigeonholes. Beads and other trinkets were placed either in small boxes or envelopes and stacked neatly. Jesse whirled to face the housekeeper and drew in a deep angry breath.

"These were my stepmother's things. Papa has never allowed anyone to touch them."

"Nonsense!" Louella scoffed. "Don't worry about it. I've not removed a thing. It's all there anytime he wants to look at it."

Jesse tried the drawer. Thank goodness it was still locked. She had no idea of what was in it or why her father kept the key on his keyring. She closed the lid on the desk.

"You should bow to my judgment on this, Jesse. It isn't healthy for Hollis to wallow in grief." She would have said more but something in Jesse's face silenced her.

"Dora's hair-saver sat here on the chiffonier. Where is it?"

"In the bottom drawer."

Jesse took the china jar with the hole in the lid from the drawer where she also found Dora's comb, brush and mirror set. She placed them on the chiffonier after first looking to see if the blond hair had been removed. It was there and she cast a warning look at the housekeeper.

Louella turned down the oil lamp and went to the door.

Jesse followed.

"Do you children want a bite to eat? I made a peach pie. It's the doctor's favorite."

"Don't refer to me as a child, Mrs. Lindstrom. I'm twenty-two years old."

"Yes, I know. I didn't want to embarrass you."

"Why would I be embarrassed?"

"Well . . . twenty-two years old, unmarried, and still living in your father's house —"

"I see. So you think there is a stigma attached to an unmarried, twenty-two-year-old woman still living in her father's house."

Jesse was seething with anger, and it showed in her face and the sharpness of her voice.

"No, of course not. Maiden ladies have a certain place in our society. But some people in town think that it's not exactly natural . . . that you show no interest in a social life or meeting a young man and establishing your own home —" Louella's words trailed as Todd, Susan and Pauline came through the dining room to the hall.

"J-Jess, can we have the p-pie?"

"Yeah, old p-poothead made it." Todd scooted behind Susan and made for the kitchen door when he saw the housekeeper.

"Of course, you can have it. I'll cut it for you. Come on, Pauline. Mrs. Lindstrom is tired and wants to retire. She's had a *busy* day." Jesse turned her back on the housekeeper and herded the others toward the kitchen.

"Gosh, Jess. You're madder than a wet hen. I can tell," Susan swung the door closed. "What's old poothead done now? I like Todd's name better."

Jesse, with her back turned to reach for the plates, tried to get her anger under control before she spoke.

"You're right. But I don't want to talk about it. I might explode."

"Was it a-a-about m-me?" Todd asked, his face anxious.

"No, sugar. Why would it be about you?" Jesse replied as she cut a large wedge of pie and put it on his plate. "You're the best nine-year-old,

223

dirty, sassy, good-for-nothing boy I know." He rewarded her teasing with a wide grin. " 'Course sometimes you're darn near perfect and at other times utterly revolting."

"I'm a-a-lmost ten."

"She rides Todd about his stuttering; that's why he thinks it's 'bout him. I heard her and I yelled for her to shut up. She said she'd tell Papa, but I guess she didn't. He never said anything."

Jesse's eyes, sparking with angry lights, caught Pauline's before they moved on to her sister. "Exactly what did she say to Todd, Susan?"

"Well, she said he could talk without stammering if he wanted to and it was his way of getting attention. She said only stupid people stammer when they talk. That's when I told her to shut up."

Although she was so angry that she was about to cry, Jesse struggled for something to say and was relieved when Pauline filled the void.

"That shows you how stupid *she* is," Pauline said heatedly. "Todd is one of the smartest pupils in the school. Many great men in history stammered. For instance, Lewis Carroll who wrote *Alice's Adventures in Wonderland.* The Bible says that Moses was slow in speech. Demosthenes, an Athenian statesman, stammered and he eventually became the greatest of ancient Greek orators."

"Ichabod told us about him. He talked with stones in his mouth."

"Just as you're doing with pie in yours, dear

little sister," Jesse said drily.

"P-Papa says I'll g-grow out of it." Todd's eyes clung to his teacher's face.

"And you will. I'm sure of it. Some think that people who stammer are extra smart, that the brain works too fast for the tongue to keep up with it. Did you notice that you didn't stammer as much today?" Pauline asked.

"I d-d-didn't?"

"You didn't because you didn't think about it. If you think about your stammering, you'll stammer even more. Just let the words flow out."

Grateful for Pauline's wise counseling, Jesse cut a wedge of pie for herself although she didn't know if she would be able to eat it. The scene with the housekeeper had upset her to the extent that her stomach roiled and her head throbbed. It had been a wonderful day. Why did it have to end on such a sour note?

She looked up as her father pushed open the swinging door.

"I thought I heard voices in here." He shoved the door back until it caught the latch and remained open. "I don't know why this thing has to be closed."

"I can tell you. It's old —"

"— Come sit down Papa. Have some pie." Jesse gave her sister a warning glance and got up to get a plate and the silverware caddy.

"We h-had fun, P-Papa. Jody's dog's got p-pups. Tell him, J-Jess."

"You tell him, you're doing a pretty good job

225

of it. Sit here, Papa. Do you want me to heat the coffee?"

The doctor sat down. "No, thanks. I'll just have some of that pie." His smile included all at the table. "Looks to me like you all had a day in the sun. Sis, I do believe that you've got a hundred more freckles on your nose," he said to Susan.

"I do! Oh, darn! Are you teasing, Papa?"

"What have you been in, Todd. I . . . smell something."

"Dog do-do, more than likely," Susan chortled happily. "He played with Delilah's pups all day."

"Delilah? I thought he said Jody's pups."

"Jody's d-dog's pups. It's fun there, P-Papa. Mr. S-Simmer's got some g-goats too."

"You spent the day at Mr. Simmer's? Did you change your mind about going to Granny Lester's or staying at the store with Mrs. Frony?"

"Mr. Simmer met us on the road before we got to the store and we went to his house," Susan explained.

"Is that so?" Hollis looked at his son and winked. Todd winked back, his eyes twinkling and his face split with a grin.

"Mr. Simmer cooked a turkey, Papa. When I said we only have turkey on special occasions like Thanksgiving and Christmas, he said it was a special occasion. I don't know what he meant by that." Susan looked knowingly at her elder sister, who threw her another warning glance. "I climbed up in the hayloft and that darkie threw a cow pie at me. Jody's not so bad if you can stand his smart mouth."

"That takes care of Susan and Todd. How about you, Pauline? What do you think of the hill country?" Hollis continued to eat his pie.

"It's pretty up there. I thought the people all lived in shacks and hogs rooted in the yard and chickens wandered into the house. Mr. Simmer's home is nice. It's as modern as any house in town."

Hollis winked at Jesse. "I take it you didn't take her to the Merfelds'."

"Mr. Simmer went with Jesse," Susan announced. "We stayed at his house with Pauline . . . ah . . . Miss Anthony."

"I-It was fun, P-Papa. Th-thank you for l-letting us go."

"You're welcome, son." Hollis placed his hand on Todd's shoulder and squeezed.

"Doctor. I didn't know you were home." Louella stood framed in the doorway. "I'll make you some fresh coffee."

"Don't bother." Jesse spoke quickly and somewhat crisply. "I asked him, and he doesn't want coffee. We'll not need you any more this evening, Mrs. Lindstrom. The girls and I will tidy up before we retire."

"Well," she hesitated and looked directly at Hollis. He glanced at her and turned his attention back to his plate. "I'm glad you got here before the pie was gone, Doctor. The other evening while we were sitting in the porch swing you told me among other things that blue was your favorite

227

color and peach was your favorite pie."

"It's very tasty, Louella, especially after that train ride. Thank you."

Louella glanced at Jesse. She wanted her to know that she and the doctor had had intimate conversations. Jesse was staring at her with icy blue eyes. Something would have to be done and soon, or the doctor's elder daughter would spoil her plans. If she could get that girl married to Edsel Harper, she would be able to handle the other two. The boy would be easy. Susan would be easy too, after a while.

"Good night, Mrs. Lindstrom," Jesse said pointedly. Her father looked at her sharply and then at the housekeeper.

"Well . . . good night." Louella allowed Hollis to see the hurt look on her face. She smiled bravely and bowed her head before backing out the doorway.

"What was that all about?" Hollis looked directly at his older daughter. She shrugged.

"We like time alone with you, Papa."

"Y-Yeah. Sh-She's al-l-ways got her n-nose in."

"We don't like her," Susan said bluntly and scooped up another piece of pie.

"You like her pie."

"She cooks good, but . . . it's not like it used to be around here."

"And how was that?" Hollis asked.

"We didn't have to walk around scared she'd pop out and accuse us of something. And we had a little time to do something besides work." Susan's resentment bubbled out unguardedly.

228

"And you, Todd. Do you feel the same?"

"Sh-she don't l-l-like me."

"That's not true. She thinks you're a fine lad — her words, not mine. I know how Jesse feels about Louella or any woman we would hire to take care of the house." He looked straight at his elder daughter. "You resent her taking over what has been your domain for quite a few years. Louella understands that. You must admit, Jesse, she's taken a load of work off your shoulders. It was unfair of me to allow you to work in the surgery, keep my home, raise my children."

"I thought it was *my* home too, Papa." Jesse fought to keep the tears at bay. "The children I have cared for are my brother and sister."

"It is your home for as long as it stands." Hollis saw the unshed tears in her eyes and wanted desperately to ease her pain. "I want you to have the freedom to enjoy your youth."

"Are you embarrassed, Papa, to have a twenty-two-year-old, unmarried daughter still living in your house?"

"Jess! For God's sake! Where in the world did you dig up such a crazy idea?"

"I . . . bet I know!"

"Hush, Susan," Hollis said angrily and got to his feet. "Jesse, if anyone is embarrassed, it must be Pauline. I'm sorry, my dear, for filling your ears with family problems. We'll talk about this later. Meanwhile, I want all of you to understand that Mrs. Lindstrom stays. She takes good care of the house, is a good cook and has refined ways.

As for you two," — he looked pointedly at Susan and Todd — "I want you to make more of an effort to get along with her. Discipline is what you need. She's had experience with children who need direction."

"Are you saying that I let them run wild, Papa?" Jesse, too, had stood. Her face was tight, her heart thudded with dread.

"I'm not saying that at all. You're too close to them to see how they manipulate you."

"Mrs. Lindstrom's words, no doubt," Jesse said drily.

"Regardless of who said it, it's true."

Jesse's heart fell with a thud. "You won't reconsider?"

"No. I suggest we all get a night's sleep before we discuss this further. Good night."

With a look of apology to Pauline, Jesse followed her father through the dining room and into the hall. She paused at his bedroom door while he turned on the gas light. She watched his face anxiously while he looked about the room. His hand was wrapped tightly around the bedpost. She saw the shock, grief, and finally resignation.

"Papa, I didn't do it."

"I know. I know. Good night, Jesse."

When he was alone, Hollis sank down on the edge of the bed, rested his elbows on his knees and covered his face with his hands.

*Dora, my love, I had a little something of you here where I could sit and dream . . . and now even that is gone.*

# CHAPTER
## • 14 •

*E*than was taking lines of type out of the frame that made up the front page of the *Gazette*. The weekly paper was printed and stacked beside the door ready for delivery. The bold headline warned women to be careful because The Looker was still about. One more woman, whose name was not revealed, had reported to Marshal Wright that she had been stripped and *looked at* in her home. She reported that it had been a most humiliating experience.

"How long has this been going on?"

"Since a month before you got here." The outspoken publisher of the paper was more comfortable now with the detective.

"That's a relief. I think I'll hang a sign around my neck saying I've only been here a couple of weeks."

"Someone giving you trouble?"

"Every woman in town runs from me." Ethan gave Ralph a cocky grin.

"Shows we got smart women in Harpersville."

"People seem to think it's a man who lives up in the hills."

"Wade Simmer. They think that because the almighty Harpers sicced them on him. It isn't Wade. I'd stake my life on it."

"You know him?"

"Hell, yes, I know him. He's a rough character. He minds his own business, but don't push him. Get him in a corner and he'll fight till hell freezes over, and he fights dirty. Must have picked it up in his travels."

"Nothin' wrong with that."

"Wander down to Ike's garage some Wednesday night and meet him."

"They say he's got plenty of money. Any idea where he got it?"

"No. He came back here about three years ago. He'd been away for quite a while. If he stole the money, it wasn't from anyone around here. I don't know where he got it or how much it is or where it is. It's none of my business."

"I'll tell you one thing. He'd better watch his back. Some fellows from that bridge crew are laying for him. One has a girl that was molested. The man just heard about it and is out to hurt someone."

"That'll be Bertha Secory's pa. When John gets some white lightning in him he's got the brains of a pissant."

"Someone should pass the word to Simmer."

"I already have."

Ethan looked up from the alphabetized boxes

where he was filing the type. Ralph was cleaning the press.

"You don't miss much, do you?"

"Not much to miss in this one-horse town. How did your interview go with the doctor last night?"

"I wondered when you'd ask."

"On print day I don't have time to go out back to the privy, much less make idle conversation."

"It went well. He told me the Public Health people think they can stamp out smallpox here in the United States within twenty years if they can get people to come for vaccinations."

"Hurrumpt!" Ralph grunted and carried the turpentine-soaked rags to a bucket that sat outside the back door. "See anything of the girls? That's what you went for, wasn't it?"

"How would you be knowin' that?"

"I'm not blind. I've seen you eyeing Miss Anthony, and you know well as I do that she's staying with the Forbeses this summer while Mrs. Poole is gone. Don't blame her for not wanting to stay alone."

"She's an eyeful. And won't give me the time of day."

"Rankles, doesn't it?"

"She and Miss Jesse were on the front porch when I got there. Miss Jesse is friendly enough, but Miss Pauline tilted her cute little nose and hardly spoke. Since I've not seen her with any man at all, I know she doesn't have a steady beau. Something's caused that girl to be man-shy."

Pauline Anthony had intrigued him from the

very first — a menace to his peace of mind. She was lovely with an innocent sensuality and was causing him to violate his long-standing prohibition against getting involved with anyone connected with a case while he was working on it.

"Doc Forbes has got that darkie doing some cleanup around the place. His new housekeeper will work the living daylights out of the kid. I can't abide the woman myself. There's something about her that doesn't ring true."

"Yeah?" Ethan's hand, holding the large tweezers he used for lifting the small type, paused momentarily. "For instance?"

"Well, for one thing she calls herself 'friend of the family.' Miss Jesse calls her 'housekeeper.' Susan calls her 'Ghost-face' and Todd calls her 'Poothead.'"

Ethan hooted. "I think I'd like those kids."

"The old girl says she was mistress of a girls' school. Then why is she here in this jerkwater town doing housework instead of getting another job at a school? And she tries to hobnob with the 'elite.' Doesn't seem natural somehow."

"Maybe she's got her eye on the doc?"

"Doc Forbes says he never set eyes on her till she knocked on the door. Seems she's a girlhood friend of Dora Forbes, his deceased wife."

"Does anyone in town remember her?"

"Dora was from Knoxville. She came here when she was a young woman and worked in the boarding house. That's where she met the doc."

Ethan mulled Ralph's words over in his mind.

He was tempted to take the publisher into his confidence but decided against it. It was too soon. He would wait until he found out if there was a connection between Pauline and Mrs. Lindstrom. Pauline had a convenient excuse for staying with the Forbeses this summer. God, he hoped it was just coincidence that she was there. When she had been pointed out to him as a teacher, his first thought was that she was someone Louella Lindstrom would gravitate to, having been connected with a school herself.

"That little darkie can run like a deer." Ralph's voice jarred Ethan back to the present.

"I heard he lives with Simmer."

"Yeah. Simmer has kind of adopted him."

"Going to the ball game this evening?"

"Might, if you stop flapping your lips and get that type sorted."

A week had passed since Jesse had seen Wade. Beside the fact he hadn't called, there were two reasons for her nerves being on edge.

The first was what happened when the housekeeper went into the parlor and found Todd with the stereoscope and several series of views.

"Put those back right this minute," she had ordered, her voice reaching down the hall to the surgery. "You are far too young to be viewing that set, and, besides, you'll break your father's stereoscope."

"B-But, I-I-I —"

"No buts. Put it away."

"N-N-o-o-! J-J-Jesseee —"

Jesse left the surgery. Todd's wail brought her scurrying down the hall. She was alarmed at the terror she heard in his voice. She paused in the doorway of the parlor to see him with the stereoscope clutched to his breast and Mrs. Lindstrom trying to wrench it from him.

"This is shameful behavior, Todd. Give it here."

"I-I-I w-w-won't. J-J-Jesss —"

Mrs. Lindstrom's hand lashed out and struck Todd's face. The slap made a sharp sound.

Jesse, with rage boiling up like a tidal wave, flew across the room and grabbed the woman's arm, spinning her around so violently that she stumbled back and stood with a chair between them.

"Leave him alone!"

Sobbing, Todd turned to wrap his arms around his sister's waist. "J-J-Jess . . . Sh-She w-w-on't —"

"It's all right, darling. It's all right."

"He'll break it. The doctor said I should discipline him."

"I'm sure he didn't mean for you to strike him."

"He must learn to bow to authority."

"Not yours, madam! And he will not break it."

"The doctor spent good money —"

"The doctor did not spend one red cent on it. I did. Todd has been using the stereoscope for years. It's not only enjoyable, it's educational."

"He was looking at the series that show men and women kissing."

"And what is wrong with that? People do it all the time. Todd, take the stereoscope and the views to your room. You can keep them there." Jesse bristled like a mama bear protecting her cub.

Louella waited until the boy was gone before she spoke.

"I'll speak to the doctor about this. He wants the children trained to be refined and genteel. Your interference makes it impossible for me to have any control over them."

"Speak to him all you want, but keep your hands off that boy." Jesse was so angry that words gushed out of her mouth like water from a fountain. "I'll tell you this and you had better heed my words. If I ever hear that you have slapped him, called him stupid or have even mentioned his stammering, I'll pull every hair out of your head. And that's not all. I'll mark up that lily-white face of yours so that you'll be putting more than buttermilk on it for the rest of your life." By the time Jesse finished she was shouting.

"You are certainly lacking in polish and grace." Mrs. Lindstrom lifted her chin and shook her head sadly. "I can't imagine why a man as refined as Edsel Harper would be interested in you."

"If you find the Harpers so perfect, Mrs. Lindstrom, why don't you apply for a job with them?"

Back in the surgery, Jesse sank down in a chair. Never in her life had she threatened anyone or come so near losing control. It would not have taken much more for her to grab handfuls of the woman's hair. She realized how short her temper had become as the days had passed and her father had continued to appear to enjoy the housekeeper's company. But that had nothing to do with the anger she felt now.

That evening she and Pauline sat in the porch swing and discussed what had happened.

"Wait," Pauline cautioned. "Wait until you have more incidents to report to your father. He may be able to find an excuse for the woman's behavior."

"For slapping Todd?"

"She could tell him that she used this method with her students at the boarding school."

"Papa wouldn't go along with that, would he?"

The conversation was cut short when Ethan Bredlow came up the walk to the house. He sat on the porch rail and tried to make conversation.

"Nice evening. I like the long days, don't you, Miss Anthony?"

Pauline's eyes lifted to survey him with unease. "Yes," she agreed, coldly.

"Soon we'll have the longest day in the year. June twenty-second, isn't it?"

He was looking at Pauline. When she didn't answer, Jesse tried to fill the void.

"It's the twenty-first or the twenty-second. And then the days will start getting shorter. I love fall, but I love summer more."

"Have you been going to the ball games? I hear Grover has a good team."

After a pause, Jesse answered. "We've been to

some. Todd, my brother, loves to go. He says he's going to be just like Joe 'Iron Man' McGinty."

"Whoa!" Ethan's laugh was warm. "I was at the game when they threw him out for stepping on the umpire's toes, spitting on him, then punching him. They not only threw him out of the game but out of the National League. He was later reinstated because the fans demanded it. The little escapade cost him a wad of cash in fines."

"Wait until Todd hears that you were at that game. You'll be his hero."

"Great. That's probably as close as I'll ever get to being one."

Doctor Forbes came to the door. "Come in, Ethan. We'll go over the information about the vaccinations." Ethan went into the house.

"Why don't you like him?" Jesse asked.

"I just don't. He's too sure of himself."

"You acted as if he were . . . were —"

"The Looker? Maybe he is."

"I don't believe it. He's just a nice man. He might be fun."

"Not to me. I'm going in. I need to prepare for tomorrow's lessons."

Jesse watched Pauline escape into the house and wished with all her heart that there was something she could do to ease her friend's fear.

Lessons with Jody were going well. He and Pauline had carried a table out to the barn — out from under Mrs. Lindstrom's eagle eye, as Pauline put it. Each morning Jody worked for a couple of hours in the yard before lessons. After dinner, they studied for a couple more hours. Then Jody quietly disappeared.

Several evenings a week Todd slipped away after dinner to go to Ike's garage. He came home before it was completely dark with greasy hands that he washed at the pump. Once Jesse brought out clean clothes so that he could leave the greasy ones in the wash house. She wanted badly to ask him if Wade had been there, but she didn't; and although she listened for any news Todd might volunteer, she heard nothing about Wade.

After a few days, when her father failed to mention the scene in the parlor, Jesse realized that Mrs. Lindstrom had not told him. She debated again about telling him herself but decided against it. He would be put in the middle again and have to take sides, but surely he wouldn't have approved of the housekeeper's slapping Todd.

Then something happened that caused Jesse to stand in the door and wait for her father to return from the depot, where he had supervised the loading of enough smallpox vaccine to vaccinate the entire county.

"Papa, I've got to talk to you," she said as soon as he had hung his hat on the rack.

"What's happened?"

Jesse closed her eyes for an instant. "I had promised myself that I'd not complain about Mrs. Lindstrom, but this time she has gone too far."

"What has she done?"

"She dumped out all the canned food that I

brought back from the hill country. Dumped every bit of it in a slop bucket and had Todd take it down to Mr. Adams' hogs. When I asked her why she did it, she said it wasn't clean. I'm not only angry, Papa, I'm furious! That food was as clean as any she cooks. Mrs. Bailey may live in a shack, but it's spotless. The Gordons are as clean as anyone I've seen in town. The Prestons are dirt-poor, but Mrs. Preston is neat and clean with her person and her cooking. That woman even threw away the dried pumpkin and peaches I bought from Mrs. Arnold." Jesse paused to take a deep breath. "Papa, those people have pride. They sacrificed to give up that food as payment, and she threw it away as if it were so much garbage."

"Jesse," Hollis took his spectacles out of the case and put them on. "Mrs. Lindstrom comes from a different background from ours. She doesn't understand the ways here. To her the people up there are trash like the ones in the slums in the cities of the world. I can understand her reluctance to use the home-canned food."

"Papa, why didn't she tell one of us her concerns about the food? I never got sick eating at the tables up there. If she didn't want to use it she could have just let it sit. She won't be here forever." Jesse's eyes were steady when she looked at her father and added, "Or will she?"

"Jesse," he said tiredly. "You're over-reacting to this. I agree that she shouldn't have dumped the food without discussing it with you, but she didn't do it maliciously."

Jesse looked into his face and suddenly realized that he looked strained and tired and old. She went to him where he sat in the chair and, bending, put her arms around him as she had done in the days following Dora's death.

"I'm sorry, Papa. I shouldn't have bothered you with this." She patted his shoulder and moved away. "I take it the vaccine came in."

"Yes. I asked the freighter to bring it over. I didn't take the buggy, and there were other supplies too heavy to carry."

"We'll have two busy Saturdays. Pauline has volunteered to help with the paperwork so that I can help with the vaccinations."

"Ralph put a good-sized notice on the front page of the *Gazette*. I hope it brings the people out. Your idea of a donation box is a good one, Jess. The folks who can pay will donate. Those who can't won't be embarrassed. It will bring out the ones who can't afford to pay."

"Jody should be vaccinated."

"Of course. We'll do it here in the office."

"He's a strange boy. Sometimes I forget that he's colored."

"How's he doing?"

"Pauline says he's smarter than all get out — soaks up everything she tells him and asks questions."

"Why is she teaching him in the barn?"

"The boy is proud as a peacock, Papa. He won't come into the house. Mrs. Lindstrom chased him from the doorstep with the broom the first time he came with my message."

"I didn't know that."

"He stays around until sundown and then disappears. I wonder if he runs all the way back to Mr. Simmer's place."

"I doubt it," Hollis said drily. "Hand me the ledger, Sis. I've got to write down some things before I forget them."

As usual after supper, Jesse and Pauline sat on the porch. This evening they watched Todd and one of his friends play "kick the can."

"What a wonderful way to wear out your shoes — and yourself." Pauline had pulled her hair to the top of her head and tied it with a ribbon. Now she wiped the back of her neck with her handkerchief.

"They're old shoes. We saved them for just this purpose. When he wore a hole right through the sole, we put a piece of cardboard inside. That's probably worn through by now."

"It's awfully hot. Do you want to go for a walk?"

"Maybe later. I'll get us some lemonade."

"Sit still. I'll get it." She leaned toward Jesse and whispered, "Old Ghost-face walked uptown. I can pilfer some ice from the icebox."

"Oh, you! How am I ever going to teach Susan and Todd to be refined with you around?"

Pauline was still laughing as she left the porch. She was back to her old flamboyancy with one exception: when Ethan Bredlow was around, she turned cold, and when he persisted in his attempts to get her to talk, she became downright rude.

Jesse rocked gently in the swing, one foot tucked under her, the other touching the porch floor. The scent of honeysuckle was in the air. Earlier in the evening she'd seen a hummingbird dipping its long beak into the blossoms to drink the sweet nectar.

Her senses swarmed with details of her last meeting with Wade. She had only to close her eyes to see his sculptured features: high cheekbones, magnificently squared jaw, and his forest-green eyes framed with thick dark lashes. His eyes were like deep pools, clear and fathomless, as though they reached to the very center of him. She had lived over and over the time they spent alone in the buggy, recalled every word and every touch. She relived the kisses they shared, the raw pleasure of his warm, vibrant body pressed to hers, the tender expression on his hard, dark face just before he kissed her.

She half-hoped he would never come to call. It would be an ordeal for her as well as for him. He was a hill man and she a town girl. They had absolutely nothing in common. To get more involved with him would only mean heartache for her.

Jesse opened her eyes.

Wade was coming around the end of the porch.

Her foot stopped pushing the swing. She blinked. He seemed to have materialized out of her imagination except that he was wearing a white stiff-collared shirt with a string tie and dark dress pants. She watched him walk toward her, unable to keep her foolish heart from fluttering like a caged wild bird. He removed his hat as he stepped up onto the porch. Her imagination could not have conjured the look of longing in his eyes or the expression of uncertainty on his face.

"Wade." Her throat tightened as she said his name. She suddenly yearned to tell him how glad she was to see him, although a minute ago she had hoped he wouldn't come.

"Good evening. Is this a convenient time to call?"

"Yes, of course." She removed her numbed leg from beneath her and straightened her skirts. "Come sit down."

He sat down beside her, holding his hat on his lap. "It's been a long time since I've sat in a porch swing."

"I sit out here for a while each evening."

The tension in his expression and the set of his shoulders told her how uncomfortable he was. Her mind searched for a way to put him at ease.

"Have you changed your mind?" he asked with quiet emotion.

"About what?" The unexpected words stirred confusion in her.

"About . . . wanting me to call?" The agony in his eyes sent a quiver through her heart.

"Of course not. Whatever gave you that idea?"

"I came by one evening and you . . . already had a caller. He was sitting there on the rail talking to you and Miss Anthony."

"That was Ethan Bredlow. He works for the newspaper and came to see Papa." She clutched his arm. "I wish you had stayed and met him."

His hand covered hers and squeezed it so hard that it hurt. He could have broken it and she would not have cared.

"This past week has been pure hell. I wanted to see you so damn bad that I could hardly wait. I was tempted to come and stand in the shadows and look at you."

"What a lovely thing to say." Her eyes were luminous, her lips trembling.

"This is strange new ground for me, Jesse. I've never courted a woman before."

"Didn't you consult with Grandpa Lester?" she asked with mock seriousness, then laughed when he smiled.

He couldn't seem to say anything. He stared into her jewel-like blue-gray eyes, which were filled with what could only be the pleasure of being in his company. His breath caught and his heart almost stopped at the thought of it. Could he really be sitting with her like this — on her front porch — in Harpersville?

"Jesse, Jesse, Jesse." He whispered her name over and over, his voice deep, resonant with longing. "I was deathly afraid to come even though you said I would be welcome."

For a moment she saw old memories, old hurts in the eyes that devoured her face. The hurt reached across the years, and she felt the pain that must have been in his boyish heart the day his father was hanged in the town square.

This great oak tree of a man was actually

trembling beneath her touch. He had come down out of the hills and into the town that had rejected him and his family for years dressed in what he thought would be acceptable to come courting. He was so vulnerable — baring his heart, his pride, offering to fit himself into what he thought she wanted him to be. His willingness to do so filled her heart with joy.

With unsteady fingers Jesse reached for the string tie and slowly pulled it from under the collar of his shirt. Her eyes held his captive while she wrapped it around her fingers and stuffed it in his breast pocket. Slowly she unbuttoned the collar on his shirt and then the second button that revealed his sun-browned throat. With utmost care, to prevent scratching his neck, she pulled free the detachable stiff high collar.

"Now . . . you look more like . . . like the Wade who met me in the woods and told me he was not the least bit disappointed in me." Her breath caught in her throat as she watched his eyes become softer, greener.

"You remembered that." He managed a dry whisper.

"I remember every word."

He fitted his palm to hers, gently threaded his large, calloused fingers through her slender soft ones, then curled them down over her hand. She placed her other hand over his as if to lock them together. They smiled into each other's eyes, then looked down at the symbol of their joining.

"Shall we walk?"

She nodded. "I know the perfect place."

They walked down the steps, his arm holding her close to his side. Feeling as light as a billowing cloud, he pulled her hand into the crook of his arm and heaved a trembling sigh of relief. At last he had found the part of himself that had been lost for such a long time.

Pauline came out of the house with two large glasses of lemonade. The first thing she noticed was the hat in the swing, then the stiff white collar beside it. She was puzzled until she saw Jesse and Wade strolling slowly down the walk, his head bent toward hers, hers tilted to his.

*Land-a-goshen! The hill man has finally come to call. The gossips will have their tongues going before dark.*

She placed one glass of lemonade on the porch railing and, sipping from the other, sat down in the swing and rocked gently. She was glad, so glad for Jesse. Her friend had been utterly miserable for the past few days even though she had not mentioned Wade's name. Pauline was reasonably sure that Jesse had not wanted to fall in love with the hill man. Yet, there the two of them were, together.

Pauline's feet continued to push the swing as weepy waves of loneliness seeped into her heart.

# CHAPTER
## • 15 •

*A*s if she were walking on air, Jesse followed the path with Wade at her side. In the distance she heard the sound of the tin can bouncing on the brick street and her brother's shouts to his friends. When a topless buggy passed by, the horse's iron shoes ringing on the brick paving, Jesse waved her hand automatically, indifferent to the gaping occupants and the heads that turned to gawk at them.

Nothing seemed real.

"How are Delilah and her family?"

"The pups are venturing out of the barn on their own."

"Todd had the time of his life with them. He told Papa you had goats. I didn't see them."

"One goat. Her name is —"

"— Don't tell me her name is New Year, or Easter."

"Would you believe Thanksgiving?"

"No! Did you or Jody name her?"

"That's what he wanted to name her, but I put

249

my foot down. Her name is Puddin'.'"

"His favorite food, no doubt."

"All food is his favorite. His stomach is like a bottomless pit."

"He's a growing boy."

They followed the walk to the end of the block and turned toward the creek that curved around the town. The sun had completed its journey across the sky and was a red globe sinking on the western horizon. The two of them could have been any place and at any time during the history of mankind as they continued to walk, aware only of each other.

Suddenly a big green horsefly buzzed across their faces. Wade lifted a hand to shoo it away. Then a horde of mosquitoes descended on them. He turned Jesse around to face him. One had settled on her cheek. He quickly brushed it aside.

"This is the wrong time of day to be down by the creek. The mosquitoes will be as thick as hair on a dog's back."

"I know another place." Jesse tugged on his arm to turn him around. "The ball park. The purple martins feast on the mosquitoes there."

"Sweetheart," he drew the word out into a long, soft caress, "I can't hold you and kiss you in the baseball park."

Jesse felt her heart jump out of rhythm. "You can . . . after dark." They started walking again.

"I don't know if I can wait that long."

"Oh, Wade." His name came shivering and sweet from her throat. "What is this wonderful thing that has happened to us?"

"I know what's struck me. I've fallen tail over teakettle in love with you, something I never thought I'd do."

"Didn't you *want* to fall in love?"

"I never thought it would be something for me. I figured someday I'd meet a woman who would be pleasant company, one I could respect, who would keep my house, give me children. Every man likes to think he has left something of himself to mark his time on this earth. I've never been loved by anyone other than Granny and my pa, to a certain extent. I had no idea that loving a woman would consume me until all I could think of was her, all I lived for was to see her again. At times, Jesse love, I was sick with longing to be with you."

Jesse didn't say anything. Her throat was clogged, her eyes misty. She breathed deeply in an attempt to get her emotions under control.

"I . . . wish it was dark," she whispered between quick breaths.

The town barber, cleaning his flower bed, paused, leaned on his hoe and watched the couple approach.

"Miss Jesse —" He had a puzzled look on his face.

"Evening, Mr. Baker," Jesse called.

Widow Armstrong, who had lost her husband during the war and never remarried, saw the couple walking arm in arm down the walk and clicked her tongue in disapproval.

The butter maker and his wife, sitting on a porch, gawked.

"What in the world is Miss Jesse doin' strollin' along, bold as brass, with that hellion from the hills?"

The wife sniffed. "I swan to goodness. What's the world comin' to? Young people now days don't have no sense of propriety a'tall. I never thought it of 'er. The doctor better watch 'er. She'll be having a woods colt, sure as shootin'."

Jesse and Wade strolled on, oblivious of the stir they were creating by being together.

The ball park was a field at the edge of town. Rows of plank seats stretched down two sides of the diamond. Jesse and Wade walked across the infield to the far side and sat down — close so that her shoulder was tucked behind his arm.

"Do you like baseball?" Jesse wiggled her fingers until they were laced with his.

"Yeah. Jody and I go over to Coon Rapids and watch a game now and then."

"There'll be a game here on Sunday." The invitation was in her voice, in the eyes that looked into his.

"Sweetheart . . . are you sure you want me to come?"

"I was never more sure in my life."

"If we're seen together publicly, your standing in this town will hit rock-bottom."

"We've already been seen together publicly. I could almost hear the tongues wagging as we walked down the street. As far as my standing in this town is concerned, I don't feel the people here have the right to choose my friends, or — my young man for that matter. I'm my own person, not an extension of this town."

Wade's arm slipped around her. "Is it dark enough?" he whispered, nuzzling her ear.

"I . . . don't care about that either." She placed her cheek against his shoulder and tilted her face to his.

"You're so . . . pretty and . . . sweet," he breathed against her mouth, his voice thick yet full of wonder.

His lips moved across hers slowly and gently, as if to savor every tiny line. His arms held her tightly against him. Then a little noise came from his throat and, drawing her closer still, he let gentleness give way to greed and his kisses became harder, more demanding. His mouth was moist and firm, forcing hers to open so that his tongue could wander over her soft inner lips before venturing deeper.

Jesse ached for him, heat gathering in the sensitive areas of her body and giving rise to an urgency that was strange and new to her. She responded to his kisses eagerly. His hand moved to her breast and closed possessively over it. His fingers sent delicious shivers through her. His kisses were breathtaking, hot and voracious. His hand kneaded and caressed her breast, her waist, her hips. He was hungry for her — starving for her. He began to tremble violently and moved his mouth to her cheek.

"Oh, love . . . oh, love. One sweet bite of you calls for another. I must stop while I can or I'll have you right here on the grass." An outpouring of love rushed in to meet their passion.

He got to his feet and reached to pull her up beside him. "Let's walk." His voice was rough. "I'm sorry —"

Jesse wrapped her arms around his waist. "You've nothing to be sorry for. I'm not a naive young girl. I know about the strong desires of a man . . . and a woman." She moved her hand up to his cheeks and forced him to look into her eyes. "I've never loved like this before. But I know that it's sometimes . . . painful to have unfulfilled desires."

"I want you so badly." He whispered as if he were talking around a huge lump in his throat. "I've dreamed of you in my house, in my bed, having my children; I've thought about growing old with you, loving you. But . . . it's not fair to ask you to give up your life here and share mine. You'd never be welcome in this town again. And your father — he's a respected doctor, mine was hanged in the town square." Jesse had never heard such anguish in a man's voice.

"Why don't you ask me if I want to share your life? Ask me and let me decide."

"You mean — ?"

"Ask me."

"Would you" — he swallowed painfully — "be willing to live with me . . . in the hills?"

"Only if you marry me."

"Oh, love —" He grabbed her, hugging her to him, lifting her off the ground. His big hard body was still trembling. He bent his head and buried his face in her neck. "I just want to . . . pull you inside me and take you wherever I go."

"You'd get tired of that," she whispered happily. "I can be stubborn and as irritating as a prickly pear at times."

She held him for a long while and smoothed the black hair at the nape of his neck. Gradually his taut body relaxed, and a strange quiet came to both of them. She held him like a tired child, as she sometimes did her brother Todd, and stroked his head lovingly, wishing she could protect him from all the problems that plagued him, wishing she could keep him safe and secure here in her arms.

Wade stirred, raised his head, and looked into her eyes, blue and shimmering and beautiful. His were filled with love. He kissed her lips, gently, reverently.

"I don't deserve you," he whispered in a softly slurred voice.

"Yes, you do. And I deserve you. You'll never be anything less than my love, the one person in all the world I want to spend my life with. I never thought I'd say that. Just a little while ago I was thinking of our different backgrounds and had decided that you had changed your mind about wanting to court me."

Wade inhaled deeply and let the air escape slowly from his lips. "I was afraid. You're so beautiful, sweetheart. Not only your face but inside you as well. I'll be the luckiest man in the world to have you by my side. I know what you're giving up. Oh, God, I hope you'll not be sorry someday." He hugged her close and buried his lips in her hair. "I'll love you and cherish you and protect you with my life. I swear it."

Jesse laughed with pure exaltation. It was all Wade could do to keep himself from lifting her in his arms and carrying her away. Her face seemed to glow with happiness. She lifted her lips, sweet and softly parted, to his. His kiss was gentle and reverent, for she was infinitely precious to him.

They began to walk.

"We have so much to talk about. I want to know all about you and I want you to know all about me," she whispered.

"You've probably heard all the bad things about me and there's very little good I can tell you. I have what I consider a great deal of money. I want to tell you about it."

They sat back down on the bench.

He told her about going to the rescue of an old man and his wife who were attacked by thieves on the wharf in New York City.

"The next morning the couple's servant came to the rooming house where I was staying. I've no idea how he found me. The man gave me a certified check for twenty-five thousand dollars. There was a note from the old man attached. The old man said for me to please accept the gift and to invest some of it in telephone and telegraph stock, and by the time I was his age I would have money to give away too. It was signed Andrew Carnegie."

"My goodness. He's a famous man."

"I took his advice, Jesse. We'll have enough money for most anything we want."

Jesse began to laugh. "I'd like to see Boyd Harper's face when he learns you have that much money. I take it you don't have it in his bank."

Wade grinned. "You take it right, lady. It's in banks in Knoxville and Atlanta."

"Oh, Wade. You can send Jody to a good school."

"Mr. Carnegie was a large benefactor of Tuskegee Institute. After reading about him and Booker T. Washington, I'd like for Jody to go there."

"I'm proud of you, Wade. You've got a heart as big as the ocean. You just don't want anyone to know it. Look what you're doing for Jody. It takes courage to go against the prejudices of your neighbors and friends."

"I want to see him grow up and not only be able to fend for himself but to do something for his people."

"You're very fond of him, aren't you?"

"Yes. He was like a frightened little wildcat when I found him in that cave. He was hungry and sick but still he spit and hissed when I carried him out. There wasn't anyone in the world that cared if he lived or died."

"You cared."

"Yes, I cared because he reminded me of myself when I was that age. But I was luckier than Jody. I had my granny when I was young. Then all too quick she was gone and I was alone."

"It didn't matter to you that he was a darkie."

"He was a human being. I've been around the world a couple of times and met people of all colors. A sailor, so black you could only see the whites of his eyes, jumped into a fight and risked his life to save mine. A Chinese hid me to keep me from being captured by the captain of a ship who was afraid I would report him for carrying dangerous contraband. The color of a man's skin does not keep him from being any better or any worse than his fellow man. I've never understood why white people think they are superior because their skin is white. There are no-good whites just as there are no-good Negroes."

"Papa says people of any color bleed red blood. I think you and Papa are ahead of your time. Papa heard Booker T. Washington speak at the Atlanta Exposition and came home saying that the only hope for the Negroes was through education, industrial skills, intelligent farming, thrift, and applying good manners and morals."

"I want to go down to Tuskegee and look the place over. Jody needs to stay there and be with other Negroes who want an education. Because of the way he was treated when he was very young, he doesn't have a very high opinion of them. He thinks all Negroes are stupid, but him."

Jesse hugged his arm tightly. "Wade Simmer,

you are a good man and I'll be so proud to be your wife."

Wade's heart swelled with pride, yet he knew it was not going to be easy. Would she be able to weather the hostility their joining would generate? In the years to come would she become resentful because of it? Most of all, would he be able to live up to what she expected of him?

Dear God, he hoped so.

Ethan Bredlow strolled up the walk to the Forbes house. Pauline was so lost in her own thoughts that he was already coming up the steps when she became aware of him, and it was too late to escape into the house.

"Good evening, Miss Pauline. I can't believe my luck in finding you alone here on the porch." He picked up the glass of lemonade from the porch railing. "Is this for me?"

"If you want it. It's probably got a dead fly floating around in it."

"You hope, huh?" He peered into the glass. "Nope. Not even a gnat. Mind if I sit down?"

"Suit yourself."

"I could sit on the porch rail, but there's plenty of room in the swing, and I promise not to pounce on you."

"Just try it, mister, and you'll get a hatpin in the belly."

"Ohhhh . . . It hurts to even think of it. Whose hat and collar?"

"They belong to a friend of Jesse's. If you came

to see the doctor, I'll tell him you're here."

"Don't get up. I didn't come to see the doctor. I came to see you."

"Me? I thought I made it clear I'm not interested."

"Yeah, you did, but it puzzles me why you're so hostile to me."

"Glory be! I'm probably the first woman you've met who's not smitten by your dazzling smile."

"You noticed — my smile?"

"How could I not notice, for heaven's sake? You grin like the Cheshire cat in *Alice in Wonderland*."

"And that's the reason you dislike me?"

"Only partly. You're the kind of man who sets my teeth on edge. You turn on the charm and expect women to fall at your feet. I've no desire to be one of those who feed your conceit."

"It's that obvious? Hummm . . . I never thought about women falling at my feet. It would be fantastic, though, wouldn't it?"

"You're impossible!"

"You're as pretty as a dish of strawberry ice cream and about as cold."

"Your tongue must be attached in the middle. It flaps at both ends."

"That's a good one. Mind if I use it sometimes?"

"Feel free to use it whenever you wish. It may get you a good hard sock in the jaw."

"Will you go with me to the Chautauqua over in Frederick on Sunday? William Jennings Bryan is going to talk on 'A Conquering Nation.' "

" 'A Conquering Nation'? That sounds about as

dry as chalk. I'm going to the ball game with Jesse and the kids."

"That sounds better yet. Mind if I come too?"

"I couldn't very well keep you away."

"Good. I'll be by about two o'clock."

"I didn't mean with me, *Romeo*," Pauline said heatedly.

"Oh, shoot! I thought you did." A buggy stopped in front of the house. "Looks like you've got company."

"It's only old . . . Mrs. Lindstrom coming back from her meeting. She got herself invited to serve on the church bazaar committee."

"You mean old Ghost-face," he whispered.

In spite of herself, Pauline giggled. "You've heard?"

"Yeah. Fits her, doesn't it?"

"Where'd she come from anyway?"

"Who knows. She talks out of both sides of her mouth the way you do. You'd make a good pair."

"You don't like her?"

"I can hardly stand the woman."

"Hmmm . . . that's interesting. The ladies in town seem to think she's right up to snuff."

"The ladies in town don't have to live in the same house with her."

"You don't *have* to stay here, do you?"

"I'm staying here for the summer. Don't ask me why." She turned to frown at him. "You're as nosy as old Ghost-face."

Mrs. Lindstrom waved a cheery good-bye to the man and woman in the buggy and came up the walk to the house.

"I didn't know you were expecting a caller, Pauline."

"Good evening, ma'am." Ethan got to his feet. "Ethan Bredlow from the *Gazette*. I met you the other night when I came to interview the doctor."

"I read the article. It would seem to me that you could have given the doctor more credit. He's the only one in town and he works from daylight to dark." She lifted her brows and looked at Pauline. "Is Susan home?"

"She's at Mary Sue's. Mary Sue and Jeff will walk her home."

"She didn't ask permission to stay out until after dark."

"She asked her father," Pauline replied drily.

"Oh, well, in that case — I'll go in and have a glass of lemonade with Jesse."

"Jesse isn't here either."

"Oh, dear. I hope she isn't traipsing around after dark by herself."

"No. She has an escort."

"Who, for goodness sake? Edsel came to fetch his mother. He and Roberta gave me a ride home."

"Ask Jesse. She's coming up the walk now."

Louella turned to peer into the near darkness. "Well, my heavens! Has she lost her wits? What in the world is she doing with *him?*"

"I don't think that's any business of yours, ma'am," Pauline said testily.

"I wonder if the doctor knows. My, my! I can't believe he'd approve of his daughter consorting with hill trash." Louella turned and went into the house.

"Old busybody," Pauline murmured.

Jesse and Wade came up the steps, Jesse holding tightly to Wade's arm.

"Hello, Ethan. It's nice to see you. Have you met Wade Simmer?"

"Well . . . no. Howdy, Wade." Ethan held out his hand.

"Ethan Bredlow works for the paper," Jesse explained as the two men shook hands.

"Howdy," Wade said, then, "Howdy, Miss Pauline."

"Mr. Simmer." Pauline's nod and smile did not go unobserved by Ethan.

"I dropped by to ask Pauline to go to the ball game on Sunday." Ethan sat back down in the swing.

"You did not," Pauline declared and stood. "You asked me to go to the Chautauqua, and I said I was going to the ball game."

"Honey, you're just being picky." He gave her a cocky grin.

"Don't honey me, you . . . masher. And get yourself out of the swing so Wade and Jesse can have it."

"No, don't bother," Wade said. "I've got to go to Ike's and get my horse. It's not wise to be wandering around Harpersville at night. I might be mistaken for The Looker."

"I'll go with you, Simmer, unless Pauline begs me to stay." Ethan cocked a brow at the teacher, who tilted her chin with indignation.

"Don't hold your breath," she said tartly, then scowled.

"I think I may have cracked the ice around her heart, Miss Jesse," Ethan said good-naturedly. "At least she's talking to me."

"I'll be glad for your company, Bredlow." Wade drew Jesse toward the corner of the wraparound porch. "Give me a minute with my lady."

*My lady.* Jesse loved to hear him say that.

"You'll come Sunday?" she asked as soon as they were alone.

"A team of mules couldn't keep me away."

"Saturday Papa and I will be at the school giving the smallpox vaccinations. The next Saturday we'll be at Fronys' store. I hope the hill people will turn out."

"You may be surprised. They're not all like Otis Merfeld. They love their children. But enough about that. I need a kiss to last me until I see you again."

The tenderness of his lips on hers bespoke a new priority, putting love ahead of all other desires. They kissed as if they had not kissed before — soft kisses, loving kisses. He cradled her face in his hands.

"I love you." His voice was quiet. They stood pressed together, heart to heart, thigh to thigh, toe to toe.

"I love you too," Jesse said and meant it with all her heart. "I'll look forward to Sunday."

"Be careful. I'll worry about you until that man is caught."

"I'll worry about you. I'm glad Ethan will go with you to Ike's."

"Bye, sweetheart."

"Bye, till Sunday."

Jesse watched him and Ethan until they rounded the corner of the porch and walked down the drive toward the alley where they would take a shortcut across the field to Ike's garage.

"Well?" Pauline said when Jesse came to sink down beside her in the swing.

"He loves me and wants to marry me." Jesse hugged herself with her arms and leaned her head against the high-backed swing.

"You've just discovered that he's crazy about you?" Pauline sighed. "Anyone with half an eye could see that when we were at his place. He couldn't keep his eyes off you."

"I'm not going to tell Papa yet. I'll not leave Susan and Todd here with Lou . . . el . . . la." She drew the housekeeper's name out the way Susan sometimes did. "Wade will understand when I tell him."

"I keep wondering how she got in so tightly with the Harpers in such a short time."

"She's probably convinced them that she's a quality lady who has fallen on hard times. But I can't see Roberta Harper hobnobbing with a housekeeper." With a toe on the floor, Jesse started the swing moving gently.

"I bet she's told them that she's a friend of the family and come to take care of her *dear* friend's children."

"How did you and Ethan get along?"

"Like a cat and a dog."

"Which was the cat?" Jesse laughed. "He's quite a charmer."

"That's the trouble. He could charm the bark off a tree."

"Are you still worried about . . . The Looker?"

" 'Course I am. I don't think I'll ever feel safe again."

"It wasn't Ethan. He hasn't been here long enough."

"I realize now that it couldn't have been him. Besides, he'd not do anything incognito. He's too much of an exhibitionist."

"I kind of like him. I hope he and Wade can be friends. Wade needs friends here in Harpersville."

The familiar squeak of the swing chains filled the silence. The thoughts of the two women were of the men who had just left them.

Jesse felt as if she were riding on a cloud. Wade loved her! All the time she was worrying that he had changed his mind about her, he was worrying about calling on her. He had actually come and left when he had seen Ethan on the porch.

*Darling Wade, you are my heart.*

Pauline's thoughts were on Ethan. In another time before the attack she might have been flattered by his attention. He was good-looking, fun, and charming. That was it, she thought as her mind mulled over the things he had said; he was *too* charming. It was as if he were using his charm to hide something. What could it be?

# CHAPTER
## • 16 •

*E*than walked alongside Wade. With an experienced eye he sized up the man. Although Ethan could match Wade stride for stride, Wade was taller and more heavily built. Obviously, he was a hard, tough, powerful man who was well able to take care of himself. He radiated energy and strength. Ethan had met others like him who seemed to be both the hunter and the hunted. Their senses were alert to a thousand possible dangers.

As they rounded the barn behind the doctor's house, Wade paused and looked in every direction before he started walking again. He was a careful man.

"I've been wanting to meet you, Simmer."

"Yeah? Why?"

"To see if you were the hellion everyone says you are."

"Yeah," Wade said again, his eyes scanning the landscape from side to side.

"You expecting someone to jump you?"

"Maybe. Can't tell about these yahoos. They'd not do it in daylight."

"Ralph said he warned you about Secory."

"He left word with Ike."

"Most folks think you're the fellow who's looking at the women."

"Yeah? They can think what they want."

"Who do you think it is?"

"How the hell would I know? I just know it isn't me."

"It isn't me either. I hit town only a few weeks ago."

"Rules you out, doesn't it?"

Suddenly Wade threw his arm out in front of Ethan to stop him. He tilted his head to listen. His keen ears had picked up a sound. An instant later he knew what it was. A horse was snorting and fighting. *His horse.* He began to run. Ethan kept pace with him.

"What is it?"

"Be quiet. Somebody messing with my horse."

When they reached Ike's garage, Wade sped around to the back and jumped over a rail fence. In seconds he was on the man who, with a cruel thin rope on the nose of the horse, was trying to pull him to the gate. Wade's fists lashed out with lightning speed and knocked the man to the ground. The frightened horse reared when the man lost his grip on the rope, his hooves coming down within inches of his tormenter. Wade grabbed the horse's mane, held his hand in front of his nose so he could smell him, and began to talk soothingly.

268

Recognizing his master, the horse quieted.

"God-a-mighty, that bastard almost killed me!" The man swore and scrambled to his feet. He reeled toward the fence and ran headlong into another fist. Ethan's.

"If there's anything that gets my dander up," Ethan said calmly, "it's a son of a bitch who abuses a horse." He hit him again and blood splattered.

Wade grabbed the man by the shirt at the back of his neck and pushed him toward the gate. "Move," he snarled, "while you can."

He hauled him into Ike's garage with only his toes touching the ground. A lantern hung over the grinder where Ike was working on a piece of metal. Wade's eyes quickly scanned the room, then turned to the man he held. He seldom forgot a face, and he had seen this man unloading a dray wagon the day he had talked to Marshal Wright.

"In the hills we hang a man for horse-stealing." His voice was low and sinister.

"I . . . wasn't stealing him."

"It sure as hell looked like it to me."

"Me too," Ethan said. "Let's hang him."

"I was . . . only goin' to turn him loose. I wasn't stealing. I . . . wasn't."

"You'd better talk fast, mister." Ethan jerked his head toward Wade. "This man is one mean son of a bitch. I don't know if Ike and I can keep him from stringing you up."

"They . . . told me to turn the horse loose so ya'd have to walk home." His eyes left Wade and pleaded with Ethan. "That's all I meant to do, mister. I swear it."

"Who's they?" Wade demanded and shook the man like a wet mop.

"I . . . I . . . I — The . . . the bridge crew. Don't shake me! Ouch! Ah . . . my neck —"

"Where are they waiting?"

"Bridge, by the creamery."

Wade opened Ike's door and shoved the man outside. "Go tell 'em I'll be along in an hour." Before he could get the door shut the man was running.

"I never heard a thin', Wade. I was workin' on the grinder." Ike was a small man with a sun-wrinkled face, squinty blue eyes and hair that had receded to the middle of his head. His hands and his clothes were covered with grease.

"That's all right, Ike. Where's Jody?"

"In the back room readin' or sleepin'. He'd not hear nothin' either with the grinder goin'."

"It's a good thing. He'd have run out there and made matters worse." Both Ike and Wade looked questioningly at Ethan.

Ethan held his hands up palms out. "You're thinkin' I'll turn the boy in for being in Harpersville after dark?"

Ike spoke. "I don't know ya, mister. I don't know what ya'll be doin'."

"It's a stupid law that wouldn't hold up in court. I'm sure Marshal Wright knows it. If he doesn't, I have contacts that will make sure he knows it damn quick."

Ethan's manner had changed so completely that Wade looked at him with a puzzled frown. Gone was the flippant, devil-may-care look. Ethan's face had sobered and a telling, knowledgeable light had come into his eyes as he weighed his words. He was getting his point across without giving anything away. Wade knew instantly that there was more to this man than the image he presented.

"Then we have your word?"

"You have it."

"Good enough," Wade said.

A moment later Ethan's charming facade emerged once again as he looked over the motor that sat on two blocks.

"What's it for? A motor car?"

"Might be," Ike said.

"*The Literary Digest* says motor cars won't catch on."

Ike snorted. "They ain't done too bad in the six years since Ford built the first one." His laugh was a dry cackle. "I'd a give a penny to a been there when they found out they'd built the thing too wide to get it out the door." He wiped his greasy hands on a rag and dropped it on the bench beside the motor. "We might put this'n on a carriage and drive 'er up and down in front of Harper's bank, huh Wade?"

Wade clasped his friend on the shoulder. "Sounds good to me, Ike." He looked toward a curtain covering a doorway and saw it move. "You can come out, Jody. Ethan knows you're here."

"Yeah. He's the smarty what works at the paper." Jody emerged and stood with his arms crossed over his chest. "Be big news, NIGGER FOUND IN TOWN AFTER DARK."

"Yeah?" Ethan looked the boy up and down. "A bigger story would be SMART-MOUTHED NIGGER BEING TUTORED BY MISS PAULINE ANTHONY."

"How'd ya know that, *toad?*"

"That's enough, Jody," Wade said sharply and turned to Ethan. "How did you find out?"

Ethan shrugged. "Wasn't hard. Doctor hired the boy when there were plenty of boys in town who would have been glad to have the job. Teacher stays with the Forbeses and disappears in the barn with an armload of books every morning about ten o'clock. Susan or Todd takes lunch basket to the barn. And you know what? Jody is nowhere in sight. It doesn't take a ton of brains to figure out what's going on."

"You've nosed around and found out quite a lot in the short time you've been here."

"My job is hunting the news."

"So that's your interest in this, huh, Bredlow? A story for the paper?" The expression on Wade's face was anything but friendly now.

"My interest in this has nothing to do with the paper. It's purely personal. Miss Pauline Anthony." Ethan grinned and to his astonishment he felt a flash of heat cover the skin of his face. "She's something I've been looking for all my life."

"That's all?" Wade asked, not quite believing.

272

"It's plenty. You of all people should understand that." Ethan's eyes caught Wade's and held them. The unspoken words about him and Jesse sparked between them.

Wade nodded. "You know she'll lose her job if she's caught. Harper controls the school board."

"It won't be me that tells. If anyone does, it'll be the housekeeper."

"Doctor Forbes assured me that she would keep quiet."

"Why would she keep quiet if it's to her advantage to get in good with the Harpers?"

"Because she doesn't want to get in bad with the Forbeses. She works for them after all. If we can rock along here a few more weeks, though, Jody and I will be going down to Tuskegee to see if we can get him into a boarding school. We'll talk to the track and field coaches. Jody'll need training if he's going to try out for the Olympic team a couple years from now."

"He's that fast, huh? The 1904 games will be in Saint Louis. I'd like to see him run, but will he be allowed to enter the races?"

"A few good men are working on it."

Ethan looked at Jody and saw resentment in the eyes that stared back at him.

"You've nothing to fear from me, boy."

"I ain't a feared a you. I ain't a feared a no man — nigger or white."

"Good for you. I can't say that. I've been scared out of my wits by colored *and* white men at some

273

time or other." He grinned cockily at Wade. "Well, shall we go tackle that bunch down by the creamery?"

Now Wade grinned. "Let 'em wait. I'll cross the creek a mile back and go home by way of a deer trail up through the woods. There's a hungry bunch of mosquitoes down by the bridge. After they've chewed on those fellows for a while, they should be ready to give it up and clear out."

Ethan smiled broadly. "Good. I wasn't in the mood for a fight anyhow. I've got on my courtin' clothes." He gave them a jaunty salute. "See you at the ball game," he said before he went out the door.

Beneath the bridge that spanned the creek four men huddled, fighting the swarms of mosquitoes that surrounded them.

"Goddamn. These sons-a-bitches is eatin' me up. Let's get outta here. He ain't comin'."

"You said he'd be here in an hour." John Secory, a big, burly redheaded man with a hot temper stood and peered over the bank. "I already got the wire stretched across the bridge."

"It's what he told me to say. Lord-a-mercy, I think my nose is busted."

"It's what ya get for gettin' caught."

"How'd I know that sissy-britches from the newspaper'd be with him?" The man tried to protect his face from the mosquitoes with his shirt collar. "He might be a comin' with him."

"Let him come," Secory growled. "Any one

274

of us can handle that dressed-up dude with one arm tied behind."

"Horseshit! He didn't bust *yore* nose. I'd just as soon been kicked by a mule."

"It would a been a sight easier if'n he'd been walkin'," Secory grumbled. "But the wire will trip up his horse. Then we'll be all over him like flies on a pile of fresh cowshit. That bastard'll pay and pay good for what he done."

"How'd you know for sure it was him that looked at yore gal?" The question came from one of the two men who stood and came to peer down the road toward town. The man with the broken nose huddled with his head in his arms.

"I jist know, that's all. He's been a thumbin' his nose at this town fer years. He's as randy as his old pa was. The bastard got hung fer it."

"I thought he was hanged for killing old Harper's brother."

"You can bet yore boots there was a woman mixed up in it somewheres."

"Was you around then?"

"Hell no. It was twenty years ago. The old timers is still talkin' 'bout it."

"He ain't comin'. It's been more'n a hour. I'm callin' it quits. I gotta work tomorrow."

"Guess he pulled a fast one," the other man said. "Let's roll up that wire and get the hell outta here."

"There'll be other times," Secory said. "Ya can bet yore life on it."

The next day Jesse hugged her happiness to her,

having told no one but Pauline that she and Wade were in love and that they planned to marry. When she wasn't busy with patients in the surgery, she was preparing the vials of smallpox vaccine to be used the next day. Just before noon Doctor Forbes was called away to tend a man who had been kicked and trampled by a mule. With fluttering concern over the doctor's missing a meal, Louella hurriedly prepared him a light lunch to eat on the way to the farm south of town.

Usually when the doctor was away, the conversation at the dinner table, with Mrs. Lindstrom presiding, was limited to "pass the butter," bread, or whatever was being served. Today, however, Mrs. Lindstrom brought up the subject of Jesse and Wade Simmer.

"Jesse, I feel it my duty to tell you that being seen on the arm of that man . . . Wade Simmer, will certainly harm your reputation in this town."

Jesse looked at her for a long moment. "Why do you feel that it's your duty?"

"Why, my dear, I've been training young women to meet their social obligations for years. I'm speaking now on behalf of your father. The dear man is so wrapped up in his medicine that he couldn't possibly know what harm you are doing to yourself and to this family."

Susan's eyes were as big as saucers, and Pauline was holding her breath as they waited for Jesse to explode. They were surprised when Jesse spoke calmly.

"It's very thoughtful of you, Louella, to be so

concerned about my reputation."

"I was sure you'd understand. Todd, dear, you have gravy on your chin." Louella blotted her own mouth with her napkin. "This family has a unique position in this town. The doctor is highly respected and his family should be beyond reproach."

"And in the short time you've been here, you consider yourself qualified to make decisions regarding whom we should and should not associate with?"

"Well, yes. My experience at the girls' school has given me an insight on character."

"Supplemented, of course, by the advice of Roberta Harper."

Rage was boiling up in Jesse and she made no attempt to allay it.

"I bet you can hardly wait to discuss my latest indiscretion with Roberta and Edsel. I'm sure they know by now that Wade Simmer called on me."

"You can't keep something like that quiet in this town," Louella said with authority.

"I was certainly not trying to keep it quiet." Jesse's voice shook with anger. "And for your information, Mrs. Lindstrom, I don't give a tinker's damn what the Harpers think or what anyone else in this town thinks, especially you. You are an employee here and that is *all*. In the future you had better remember that and keep your nose out of this family's business."

With Jesse's words, it was plain that open war had been declared between the two women.

Louella's white face turned a brick red. "I can see, Jesse, that your education was sadly neglected. Your lack of refinement appalls me. If you have no care for your reputation, think of your father."

"My education is far broader than yours, Mrs. Lindstrom. Beside my schooling and my nurse's training, I learned from my father and my step-mother to have compassion for those less fortunate than I. And that all persons are indeed created equal and that each has the right to express himself. I learned to stand up for myself, make my own decisions, choose my own friends and honor the right of others to do the same." Jesse scarcely paused to take a breath before continuing.

"As far as my father is concerned, ma'am, I think you do enough thinking about him for both of us. Todd, will you please pass the pickled peaches."

Todd couldn't keep the grin off his face, and Susan barely suppressed a giggle.

The meal was finished in total silence.

Doctor Forbes returned from his call in the middle of the afternoon. Jesse waited for her father to say something about Wade calling on her; but the afternoon waned, suppertime came, and he had not mentioned it.

Louella was charming during the evening meal. She asked about the patient the doctor had visited and seemed to be genuinely concerned. If the doctor noticed that the rest of the family and Pauline spoke only when spoken to, he didn't acknowledge it. At the end of the meal, however, he stood and beckoned to his elder daughter.

"Come to the surgery, Jesse. We have a few things to go over before tomorrow."

Jesse glanced at Mrs. Lindstrom. She had a satisfied smile on her face. The woman was sure that Doctor Forbes was going to give Jesse a good dressing down for her behavior. Jesse lifted her chin and followed her father.

The doctor slumped tiredly in his chair and Jesse closed the door.

"What the hell is going on between you and Mrs. Lindstrom?"

"She criticized me at the dinner table in front of Todd, Susan and Pauline because I was seen walking with Wade Simmer." Jesse crossed her arms over her chest and leaned back against the door.

To her surprise her father laughed. "That got your temper up, did it?"

"It certainly did. I reminded her that she was an employee in this house and nothing more."

Her father was thoughtful for a moment, then asked, "Do you like Simmer?"

"I love him."

"Does he love you?"

"He says he does."

"You plan to marry?"

"Someday."

"What does that mean?"

"It means I'll not go off and leave Todd and Susan with Mrs. Lindstrom."

"Good grief. I thought you'd get over being so

possessive about this house and your brother and sister."

"You see only the side she wants you to see, Papa. I believe her to be a cold, calculating woman."

"I enjoy her company, Jesse. Give her some credit for being able to put up with the opposition she has faced here." The doctor leaned back and hooked his thumbs in his vest pockets. "My fondest hope for both my girls has been that they meet strong men who will love them and whom they will love in return."

"You have no objection to Wade?"

"Why should I? I'm not going to marry him."

"Oh . . . Papa —"

"I'm glad for you, Jesse. Wade is a good man. Better than most. He's had a hard time, but it's only made him stronger. He'll take good care of you."

"You don't care that the town hates him and calls him hill trash? Mrs. Lindstrom thinks that my seeing him puts a blight on your reputation."

He chuckled. "I've had blights on my reputation before and survived."

"We're going to the ball game together on Sunday. It'll create quite a stir."

He chuckled again. "This blasted town needs shaking up."

"Oh, Papa. I love you." Jesse crossed the room and put her arms around his neck. "How was I so lucky as to have a papa like you?"

"You've not been a disappointment to me either,

girl," he said as if he had a frog in his throat, and patted her back.

"That's what Wade said the day we first met."

"He did, huh? Somehow I knew that you two would hitch together. I ran into him a couple years ago and liked him from the start. He's a man who stands on his own two feet and depends on no one but himself. Just like you, daughter. For choosing him you'll take some guff. You know that. But you'll weather the storm."

"Thank you, Papa." She kissed his cheek.

After Jesse left the surgery, Doctor Forbes rocked for a while in his rolling desk chair. Things were working out just as he had hoped. His Jesse had met a good man and fallen in love.

On Saturday, Jesse, Pauline and the doctor were at the schoolhouse at seven o'clock preparing for the mass smallpox vaccinations.

Jody had been vaccinated the evening before, after Susan had teased him for being a coward and a crybaby. She and Todd had been vaccinated several years earlier and proudly displayed the scars on their upper arms. By morning Jody was running a slight fever which was sure to rise during the day. Doctor Forbes had sent him back to Ike's with orders for him to take it easy for the next two days.

The number of people who came for vaccinations far exceeded what the doctor had expected. The townspeople came early. Wagons loaded with families from outside of town started coming in by mid-morning. Some came later after the farmers had done their day's work. The doctor welcomed all in the same manner whether they could pay or not. Most everyone dropped a few cents into the donation box.

By late afternoon Jesse was tired of hearing the sound of her own voice saying the same words over and over.

"There will be a festered sore on the arm. Cover it loosely so that air can get to it. You may wish to have one of those little celluloid bubbles to put over it. The druggist has them for two cents each. There will be a fever for a few days. Be sure the patient gets plenty of rest and drinks plenty of water. Should the fever be very high and you cannot bring it down with a sponge bath or if the sore should become infected and you cannot bring the patient to the surgery, send word. The doctor or I will come out."

Mothers held screaming younger children. Boys and girls of school age tried to act nonchalant about the vaccination but cringed when the doctor approached them with the instrument he used to scrape their arms. Fathers shuffled their feet and talked crops with the other farmers as they waited for their families.

Finally the day ended.

Tomorrow, Jesse thought, as they trudged home after having inoculated more than three hundred people, she would see Wade. All day long, as busy as she was, eagerness for the sight of him had crept into her bones like an ache.

282

Pauline's thoughts were also on the morrow. She wondered, as she walked beside her friend, if Ethan would show up to go with them to the ball game after she had pointedly told him she did not want to go with him. Frustration throbbed in Pauline's throat. That damned man had skin as tough as an elephant's and didn't know how to take no for an answer.

Sitting on the porch of the rooming house, Ethan saw Jesse and Pauline come down the street at the end of the block, then turn to go toward the doctor's house. It was a puzzle to him why he was so attracted to the blond beauty who was so cold to him. It was irritating too. He was here to do a job, but she was constantly in his thoughts. Inside that cold exterior he was certain there was a passionate woman; if only he could break down the barriers she put around herself, she would be warm and loving in his arms.

After the women were out of sight, Ethan mused about the conversation he'd had that day with the postmaster. Ralph had assured him that Dick Efthim was a trustworthy man and that he and his wife Patricia ran the post office and store completely free of Harper control. The Emporium across the street from the store was Harper-owned and-operated.

After introducing himself, Ethan had shown Dick his credentials and said that if he wanted verification he could talk to Ralph at the paper. After that they had talked quietly for several minutes.

"I've never done anything like this." Dick was a careful man. His being a competitor of the Harpers and the fact that the Postal Department had refused Harper's request to have the post office moved from Efthim's store to the one Harper owned had put Efthim in a precarious position.

"It's important, or I wouldn't ask you to do it."

"What's she done?"

"I can't tell you that. The less you know the better off you'll be. If she gets a letter or if she mails one, lay it aside and get word to me. There's a reward out for information about this woman. I'm not sure of the amount, but if she's who we think she is, you'll be in for a slice of the reward."

"I'm just worried I'll lose my job."

"I can assure you that you won't. I've been with the Bureau for nine years. They take care of their own."

"All right, Mr. Bredlow, I'll do as you say. The woman seems nice enough, but kind of snooty for my taste. She comes in and talks to Patricia, but she buys very little. Asks a lot of questions as if she plans to stay in town for a long time."

"Not a word to your wife."

"I won't." He shook his head vigorously. "I don't want her involved in this. Not that she'd say anything, mind you. I just don't want her to worry. She's expecting."

Ethan thought over his conversation with the postmaster and felt he was on the right track. Louella Lindstrom would have connections, and they would try to get in touch with her, or her with them. He needed just one little thread to tie her in and his job would be done.

His thoughts turned again to Pauline. He'd never had to fight so hard for a woman, and he relished the challenge. One day she would goad him too far, and he would kiss that defiant look off her face. He grinned. Damn the woman. Maybe it would happen tomorrow.

# CHAPTER
## • 17 •

Supper was scarcely over when the knocker sounded on the front door. Louella answered and after a few minutes came into the dining room to announce that Jesse had a caller.

Thinking that surely it was Wade, Jesse hurried to the parlor. Much to her disappointment and surprise, Edsel Harper rose from the settee to greet her.

"Evening, Miss Jesse." Edsel was dressed as he was each day when he went to the bank: dark serge suit, white shirt and high stiff collar. He looked hot and uncomfortable.

"Evening, Edsel. Did you come to see my father?"

"No. Oh, no, Miss Jesse. I've come to take you for a ride. After such an exhausting day, you are in need of some relaxation, I'm sure, and I have the means to provide it."

"I'm glad you've a buggy of your own, but I'm not really interested in a ride. Thank you anyway."

"Let me be the judge of what's best for you.

286

That's a man's role, you know. My buggy is waiting. Shall we go?" He reached to cup her elbow in his hand.

Jesse stepped out of his reach. "I said no, Edsel, but thanks again for the kind thought." That is if it was your thought, she wanted to add. "I do not want to go."

"Oh, but a ride would cool you off."

"A bath will do the same thing."

"Then will you sit on the porch with me for a while?"

"No. I have things to do —"

"Just for a while," he coaxed. His eyes had a brightness to them as they roamed her face and lowered to her breasts. His red lips turned down in a pout. Jesse couldn't help but compare his lips to Wade's wide firm mouth.

"I told you I have things to do," she said in a firm, no-nonsense manner.

Her words wiped the smile from Edsel's face and a flush of red covered his cheeks. He straightened his shoulders and threw back his head just as she had seen his father do when he was talking to a farmer who was asking for a loan.

"Miss Jesse, maybe you don't realize it now, but your reputation has suffered a severe blow. I'm here to help you recover it. You have very few friends left in this town. If you're seen riding or sitting on the front porch with me, the gossip will soon die down."

Anger caused Jesse's cheeks to flush, but she spoke calmly.

"I appreciate your willingness to sacrifice your reputation to help me, Edsel, but I can't allow you to do it. Gossip is like the poisoned fangs of a rattler. It leaves its venom to work in the wound. It may be years before my name is even mentioned by the *decent* women of this town because I am considered . . . flawed." She finished dramatically but her sarcasm failed to register with Edsel.

"I'm willing, Miss Jesse. I'll do whatever it takes to see that you are vindicated. It wasn't your fault. You were trying to be kind and gentle as you were raised to be. A refined young lady is no match for that hill trash. Why, there's no telling what harm you could have suffered. Heaven forbid" — Edsel lifted his hands palms up — "in that dark ball park he could have ravished you."

Anger, with a full head of steam, boiled up in Jesse. With her hands on her hips and eyes blazing she cast aside all pretense of politeness to a guest in her home.

"Don't you dare call Wade Simmer hill trash, you . . . you mealy-mouthed worm!" The words exploded from her mouth in a high screech of indignation.

Edsel's face registered first shock and then disbelief. But it didn't stop Jesse's tirade.

"You snooped and found out we went to the ball park. How dare you spy on me!" She stepped up to him and thumped his chest with her forefinger. "Wade is worth a hundred of you. What have you ever done for your fellow man? You think you're better than anyone else because your name

288

is Harper. You sit in your bank lording it over the poor souls who come in seeking a loan so they can keep body and soul together. Wade Simmer is the most decent man I've ever met. He cares about his neighbors. He cares about those less fortunate than he is, and he's had to tolerate this town's hostility because you Harpers keep stirring up things that happened years back."

Edsel backed toward the door and Jesse followed.

"Now, just a minute, Miss Jesse, I didn't spy —"

"Don't Miss Jesse me, you . . . you . . . sappy, stuck-up jackass." Her voice was loud enough to be heard all over the house.

"Now just a minute —"

"Just a minute is all you've got to get out of this house. But before you go, I want you to know that as far as my reputation in this prissy, small-minded, Harper-controlled town is concerned, I don't give a hoot and a holler about what anyone thinks, and that includes the almighty Harpers. I *love* Wade Simmer. Love him, love him, love him," she repeated in a high screech. "I'm going to marry him. Now go home and tell your mamma and papa that the doctor's daughter is going to hell in a hand basket. Then you can cry on your mamma's shoulder."

Edsel stood as if frozen. His eyes narrowed, his lips were pressed so tightly together they looked like a thin red line. The hands holding his hat shook.

"You're making a terrible mistake." When he spoke his voice was low and controlled. "A mistake you'll regret for the rest of your life."

"If my marrying Wade is a mistake, it's *my* mistake."

"You'll be sorry for this," he said quietly. "Mark my words, Jesse," he said, deliberately leaving off the polite "Miss" he had always used.

He looked at her with eyes filled with hatred. Then he turned on his heels and left, closing the door softly behind him.

Jesse stood motionless with her hands clasped in front of her. Suddenly she realized what had evaded her before. There was something deep and evil working in Edsel Harper. His eyes had glowed as he looked at her breasts although the dress she wore was not tight-fitting. It was as if he couldn't take his eyes off them.

Susan bounded into the room.

"You sure told him off, Jess. Old Louella is mad as a hornet. She said your behavior was *disgraceful!* You are ruined in this town . . . and on and on. Well, la-de-da! I thought it was . . . heavenly. It's about time someone put that stuck-up toad in his place."

"Did everyone hear?"

Susan nodded happily. "Papa got up in the middle of it and went into the surgery. I'm not sure, but I thought I saw a grin on his face before he shut the door."

"I lost my temper, Susy. Heavens to Betsy, three times in the last two weeks I've lost it."

"He's a nasty old thing anyhow. Jeff Stealy found a dirty magazine in the back of his buggy. Mary Sue and I just got a peek when he took it away from us. There were pictures of naked women —"

"For goodness sake. When did this happen?"

"A week ago. Edsel's buggy was behind the bank. Jeff saw some papers sticking out from under the seat in the back. He pulled them out and found the dirty magazine. He's had fun showing it around to the boys, but he won't let me and Mary Sue see it."

"I hope he didn't show it to Todd."

"He didn't. He said Todd was too young to appreciate it. Imagine old Edsel having a dirty magazine." Susan wrapped her arms about her sister's waist. "Jess, did you mean it when you said you were going to marry Mr. Simmer?"

"With all my heart I meant it. I'm going to marry him someday. But don't worry. I'll not go and leave you and Todd with Mrs. Lindstrom."

"Does Papa know?"

"He knows."

"Could Todd and I come with you?"

"And leave Papa at the mercy of Louella? No, I'll not leave until she's gone."

"She wants to marry Papa. I know she does."

"Don't worry about Papa. He's smart enough to see through her sooner or later."

"I wish she'd go."

"So do I, but we've got to trust Papa, Susy. We both know that he'd never do anything to hurt his children. He hired her to relieve me of the household chores. But he's bound to realize she's more trouble than she's worth. We've got to wait it out. I'll make you a bet that she'll be out of here by Christmas."

"Christmas! We gotta put up with her that long?"

"Maybe not. Where's Pauline?"

"She took a few of the dishes to the kitchen. But when she heard what you were saying to Edsel, she laughed, and Ghost-face said that you and Pauline were two of a kind. Pauline ran up to her room giggling all the way."

"I want to talk to her." With Jesse's arm across Susan's shoulders they walked to the foot of the stairway. "Keep an eye on Todd," Jesse said in a low voice. "See that he stays out of Louella's way. I'm sure she set up the arrangement for Edsel to call on me; and after what happened, she may take her spite out on Todd."

"If she does, I'll fix her wagon!"

The door of Pauline's room was ajar. Jesse pushed it open. Pauline was taking down her hair.

"May I come in?"

"Do." Pauline burst into laughter. "I've never enjoyed anything as much as hearing you put down one of the mighty Harpers, especially Edsel. I'd love to have seen his face when you called him a sappy, stuck-up jackass."

"I lost my temper." Jesse closed the door and sat down on the edge of the bed. "It really riles me when people talk about Wade in such a nasty way; they don't even know him."

"It's the Harpers' town. They control the money so people listen to what they say. Jesse, there's no way I'll stay here another school year."

"Not even if The Looker is caught?"

"Face it, Jesse." Exasperation was on Pauline's face and in her voice. "If he's caught, he'll brag about all the naked women he's fondled. He might even name them, too. I couldn't bear that."

"I don't believe Marshal Wright would allow that to happen."

"We'll see. I looked at each of the men who were at the school today and none of them looked back at me as if he knew what was under my dress. Of course, if it was a man with a wife, he'd have no need to look at naked women." Pauline's laugh was more of a snort. Then in a lighter vein, she said, "You sure blew away your chances with the Harpers tonight. When word gets out that you're going to marry Wade Simmer, they may tell all the people they give loans to that it would be better to doctor someplace else."

Jesse snorted in disgust. "Where would they go? When they're sick they want a doctor. Papa would be the first to say that if they want to go to Frederick, or Knoxville, let them go." Jesse went to the door. "Tomorrow I'm going to be seen with Wade by half the people in this town. I'll be proud to be seen with him. If they are so narrow-minded that they turn against me, I'll not lose any sleep over it."

"You've got a lot of hurt coming, girl," Pauline said seriously. "It would be better if you married

293

Wade right away and moved to the hills."

"I'll not go and leave Todd and Susan with Louella. And I'll not let the people of this town run me out like a dog with its tail between its legs. I'm sure that not all the people feel about Wade as the Harpers do. I'll stay here and hold my head high. I've nothing to be ashamed of."

"Good for you. It sounds like we'll have an interesting summer."

The family attended church as usual on Sunday morning. Jesse, Susan and Pauline sang in the choir. Doctor Forbes and Todd sat in a pew toward the back of the church. Just before the service was to start, Mrs. Lindstrom came in, looked around and sat down beside Todd.

"That old biddy wants people to think she's part of the family," Susan whispered to her sister.

"I wonder why she's here?"

"Last Sunday she went to the Methodist church and managed to get herself on the bazaar committee."

"I hate her!"

"You shouldn't say that . . . in church." Jesse grinned and picked up the hymn book.

If the people in the congregation were incensed because Jesse had been seen with the notorious "hellion" from the hills, they didn't show it. Much to Jesse's relief, they greeted her as usual. Most of them owed Doctor Forbes in one way or another, either in money or gratitude. The gratitude extended to his daughter.

Jesse had spent nights in their homes when they had had serious illnesses. She or the doctor had always come as quickly as possible when there had been an emergency. Jesse was as handy as the doctor at stopping blood and stitching wounds. Both of them gave generously to the church. If she strayed a little, it was forgivable. She would soon see her mistake and be back in the fold.

When the service was over, Louella left immediately. Doctor Forbes and Todd stayed inside to visit for a few minutes and the girls inquired about choir practice before they left the church. Outside, Susan scanned the area. Louella was nowhere in sight.

"She's hurried home to impress Papa with what a wonderful, reliable housekeeper and cook she is," Susan said as she walked alongside her sister.

"That means we'll have a good dinner on the table."

"I can hardly wait to go to the ball game." Susan moved ahead of Jesse and Pauline and turned to walk backward. "Can I walk with you and Mr. Simmer? Pauline, are you and Mr. Bredlow going to walk with them?"

"I doubt Sir Galahad will show up. He's all talk," Pauline answered drily.

"He's handsome as sin. Mary Sue almost swooned when she saw him. When Jeff was having trouble with his bicycle chain, Mr. Bredlow fixed it."

"Hurrah for him. I'm glad he's good for something. As far as I'm concerned, he's a masher, a lecher and a blowhard."

"What's a lecher?" Susan asked, still walking backward.

"Ethan Bredlow!"

Jesse could see Pauline's lips in a tight line and her chin raised.

"I wish I'd asked Ethan and Wade to dinner."

"Ha! I'm extremely glad you didn't."

Susan whooped with laughter. "Old Ghost-face would've had a cow if you did it without telling her at least a week ahead. She had one when I made a picnic for me, Mary Sue and Jeff. I said I'd go ask Papa if we could take a picnic down by the creek and she shut up. She doesn't want us to tattle to Papa."

They went up the steps to the porch.

"I love the smell of honeysuckle," Jesse said and broke off a small bloom to tickle her nose.

The meal Louella had prepared was delicious. She had baked a hen, made cornbread dressing and chicken gravy, mashed potatoes, creamed peas, scalloped corn, apple-walnut salad, and pickles. Peach cobbler completed the meal.

And Louella was on her best behavior, as well. She was gracious even when Todd dripped gravy on the tablecloth.

"Accidents will happen." she said lightly. "More dressing, Doctor?"

"Don't mind if I do, Louella. You outdid yourself with this meal."

"Thank you. When I was a child at home, Sunday dinner was always special. We used the best china, silver and, of course, the lace tablecloth. It was my duty to keep the silver polished and I took great pride in doing so." She looked meaningfully at Susan who, when her father was not looking, tightened her lips and rocked her head in a haughty manner.

They had just finished eating when the knocker sounded on the front door. Susan reached it a half dozen steps ahead of Louella, who stood in the hallway with a disapproving look on her face. It turned into a scowl when Susan threw the door wide.

"Hi, Mr. Simmer. Hi, Mr. Bredlow. Come in. We're done with dinner. Jesse and Pauline just went upstairs to take off their cor . . . to change into something . . . to get out of their church clothes."

"Howdy, Wade. Howdy Ethan." Doctor Forbes came out of the dining room. "Come into the parlor. Susy, get the gentlemen some lemonade."

Hollis and Ethan sat on the settee. Wade perched on a chair, his hat in his hand. He wore a soft white shirt open at the neck and tan britches. His shoes were polished as was his belt buckle. Ethan also wore a soft white shirt but had added a black string tie.

"Doc, we just came from Ike's. Jody is running a high fever," Wade said worriedly.

"Is the vaccination infected?"

"Doesn't appear to be. It's about the size of a dime and has a white scab. We put one of those celluloid bubble things over it to keep him from bumping it."

"It's normal for him to run a fever and even have a few spots, but I'd better go over there and and take a look. Is Ike giving him plenty of liquid?"

"He says he hasn't eaten much for a couple of days, but takes the water all right."

"Can I g-go?" Todd slinked from around the corner where he'd been listening.

"Say hello to our guests, Todd." Doctor Forbes smiled fondly at the boy who was already standing beside him.

"H-howdy, Mr. S-Simmer. Howdy, Mr. Bredlow."

"Howdy, Todd," Wade said. That he seemed genuinely glad to see the boy and that his face lost some of its remoteness when he smiled at him was evident to Doctor Forbes.

"I want to g-go see Jody. He's my friend. If he's s-s-sick, it's my fault. I talked him into l-letting Papa vaccinate him." He looked quickly at Wade. "I-I-I ain't told no-nobody 'bout Jody b-being at Ike's."

"We knew you wouldn't tell and get Jody in trouble. We've had secrets before, haven't we?"

"Yeah." Todd winked at Wade.

"I thought you wanted to go to the ball game, son."

"To heck with th-the ball game, Papa. I want to see J-Jody. I could b-b-bring him water and put a wet cl-cloth on his h-head like Jesse does when I get a f-fever."

"We'll go see him together. We'll have Mrs. Lindstrom fix up a basket of lunch and a big jar of lemonade for Jody and Ike. How's that?"

"Jody'll l-like that."

Wade felt a stirring around his heart. He had never dared hope that he would be a welcome guest in the doctor's home or that Jody would be treated so decently. He heard footsteps on the stairs and glanced at Ethan, who had heard them too. He was on his feet, alert as a deer, Wade thought. The man was in love. There was no doubt about it.

Susan brought the lemonade.

"The reason it took me so long was old Ghost . . . ah . . . Mrs. Lindstrom made me squeeze the lemons."

"I thought there was something special about this lemonade," Ethan said after taking a sip. He turned the full force of his charm on the young girl and she blushed to the roots of her hair.

Wade stood when Jesse came into the room. She was lovely in a soft pink shirtwaist and a light blue walking skirt. She came directly to him and took his hand in a possessive, intimate way.

Wade's eyes flicked from her face to her father. *Here it comes. Here is where I get thrown out on my ear.*

"He knows," she said simply and hugged his arm to her. "I wish I had thought to ask you and Ethan to dinner."

"It's all right. I'm not the least bit hungry."

Hollis got to his feet. "Well, son, it seems you

and I are not needed here. Where's Pauline?"

Jesse glanced at Ethan. "She went through the kitchen and out the back door."

Ethan jumped to his feet. "That blasted woman makes me so mad I could spit nails!" He took off down the hall toward the kitchen.

Doctor Forbes laughed. "She's sure got him all bumfuzzled. He's like a love-sick calf."

"Ugh! I g-guess they'll get a-a-ll k-kissy and mushy."

"What do you know about mushy, son?"

"Mary S-Sue and Jeff k-kiss when they think no-nobody's lookin.' Phew! I bet it's aw-awful."

"It's not awful at all. Kissing feels pretty good sometimes. You'll learn all about it when you're a little older." He turned to Jesse and Wade. "Have yourselves a good time at the ball game. Come on, son, we've got to battle old Ghost-face for a lunch basket."

Jesse's mouth dropped open and so did Todd's and Susan's. They stared at him in astonishment. Doctor Forbes grinned devilishly.

"I ain't no dummy, ya know. Come along, Susan. Jesse and Wade don't need you in here," he said over his shoulder as he went out the door.

As soon as they were alone, Jesse raised her face to Wade's. "Are you going to kiss me, Wade?"

"And go all mushy?" he teased.

"Sure. I like being mushy with you."

"Sweetheart — love —" The words were a groan. "I've thought of nothing but kissing you since I kissed you out there on the porch."

He kissed her then, taking away what breath she had. His mouth was firm, his body was hard and smelled of cool green forests. She clutched his arms for support when her knees went weak. He was so male yet so tender and sweet.

She was dazed. "I don't think we'd better kiss again while we're here in the house. I'll wait until we can go to that cool green place beside the creek where we had our picnic the day I left the hills. Remember?"

They were standing close together, her hands on his shoulders. His trembling arms made her aware of how big he was, how strong, yet as vulnerable as a young lad.

"How could I forget? I was in heaven and hell."

"Hell?"

"So afraid you'd think I was just hill trash being fresh with you."

"I didn't think that at all. Right from the start I felt safe with you and wanted you to go with me when I made the rounds the next day."

"I thought that if I stayed away from you, I would forget how sweet you are and how much I wanted you to like me."

"Oh, Wade, I would have sat there on that blanket all day if we hadn't run out of food," she said with a chuckle in her voice.

"Next time we'll have things to do beside eat."

"Promise?" She smiled into his eyes.

"I swear it," he replied and kissed her nose.

Ethan caught up with Pauline by the clothesline

that stretched across the back of the property.

"Pauline!" he called and ran the few steps it took to reach her. He was hot and angry. "You're the damndest woman I ever met. Where the hell are you going?"

"Don't swear at me, Ethan Bredlow. Where I go is none of your business." She stood proud and defiant. "Come near me and I'll kick you."

"We were going to the ball game with Jesse and Wade."

"We? You're ahead of yourself, mister. I never said I'd go with you."

"Then don't go with me, damn it. Go with Jesse and Wade and I'll tag along."

"Why?"

"Why what?"

"Why do you keep . . . hanging around?"

"Because I like you, you muddle-headed female. Is that such a sin?" Ethan shouted so loud that she flinched.

"The only reason you like me is that I haven't fallen at your feet in a swoon."

"I never wanted you to fall at my feet. I wanted your friendship. What's happened to make you so cold? You're beautiful when you smile, which is seldom when you're with me. You're intelligent and have a sense of humor. You're also compassionate or you wouldn't be helping Jody. I sense that you've been greatly disappointed in a man, or that some man has hurt you."

"Well now, you're a regular fortune-teller. And how'd you know about Jody?" She folded her arms over her chest and glared at him although her face was not quite as frozen as before.

"I just know. Wade knows that I know." He reached to put his hand on her arm.

"Don't you dare touch me, you . . . lecher."

"For God's sake! Now I'm a lecher. I'll never understand you. Come on, let's go to the ball game before I get mad enough to throw you over my shoulder, carry you down to the creek and paddle you."

"You wouldn't dare! I'd fight you every step of the way."

"No doubt," he said drily. "Come on and behave yourself. I promise not to touch you, but I won't promise not to look at you. That's it! Take it or leave it."

"Oh, all right." She marched ahead of him down the drive past the surgery door and around to the porch, where Jesse and Wade were waiting.

"Ready to go?" Jesse looked from Pauline's set features to Ethan's scowling countenance. *Oh, boy, they've had a set-to.*

"As soon as I get my parasol." Pauline marched up the steps and into the house. She came out an instant later and she and Ethan fell in step behind Jesse and Wade.

# CHAPTER
## • 18 •

Jesse walked beside Wade, holding onto his arm.
Today they would be seen as a couple, and she
was so proud of him. He stood head and shoulders
above the majority of the men who passed them
on their way to the ball park. A few spoke to Jesse,
eyed Wade and walked on.

Jesse sensed his reluctance and understood it.
This was a new experience for him and for her
too. It seemed unreal to her that the big handsome
man who walked beside her was going to be a
permanent part of her life.

Wade's heart did an odd little dance when Jesse
moved her hand from the crook of his arm down
to his hand and squeezed it. His gaze moved down
to her face, and the love he saw there made his
knees weak. She had given her heart to him. The
thought brought both ecstasy and torment to him
because he knew that there was such a great difference between the life he had lived and hers.

Wade had never felt so uncertain before. He
had spent many of his years among rough men.

His granny had been the only feminine influence in his life, and she had been gone for so long he couldn't recall her face without looking at the tintype he had on his chiffonier at home. He was a rough man too, in his own way, impatient with prejudice and stupidity. Experience had hardened him, yet his chest warmed with the quickening of his own heart at the thought of this woman's love. He questioned himself while holding tightly to Jesse's hand. Could he live up to her expectations? After a while would she regret marrying him?

The clear sky promised a perfect day and it was — almost.

Wade spread a blanket on the ground at the end of the bench that stretched almost to third base. Jesse sat close enough to him to let people know they were together. Some who passed greeted Jesse but not one person spoke to Wade except for the postmaster and his wife, who sat on the end of the bench. Patricia Efthim was seven months pregnant and looked as if she would rather be anywhere but here at the ball game.

Ethan went for cold drinks and brought some back not only for the four of them but also for the postmaster and his grateful wife who was perspiring profusely despite the parasol she held over her head. For the most part Ethan ignored Pauline and visited with Mr. Efthim.

It was not an exciting game. The Grover team had moved ahead of Harpersville six to nothing by the second inning. The crowd from Grover hooted and yelled taunts at the Harpersville players.

Mr. and Mrs. Harper sat in their unhitched buggy. Their horse grazed on the grass beyond the playing field. Jesse was relieved that Edsel, self-selected manager of the Harpersville team, sat just left of home plate with the team. More than likely he wouldn't come down this way and she wouldn't have to face him.

Giddy with happiness, Jesse almost failed to notice when the game ended. She held Wade's hand and smiled into his eyes, then whispered to him.

"I'm as happy as a dog with two tails."

He laughed. *And oh, he was so handsome when he laughed.*

"I can top that. I'm as happy as a drunk hoot-owl."

"Oh, Wade, I didn't dream that it would be so wonderful to be in love."

"We've got lots to learn about each other, sweetheart."

"I'll not have to learn to love you or learn how wonderful you are, or how worldly and intelligent and kind and . . . sweet. I'll not have to learn to love your kisses —"

Wade grimaced. "Honey, why do you have to say things like that in a place like this where I can't grab you and kiss you?"

Jesse squeezed his arm. " 'Cause I'm mean and cantankerous and stubborn, and I can be a real pain in the neck at times."

"Hush, I'll not hear you saying things like that

about the woman who will be my wife. Besides, the ball game is over."

"It is? Who won?"

"Grover. Twenty to eight. Harpersville needs some new players." He stood and extended his hand to help her up.

"They need a new manager too."

Jesse shook out her skirt and glanced at Pauline. She had sat quietly throughout the game holding her parasol over her head. She rose to her feet, ignoring the hand Ethan held out to help her. Wade shook the blanket, folded it and tucked it under his arm.

They said good-bye to the Efthims and with Jesse's hand snug in the crook of Wade's arm, they walked back across the playing field. Most of the crowd had dispersed by the time they reached the dirt road that led into Main Street and turned toward home, but there were a few stragglers behind them.

Susan and Mary Sue passed them, hurrying to catch up with Jeff who rode his bicycle.

"Wasn't the ball game fun?" Susan yelled as she went by. "Did you see old Edsel's face when the Grover manager said the team was good, but they needed a manager with more than air between his ears? Mr. Simmer, make Jesse tell you what she called old Edsel. You'll laugh all over yourself. Bye. See you at the house." She ran ahead and caught hold of the back of Jeff's bicycle.

"That girl is more fun than a barrel of monkeys," Ethan said as the girls raced ahead.

"I can't imagine a barrel of monkeys being fun."
Pauline snorted. "Poor things all scrunched together."

"Just what did you say to Edsel?" Wade tilted his head close to Jesse's.

Jesse knew Wade would not let Susan's remark go by. She was tempted to give her sister a pinch for mentioning the incident.

"Not much. He came by and wanted to take me for a ride. I refused and he left."

"That's all?"

"No that's not all." Pauline actually giggled and tilted her parasol so she could see Wade's face. "She called him a sappy, stuck-up jackass and all of it fits perfectly."

Ethan hooted. "Godamighty, I'd like to have heard that. I bet Edsel was struck to the heart."

"He was more than struck," Pauline said impatiently. "He was boiling mad."

Jesse looked up at Wade and caught a grin on his face.

"It's funny now, but at the time it was not very pleasant. He was so insistent and so sure I'd be grateful to be seen with him. The puffed-up baboon."

"Was it because of me?"

"Not necessarily," Jesse lied. "He's been trying to court me for a long time. The thought of his kissing me is enough to make me throw up."

The two couples strolled slowly along the dirt road. In her haze of happiness Jesse was slow at realizing that four men had come out of the bushes that lined the road and stood blocking their path. Wade had noticed. He became instantly on guard and his muscles tightened. One of the men was John Secory, Bertha's father. He was a rough-looking man, tall, with legs that were as thick and solid as a tree trunk. The other three were of the same ilk. Bridge workers, Jesse presumed.

"Looks like we got a bit of fun coming up, Wade," Ethan said with a grin.

"Aren't you ever serious about anything?" Pauline snapped.

"Sure. About you, honeybun."

"Wade . . ." Jesse was holding his arm with both hands. He was watching the men with narrowed eyes and a grim mouth.

"If you're wanting a fight, you could have waited until we got the ladies home."

"Ya bastard! Ya didn't wait to strip my little girl 'n' look 'er over. It's time somebody put a stop to what yo're doin' to the womenfolk of this here town."

"John Secory, you're as crazy as a bedbug if you think Wade is the one —"

"Hush, honey. They won't listen. Take the blanket and get over there beside the road." He gave her the blanket and his hat and gently pushed her out of the way.

Ethan had snatched the sleeve garters off his arms. He shoved them, his black derby hat and his gold watch in Pauline's hands.

"Stand aside, sweetheart, and watch your man in action." He grinned as he rolled up his sleeves.

Pauline snorted but moved to the side of the road with Jesse.

"We ain't got no quarrel with you, mister," Secory said to Ethan. "We ain't wantin' to hurt ya."

"But I've got a quarrel with you. It fairly sets my teeth on edge to see four against one."

"Ethan, you don't have to mix in this."

"Sure I do, Wade. That yahoo bled all over my Sunday best shirt. I figure he was part of this bunch. It cost me two bits to get that shirt washed. I intend to get two-bits of hide. I'll take the two on the left. They look kind of soft and easy-like. It'll take no time at all to whip their behinds."

"I heard that you were waiting for me down at the bridge . . . in the dead of the night . . . like a coward, Secory." Wade's voice showed the contempt he felt for the men. "I decided not to oblige you that night. What happened to the man who tried to steal my horse?"

"He warn't stealin' it."

"Was he going to borrow it? I haven't filed charges with Marshal Wright yet. I'm still thinking about it."

"File all the damn charges ya want. Yo're jist wastin' time a-talkin', Simmer. We mean to beat the shit outta ya and make ya a new asshole."

"That's no way to talk in front of ladies." Wade's tone was sharp and he choked down the anger that gripped him so tightly.

"Ladies? I ain't seen no ladies. To my notion, ladies don't run with big-peckered hill trash."

"That's it. You've shot off your mouth enough.

Before we go any farther, I want you to know that I've fought in street fights with no holds barred. I've fought my way out of taverns in the meanest cities in the world. I know how to protect myself, and if you don't apologize to the ladies for what you said, I'm going to hurt you . . . and hurt you bad."

"Ha! I ain't apologizin' to loose women and I ain't a worryin' you'll hurt me none."

"Then come on, windbag, let's get this over with."

With that Secory and another man charged Wade and the other two charged Ethan. As soon as Secory was within a few feet, Wade spun with lightning speed. His booted foot lashed out and he kicked the man viciously in the groin. Wade heard Secory scream in pain as he ducked down to meet the other man's charge. Wade hit the man in the belly with his shoulder, throwing him over to land on his back on the hard ground. The air went out of his lungs with a poof. Secory had sunk to his knees, yelling with pain. He rolled on the ground holding his privates in his two hands.

"I'll . . . I'll kill ya —" he gasped.

The second man regained his breath and sprang to his feet to jump on Wade's back. Wade struck him a severe blow in the Adam's apple with his elbow. The bully gasped, grabbed his throat, staggered back and fell to the ground.

"I could have killed you with that blow had I wanted to." Wade looked without pity at the ruffian on the ground. "I could have crushed your windpipe. Don't mess with me again."

Secory cursed. "Ya dirty son of a bitch —"

Ethan, in a boxing stance, danced around the other two men and jabbed at their faces while constantly moving to ward off the other men's flailing fists. The first blows from Ethan's fist gave both men bloody noses. He struck one of the men a blow so powerful that it knocked him off his feet.

Pauline was on the fallen man in an instant with the point of her parasol pressed tightly against the base of his throat.

"Lie still or I'll poke this right through your rotten neck and pin you to the ground." The man looked at her with terror in his eyes. When he lifted his hand toward the parasol, Pauline stamped on his arm and held it down. "I'm not fooling, you worthless son of a biscuit eater. Move again and you'll not be singing 'Dixie' for many a year, that is if you can sing at all."

Wade looked at the two men he had laid low and the one on the ground and grinned at Pauline.

"Need any help, Ethan?" he called. "Pauline's taken care of one of them for you."

"Naw. This one's duck soup. He's just too bull-headed to quit."

With a tight fist he jabbed at the only man standing. More blood spurted from his nose.

"I'd knock your teeth out, but I don't want to cut up my hands," Ethan remarked in a conversational tone.

The man looked at his three companions on the ground and backed away, then made for the bushes beside the road. The fight was over.

Jesse, with indignation in every line of her body, marched over to where John Secory was trying to get off the ground.

"You should be ashamed of yourself. Bertha must be mortified knowing what you're up to. Wade Simmer was in Knoxville the night the man came to Bertha's room." Jesse didn't know if the statement were true or not and didn't care. "Even if he was right here in town, you don't have one bit of proof that he was the one. You're a disgusting man, John Secory."

"I don't need a preachin' from the likes of you," he gasped. "That bastard ruint me." He stood spraddle-legged and picked up his hat.

"I don't feel a bit sorry for you. He warned you that he would hurt you and he did."

"This ain't the last of it. He hadn't ort to a hurt me like he done. It warn't a fair fight."

"How can you talk about fair? The four of you would have jumped him if Ethan hadn't been along."

"He isn't worth a spit in the wind, honey." Wade put his hand against Jesse's back, then said to Secory, "I told you that I'd hurt you because of what you said to the ladies. I know a hundred other ways to cripple you, Secory. If you're interested in carrying this thing farther I'll be glad to oblige you. For your own good, I suggest that you go about your business and stay away from me and Miss Jesse."

Jesse turned to see that Pauline still held the

man down with the point of her parasol. She clapped her hands and laughed.

"Oh, Pauline, I wish I had a picture of that."

Ethan was wiping the blood off his hands with his handkerchief and smiling proudly at Pauline.

"I knew that you were my kind of woman the minute I laid eyes on you. Might as well let him up, honey. Your parasol took the fight right out of him."

Pauline stepped back. The man scrambled to his feet. He looked around and hurriedly followed his friends down the road. It was then that Jesse noticed the dozen or more spectators that had stood back to watch the fight.

"Well," she exclaimed in a voice loud enough to carry to the group watching. "It seems we have some cowards here who stood aside and let two men defend themselves against four."

"It wasn't our fight," a man called.

"You see what you're in for, Miss Jesse," another said. "Fightin' and feudin' is all them hill people know."

"Never mind, honey." Wade said. "We didn't need their help."

"That's beside the point. It's the principle of the thing that makes me furious." She glared at the group and vowed that the next time one of the men came to the surgery to have a cut sewn up or anything else tended to she was going to be less than gentle. Much less.

"I've not had so much fun in a month of Sundays." Ethan rolled down his sleeves. Pauline handed him the sleeve garters, his hat and his watch. "We make a pretty good team, Miss Pauline. I punch 'em out and you hold 'em down."

"Don't read anything into that. I still think you're a lecher." She opened the parasol and started down the road. Ethan hurried to catch up with her.

"Can I get under that weapon you're carrying before I get an eye gouged out?"

"I guess so."

"You'll have to take my arm —"

"What for?"

"So we can walk close together under this thing."

"— Oh, all right."

Walking behind them, Jesse smiled up at Wade and hugged his arm close to her.

"The man was right, Jesse, that kind of trouble is what you're in for. There's always going to be someone in this town who wants a piece of my hide."

"We'll deal with it when it comes, my love. I'm convinced that you can take care of yourself . . . and me too."

By nightfall the story was all over town that Wade Simmer and the new man at the newspaper had beaten John Secory and his friends and sent them off with their tails between their legs. Wade, however, felt less than proud of what he'd had to do in front of Jesse.

"Run along with Ethan, Pauline," the doctor

said when they had finished the evening meal. "Susan will help clear the table."

"Papa," Susan protested.

"Run along," Doctor Forbes reiterated when Pauline hesitated.

"I'm not going out on that porch with this . . . this . . . lecher."

"If he gets fresh, just sing out and I'll be right out to put him in his place."

"Come on, sugarfoot. I'm not a boogyman." Ethan winked at the doctor as he put his hand in the small of Pauline's back and gave her a gentle push.

"I'm not so sure — and stop calling me that stupid name."

"You don't like sugarfoot? All right, I'll shorten it to sugar. How's that?"

The screen door slammed behind them. It was dark and cool on the porch. The sweet smell of honeysuckle was in the air. Pauline hurried to the swing and sat down in the middle.

"Move over, sugar, and make room for me."

"You can sit in a chair or on the railing."

"I'll not do either. I going to sit in the swing with you. If you don't move over, I'll sit on your lap."

"Oh, all right! You're an insensitive boor or you'd not go where you're not wanted."

"I never go where I'm not wanted, sugar. I know you were hoping and praying that I would come to take you to the ball game."

"Ha!"

316

"You've said that three times tonight. What does it mean?"

"It means I don't believe you."

"Well, never mind that now. I'm going to kiss you, sugar."

"No you're not!"

"Yes, I am."

"I'll bite you."

"I'll risk it."

Ethan pulled her up close and held her chin in a firm grip. With a wide-eyed gaze she watched as his face came closer to hers. He tilted her face up to his and fastened his lips on hers. At first her mouth was as tight as a miser's purse. Ethan's lips were firm; and when she didn't resist, they gentled and he placed small kisses on her mouth, her chin, her cheeks. When he returned to her mouth it had softened. He no longer held her chin in his hand and she didn't move.

His chest was firm against her breasts, his hip and thigh pressed tightly to hers. His hands began to caress her through her clothes in desperate seeking. Pauline shuddered uncontrollably at the wonderful sensation that passed through her. A hot, delicious feeling coursed through her and a pleasure-pain curled in her stomach.

When her arms slid around his neck, a low growling sound came from his throat, and then his warm, wet lips claimed hers again. Pauline felt a sweet singing in her blood. He lifted his head and looked down at her. Her lids fluttered open. He was looking at her with so much love and passion that she was speechless for a moment. When she spoke it was low and breathless.

"You do strange things to . . . me."

"Honey, you are as sweet as honey —" Ethan murmured as he placed soft kisses on her face. "Please . . . don't fight me. I hung around because I knew what was beneath all that bluster — the sweetest, dearest girl in the world."

Tears came to Pauline's eyes and rolled down her cheeks. Ethan was surprised to feel the wetness.

"Honey, you're crying!"

"I . . . am not!"

"I'll never hurt you. Don't you know that?"

"You'll honey up to me. Make me like you and you'll . . . leave."

"I won't leave. I'm going to marry you."

"I'll not marry a smart-mouthed lecher who probably has women in every town." Her delivery was not convincing and Ethan smiled into her hair.

"Honey, whatever gave you that idea?" If this moment hadn't been so important to him, Ethan would have laughed.

" 'Cause you're so . . . smooth. You've got a quick answer for everything."

"You bothered and confused me so, sweetheart. I didn't know of any way to talk to you. And besides, you gave me a cold shoulder every time I came near you."

"I didn't want to . . . like you."

"But you do, don't you?"

"I . . . guess so."

"After we're married, I'd like to start a newspaper in a town about this size."

"What do you know about the newspaper business? Setting type and writing stories is only a part of it." Her head was resting on his shoulder and his arms were around her. Her palm rested at the base of his throat. Pauline had never felt so loved, so protected.

"I could learn everything I need to know. Sweetheart, why have you been giving me such a bad time? You knocked me right out of my socks that first day when I met you and Jesse on the sidewalk. You looked so beautiful and so . . . sad. Did you love someone who left you?"

"No. I've never been in love."

"You are now. Tell me you are."

"I don't know. I . . . like you a lot."

"I love you, Miss Pauline." As Ethan said the words he tightened his arm around her and placed a gentle kiss on her lips. "I love you so much. I know I sound sure of myself, but I've been scared to death that you'd never love me back."

"Please, Ethan. If you don't mean what you say . . . don't say it. Don't break my heart. I don't think I could bear it."

"Honey, I won't do that. I just want the name of the bastard who hurt you and caused you to close your heart against me."

"I don't know who he is, but we're going to find out." Pauline hid her face in his neck. "He . . . he stripped me . . . naked and looked at me. I felt like a piece of meat lying there. Like

I was . . . nothing but a curiosity." She began to tremble violently.

"Godamighty! The Looker got to you? Oh, precious girl. Nothing like that will ever happen to you again. I swear it!" Ethan held her tightly until she calmed.

"No one knows about it except Jesse and the doctor. It happened just before school was out. I was going to leave town, but Wade asked me to tutor Jody. The only way I could do it was on the sly. I'd not get a recommendation from the school board if they knew I was teaching a darkie. This town and everyone in it, with the exception of Doctor Forbes' family, are run by the Harpers, and they hate darkies."

"If you don't like this town, we won't stay here when we're married. We'll go wherever you want to go, just so we stay together."

To Pauline it was a wondrous dream come true to have someone of her own. To Ethan it was like a new beginning. He knew deep in his heart that he would love this spunky, daring, mouthy woman for the rest of his life and not a day of it would be dull.

# CHAPTER

## • 19 •

*O*n the following Saturday Jesse, Doctor Forbes and Susan went to Frony's store and vaccinated the few people who came in. By mid-morning they had treated fewer than two dozen children. As noon approached, Wade arrived in a wagon that held Mrs. Merfeld and her children. He helped Mrs. Merfeld down and she waddled into the store followed by Wade and her brood.

Jesse's eyes caught his the instant he filled the doorway. She smiled and blushed with pleasure at the sight of him. Her face glowed. Wade had a moment when his mouth went dry, a moment when he knew that this woman was dearer to him than life. He couldn't stop looking at her. She was starchy clean in her blue dress covered with the white nurse's apron. The little round cap was perched atop her head. Lord, she was lovely. And she loved him!

Jesse talked to the children while she worked, soothing their fears. Once she looked at Wade and mouthed, "Don't leave."

He grinned at her and nodded. He had waited all week for this day, knowing she would be here at the store and that he would have a chance to be alone with her.

After the children were vaccinated, Doctor Forbes took Mrs. Merfeld to the back room to talk about her pregnancy. It was only then that Jesse had a chance to speak to Wade alone. She went to him, took his hand and pulled him outside. They stood beside his wagon.

"I'm so glad to see you. I was afraid you'd go before I had a chance to talk to you."

His green eyes smiled down at her. "I'm glad to see you too. I wasn't going to leave. I'm hoping to take you away for a while this afternoon. Do you think you can come?"

"We're not nearly as busy as we thought we'd be. Why haven't more people come in?"

"It might be the distance they have to come. The doctor might want to go over to Violet, the colored town. People over there get sick too, and they would welcome him."

"I'll tell him. Where did you want to take me?"

"For a little ride so we can talk."

"Talk?" A worried frown came over her face. "What about, Wade?"

At that moment the sound of a rifle shot split the silence. Wade looked quickly toward the direction from which it had come and saw a straw-haired man run out of the woods and jump upon a mule. A rifle was in his hands. Otis Merfeld!

He ought to have killed the son of a bitch today when Otis had threatened him for taking his family to get their vaccinations.

"Wade —" Jesse gasped.

He turned to Jesse and in horror looked down at the blood that had blossomed on her dress. Her knees began to give way. Terror clutched at Wade's heart.

*Godamighty! His love had caught the bullet meant for him.*

"No!" he shouted.

"Wade . . . I think . . . I've been . . . shot —"

"No!" he shouted again. Then, "Oh God, sweetheart. My love —"

"Take me to Papa —"

He swung her up in his arms and headed for the store.

"Doc!" he shouted. "Doc!"

Doctor Forbes came hurrying out through the door with Susan not far behind. She ran past her father.

"What's the matter with Jesse? Oh . . . she's all bloody!"

"Out of the way, Susan," Wade said sharply. "She's been shot, Doc. The bullet was meant for me." The anguish in Wade's voice transferred to Susan and she screamed.

"Jesse! Jesse! Papa do something —" Susan began to sob.

"Get hold of yourself, girl," Doctor Forbes said crossly. "You'll have to help me. Go clear off a place on the table and spread it with one of the cloths from our bag. Go!" he shouted when Susan hesitated.

"Open the door, Doc, and I'll carry her inside."

Wade kissed Jesse's forehead and her lips as he carried her into the store. He didn't care who witnessed the caress. His heart felt like lead in his chest. He placed her on the table and moved out of the way to allow her father to examine her. It was then he realized that Doctor Forbes's face was deathly pale and his hands shook.

"Move over by the door, Wade. I've got to take down her dress."

Wade moved away and Susan, with bandages and the doctor's bag, came to take his place. Still sniffing, she opened the bag for her father and placed it where he could reach it easily.

"Who did it?" she asked.

"That's not important now," Doctor Forbes snapped. "I'll lift her shoulders and you pull off the dress. I want to see the damage before she comes to."

Knowing that there was nothing he could do, but determined to stay close by, Wade went to stand in the doorway and answer the questions of the curious and concerned folk who gathered in the yard.

"Who done it, Wade?" Mr. Frony asked.

"Otis Merfeld. He was shooting at me. We had a set-to a few weeks ago about him beating his kids, and when I went to get them this morning we had another. He didn't want his kids to be vaccinated. Mrs. Merfeld did, so we loaded them

324

in the wagon. I intend to beat the son of a bitch to within an inch of his life when I get my hands on him. If anything happens to Jesse, I'll kill him and save the law the trouble." Wade spoke with rock-hard certainty, and none who heard his words doubted that he would do exactly what he said he would do.

"Is she bad?" Mrs. Frony asked.

"I don't know. The bullet went in about here" — Wade put his hand on his chest — "and came out the back."

It seemed hours before Doctor Forbes told Wade he had done all he could for Jesse here and that they had to get her home.

"She's going to be all right, Wade. We were lucky that I was close by."

"A wagon will be too bumpy. That buggy of yours has good springs. I'll hold her, if Susan will ride in the boot."

"Then let's get going."

Wade and Susan wrapped a blanket around Jesse before Wade lifted her off the table. Susan looked anxiously at her sister's pale face and began to cry again.

As he was carrying Jesse to the buggy, she moved her head.

"Wade . . ."

"I'm here, sweetheart — holding you. You're going to be all right. Your Papa said so, and you told me that he's the best doctor in Tennessee."

"Wade . . ." she said again, and lapsed into sleep.

Wade held her as the doctor drove. The precious

bundle in his arms was his life. His mind raced ahead. If the bullet had been a few inches lower, she would be dead now. Dear God, there was no way he could have lived if he had been the cause of her death. Wade held her tenderly. Her head rested on his shoulder; and, unmindful of her father, he kissed her forehead again and again.

"Why did Merfeld shoot at you?" Doctor Forbes asked.

"He didn't want his kids vaccinated. Mrs. Merfeld did, so I brought them."

"That's a pretty flimsy reason to shoot someone."

"There's a little more to it than that. I'll tell you sometime. As soon as I know Jesse will be all right, I'll go to Marshal Wright and let him handle it. Although if I know Merfeld, he's scared that he's killed Jesse and he'll hightail it out of the county."

"What will his family do?"

"They'll get along. The kids do most of the work anyway, and the neighbors will help them some."

The main street of Harpersville was filled with wagons, buggies, bicycles and farmers who had come to town on Saturday night. All gawked at the doctor's buggy as it passed.

*What was Simmer doing in Doctor Forbes's buggy? And whom was he holding?*

Wade had flipped the blanket over Jesse's head. He was sure that she wouldn't want her pale face and loose hair exposed to the curious.

Doctor Forbes drove the buggy to the door of

the surgery. Susan ran around and yelled for Jody and Todd to come take care of the horse. The doctor got down and opened the surgery door.

"Need help, Wade?"

"No." He didn't want to surrender his precious burden before he had to. He wanted to hold her for the rest of his life.

Jesse's father directed him to a small room off the surgery where there was only a washstand and a single bed placed on blocks so that it was waist-high. Wade laid Jesse on it. She appeared to be in a deep sleep.

"Doc," Wade said anxiously. "Is it normal for her to sleep this long? It's been a mighty long time." His worried face turned to the doctor.

"Sometimes. She's lost a lot of blood. I've got to be careful that she doesn't go into shock."

Pauline came rushing into the surgery. "What happened? What happened to Jesse?"

"She was shot, but Papa says she'll be all right," Susan answered.

"Oh, my goodness. Who did it? And why?"

"It was Otis Merfeld. But Wade will have to tell you why. Don't ask him now," Susan whispered. "He's wound as tight as a fiddle string. He even kissed Jesse right in front of everyone."

Louella, her dress and apron freshly ironed and without a single strand of her high-piled hair out of place, stood in the doorway to the surgery. When she saw Wade, she looked at him as if he were manure on her white shoes, then tilted her nose and went past him to the doorway of the small room where Jesse lay. She clucked her tongue in a gesture of sympathy, returned to the surgery and surveyed Susan's tear-streaked face with a small grimace.

"Is Jesse's condition serious, Hollis?" Louella asked as the doctor was checking Jesse's bandages.

"Gunshots are always serious."

"Well . . . she's a strong girl. Worrying won't help. Supper will be at the usual time," Louella announced and placed her hand on Doctor Forbes's arm to get his attention. She spoke the last sentence in a confidential tone as if to exclude Wade.

"All right. Thank you, Mrs. Lindstrom."

Still Louella lingered as if reluctant to leave for fear she would miss something.

"What happened, Hollis? What in the world has that girl got herself into now? My, my, it's just one thing after the other with her. She just can't seem to settle down, act her age, and learn the ways of a lady as befitting her station."

"She didn't get herself into anything of her own making," Susan spoke in a heavy sarcastic tone. "Someone shot her."

"Well, what can you expect with her going up there and traipsing around with that kind of . . . folks?"

Wade had to bite his tongue to keep from telling the old biddy where she could put her opinion of hill people. Godamighty! He would never fit in here. Why in God's name had he ever imagined he would?

Susan had no such restraints about expressing her feelings. Her temper erupted with the force of a tornado.

"You nasty, mean old thing!" Susan blurted in a loud and angry voice. "You've no right to come in here shootin' off your bazzoo about my sister or what she does or does not do! You've been trying to make it so miserable for Jesse that she'd marry that sissy old Edsel just to get away from home. Flitter! We know what you're up to. You're after Papa." Susan's voice rose even higher. "You plan to feather your nest right here and you'd be glad if all of us kids got shot!" She paused to take a breath and saw the grin on Wade's face. It goaded her to say more. "I'd rather have Wade and Jody as my friends than a hundred bigoted, mean old women like you and the Harpers. So there!"

"Well, my land! Someone should take a hand to this rude undisciplined child. You need to be taught some manners." Louella's usually white face was red with anger. She longed to slap the silly girl's face, but didn't dare. She had pressed too hard already.

"It won't be you," Susan replied nastily. "I'll leave home first."

Doctor Forbes came from Jesse's room. "That's enough, Susan. Go back to the kitchen, Mrs. Lindstrom."

"You're right, Hollis. I'm terribly sorry about Jesse. You know that. Susan, I'll expect your apology before you come to dinner."

After Louella left the surgery, Susan continued

to sputter. "Cows will fly before I apologize to that old hen. I'm sick of her, Papa. She's a mean old white-faced fart-knocker."

The doctor's face showed a brief flicker of sadness as he surveyed the angry face of his younger daughter. He stood with his hands in his pockets rocking back and forth on his heels.

"What's that?" Pauline asked trying to bite back her grin.

"What's what?"

"What you just called Mrs. Lindstrom."

"I don't know, but that's what she is. I wish you would get rid of her, Papa. She hates Jesse and makes her life miserable when you're not here. Todd stays away from the house because she's always on him for his stuttering. One day she had him cleaning out from under the back porch because he sassed her. There wasn't even anything there but a few weeds. He's just a kid and needs time to play." Susan's voice was a pathetic croak at the end and tears began to flow again.

Doctor Forbes put his arm around his youngest daughter. "I didn't realize you were so unhappy with her, punkin'. Be patient just a little while longer and we'll work things out. Hmmm?" He went back into the room to stand beside Jesse's bed.

Wade wiped his forehead with his sleeve. He was embarrassed to be a witness to what was a family affair. Things were going on here that he didn't understand, especially the part about the housekeeper's dislike for Jesse. Susan had said that the housekeeper hated her. Now he understood why Jesse didn't want to move out of the house and leave her brother and sister at the mercy of the woman.

"Wade," Doctor Forbes called from the patient's room. "Jesse's awake and asking for you."

Wade's feet couldn't carry him fast enough. He was beside the bed in a half-dozen strides. Doctor Forbes left the small room.

"Wade . . . are you all right?" Jesse's eyes were concerned, and she looked as if she would cry.

"I'm fine, sweetheart." He took her hand and held it to his lips. "Not a scratch on me."

"I'm so glad. I was worried about you."

His heart flooded with love for her. Not since his granny had anyone worried about him.

"I was the one who was worried half out of my mind. I never dreamed that being with me had put you in danger."

"I . . . loved being with you."

"How do you feel, sweetheart? Are you in pain?"

"I'm not in pain. Papa gave me something for that. I just feel like I'm all by myself and lost in a fog."

"You're not lost, honey. I'm here, your father's here . . . and Susan and Pauline. Everyone is anxious about you."

"I wanted to see you before I went to sleep. I was afraid the bullet hit you before it hit me. It was Mr. Merfeld, wasn't it? I think I heard you tell Papa it was him. Why did he shoot me, Wade?"

"He meant to shoot me, honey."

"Oh, no!" She squeezed his hand and tried to lift it to her lips.

"Don't worry, love. He won't try again. He was mad because I brought his kids and Mrs. Merfeld to the store to get the vaccinations. He knows that everyone will be up in arms about what he's done to you. I bet he's left the county by now."

"Poor Mrs. Merfeld." She began to doze. "Wade, I love you." Her voice trailed but she forced her eyes to stay open so she could see him.

"I love you too, sweetheart."

"Kiss me —"

He leaned down and gently pressed his lips to hers.

"That was . . . nice —" she murmured. Her eyes drifted shut and she didn't open them again. Soon she was sleeping soundly.

Wade stood for a minute looking at her. She seemed so small and fragile with her hair loose and pulled back from her face. He spread it on the pillow, recalling how silky it felt when he had buried his face in it. Jesse's eyelids were thin and blue-veined. They seem too fragile to hold the heavy weight of her lashes. Her mouth was relaxed and sweet. One arm was secured below her breast so that she couldn't move it. He kissed the hand he held and placed it on the bed beside her. He looked at her a minute longer, then bent and kissed her lips again before he left the room.

"Doc, why is her arm bound?"

"The bullet went through her shoulder blade. She must keep her arm from moving so that it will heal."

"Are you sure she's going to be all right? She looks so pale. And her voice is . . . weak."

"Of course she's weak. She lost a lot of blood, but not as much as she would have if you hadn't acted quickly. She's a strong, healthy woman. I see no reason why she can't recover completely."

"Lordy! Those are soothing words to my mind, Doc. I was never so scared in all my life as when I saw the blood on her dress."

"It's natural. Shook me up some too."

"Doc, listen. While she's asleep, I'm leaving. Tell her that I'll not be back. Because of me she was almost killed. I failed to protect her. A hill man can only bring her trouble and heartache."

"You're not thinking straight, Wade. Come back and spend the night."

"Thanks, Doc. But coming down out of the hills, holding her in my arms, made me realize that there are a million miles between Harpersville and the hill country. It's best to end it now so Jesse can get on with her life."

"Jesse will be hurt —"

"Better a quick hurt now than years of hurt later. Would it be all right if I borrowed a horse to go home? Jody'll bring it back in the morning."

"Take the horse, Wade. I just hope you know what you're doing."

Dusty Wright sat behind his desk, a cup of coffee in his hand. From the look of him, he could have been sitting there since the last time Wade was in to see him. Dusty was a man who did a lot of thinking before he took any action.

"Come in, Wade. Figured you'd be down to tell me what happened to Miss Jesse."

"You already heard about it?" Wade poured himself coffee from the pot on the round wood stove.

"No, but I got eyes. Miss Jesse left here this morning with Doc and Miss Susan. They came back with you holding someone that had to be Miss Jesse because Susan was in the boot."

"Jesse took a bullet meant for me."

"She going to be all right?" Dusty asked hastily.

"Doc says so. Bullet went into her right breast and out through her shoulder blade. Dammit, Dusty, it was that blasted Otis Merfeld. His mule had wandered out onto plowed ground and I saw him running for it. He was at the edge of the timber when he shot."

Wade told Dusty the history of his run-ins with Otis and they discussed the possibility of his running scared.

"He could do more damage with that rifle. What's he got to lose?" Dusty moved his chair back and his feet left the desk. "I'd ride up there tonight, but it'll be pitch dark in a few hours and I don't like the idea of that bastard standing behind a tree with his sight on me. I'll leave at dawn."

"Don't worry, marshal. He's not a very good shot."

"That's comforting." Dusty snorted. "Now I've got a would-be murderer running loose as well as a pervert."

"Any closer to catching The Looker?"

"Got a couple of things in the wind."

Wade rinsed his cup and turned it upside down on the shelf and headed for the door.

"So long, Dusty."

"Tell Miss Jesse I'm mighty sorry about the shootin'."

Wade nodded and stepped out the door.

The marshal watched him mount the doctor's horse and ride toward the hills. If Miss Jesse was going to be all right, what had caused that dejected slump to Wade's shoulders and the look of misery in his eyes? He looked as if he didn't care if the sun came up tomorrow or not. He had been a changed man since he met Miss Jesse. There was no doubt that the man was totally in love with her. He had been glad for Wade. The boy, man now, had had a rough life, and it was time something good happened to him.

# CHAPTER
## • 20 •

*I*mmediately after supper, Doctor Forbes called Louella into the parlor and told her, that while he wanted his younger children to have some training, she was bearing down too hard on them. It was causing them to dislike her. He was especially concerned about her behavior toward Todd and its effect on his stammering.

"You are only making it worse, Louella. Do not mention it to him again if it takes him half an hour to say what he wants to say."

"Well . . . I only —"

Doctor Forbes cut off her words with a raised hand.

"I realize that this is a difficult position for you and unless things change, I'll be forced to terminate your employment."

"Very well, if that's what you want. But, Hollis, you told me that the children needed a firm hand, and that was what I was trying to provide. You have a standing in this town, and I'd hate for you to be looked down on because of the rudeness of your children."

"I doubt that someone who was sick would concern himself about how rude my children are," he said drily.

"Furthermore, I don't believe they've had much guidance during the last few years. Todd and Susan have had a free hand and they've not had to account for their time away from home. And they spend too much time with that nigger boy. It's just too revolting to think about. My Lord! I hate to think what the Harpers would say if they found out."

"Tell them, Mrs. Lindstrom," the doctor said, his voice rising. "And then catch the next train out of town. I don't give a hoot in hell what the Harpers think, but I do care about my children, Jody and Pauline, and the repercussions they would face in this town if it became known that Pauline was teaching a colored boy right here in my home and Susan was helping."

"You know that I would never do any such thing. My goodness, Hollis, I thought you trusted me more than that." Louella's voice had softened seductively but she was shaken. Rivulets of sweat ran from her temples down the sides of her face, making little grooves in the coat of face powder she had applied so generously.

The kids had named her Ghost-face. By damn, the doctor thought, the name fit the woman like a glove. Dora, you'd be proud of the two smart kids we made together and also of Jesse, who has found herself a fine man who loves her enough to give her up because he worries he's not good enough for her. And, to think, I felt for a while that Louella would be a good companion to help fill the lonely years after the children were grown!

"Hollis, I really do think that I have met the requirements for the job to the best of my ability," Louella protested, intruding on his thoughts.

The doctor gave her a long searching look, then said, "That will be all, Mrs. Lindstrom. I need to look in on Jesse."

He walked from the room wondering why he had been so blind as to not see the woman for what she was. Her presence was too much for his children. It had to end.

If the doctor had looked back over his shoulder, he would have seen the ugliness on Louella's face. Her eyes put daggers in his back.

She could hardly restrain the desire to slam the door when she entered her bedroom after cleaning the kitchen all by herself. Susan and Pauline had made themselves scarce.

The nerve of that man to backtrack so suddenly. He had told her specifically that the children needed discipline and that Susan needed lessons in housekeeping. That was exactly what she had tried to give them. In almost any other home her methods would have worked. Here the parent let the children run as wild as deer. Associating with darkies — now that was the limit.

Louella stood in the middle of the room and silently cursed the day she had come here. It was clear now that whatever harmony had existed between her and Doctor Forbes was over and that there would not be a permanent place for her in this house where the doctor still worshiped his dear wife and thought his children could do no wrong.

What to do now? She weighed her options and decided that she had to swallow her pride and stay. Maybe she would hear from Jack soon and maybe — just maybe — she could persuade that handsome rascal to take her with him. It had been a while since she had posted the letter to him in care of the rooming house in Buffalo.

But when she left, she thought now with much satisfaction, she would leave a surprise for the self-righteous doctor who had spurned her attentions so cruelly. The note his wife had received just months before she died was carefully hidden beneath the dresser scarf. She took it now, read it again and almost chortled.

*When she presented this, it would certainly tarnish the image of his precious Dora!*

In the night Jesse awakened to find her father sitting beside the bed.

"Papa?"

The doctor shook himself out of a half sleep. "Do you want some water, honey?"

"Yes, please. Did Wade go home?"

"He had animals to tend. I assured him that you'd be all right."

Jesse drank the full glass of water. "He'll be back tomorrow," she said and drifted off to sleep.

Sunday morning the neighbors began to call.

Pauline left Jesse in Susan's care and sought out Jody in the barn.

Jody's first words were, "Is Miss Jesse goin' to be all right?"

"Doctor Forbes says she will. Have you been home?"

"Yes ma'am. The marshal was snoopin' round early. He ain't goin' to find nothin' though. Dude Merfeld brought the wagon back and told Wade his pa had took the twenty-nine dollars, ever' cent they had in the world, and skedaddled. Dude hopes he don't come back."

"He left his family destitute?"

"What's that mean?"

"It means he left them without a cent to their names."

"Wade gave Dude some money, said to tell his ma it was what he owed Otis for whiskey. But Wade ain't . . . he don't —"

"— Doesn't. Speak correctly, Jody. I know you can. Listen, I've heard from the people at Tuskegee. They're expecting you the middle of the month. What do you think of that?"

"Scares the waddin' out of me, is what it does. I don't know, Miss Pauline. I've never seen a darkie that had enough sense to stay out of the rain except that Mr. Washington that Wade took me to hear."

"Then it's time you became acquainted with darkies that are smart and want to make life better for their people. But remember one thing — you're just as smart as they are. Smarter than most."

"You think so?" Jody had a bewildered look on his face.

"I know so. Think I'd put up with a dumbbell?" Pauline threw her arm across the boy's thin shoulders. "Now get your head into those books. I must get back to the house."

The Forbes' home was full of visitors for most of the day. It was evening before the doctor had uninterrupted time with Jesse. He sat down beside the bed.

"Lordy! I'm glad they've all gone. This house has been a beehive all day."

"I was sure Wade could come today."

Doctor Forbes took his daughter's hand. "Honey, he waited last night until he was sure you were going to be all right. When he left, he told me to tell you that he wasn't coming back. He thinks it's better to break it off now rather than later. He feels guilty that people in town are looking down on you because of him. He thinks it's his fault that you were almost killed."

"Papa! What are you saying?" The anguished cry tore from Jesse's throat. "Are you saying that he doesn't want to marry me now?"

"He didn't say that. He feels that his reputation has soiled yours. He's sure that after a while you would come to resent him. He's a hill man born and bred and has more than his share of pride. He's a rough character and he knows it."

"He wasn't rough with me. He was gentle and sweet and l-loving."

"He feels he's doing the right thing for your sake."

"Well, I don't! I love him." Huge tears rolled down Jesse's cheeks and she began to cry. "He changed his mind about loving me and that's an excuse," she said between sobs.

"No, honey. I'm sure he loves you. He's worried that someday you'll be sorry you married him and he couldn't bear that."

"Papa, I wouldn't have ever been sorry. I wanted to marry him more than anything in the world."

"Maybe he'll reconsider and come back."

"No, he won't. Once he's made up his mind, it's set. And I don't want him if he doesn't want me."

"Honey, he thought long and hard before he made the decision."

It had been years since the doctor had seen his elder daughter cry. It tore at his heart. He wanted to hold her in his arms as he had done when she was a little girl and comfort her, but she was a grown woman and nothing he could say would ease her pain.

He went silently from the room and closed the door.

Louella Lindstrom was very much on Ethan's mind. That Saturday morning Dick Efthim, the postmaster, had come hurrying down to the newspaper office with a letter in his hand.

"This came in on the morning train."

Ethan took the letter. "Well hallelujah!" he exclaimed happily. "It's from Jack Dinsmore, Buffalo, New York. I'm going to steam it open, Dick. I'll bring it back to the post office all resealed and Louella will never know it's been opened."

"Well, I've never been involved in anything like this. It's tampering with the mails . . ."

"You've been a big help and I appreciate it."

"You know about this, Ralph?" Dick said.

"I know. In my young and foolish years, I was in the Bureau. They won't let me forget it. The boy here has a good head. He knows what he's doing."

"I'll go on back to the store then. I don't want to leave Pat any longer than I have to. She's nervous about being left alone."

"When's the baby due?" Ralph asked.

"In about three weeks."

"That's enough to make any woman nervous."

"I'll be there shortly," Ethan said, as Dick headed for the door.

Using the boiling teakettle, Ethan expertly steamed open the letter as if he had done it hundreds of times before. He took out the single sheet of paper, read it and whistled with satisfaction.

My dear Louella,

I'm happy to know that you've got a good place and a chance at marrying a well fixed man. But dear lady, I'll miss you and the many enlightening chats we've had over the past few years, not to mention our dalliances

343

between the sheets.

Since Leon's execution things have been quiet. No one has been prowling 'round asking questions, so I'm told.

The coast is clear for you to come back to Buffalo if things do not work out for you there. The officials think that because Leon confessed he had the brains to do the deed by himself.

There is nothing to worry about now. The reason that I'm writing is to tell you that I'll be coming to Harpersville July first for the day before I go on to Atlanta. I'll be standing in front of the post office about half past noon. Walk by and tell me where I can meet you later.

Jack

Ethan chortled happily after he read the letter and passed it to Ralph, who read it quickly and handed it back.

"Now tell me what this is about."

Ethan sobered. "It's a big case. A really big one. When President McKinley was shot and killed up in Buffalo last September everyone thought that Leon Czolgosz had acted alone. He even said he did. But a few of us in the Bureau thought he must have had some outside help. In other words, a conspiracy. We concentrated on the rooming house where Czolgosz lived. The day McKinley was shot, one of our men took a room there. The only boarders packing up to leave were Louella

Lindstrom and this bird Dinsmore. We figured that they were afraid that Czolgosz would talk. He was executed a month later, but even with all the grilling, he still contended that he had acted alone.

"I trailed Mrs. Lindstrom to Knoxville, where she took a room in a rooming house and stayed about a month. She moved around several times and mailed several letters to Dinsmore but received no answers. I was really surprised when she came here and settled in.

"Another man in the Bureau trailed Dinsmore. He went to a place in New Jersey and then into the boroughs of New York City. He was hard to keep track of there. After a while he went back to Buffalo, where he must have received Mrs. Lindstrom's letter. Dinsmore has done about everything criminal, including fleecing old ladies out of money. He worked in Sweden for a while, and probably met Mrs. Lindstrom there. He also signed aboard ships making the Atlantic crossing. We figure that's where he got acquainted with Czolgosz. Dinsmore is a handsome guy, a snappy dresser and a charmer. I imagine he charmed the prissy Mrs. Lindstrom right out of her drawers."

"What would the motive be for killing the president?"

"Who knows. The president made a lot of enemies by supporting high tariffs to protect the U.S. industry from foreign competition. He was not popular abroad."

"I'm surprised Mrs. Lindstrom didn't catch onto

the fact she was followed."

"You don't have much faith in my ability, Ralph, or in my talent for disguising myself." Ethan was in a good mood. This was the break he had been waiting for.

"You're the one with the gift of gab. I suspect if you put your mind to it, you could charm the skin off a snake." Ralph shook his head thoughtfully and went back to setting type.

Ethan was so lost in thought that he scarcely heard Ralph. He was busy copying the letter word for word and resealing the envelope, making sure it didn't look as if it had been tampered with.

"I'll take this back to Dick," he said over his shoulder as he went out the door. "Then I'm going down to the depot to send a wire."

# CHAPTER
## • 21 •

*W*ednesday morning came and, with it, the early morning train. Black smoke rolled from the smoke stacks on the engine and the wheels sang a protest as they sent out sparks and screeched to a stop on the iron rails. Mail bags were tossed onto the platform, and two men alighted from different cars on the train. One carried a large case of the kind that a drummer would use. The other man wore well-worn clothes and appeared to be a down-and-outer looking for work. The two men walked away without looking at each other and met again behind the newspaper office. A door opened and they slipped inside. Ethan greeted them with a handshake and introduced them to Ralph.

"Peterson, McGarvey, meet Ralph Marsh. He's been a great help."

"Howdy." The men shook hands. "Thanks for the help. This wet-eared kid needs all the help he can get." Peterson grinned at Ethan.

"I remember a time or two when this wet-eared kid saved your bacon, huh, McGarvey?"

"Yeah. I remember the time he was chasin' —"

"Whoa!" Peterson said. "If we get into reminiscing about the tight spots we'll be here all day. I hear you're about to be a *former* Bureau man, Bredlow."

"Yeah, kid." McGarvey removed his billed cap and scratched his head. "What caused you to change your mind about staying with the service?"

Ethan grinned. "It's about time I settled down. Hell, I'm not getting any younger and I don't fancy catching a bullet. I want a loving wife and kids before I turn up my toes."

"So do I," Peterson said. "I keep thinking I'll turn in my badge, but something like this comes along and the juices flow."

"Dinsmore should be on the noon train. He said he'd be here the first of July." Ethan showed the men a copy of Dinsmore's letter to Louella Lindstrom. They read it and "the drummer" tucked it away.

"And the woman — ?" Peterson asked.

"She's still here. She has been employed by a doctor as housekeeper."

"Is there a connection?" McGarvey asked.

"None. I'm absolutely sure. I had to give Ralph the story and he vouched for the doc. I've been afraid the doc would send her packing. His children are upset, and his home is in turmoil. That Louella has got more gall than any woman I've ever met."

Peterson, the man with the large black case, chuckled. "She's gutsy all right, and she's got an air about her that makes folks think she's some-body. I'm surprised she'd take a job as house-keeper."

"She explains it to people around town that she's a friend of the family and that she's tutoring the children." Ethan silently hoped Pauline, with her explosive temper, didn't hear about that until they had Louella in custody.

"We need to tie her and Dinsmore together," Peterson said. "We'd better wait until they meet to make the arrests."

"I agree to that. Meanwhile, you two have been on the train all night and need some rest. Ralph won't mind if you flop down in the back room."

"Make yourself to home," Ralph said and handed each of the Bureau men a bedroll. "I'll go to the bakery as soon as it's open. Ethan will make coffee. He ought to know how — he's drunk ten gallons since he's been here."

The morning dragged until the whistle of the noon train sounded. Ethan took up watch at the window of the newspaper office. The passengers had to come this way to get to the hotel or the rooming house. Several buggies were lined up be-hind the depot. Ethan was sure none were waiting for Dinsmore. Several drummers passed by before Ethan spotted the man he was waiting for.

Jack Dinsmore, carrying a small carpetbag and dressed in a black serge suit, a stiff derby hat and shiny black patent leather oxfords, stepped up on the boardwalk. He had a neatly trimmed mustache and black slicked-down hair. His appearance was that of a well-to-do businessman. He paused to wipe the tops of his shoes on the backs of his trouser legs.

"Vain bastard," Ethan muttered as he watched him swagger down the street.

Ethan stepped out the door fanning himself as if he were out getting a breath of air and watched Dinsmore enter the hotel. Remembering that the suspect planned to be standing in front of the post office at half past noon, Ethan looked at his pocket watch and then down the street toward the doctor's house. In the distance he saw a woman coming toward town carrying a parasol. It was Louella Lindstrom. He stayed to watch Dinsmore come out of the hotel without his carpetbag, light a cigar, and casually amble toward the post office.

McGarvey, in his worn pants and shirt and with a billed cap pulled low on his forehead, was no more than a dozen yards behind Dinsmore. His intention was to catch up with the man when Mrs. Lindstrom met him and overhear the conversation that passed between them.

He was lucky; for when Louella attempted to pass Dinsmore, he laid a hand on her arm to stop her.

"Well, forevermore, if it isn't Louella Lindstrom," Jack proclaimed pleasantly and tipped his hat. "How are you, ma'am? Imagine seeing you after all these years."

"As I live and breathe, Jack Dinsmore. What in the world are you doing here?" Louella said, then whispered, "Where are you staying?"

"The hotel, room thirty-one. Don't worry, dear lady, nobody in this hick town knows about us," he whispered back. He glanced at the tramp looking in the store window, then spoke in a normal tone. "You are looking extremely well, Mrs. Lindstrom. Will you allow me to treat you to a cool drink in that quaint little establishment across the street?"

"I don't know . . . I'm on an errand for the doctor."

"Come now. You can spare me a few minutes of your delightful company — for old times' sake."

Without waiting for an answer, he cupped her elbow and they walked to the corner and crossed the street. As soon as they were inside the restaurant, McGarvey entered the store that housed the post office and walked rapidly through to the door leading to the alley.

"They're together in the eatery across the street," he said as soon as he entered the newspaper office. "We don't have to wait until night." Then he repeated word for word the conversation he had overheard.

"All right, let's go," Ethan said. "Ralph, do you want to be in on this?"

"No. Keep it as quiet as you can. I'll run head-lines tomorrow and shock the hell out of this town."

"I'll go in the front and greet Mrs. Lindstrom and chat a minute. She knows me. While I have their attention, you two come in from the rear of the building."

"If this goes well, we can be on the six o'clock back to Buffalo," Peterson said gleefully.

It did go well.

Ethan walked into the restaurant and acted surprised to see Louella.

"Well, hello. It's nice to see you out of Doc's kitchen for a change. Are the kids giving you fits again? Who's your friend?"

"Mr. Dinsmore, Mr. Bredlow. He works for the newspaper." Louella made the introduction reluctantly.

"How do you do?" Dinsmore said politely.

"Are you going to be in our town very long, Mr. Dinsmore?"

"No, I'm just passing through."

"Did you know that this woman makes the most delicious pies you ever ate in all your born days?" Ethan said, moving closer to Louella after seeing his fellow officers enter from the back door and move up behind Dinsmore.

"Well, I guess this is it."

As soon as the words were out of Ethan's mouth, Peterson slapped the handcuffs on Dinsmore. At the same time Ethan grasped Louella's arm.

"You're under arrest," Peterson said and jerked the man to his feet.

"What the hell is goin' on? Is this a joke?" Dinsmore asked belligerently.

"It's no joke. Move."

Ethan cuffed Louella and snapped the other cuff around his own wrist. He placed money on the table to pay for the drinks the couple had ordered.

The diners sat in stunned silence as Ethan opened the screen door for Louella to pass through.

"This is an outrage. You've embarrassed me to death," Louella protested when they reached the walk in front of the eatery. "You have no right —"

"I've every right. The United States Board of Inquiry wishes to chat with you, dear lady."

"It's about McKinley, isn't it? I had nothing to do with that. I was unfortunate enough to live in the same rooming house as that . . . fellow."

"Save your breath, Louella. My job was to bring you in and not to judge you. Peterson, the city jail is there at the end of the street. You can stash Dinsmore there until time for the train. I'll take Mrs. Lindstrom to the doctor's house to get her things."

Ethan's heart was light. The job was done and now he was free to make a life with Pauline.

Louella was sullen and quiet as they walked the few blocks to the house. Luckily, they passed no one on the way. Ethan was glad. It wasn't his intention to embarrass the woman.

All was quiet at the doctor's house when they reached it. Since the front hall was empty, Ethan knocked on the surgery door. Doctor Forbes opened it and saw the handcuffs. He looked at Ethan with a puzzled frown.

"What's going on, Ethan?"

"I work for the United States government, Doc. I've been trailing Mrs. Lindstrom for months. I'll explain after I see her off on the train with my two partners. We're here to get her things."

"Go ahead. Do what you have to do. I guess my children were right about this woman."

"You didn't appreciate a thing I tried to do here, did you, Hollis?" Louella declared angrily. "I took your brats' back talk and Jesse's interference and tried to bring refinement into this home. The fact that you let your children associate with a nigger was appalling. I never told a soul about that. I wish I had now."

"Your definition of refinement is different from mine, Mrs. Lindstrom. My children were happy before you came here. I will say that the meals you served were good, and I enjoyed them, but my family and I will be glad to see the last of you."

"Bastard! Well, I've got a surprise for you."

"We'll get her stuff, Doc," Ethan said and tugged Louella toward the stairway.

Ten minutes later they came down. Ethan carried her suitcase, which had already been half-packed. Doctor Forbes waited at the bottom of the stairs.

Louella stopped and looked at him, her face a mask of hatred.

"You thought your Dora was so righteous. You couldn't see me for her. You considered her far above me. Well, I've been welcomed into homes of royalty. And I'll tell you another thing. I knew your precious Dora long before you did and believe me she was no angel. As a matter of fact I found a note from her lover in her secretary." She enjoyed seeing the color leave the doctor's face. "Here it is." She drew the note from her pocket and handed it to the doctor. He took it and crushed it in his hand.

"We'll be going, Doc. This she-cat and Dinsmore will be leaving on the six o'clock with the two agents that came in this morning. Tell Pauline I'll see her tonight."

Doctor Forbes scarcely heard the words. He walked stiffly down the hall to his bedroom. It was hard to breathe. His heart thudded painfully. The paper in his hand crackled as his fingers tightened around it. The woman's words echoed in his head. He would have scoffed at them if not for the unread note he held tightly in his fist. He was tempted to destroy it, but he could not, because not knowing would haunt him for the rest of his life.

# CHAPTER

## • 22 •

*D*octor Forbes smoothed the crushed paper. As it was written in pencil, he had to put on his spectacles to read it.

Dora,
I saw Hollis get on the train a few minutes ago and if Jesse takes Susan to the May Day party at the school, I'll be over. I have something for you. Take heart. I'm sure Hollis doesn't know.
    Dusty

The doctor looked at the note for a long time. He felt sick. Sick at heart and sick in his stomach. No, he hadn't known or even suspected. Dusty had been in their home, and had eaten at their table time and again. He had considered him an honorable man — until now. He could not imagine his Dora practicing deception. Someone had delivered the note. Was it a stable boy who had bragged to his friends that the doctor's wife had a lover? Lord! Why did that wretched woman have to find the note and shatter his belief in the wife he had adored?

He heard the sound of the screen door being slammed and hurrying footsteps coming down the hall. They paused at the surgery door, then came to his room. Susan appeared in the doorway, not really expecting him to be there.

He was sitting in his old chair beside the bed where he had spent hours, days and weeks before her mother died, his head sunk on his chest. The hands that had saved so many lives lay limp in his lap.

"Papa! I saw Ethan walking with Mrs. Lindstrom. He had her suitcase. What ever has happened? He's not running away with her, is he? Pauline would die of heartbreak. She likes him a lot. But you know Pauline, she doesn't want anyone to know and acts like she don't like him a'tall."

Doctor Forbes lifted his head and stared at his daughter as if she were a stranger.

"Papa!" Susan went to him. "What's the matter? Is it . . . Jesse?" There was a sharp edge of panic in her voice.

He shook himself and cleared his throat.

"Jesse is doing fine. Ethan is a federal agent. Mrs. Lindstrom is a suspected criminal. He's taking her away."

"Well! I'll be a hornswoggled billy goat!" Susan said excitedly. "Did you know, Papa?"

"No, I didn't know. I took her on thinking —

well, never mind that now. After I realized that you, Todd and Jesse were unhappy, I was trying to figure a way to ease her out without causing a to-do about it."

"Oooh! A real honest-to-goodness crook living right here in our house! I can't wait to tell Mary Sue and Jeff. You don't mind if I tell, do you, Papa?"

"Tell whoever you want. It'll be all over town by nightfall."

"You're not to worry about the house, Papa. We won't depend on Jesse like we used to. I think Mrs. Klein will come days and she'll do the washing too. Half-days would be fine until school starts because I can help. She'll want to go home nights. That's all right with me. I want my room back." Susan stopped talking when she realized that her father wasn't listening.

Something else had happened. Her heart beat faster. Surely her father wouldn't be sitting like this and hurting because old Ghost-face had left. Maybe it had something to do with the old piece of tablet paper with writing on it that lay on the table beside the chair. Even as her eyes found it, her father reached for it, folded it and put it in his pocket.

"Where's Pauline?"

"She took Todd and Jody down to the creek to give them a science lesson. Do you need her?"

"No. I'm going to walk uptown for a little bit. Stay with Jesse." He looked at his pocket watch.

Susan followed him out into the hall. "You won't

be gone long, will you?"

"No, no," he said absently. He took his hat from the hall rack and went out the door.

Susan watched him walk down the steps and head toward town, his hands in his pockets and his shoulders bowed. Somehow the joy of being rid of the hated housekeeper faded and in its place was a deep, troubling worry about her father.

She turned back and walked slowly up the stairs to Jesse's room. She opened the door quietly in case her sister was sleeping. Jesse sat by the window, her head resting on the back of the rocker.

"You'll never guess what happened, Jesse." Susan came into the room and stood beside the rocking chair. "Ethan is a law man. Did you know that? He came and took old Ghost-face away. Jesse, are you listening?"

Jesse's cheeks were wet. She tried to avoid her sister's eyes.

"Oh, Jess." Susan squatted down beside the chair. "He isn't worth crying over. The toad, the blackguard, the . . . hellion." She stood. "That's what people call him and that's what he is. I hate him," she said on the way to the door.

Without conscious thought, Jesse heard what her sister had said. It didn't matter. Nothing mattered. She had given a man all the love she had to give, and he had left without even the decency to tell her to her face that he had changed his mind and didn't want to marry her. She supposed that she would get over it. People got over the death of a loved one. But this was worse; he lived just ten

359

miles away, and she was bound to run into him from time to time.

She got up from the chair and paced back and forth across the room. She had to get her strength back and do something or she would lose her mind. What was it Susan had said about Ethan taking Louella away? Jesse wiped her eyes on her handkerchief, vowing that there would be no more tears. She opened the door and went slowly down the stairs.

# CHAPTER
## • 23 •

*D*octor Forbes hadn't decided exactly what he was going to say to Dusty Wright, but he knew that he had to confront him. He remembered someone saying to him that when a person like Louella Lindstrom was cornered and didn't get her way, she would retaliate. She had done that all right. The woman had gone through Dora's things and found the note. Had Dora kept it because she treasured it? Hadn't she been afraid he might find it? Or hadn't she cared if he did? No. She trusted him and Jesse. The younger ones would not have been interested in a scrap of paper with a few lines written on it.

He nodded to people who nodded and waved to those who waved. Edsel Harper came out of the bank and in the usual Harper fashion nosed right in to see what he could find out.

"What's going on with Mrs. Lindstrom? I saw her with —"

Without answering, Doctor Forbes strode on, leaving Edsel standing on the walk with his hands on his hips and a puzzled look on his face. Rarely was he ignored by the town folk because most of them had money in his bank. Come to think of it, the doctor had very little left in his account. He'd not been surprised when Miss Jesse had closed her account. She had been angry with him, but she'd get over it. She'd see that Simmer was not for her. He was hill trash and she was quality.

What the doctor wanted to do was to punch Edsel in the nose. It was the first time they had come face to face since he and Jesse had squared off in their parlor. Bastard! How dare he come into his home and question his daughter's respectability because she was seen walking with Wade Simmer. Simmer was ten times more man than Edsel would ever be.

The doctor crossed the street to avoid a woman who in the past had stopped him and talked a mile a minute about her ailments. He passed the schoolteacher, Mr. Crane, the one the kids called Ichabod. The teacher, loaded with books from the school library, paused as if to speak, but the doctor walked on.

The door and the windows of the marshal's office were open to allow the breeze to circulate. June bugs buzzed around the hollyhocks Dusty planted each year in front of and beside the building. A hummingbird hovered over the blossoms of a honeysuckle bush. All went unnoticed by the doctor. He stepped into the office and stopped short at the door. Wade sat in the chair in front of the desk.

"Come in, Doc," Dusty invited. "Wade and I were just talking about you."

"Yeah? What about?"

"Pull up a chair. We're trying to work up a plan to catch the fellow who's been going around looking at naked women."

"What's that got to do with me?" Doctor Forbes asked belligerently. He stood by the door with his shoulder hunched against the wall.

"Sit down, Doc. You're sweatin' like a preacher in a whorehouse." Dusty got up and moved a chair near the window to catch what breeze there was. "Here's a fan. Sit and cool off."

Dusty went back to the chair he had sat in for so many years that it was shaped to fit his husky body. The way his long-time friend stood beside the door staring at him made him uneasy.

Even Wade was aware of something different about the doctor. Immediately he thought of Jesse.

"Is Jesse all right, Doc?" Wade held his breath while he waited for an answer.

"Other than crying her eyes out, she's fine. She was up and around this morning."

Wade's shoulders tensed. The doctor had something serious on his mind. Thank God it wasn't about Jesse.

"As I said, Doc, we're trying to hatch up a plan to catch The Looker," Dusty repeated. Hollis continued to stare at Dusty, remembering how he had looked twelve years ago and wondering if his good looks were what had attracted his Dora to him.

"Well, what do you say, Doc?" Wade asked uneasily. "Got any ideas? I want to see this fellow caught so folks will get off my tail. I get hard looks everywhere I go — even from people who used to be half-way friendly."

"Leave it to Ethan Bredlow. He'll come up with something."

There was a prolonged silence while Dusty's face turned a dull red.

"It's my job, Hollis. I'll be the one to make the arrest."

"Ethan can make the arrest. He's a federal marshal."

"It's still my place —" Dusty insisted.

"Then do it, damn you!" Doctor Forbes blurted angrily.

Wade's eyes caught Dusty's and what he saw was surprise and bewilderment. Whatever was bugging the doctor was between him and Dusty.

"I've got to be getting on home." Without a farewell to either man, Wade walked to the door and stepped out into the sunshine.

As soon as Wade left, Doctor Forbes pulled the note from his pocket. After smoothing it out, he tossed it on Dusty's desk.

"Explain that, you deceitful son of a bitch."

Dusty, taken aback by the words and the venom in the doctor's voice, glanced down at the paper. He read it through, then read it again.

"Jesus, Hollis, Dora never wanted you to know about this."

"That's obvious. Just how many times did you sneak into my house to visit my wife?"

"Oh, hell! What's got into you? You think we were lovers? Climb off your high-horse, Hollis. It was nothing like that. If you're in the mood to listen I'll tell you what this is about. If not, to hell with you. Dora sweated blood to keep you from knowing that her twin brother was about to be hanged for a murder. If that's not enough for you, get the hell out of my office."

"Dora had no brother. No family."

"That's what she wanted you to think because she was ashamed and afraid you'd not love her if you knew. Godamighty, I never dreamed you'd accuse me of having an affair with Dora. She worshiped the ground you walked on, you stupid fool."

"Then explain that." Doctor Forbes pointed to the note still on Dusty's desk.

"All right, I will. But sit down and be civil." Dusty's breathing was ragged and his hands shook. "Mind you, I promised Dora I'd never tell you this. She was a good, decent woman and trusted me. It goes against the grain to break my promise, but what the hell! Dora's gone and I don't want you to be my enemy." When the doctor was seated, Dusty continued. "Dora didn't want you or her children to know that her father and two of her brothers were in prison. Her folks were a wild bunch. They were run out of Knoxville more than once. They considered it easier, Dora said, to rob and steal than to work. After her mother died, Dora worked her way up to a supervisory job in a glove factory and saved enough to break away from them. She came here to Harpersville. She met you and fell in love with you. Finally she had respectability and someone who loved her.

"Donald, her twin, was not quite so wild as his father and brother. Dora kept in touch with him and hoped that he would settle down. But he got mixed up with a bunch in Pittsburgh and a whore ended up dead. He wrote to Dora from the Pittsburgh jail, begging for help, telling her that he was innocent and one of the men with him had done the killing. She came to me to ask what she could do to help her twin without you finding out she was the daughter and sister of criminals.

"Hell, I didn't know what to do. I'm just a hicktown marshal. Because she was so torn up, I agreed to go to Pittsburgh and see what I could find out. When I got there the bunch Donald was with had broken up and one of the men had pointed a finger at the killer. The man was tried for the crime and hanged before I got there. When Donald was set free, he went straight to the docks where he sailed out on the first ship that would take him on. I doubt if Dora ever heard from him again. The news that Donald had escaped the hangman was my reason for going to see Dora that day. Knowing how upset she was when she came to me, I didn't want to keep her in suspense any longer than necessary.

"Now, Hollis, you can believe this or you can go to Pittsburgh and check the records. I really don't give a damn what you do." Dusty propped his feet up on the desk and leaned back in his chair. To his surprise, the doctor took a handkerchief from his pocket and wiped his eyes.

"I'm sorry, Dusty. I appreciate what you did for her. I only wish she had come to me. It wouldn't have mattered to me if her family had been disciples of the devil. She filled my life with more joy than I had ever known or thought possible. Now all I have are my memories, and the thought of their being . . . sullied was almost more than I could endure."

"She probably stuck this note in a drawer, Hollis, and forgot about it." Dusty handed over the paper.

"She probably did." The doctor put the note in his pocket and headed for the door. "I'm sorry about accusing you, Dusty, and thanks again for what you did for Dora."

Doctor Forbes stepped out the door feeling as if the weight of the world had been lifted from his shoulders. His dear Dora had been worried he wouldn't love her if he found out about her family. She had forgotten how important she was to him and how much he loved her. It would not have made a speck of difference to him what kind of family she had come from and it wouldn't have mattered to Susan and Todd. But she had taken such pains to keep it from them, and now for her sake they would never be told.

Ethan was standing in the doorway of the newspaper office when Doctor Forbes reached it. He stepped out and walked alongside him.

"Well, Doc, your housekeeper and her cohort are on their way to Buffalo to be questioned as possible co-conspirators in the assassination of

President McKinley. We are sure that they had at least a minor part in sheltering the assassin. It was our job to bring them in."

"How come you're still here?"

"Didn't I tell you? I've resigned from the Bureau. I want to stay here for a while and then go to a town this size and start a newspaper."

"I suppose Pauline has nothing to do with your decision?"

"She has everything to do with it," Ethan admitted with a grin.

"Come to supper. I don't know what we'll have, but Pauline and Susan will scrape up something."

"I'll take you up on that invite, Doc. I was on my way to call on Pauline if she's finished with tutoring for the day."


By July the Fourth Jesse had regained most of her strength and was able to use her right arm a little. Mrs. Klein, the washer woman, was as happy as everyone else that they had seen the last of Louella Lindstrom. She came to work at the doctor's house the day after Louella left.

Independence Day was a big day in Harpersville. Church circles, along with quilting and social clubs, set up stands around the edge of the town park where they sold lemonade, food, fancy needlework, and more practical things such as handmade brooms and leather goods. The usual number of patent medicine salesmen would be there with their brightly painted wagons and an attraction such as a monkey or a chained bear to draw the crowds.

After the flag was raised, gunshots would sound announcing the beginning of the festivities, then the speaker of the day, usually Boyd Harper or his son Edsel, would hold forth with patriotic platitudes. Once the town had had a former senator, but the best speaker they ever had had was Mr. Crane, the schoolteacher. He had been so good and had received so much praise that he had stirred jealousy in the Harpers and had not been asked to do it again.

Jesse generally enjoyed the celebrations, but this year she had no desire to mingle with the crowd around the town square. Tears were always close behind her lids. Nothing would ever be the same again. She greeted each day with a heavy heart.

Pauline helped Jesse dress. Her bright blue eyes were shining and her mouth was turned up in a perpetual smile.

"Have you and Ethan come to an understanding?" Jesse couldn't help asking.

Pauline blushed. "I guess you'd call it that. He resigned from his job and is going to try to start a newspaper somewhere. We've talked about getting married."

"Pauline, that's wonderful. I liked him right from the start. Wade said" — Jesse paused to take a deep, hurtful breath — "that Ethan was real hickory beneath that devil-may-care attitude he puts on."

"We won't get married for a while. He says he

really loves me. But —"

"He does. I know he does. He had a crush on you the first time he saw you."

"I told him about The Looker," Pauline said in a soft, miserable voice. "I thought it might make a . . . difference in the way he felt about me."

"Did you think he might not want to marry you? Oh, Pauline —"

"He said it didn't matter. But I had to tell him."

"It's grand the way things have turned out for you."

"Oh, Jesse, I wish . . . I know Wade'll come back. He doesn't want to see you hurt —"

"I don't want to talk about it, Pauline." Jesse got up and moved out of the room, telling herself that her father, Susan and Todd were happy now that Mrs. Lindstrom was gone and there was no longer a reason why she should stay in Harpersville and serve the people who had ruined her life by being so bigoted. When she was fully recovered she would speak to her father about finding a position in Knoxville or some other nearby town.

Later, sitting in the porch swing, waiting to see the foot race that would finish a short distance from the house, Jesse watched Ethan come up the walk. He was a handsome, strong-minded man and she was happy for Pauline. Of course, Wade was handsomer and smarter and dearer, she thought, and swallowed the sobs that came up in her throat.

"You're looking fit today, Miss Jesse."

"Thank you. Pauline is in the kitchen, Ethan, guarding the deviled eggs."

"She just might need some help with that," he said and headed for the door.

Jesse had told Todd to tell Jody about the picnic on the porch. Todd was hoping he'd come. Susan and Mary Sue were waiting to cheer Jeff on. He was running in the race that brought the best runners from miles around, all vying for the silver dollar that went to the winner.

At that moment, Todd came tearing around the house and sank down on the porch steps to catch his breath. His face was covered with sweat, as was the back of his shirt.

"Where's Jody, Todd?" Jesse asked.

"He's . . . he's . . . he'll be along. I g-g-gotta go."

"Todd, wait and get something to drink."

"Can't."

He heaved himself off the porch steps and ran up the street to where a crowd had gathered around a small platform draped with the American flag. A paper ribbon had been stretched between two poles to mark the end of the race. Todd sank down on the grass to rest.

"He's been so excited today," Jesse said to Pauline and Ethan, who had come out onto the porch. "He wants to be in on the end of the race. He can hardly wait until he's old enough to enter some of the contests."

They heard the sound of the shot that started the race.

"I'll get chairs and you girls can sit in the shade of that chestnut tree." Ethan indicated the tree close to the street.

"And bring a chair for yourself unless you want to sit on the ground," Pauline called.

"I thought you'd sit on my lap, honeybun," he replied.

Instead of bristling, Pauline blushed prettily and turned her face away.

Being in love and having her love returned had completely changed her friend from a withdrawn, unhappy girl to one who glowed with happiness. Jesse wondered if her own joy had been so obvious during the weeks she and Wade. . . . Sternly, she cut off her thoughts. It didn't pay to dwell on what might have been, she told herself.

Minutes later they were seated and watched as people streamed from town to see the end of the race. Several neighbors passed and some stopped to chat with Jesse. It was hard for her to be civil with the ones who had stood by and watched as Ethan and Wade had fought the four men the day after the ball game.

"Godamighty! That kid is the limit. You never know what he'll do next."

Jesse followed Ethan's gaze and saw one runner well ahead of all the others. It was Jody, shirtless and running barefoot. She heard a cheer from Susan and Mary Sue. Then Todd was on his feet shouting, "Come on, Jody. Come on." And he wasn't even stammering.

The little toad, Jesse thought. Todd had known that Jody was going to run in the race when he sank down on the steps after running from the starting line.

With sweat streaming down his face, his arms and legs pumping, Jody passed the house without a glance. He broke the paper streamer to the cheers of Todd, Susan and Mary Sue. The rest of the crowd was silent. Fifty feet behind Jody came the man from Grover who had won the race two years in a row. The rest of the pack followed.

Jody stood well back from the crowd.

"You showed 'em, Jody. You beat 'em all." Todd was dancing with excitement.

"I'm afraid there's going to be trouble. I don't suppose Wade is anywhere around." Ethan got to his feet and walked rapidly up the walk to where Todd, Susan and Mary Sue were congratulating Jody.

After all the runners had crossed the finish line, Boyd Harper began to speak from the platform at the side of the street.

"Ladies and gentlemen. Once again I want to welcome you to Harpersville's celebration. My granddaddy, Julius Harper, the founder of Harpersville, was one of the first to hold an Independence Day celebration in eastern Tennessee. I'm proud to keep the tradition alive. We have a grand turnout today. People have come from a great distance to enjoy our hospitality. This mile race is the first contest of the day. It is my pleasure to present this silver dollar to the runner from Grover who has won this race for three years in a row. Come up here, young fellow."

"No!" Susan shouted as she, Mary Sue and Todd worked their way through the crowd to the platform. "Jody won the race fair and square."

"You're being m-mean 'cause he's a darkie." Anger made Todd's voice shrill.

"Young man, watch your mouth or I'll speak to your father."

Susan waved a piece of paper. "You said the race was open to anyone. You never said whites only. Jody won."

"In all the years since my granddaddy founded this town, niggers have not been allowed to enter the contest." Boyd's face was red and his fat jaws quivered. He had not been challenged before and it was humiliating.

"Why not?" Susan demanded.

"Well, it's just not decent, is what it is. We've got to keep our celebration . . . clean for white folks."

"You think that Jody dirtied it?" Mary Sue asked.

The tall mustached man from Grover elbowed Susan aside. "Hell, yes, he dirtied it. Want to make something of it?"

Jeff stepped up beside Susan. He looked young and small beside the Grover man, whom he ignored.

"Mr. Harper," he said, looking up at the banker, "Jody was more than fifty feet behind the starting line when the race started. He overtook us. This man tried to trip him, but Jody jumped over his foot and took the lead. He won the race and deserves the prize."

"That's right," one of the men who ran the race called out. "The nigger won. I ain't never seen anyone move that fast. It was pure pleasure to see him run."

"Jeff Stealy," Boyd Harper looked sternly at the boy, "your daddy will thrash you good when he hears that you're interfering in this."

"I don't think so, Mr. Harper. My daddy is a fair man."

Mary Sue clung to Jeff's arm. "My daddy is too." She flung the words up at Boyd Harper.

Jody circled the crowd and came to the side of the platform.

"Keep your dollar, Mr. Harper. I didn't run in order to get your prize. I ran because I knew I was the fastest runner in this county. I challenge any man here to stay with me in a *five-mile* race."

The crowd was quiet for a moment; surprised by the boy's dignity and the intelligent way he spoke.

"Well, what'er you goin' to do?" the Grover man broke the silence. "Do I get the dollar, or are you going to give it to that nigger?"

"Jody won fair and square, Mr. Harper," Susan said and held out her hand. "I'll give him the dollar if you can't bring yourself to do it."

"All right. But next year the billboard will clearly state, 'no darkies.' "

"You're givin' it to him?" the Grover man said angrily. "You're chicken shit, but I'm not."

He began to elbow his way through the crowd to where Jody stood with Susan, Todd, Mary Sue and Jeff. Ethan stood a small distance away, watching. Jody had a frown on his face as Susan held out the silver dollar.

"Take it, Jody. You earned it."

"I knew you could do it, Jody," Jeff said. "I just entered to keep an eye on you. I knew I didn't have a chance of winning."

"Yeah. Jody, you're the b-best runner in the whole w-world."

The Grover man reached them. He put out both arms and shoved the children away from Jody.

"Where you from, nigger?"

"Leave him alone," Susan said.

The man ignored her. "If you enter another one of my races, I'll break both your legs."

"You touch him and I'll have Marshal Wright on you. He hasn't bothered anyone and he broke no rules. You're just a sore loser."

"What do you know? We got us a white girl here cozy with a nigger." The man looked at Susan with an insulting leer.

"That's what bothers you, isn't it? A colored man beat you. Let me tell you something, mister. Jody is going to run in the Olympics someday. What do you think of that?"

"I think it's a pile of horse shit. They'll not let this black bastard even try out."

"That's enough." Ethan spoke from behind Susan, then stepped around to stand beside Jody. "Spout any more insults and you'll get more than you bargained for, mister. If you're smart you'll mosey on."

"You a nigger-lover too? Shit, this town's gone straight to hell." As he spoke he doubled up his fist and swung. Ethan caught his wrist easily and at the same time stamped his heeled boot down hard on the man's moccasined foot and held it there.

"E-E-E-ow! Hell and damnation! Get off my foot! You're breakin' it."

"I don't think so. Maybe just a toe or two," Ethan said calmly. "When you get ready to bully someone, pick on someone other than kids. If you as much as speak to them again, you'll leave town with more than a broken toe. Understand?"

The man ducked his head and looked back to see that his friends were heading for town. Swearing at the pain in his foot, he hobbled after them.

Ethan rubbed his knuckles over Jody's head and grinned at him affectionately.

"You didn't do bad for a skinny, ugly kid."

"I showed them, didn't I, Mr. Bredlow? I wish Wade —"

"He was here. Standing over there by the bridal wreath. He didn't interfere because he knew I would."

Jody's head swiveled around. "Where is he?"

"He took off when the Grover man left. It was great to see you run, Jody, and to see the look of irritation on Harper's face. How is this going to sit with your folks, Jeff?"

"As I told Mr. Harper, my daddy is a fair man."

"Well, let's get back to the house and eat that picnic dinner the women have been fussing over.

I know they are eager to hear all the details."

On Monday after the Fourth, Pauline and Ethan stood on the platform with Wade and Jody as they waited for the train to take them to Tuskegee. The boy fidgeted in the shoes Wade had insisted that he wear. On the way they would stop in Chattanooga and buy a complete wardrobe for Jody to take to school.

It was the first time Pauline had seen Wade since he had so abruptly broken off with Jesse. She was somewhat cool to him.

"Hello, Miss Anthony. Thank you for coming to see Jody off."

"Why wouldn't I? He was my student."

"How . . . is Jesse?"

"Miserable."

"She's recovering from the . . . wound?"

"Oh, yes. And she'll recover from her broken heart too. It'll just take time." She turned her back on him and spoke to Jody.

"I know you're going to do just fine." She tried to reassure the boy. "You're one of the brightest students I've ever taught."

"I ain't . . . I'm not worried so much about the learning part, Miss Pauline. It's the other. I can't hardly remember what it was like not being with Wade."

"He'll be here if you need him. So will Ethan, Jesse and I. You'll always be important to us. But if you want to help your people, you'll need an education."

"I'm not sure why I want to help them. I've not seen one that knew much of anything."

"You'll meet plenty of smart ones where you're going." The train whistle sounded. Pauline held out her hand. "Good luck, Jody. Write to us."

Jody clasped her hand. "Tell Todd and Susan and Miss Jesse good-bye."

Pauline, touched by the tears in the boy's eyes, turned a hostile glare at Wade. "He's . . . scared," she snapped.

The train screeched to a stop; the wind blew the thick smoke back toward them. Wade picked up his suitcase.

"Bye, Ethan, Miss Pauline. Thank you for coming."

Wade and Jody walked back toward the end of the train where people of color were hanging out the windows and standing on the coach steps. Pauline and Ethan were still standing there when the coach passed. Wade and Jody were sitting on a seat together.

Wade was the only white man in the "Colored Only" coach.

# CHAPTER
## • 24 •

*S*everal weeks of lonely days passed slowly. Jesse, fully recovered, had taken up her duties in the surgery. The renewed friendliness of the people who had shunned her when she was walking out with Wade irritated her. She worked hard and seldom left the house. She wanted to leave Harpersville soon, but she could not bring herself to tell her father and kept putting it off.

She was lancing a large boil beneath a drayman's arm and wondering how he had managed to drive the team all the way from Frederick when a boy came to the surgery with a sealed note from Dick Efthim, the postmaster, asking her to come to the store. His wife had had a shock, he said, and he was worried about her and the baby she carried.

Jesse finished with the drayman and went to find Mrs. Klein to tell her that she was leaving for a while. She looked for her straw hat and, not finding it on the hall tree, picked up her parasol, left the house and walked quickly up the street toward town.

When she reached the store, Patricia was sitting

in the back room with a cloth in her hand to dry her tears. She hadn't combed her hair, and evidently she had come the half block to the store in an old wrapper.

"Pat, what in the world is the matter?" Jesse knelt down beside the woman while her husband hovered nearby.

The bell on the door jingled and Dick had to leave the room.

"Pat, tell me," Jesse urged.

"It was . . . it was . . . that man. Dick went to meet the mail train about four o'clock this morning. After he left, I dozed off and the next thing I knew . . . he had covered my eyes and my . . . mouth."

"Oh, my God! That beast has got to be stopped. Did he hurt you?"

"Not really. He stripped me naked and looked at me. He said he wanted to see my . . . stomach and touch it. He rubbed his hand on it and felt the baby kick. I was so . . . scared."

"Of course you were. Did you see any part of him? Do you have any idea who he is?"

"No. But his face was smooth. He rubbed it on my . . . stomach. Oh, Jesse, I was afraid he'd do something to harm my baby."

"But he didn't?"

"No."

"Did he put his fingers inside you? If he did we must tell my father."

"No. But he asked a lot of questions."

"About what?"

"He wanted to know if the baby could hear in there. And he asked if the baby would . . . split me when it came out."

"That's all?"

"He wanted to know if I like it when Dick . . . when Dick and I —"

"It's all right. I know what you mean. Are you going to tell the marshal?"

"I'd die of embarrassment. Please don't tell."

"I'll not tell anyone but my father. He should know because he'll deliver your baby. You can trust him not to say a word to anyone."

Jesse stood. "This pervert has got to be someone who knows that Dick leaves early to meet the train."

"Everyone knows what time the mail train comes in. Do you think he saw me . . . at the ball game?"

"He could have. But you don't have to be afraid now. I've not heard of him visiting a place twice."

Dick came back and went straight to his wife and hugged her. "Is she all right?" His worried eyes looked up at Jesse.

"She's distraught as any woman would be who has gone through what she has. But I don't think there is any permanent damage to her or the baby. She needs to get back in bed and rest."

"I'm not going back there by myself," Pat protested.

"You don't have to, love. I'll send for the Johnson girl to stay with you. I'll tell her that you're tired and that Miss Jesse suggested that you rest in bed today."

"I'm sorry that I'm not much help to you."

"Don't worry about it. You're my sweetheart and I love you . . . and our baby. Miss Jesse, will you walk her home? I can't lock up and leave just now. People are coming in for their mail."

"Of course, I will, and I'll wait until the Johnson girl gets there."

Jesse went directly from the Efthim house to the marshal's office. On the way she encountered James Crane, the schoolteacher. She felt a little guilty thinking of him as Old Ichabod. Susan had good reasons for her nicknames usually, but this poor, shy man should not be ridiculed. He glanced up, nodded and lowered his head. He walked as usual with his long stride and awkward gait. His arms held several books. Poor man, she thought, books instead of friends. She was going to have a talk with Susan about him.

Edsel Harper was standing in the doorway of the bank when she passed.

"Miss Jesse, I'm glad to see you looking well again . . . and so pretty. I declare. You're the prettiest girl in Harpersville." His eyes swept over her as if he were looking at a horse to buy.

"What you mean is, I'm not tainted anymore and my reputation has been restored now that I'm not seeing Wade Simmer."

"Now, I didn't mean —"

"Yes you did!"

"Miss Jesse, I —"

383

"Oh, shut up, Edsel," Jesse almost shouted and kept walking.

She found the marshal at his desk.

"Mornin', Miss Jesse."

"Morning."

"What brings you out so early? You look as mad as a hornet."

"I am mad. Something has got to be done to catch that mangy polecat who's stripping women. He did it again early this morning."

"Who?"

"I promised I wouldn't tell. The poor woman has been humiliated enough."

"How will I ever catch him if the women don't cooperate?"

"I can tell you as much as she can. I've talked to four of the women. He uses the same pattern every time. He knows when the women will be alone so he must be someone who lives or works in town. He gets in and out of the house without being seen. Does that tell you anything?"

"Sure. It tells me that he's no dumbbell. What we need to do is set a trap for him."

"You mean let it be known that some woman will be alone and lie in wait for him?"

"I don't know of any other way."

"Hmmm . . . that might work."

"It would take some doing. If one word got out, it would be all over town."

"I know that. I'll think on it and get back to you." Jesse paused. "I'd like to be the bait."

"Your pa wouldn't allow it. Wade would be mad

enough to kill me."

"What I do is none of his business."

"How are you two getting along?"

"We're not and you know it."

To her surprise the marshal laughed. "I'll be at your wedding."

Jesse looked directly into his eyes. "You'll not live that long," she replied and went out.

Jesse passed the bank with her nose in the air knowing that Edsel sat at his desk looking out onto the street. Damn him, why was he always watching her? Now that Wade had stopped coming to town to see her, Edsel seemed determined to pursue her again. He was so darn sure she would he unable to resist him.

Three days later, Jesse went again to the marshal's office.

"Miss Jesse, come in. You just missed Wade." Dusty noticed the color leaving Jesse's face on hearing Wade's name. "He was telling me that Jody has settled in at the boarding school. He had a few bad moments at first, but things worked out or Wade wouldn't have left him there."

"I came to talk about The Looker," Jesse said frostily.

"Yeah. Well, sit down. What's on your mind?"

"Mrs. Pennybrook's daughter, Martha, wants to go to Knoxville for a few days. The problem is her mother. The old lady is deaf as a stone and Martha is reluctant to leave her alone. She asked my father if he knew of someone who would spend a few days and nights with her. I volunteered."

"And — ?"

"Don't you see? It's a perfect setup. We can have Ralph put a small news item in the paper about Martha leaving town and that I will be staying with her mother. The Looker is bound to see it. If he comes, you can be nearby to catch him."

"What does your father say to this?"

"He doesn't like it. But I'm of age. I want this man caught."

Dusty looked at the girl across the desk from him. Jesse had lost weight, but more than that she had a hard, cold look about her that she hadn't had before. Her breakup with Wade had had as much effect on her as it had on him. Dusty knew, although he hadn't mentioned it to Wade, that the man came to town purposely to find out how Jesse was doing. He had been here this morning and had asked a half- dozen questions about her before he had even sat down.

"If we do this, I want you to have plenty of protection. I'll have someone with me," Dusty said.

"Do you have anyone in mind?"

"Yes, the best man I know for such a job."

"Ethan Bredlow?"

"Wade Simmer."

"No!" Jesse stood suddenly. "I'll not do it if you have him."

"Don't get all riled up. I'll ask Ethan."

"All right. Martha wants to leave at the end of next week. That will give me time to get an item in the paper and to spread the word. The way the people in this town gossip, every person within forty miles will know that I'll be spending a few days with Mrs. Pennybrook," Jesse spat out the words contemptuously.

The girl had been hurt and hurt badly. Dusty didn't know the reason for her breakup with Wade, but both of them were suffering. As he stood in the doorway and watched Jesse leave, his mind was busy with a plan. He would ask Ethan Bredlow to keep watch with him, as he had told Jesse he would do. And he'd also ask Wade, who would be mad as hell when he found out Jesse was going to be used as bait to catch The Looker.

On the following Friday morning, Jesse packed a small bag and headed uptown. That morning she'd had a lengthy session with her father.

"Jesse, I wish you wouldn't do this. Every woman who has admitted to being visited has said the man carries a knife."

"I'll be all right. If The Looker comes, the marshal and Ethan will be there."

"I had a long talk with Dusty. He said he and Ethan would be in an adjoining room, not twenty feet away. That may be too far if the man intends to hurt you."

"He hasn't hurt any of the women yet."

"Don't resist him, whatever you do."

"Don't worry, Papa —"

"Jesse —" Pauline stood in the doorway. "Be careful. He may decide to do more than look."

"He might not even show up. I've got to be going." She kissed her father on the forehead. "Don't worry, Papa," she said again.

Pauline walked with her to the door. "Part of me hopes you catch him, and part of me hopes he doesn't show up."

Jesse laughed. "He may not want to look at my old disfigured body."

"Old? You're not as old as some he's looked at."

"Yeah, but they didn't have a breast with a side drawn in with a puckered scar. Maybe he'll want to see it."

Pauline watched her friend walk down the street. Her reddish-brown hair was coiled neatly at the nape of her neck, her shoulders were squared and her chin raised. Jesse had changed since she had been abandoned by Wade, and Ethan was sure that misery was eating the man alive. Pauline hadn't laid eyes on Wade since she and Ethan had gone to the train station to see him and Jody off to Tuskegee. He had looked hollow-eyed and gaunt even then.

Jesse stepped onto the boardwalk that ran the length of the business district. She passed the newspaper office and waved to Ethan through the window. Proceeding on, she entered the mercantile. Pat Efthim was seated in a chair behind the counter.

"You're looking chipper," Jesse said by way of a greeting.

"If this baby doesn't come soon, I'll be as big as a cow," Pat said with a little laugh. "Dick can hardly wait. You'd think that this was the only baby ever to come into the world."

"He'll probably decide to meet his parents in the middle of the night, and Dick will run all the way to our house," Jesse said teasingly.

"I hope not. I'd hate having to disturb the doctor's rest."

"He's used to it. Send someone right away. He hates coming in at the last minute."

"I hear you're staying with Mrs. Pennybrook for a few days."

"Her daughter told Papa that she was worried about leaving her mother alone, and Papa asked me to stay with her. It'll be a nice vacation. I can catch up on my reading."

"Be careful." Pat gripped Jesse's hand. "Lock all the windows and doors."

"I will."

The jingle of the bell on the screen door sounded.

"Mrs. Harper," Pat whispered. "She comes in to check prices so she can compare with the prices in their store."

Jesse waited, thinking she would slip out the door when Mrs. Harper went to the back of the store. She wasn't that lucky.

"Jesse, dear. I didn't see you at first. We're all so glad you've recovered from your terrible . . . ordeal."

"— And come to my senses, huh, Mrs. Harper?"

"That too, dear. We would like for you to come to dinner Sunday after church. Edsel has been so concerned about you."

"I'm busy this Sunday, Mrs. Harper, and every Sunday for the rest of my life. Tell Edsel he needn't be concerned for me. He should be concerned for his own reputation. The kids found the dirty magazines he had hidden in the back of his buggy. They're having a high old time looking at the pictures of naked women."

Mrs. Harper's mouth opened and closed, opened and closed, like a fish out of water. She gasped for breath. Jesse, looking her straight in the eyes, felt not a whit of sympathy for the woman.

"I've got to be going. Bye, Pat. See you in a day or two."

Jesse took her leave feeling a little guilty about leaving Pat with the town's "first lady" as Mrs. Harper liked to be called. She hadn't meant to tell about the dirty magazines, but the viciousness of the Harper attack on Wade, the snubs she had received when she was keeping company with him, had caused her to want to bring the woman down a notch. The revelation did a mite more than that, Jesse thought. It had shocked her speechless.

A light shone from the front bedroom window of the rambling old house. Jesse moved about the room just as the marshal had told her to do. Wade and Ethan squatted in the bushes in the back of the house until the light was extinguished. When they slipped in the back door, Dusty was waiting for them.

"Any trouble?"

"None," Ethan said.

"Where is Mrs. Pennybrook?" Wade asked in a whisper.

"She sleeps upstairs," Dusty replied. "If the guy comes, he'll come in the front window. I told Jesse to leave it open as we did the side window. It's too hot to close them anyway. There's a split in the screen on the front window, and it can be opened easily. If he comes, he'll pull down the shade and after he blindfolds her, he'll light the lamp. All we can do is sit tight and wait."

"How's Jesse holding up?" Wade's anxious whisper came out of the darkness.

"Good. She's got grit. She's ready for him to come. She doesn't know you're here, Wade. She said she'd not do it if you were here."

Dusty heard an indrawn breath before Wade sank down on the floor just outside the doorway to the room where Jesse was sleeping. Just before dawn he nudged Dusty awake.

"It doesn't look like the bastard is going to take the bait tonight."

"We'll wait a while longer. Jesse said he came to one woman just before daylight."

They waited until daylight, then left the house one at a time. Dusty was the last to leave. He went into Jesse's room and gently shook her shoulder.

"I'm not asleep, marshal. He didn't come."

"No, but there's the chance he'll come tonight. You didn't get much sleep. It's daylight. It's safe to sleep now. I'll be leaving by the back way.

You're a spunky woman, Jesse. Your pa must be proud of you."

"You and Ethan will be here tonight?"

"As soon as you turn out your light we'll slip in the back door. You're not to worry. One of us will have our ear to the door all night long."

The next night went by, and, much to the disappointment of those who waited, The Looker didn't show up.

On Sunday night, the last night Jesse was to stay with Mrs. Pennybrook, Wade, Ethan and the marshal slipped into the house just after dark. They had circled the town on foot and had approached the Pennybrook house from the rear.

"If he doesn't come tonight, we'll have to think of another setup."

Ethan whispered. "He may have gone out of town. How long has it been since he's looked at a woman?"

"It's hard to tell. Most women keep it to themselves." Dusty put his hat on the table and ran his stubby fingers through his hair. "That Jesse is a spunky woman. She's done the same thing each night — paraded around in her nightdress before she shuts out the light."

Wade sat on the floor and stretched his long legs out in front of him. Both he and Ethan wore moccasins. Ethan had grinned when he caught Wade eyeing his well-worn, unadorned, knee-high leather boots.

"I've had these a long time. They're good for sneaking about."

Wade had not really had a close friend other than Ike Spangler and Jody. He liked Ethan. He knew that his lighthearted manner was a cover-up. That was what made him such a valued agent. Ethan was a man of principle and Wade liked that. He and Pauline were in love and planning a life together. If only he and Jesse had been able to. When Wade thought of how sweet and trusting Jesse had been when she had lain in his arms, he felt an acute pain around his heart.

Through the crack in the door that was slightly ajar, Wade could hear the bed springs squeak as Jesse rolled over in the bed.

*Jesse love, Jesse love. Not being with you is killing me.*

"If you two want to sleep, I'll keep watch until midnight," Dusty whispered.

"You go ahead and catch a few winks. I've got too much on my mind to sleep." Wade crossed his legs and leaned back against the wall.

Lord, but he wished the bastard would come. The Harpers were still spreading it about that he was the one. Now that he came to town every day or so to ask the marshal, Ethan or Ike Spangler about Jesse, the rumors were thicker than ever. He didn't care for himself, but . . . Jesse, his love, who had acted as if the opinion of the town people didn't matter, had been hurt because of her association with him. People would be more inclined to *forgive* her for her indiscretion, if the intruder were caught and it was proved that The Looker was not Wade Simmer.

During the night, Wade had to nudge Dusty. He came awake instantly.

"Nothing has happened," Wade whispered. "You were snoring."

"Hellfire. I had forgotten that I snore like a buzz saw. Glad you woke me. I'll take a turn —"

"Shhh —" Wade put his hand on Dusty's arm. His sharp ears, used to sorting out the usual sounds from the ones that did not belong, had heard a faint scraping. A few seconds passed and they heard the screen being lifted away from the window. The intruder entered the room silently, then came the sound of the shade being drawn.

"It's him." Wade barely breathed the words. He touched Ethan on the shoulder before silently getting to his feet. Ethan was beside him in a second, and the three men waited. Fear for Jesse made Wade's muscles tighten. His ears strained for the slightest sound.

The man followed his regular pattern. After a gasp from Jesse, they could hear his husky whisper as he talked to her.

"I won't hurt you. I'm going to take my hand from your eyes and tie a cloth over them. No, don't fight me. I don't dare let you see me. Understand? Now don't be scared and don't cry out or I'll have to put a gag in your mouth. I don't want to do that. I may want to kiss your sweet lips."

On hearing that, Wade made a move to push open the door. Dusty caught his arm.

"I'm going to tie your hands to the head of the

bed. That's a good girl. I've got a knife in my hand. If you don't behave I'll have to put my mark on you. You've been wanting this. I've watched you walking back and forth in your nightdress with the light on. You wanted me to come and look at you. I've waited so long to see your pretty breasts. I don't care that one of them is scarred. I'll kiss it first. Now be still. I'm going to light the lamp. You're so pretty and . . . sweet. I've just got to see all of you and . . . touch you."

Wade slowly and carefully eased the door open. He slipped through. The man was bent over the bed, his knife at Jesse's throat ready to cut away her nightdress. Wade crept up behind him, locked an arm around his neck and jerked him away from the bed. Ethan grabbed the hand with the open knife and it fell to the floor.

"Marshal? Ethan?" Jesse cried in a choked voice. "Untie me. I can't stand it. Hurry, please."

Wade spun the man toward Dusty, stuck out his foot and the man sprawled on the floor.

"Jesus!" Dusty exclaimed when he saw the man's face.

Wade took the knife from Ethan, went to the bed and cut the cloth binding Jesse's hands. He gathered her in his arms and held her so tight she could scarcely breathe.

The smell of his skin, the familiar strength of his arms and the pounding of his heart told her who it was that held her.

"Wade! Wade, it's you!"

Wade pulled the blindfold from her eyes and buried his face in the curve of her neck.

"Don't send me away," he whispered frantically. "Please. I'm dying inside."

Frightened, she clung to him, welcoming the protection of his arms. "Take a look at The Looker, Miss Jesse," Dusty's voice reached them. "You'd never guess who he is."

Wade lifted his head. Jesse looked into his face and saw the ravages of sleepless nights and restless days. A mist in his eyes made them look like green mountain pools. Jesse felt naked, inside and out, before this man who had rejected her. But she couldn't seem to pull away. She turned her head to look at the man Dusty was handcuffing.

Jesse stared speechless with shock, until anger bubbled to the surface.

"Good heavens! Mr. Crane. How could you do such a despicable thing? The people in this town liked you, trusted you."

The teacher hung his head and wouldn't look at her.

"I'd like a minute or two alone with him, Dusty, but I've been in law enforcement long enough to know you can't allow it." Ethan grabbed a handful of hair and lifted Crane's face. "You miserable bastard. What you've done to these women will stay with them for the rest of their lives."

"I'm . . . sorry," James Crane began to cry. "I didn't hurt them. I just wanted to . . . look at them."

"You violated them. You raped them with your

eyes, you stupid son of a bitch," Ethan growled.

"Need any help, Dusty?" Wade asked, his arms still locked around Jesse although she was trying to push away.

"Naw. Come to think on it, maybe I'd better catch the morning mail train and take this bird on down to the county jail. Folks in this town are mad as a hive of stirred-up bees. I'm afraid that when word gets out, they'll swarm all over him. I might have trouble getting him out of town."

"I didn't hurt anyone," James Crane babbled. "I didn't hurt anyone."

"Tell it to the judge," Dusty said. "I'll take him down to the jail and go buy a couple of tickets. You two were a big help, but we couldn't have pulled it off without Jesse. Thanks, girl."

"I thought sure it was Edsel," Jesse said, looking over Wade's shoulder.

"I wouldn't have minded that at all," Dusty said with a laugh. " 'Course I'd have lost my job, but it would have been worth it."

"Where do you plan to spend the rest of the night?" Ethan asked after Dusty had left with his prisoner.

"I couldn't talk you into going to the livery and renting a buggy, could I? I'm taking Jesse home . . . to our house."

Shocked by Wade's words, Jesse began to protest.

"No! I've got to stay here with Mrs. Pennybrook."

"Ethan will stay . . . after he brings the buggy."

Ethan threw up his hands. "All in the name of love. If I don't do it, Pauline will have my head in a basket."

# CHAPTER
## • 25 •

*J*esse pushed against Wade's chest and his arms fell from around her.

"I told Dusty I didn't want you here."

"He told me."

"Then why did you come?"

"Because I couldn't stay away." Wade stood and looked down at her. "I'll go in the other room while you get dressed."

"I'm not going anywhere with you. You didn't want me. Remember?" Something vulnerable inside her began to withdraw behind the protective screen of anger.

"We're going someplace where we can talk. You can go in your nightclothes or you can dress. It's up you. These last few weeks have been pure hell. Longing for you has turned me inside out."

"You should have thought about that before you . . . abandoned me."

"Is that what you think I did?"

"What else? I was weak from loss of blood and . . . hurting. You could have waited until I was

399

stronger before you . . . you left me at the mercy of the gossips who delighted in saying I told you so."

"At the time, I did what I thought was best for you. I saw your friends turn their backs on you. I almost got you killed."

Jesse was desperately trying to keep her anger alive, or she would cry. Hugging the bedclothes to her, she glared up at him. His dark hair had fallen down on his forehead. He raked it back with spread fingers.

"You didn't even take the trouble to talk it over with me," she said, her voice quivering. "You made the decision that affected my life as well as yours. You had no regard for my feelings in the matter at all, only yours."

"That's not true. I came to believe that someday you'd regret marrying me. I thought it better that you be hurt a little now —"

"— A little?"

"Yes, I thought you'd get over it quicker. It would be better than having a lifetime of hurt. My mother was a town girl. She despised living in the hills. Life there is much different from what you're used to. People are different."

"You don't know me at all, Wade. I didn't give my heart lightly. I knew that you were a hill man and that you'd never be happy living in town, especially Boyd Harper's town. I'm not a young, naive, adolescent girl." Her eyes glistened with tears. "Is this what you wanted to talk about?"

"Yes, and how empty and miserable I am without you."

"In other words, now you're willing to take the risk that someday I'll regret marrying you."

"I want you so much I'd cut off my right arm if I thought it would bring you back to me."

Tears spilled from Jesse's eyes and ran down her cheeks. "Oh, Wade —"

"I want to take you to my home, show it to you, and you can decide if you want to live there with me. I was going to take you there the day you were shot."

"I've seen your house."

"Not all of it. Please —"

The look of longing in his eyes melted all her resistance.

"Oh, dog-gone-it!" she exclaimed, trying not to cry. "Get out of here so I can get dressed."

The sun was up and shining brightly when the buggy from the livery pulled into the yard behind Wade's house. He hadn't touched Jesse since he had helped her into the buggy. Nor had they talked very much.

"Here we are," he said, his voice strained with uncertainty. He alighted from the buggy and tied the horse to a ring in a fence post. By the time he came to help Jesse down she was already on the ground. He took her elbow and led her toward the house.

Wade opened the door and they stepped into the kitchen. The first thing Jesse saw was a huge bouquet of honeysuckle in a pitcher on the table that was covered with a new white oilcloth. The room was clean as a pin from the freshly washed curtains on the windows to the shining lamp chimneys to the stove that appeared to be newly blackened. The fireplace was cleaned, and on the mantle shelf was a small crock filled with wildflowers.

Jesse turned her shining face to his. "It's cozy and . . . beautiful."

"I spent the last week cleaning. I had to do something or . . . go out of my mind," he admitted sheepishly. He opened a door next to the stove. "This is the pantry. The cellar entrance is outside, but I plan to put a door in here and steps going down so you . . . so a person could get to the cellar without going outside. We have a tank that catches rainwater to use for washing, but the drinking water is pumped up from the spring."

He led her to the parlor. At one end of the room was an upholstered parlor suite. The high-backed couch and chairs were covered with Turkish silk fabric. The set looked so out of place that Jesse wanted to smile. At the other end of the room was a combination bookcase and desk. On the floor was a rust-colored woven carpet in a scroll design.

"I bought the furniture for Granny while on one of my trips home," Wade said by way of apology. "I don't think she liked it much. I don't like it either."

"I'll admit the room needs lightening up."

"I can build another house," he said quickly.

"No!" She turned and looked at his worried face.

"Your ancestors built this house, lived here, loved here and died here. It's part of your heritage."

"But if you don't like it —"

"I like it."

"You're sure?"

"I'm sure. Don't worry about your home not being good enough. It's a wonderful home. It looks as if it grew here with the trees."

"I want to show you something." With his hand in the small of her back he guided her to a door tucked under the stairway. He pushed open the door and stood back for her to enter.

Jesse's hand flew to her mouth. "Oh, Wade —"

The small room had been converted into a miniature of the surgery at home. It contained a rolltop desk, a tall glass-fronted cabinet for medicine and even a sink with a pump. In the center of the room was a small examination table and on the desk were several medical books.

"You don't like it? You'd rather have picked the things out yourself?" Wade's heart dropped like a stone.

"No! No! It's perfect. I just don't understand how you managed to get all . . . this."

"I wired a friend in Chattanooga. He wired someone in Atlanta and the things came in on the train. I did some humping to get it ready by the time you were to come to the store to vaccinate. It's what I wanted to show you that day."

"I've always dreamed of a little surgery of my own where I could help people in need."

"I'm going to make a door where that window

is so folks can come in from the outside. It would keep them from traipsing through the house."

"You've thought of everything."

"I want to show you the upstairs." He held out his hand and she put hers into it.

They stepped up into a center hall. On one side was a large room and on the other two smaller rooms. Wade led her into the large room. Jesse paused and gazed with admiration at the furnishings. The head of the bed reached almost to the ceiling. The walnut wood was polished to a high gloss. The matching washstand and dresser were handsomely carved to match the headboard of the bed. A free-standing, beveled glass mirror stood against one wall and a roomy wardrobe against the other. On the washstand were a china pitcher and bowl. Lamps with ornate shades completed the furnishings.

Wade moved behind Jesse and put his arms around her. When she offered no resistance, he pulled her back against him.

"This will be our room if you marry me," he whispered, kissing her ear. "This is where we'll share our dreams and make our babies."

Jesse turned in his arms. "When did you buy all this? It's new, isn't it?"

"Yes, it's new. I . . . I bought it for us. I wanted to buy a set for Granny, but she didn't want it."

"I bet she loved you a lot."

"I think she did."

"I love you a lot too," Jesse whispered, her eyes on his mouth. "Don't ever, ever leave me again."

A groan of relief came bubbling up out of him. "You mean it? You forgive me?"

"I mean it with all my heart. Even if you had never come back to me, I would still have loved you for as long as I lived. Oh, Wade, I thought I'd die of grief, and I wanted my love for you to die, but it wouldn't. It was there gnawing a hole in my heart."

They clung to each other for a long time before they kissed.

"Oh, love, I thought I could give you up to save you the humiliation you've endured because of me."

At that moment Jesse realized what love truly was — a desire to do whatever was necessary to protect the one you cared about. She looked deep into Wade's eyes and saw aching tenderness there.

"I was never for an instant humiliated," she told him. "I was proud to be with you. I want more than anything in the world to be with you for the rest of my life."

"I am what I am, love. I can never be anything else. But I'll love you, cherish you, and protect you with my life," he vowed, his voice thick and sultry.

He kissed her then; a hungry kiss, a kiss of explosive passion held back too long. His mouth covered hers; hers bloomed beneath his. He felt surrender in the taste of her warm, sweet mouth, heard it in the low wordless sounds she uttered as she strained against him. His hands moved up her sides to the soft swell of the sides of her breasts.

He felt her splayed hands on his back, holding him tightly to her. He lifted his head to look into her glazed eyes and at her swollen lips wet from his kiss.

Their passion was almost out of control. He couldn't get enough of her sweetness. Their kisses were deep, yet they both wanted more. His hand moved between them, unbuttoned her shirtwaist and slipped under her chemise to cup a soft bare breast. He could feel her heart knocking against his palm. A little sound came from her throat; a little growl of female pleasure.

She was so open, so loving, and as innocent as a babe in her wanton movements against him. His extended member was pressed tightly to her soft belly and he felt as if he would explode at any moment. With all the willpower he still possessed, he pulled a little away from her and stared down at her wet lips and passion-glazed eyes.

"Please, Wade —"

"Please, what?" he asked in a strangled whisper. He felt as if he could hold back no longer. The heat in his loins was becoming unbearable.

"I want to be with you . . . in the bed," she whispered back, her fingers stroking his cheeks.

"Oh, love, do you know what you're saying? I swore I'd never take you out of wedlock."

"You want me . . . like that, don't you?"

"I want you so bad it's killing me, but I can wait until we're married."

"You don't have to wait. I want you as much

as you want me. Make me yours and . . . let me make you mine."

For an answer he caught her close and his mouth sought hers in demanding possession. She moaned against his mouth, trembling with emotion.

He raised his lips and murmured, "My love, my sweet love. I was afraid I'd driven you away from me forever."

He lifted her and carried her to the bed, placed her gently on it, sank down beside her and gathered her in his arms.

"You don't have to —"

"— I want you. Love me, Wade."

"I will, sweetheart," he whispered tenderly in her ear and kissed her so gently that her whole body cried out for him.

She never knew how it happened, but first her shirtwaist and skirt were off, then her chemise was pulled down exposing her bare breasts. Wade kissed and nuzzled the breast with the deep puckered scar.

"Does this hurt you?" he whispered.

"No. I love it. I love you —"

His hand found the drawstring of her bloomers. His lips moved up to hers and he whispered against them.

"These will have to come off."

Jesse lifted her hips so he could dispose of the barrier. When his fingers found the moistness between her legs, a little whimper of pleasure escaped her lips. He quickly removed his clothing, lay down beside her and pressed her naked body to his.

It was all so sweet. Wade was considerate and gentle. The stroking of his hands on her flesh sent waves of pure pleasure up and down her spine. Then her loins were cradling him. Her low cries of delight mingled with his as he entered her sweet, hot depths. There was a moment of pain. He groaned when she flinched, and held himself still. When the pain passed, Jesse gave him every inch of herself.

Nothing mattered except the need for him that blazed crazily in her brain. Her arms clutched him frantically as his mouth moved from hers to her pulsing throat, kissing the soft skin. His breathing came fast and irregularly and his powerful heart thudded against her breast as his movements quickened. He whispered softly, words that were muffled as he kissed her eager lips.

"Oh, love . . . Oh, love — How could I have thought I could live without you?"

The violent force of Jesse's feelings took her beyond reason, beyond herself. Her fingers curled tightly into his thick dark hair. *How wonderful this is! How wonderful he is!* Over the singing in her blood she heard sounds of Wade's smothered groans as if they came from a great distance. Her joy rose to intolerable heights, and then she was conscious of nothing but her own sensations. Feverishly, she clung to Wade as he poured himself into her. When she came slowly back to awareness, she found that his dark, damp head rested on her shoulder.

After a while his breathing slowed and his heart

became quieter. Her fingers combed through his hair. She felt warm and lazy, her arms holding him as they would a tired child. He turned to his side and she snuggled against him, rejoicing in the thought that she would be sleeping in his arms, in this bed, for the rest of her life.

"Can you stay all day?" Wade's arms held her tightly to him. "I don't think I can let you go even for a day, an hour, a minute."

"If I stay, will we do again . . . what we just did?" She laughed when a look of surprise crossed his face before it was transformed by a huge smile.

"Again and again and . . . again."

"Then I'll stay."

With his face buried in her hair, Wade moved his caressing hands down her back to her buttocks and pressed her tightly to him. How he loved the feel of her against him. He inhaled her womanly fragrance and felt as if his heart would burst with love for her.

"I wish we could marry today. I don't want to sleep in this bed ever again without you."

"How about Sunday? That's just three days away."

"Three whole days. It will seem like three years. I'll sleep in Jody's bed until then."

Jesse's happiness shone in her bright eyes and sweetly curved lips. Wade was her life's mate. She would spend the rest of her life here . . . with him. They would live here, have their children here, grow old together here.

"Wade," she whispered with her lips against his

cheek. "I'm so sleepy, but I'm afraid that when I wake up, I'll find this was all a dream."

"Go to sleep, sweetheart." Holding her tightly in his arms, he kissed her forehead tenderly. Then he lifted her hand and nipped her thumb with his teeth.

"Why did you do that?"

"To prove that this is no dream, sweetheart. This is *real!*"

# EPILOGUE

*J*esse and Wade, together with Pauline and Ethan, were married on a bright Sunday afternoon. It didn't matter to them that only a handful of wedding guests came to see them take their vows. All the people besides family who mattered were there: the Efthims, the Marshes, Mrs. Klein, Mary Sue and Jeff, Ike and Dusty. A few townspeople who were not connected with the Harpers also came to the church. The Harpers had held a free picnic that day for all the depositors in their bank. It was amusing to Jesse and Wade that it had cost the Harpers a pretty penny to keep people from attending the wedding.

Wade's mare, Christmas, had been brought down and hitched to the new buggy that was decorated with streamers, tin cans and old shoes. The buggy was a two-seater. The back seat, designed to be let down so Jesse could transport ill patients to her father, now held Mr. and Mrs. Ethan Bredlow, who were catching the two o'-clock train to Chattanooga for a brief honeymoon.

After seeing their friends off, Wade turned the horse toward the hill road knowing that he would have his love close by his side for the rest of his life. He looked at his beautiful bride and his heart almost burst with happiness.

They lived a long and happy life together, producing three boys and two girls. Jesse was called the "Angel of the Hills" because of her devotion to the health of the community. Jesse and Wade paid tuition for Julie Merfeld to attend nursing school and she worked for Doctor Forbes until he retired.

Edsel Harper died a young man. He was too stubborn to ask Doctor Forbes for help and died on the train to Knoxville from an infected insect bite. The Harpers were left without an heir. Eventually their estate went to a distant cousin who was as different from Boyd and Roberta as daylight and dark. After a few years, Jesse and Wade moved some of their money closer to home and deposited it in the Harpersville bank, something they had thought they would never do.

Ethan and Pauline bought out a small newspaper in Frederick and the couples got together often. It bothered Ethan that Louella Lindstrom and Jack Dinsmore were found innocent of any wrongdoing in the death of President McKinley. He still felt that Jack Dinsmore had brought the killer to Buffalo and that Louella Lindstrom knew something or she would have never left Buffalo and taken such care to cover her tracks.

Susan married a farmer and horse breeder. They

built a race track and worked to make it both a profitable venture and a showplace.

Todd's stammering disappeared gradually a few years after Wade and Jesse were wed. He went to medical school, but instead of establishing a practice, he chose to teach and give lectures at various colleges.

Mary Sue and Jeff Stealy, sixteen and seventeen, married as soon as they were out of school. With the help of their parents, they established the first automobile dealership in the county. Dusty, at age seventy, was their first customer. He bought a Ford that was soon to be called the "Tin Lizzy."

Jody graduated from Tuskegee Institute with honors. His love of running was replaced by his love of learning. He was passionately interested in gardening and worked with his people to produce food not only for their families, but also to sell. He visited Wade and Jesse at every opportunity and bounced their children on his knee. Wade wanted his children to be comfortable with people of color and when his son asked him why Jody's skin was black, he replied:

"Son, God made all of us, but he thought it would be interesting to make some white, some black, some with slant eyes, some small, some tall. But under our skin we're all the same. Remember that."

And he did. It was a beginning.